RETURN TO ROOTS

ANNE ELIZABETH

ALSO BY ANNE ELIZABETH

The Roots Trilogy

A World Within Roots

Roots Unearthed

THE ROOTS TRILOGY
BOOK THREE

RETURN TO ROOTS

ANNE ELIZABETH

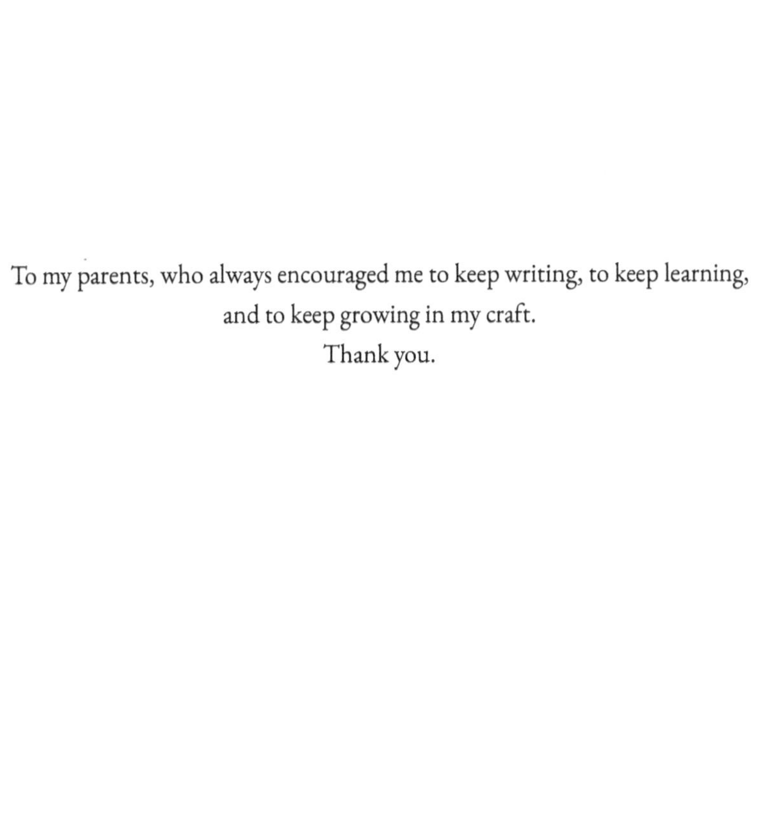

To my parents, who always encouraged me to keep writing, to keep learning, and to keep growing in my craft.
Thank you.

Chapter One

The air grew colder as I walked, feeling the weight of the katana thwack against my hamstring with each step. Clouds billowed across the sky, large and silvery. I tried to ignore the chill pervading the air, which drove its way through my clothes until I shivered. Winter had gripped the forest with her icy fingers. Silence blanketed the ground like snow, all except the trees creaking, an eerie sound carried by the breeze. Gray, brown, and faded greens filled my surroundings. The air was crisp.

A cloud passed, and the sun shone down on me again, surrounding me with yellow, though it did little for the cold. The ground, the trees, and the leaves lay dappled by the sunlight and glowed golden. When I'd left my world, this world, we hadn't even reached fall's beginning, but now ...

I swallowed past the lump in my throat. It had been months. February had greeted us soon before I'd left Ryujin. The cherry blossom trees had begun to bud. Eyes shut tight, I inhaled and forced my shoulders to drop.

What day is it?

I shot a quick look to my right. Wincing, I shaded my eyes as a shaft of light drove through the giant sequoias. The bright sun was dropping fast, yet the endless number of trees, with trunks so large it seemed a journey to even travel around one, kept my trek south slow and unsteady. My pace quickened without thinking as the sun neared the western horizon. I wanted to run, but I had no energy—no willpower—left.

I licked my dry lips. It wasn't the first time over the past few months I'd longed for water. But I shook my head. Right now, I just had to survive.

The breeze picked up, another wave of brisk air cutting across my face. I sucked in a breath as I turned my face and continued on. Cradling my broken wrist against my chest, I winced against the pulsating ache that had increased from the cold air. The pale white bandages were a reminder of the events only days before. *Tristan ...* When I'd leapt off the fortress walls in my effort to get away, I'd landed wrong on the ground. With a grimace, I inhaled, letting my wrist relax. As the tension faded, so did the wracking waves of pain. *Keep going, Juliet.* Forcing the memories of that night from my mind, I focused on placing one foot in front of the other.

A few months before, I had hiked through the Redwoods with Cam. Now, I was alone. Adnan had been with me in the portal, but not with me when I arrived. And like the first time, when I had entered Ryujin, the portal wouldn't let me back through. Tears stung my eyes.

My legs felt like jelly as another giant of the old forest faded, but excitement fueled my pace when I finally swung my gaze forward again. *The road.* I could see the curve of gray asphalt just ahead, and I stumbled as I began to jog.

I had energy left after all. *No,* a small voice urged me. *You have hope.*

The movement forced my blood to pump, warming my body. Taking the hilt and angling the sword away, I fell to my knees beside the narrow road. Relief swept over me so strongly I almost cried. Laying my palm flat against the ground, I sighed. It was icy to the touch. But satisfaction had already begun to creep its way through me. It was pavement. *Pavement.*

My head buzzed from exhaustion and dehydration, but I laughed and laughed.

<hr>

Tall forms towered over me, tall and magnificent, their green tops rustling in the slightest of breezes. *Giants.* I blinked and focused. No, trees.

Redwoods.

My eyelashes fluttered as I fought back a yawn. I struggled into a standing position from where I had been resting. *Oh, my head.* Tightening my jaw against the pain, I took in the darkening sky. At any moment, the park's gates would be closing, unless they already had.

Despair grew. *No, keep going.*

Gritting my teeth, I stood and squared my shoulders. I took a moment to breathe as I squinted through the shadows that had fallen under the thick canopy of trees. Even the road cutting a narrow swath through the forest failed to let in much of the dying light. There were no sounds from wildlife, other than the odd chirp of a bird. It was an eerie silence, echoed by the droning whistle of the wind in the trees.

A mechanical hum beat a steady rhythm alongside the faint trill of the wind. When it crescendoed into a growl, I cocked my head. The pavement beneath my feet vibrated.

Headlights rounded a corner up ahead, speeding forward like two eyes without a face. My heart raced with the relief flooding my body. Eyes wide, I signaled for the car to slow down.

For a moment, I thought it was speeding up rather than slowing down. My movements grew wild as I waved the driver down. *Please, please, please.*

They slowed.

"Thank God," I choked out as the windowless Jeep rolled to a stop next to me.

Chapter Two

I stared out over the lake. The waters barely moved in the still air. Here and there, light shone from headlamps and phone screens. The few people who wanted to take advantage of the early morning. A bird called, heralding the arrival of dawn. A runner disappeared around the curve, and I was left alone. I lifted my head. Relief flooded me as I basked in the quiet surrounding me.

Stepping forward, I halted on the sidewalk curving around the lake's edge. Water lapped the concrete wall in gentle waves, and the rushes rippled in the breeze. My hair brushed against my face, a tickling sensation following. I was alone, but I hadn't been before. My heart clenched inside my chest. Adnan had been there. The hope that had burned bright in me while in the Redwoods had now died out. *Something happened.* He was with me when I fell through the portal into this world, my world. My eyes drifted closed. *I could smell him, feel him ...*

The thrum of an engine nearby startled me. I watched as it drove away. Adnan was not here. But my family waited for me. Cam waited for me. *Or are they?* First, my parents had lost their son, and now their daughter. The pain of Eddie's death came rushing back, more potent now that I was home. It wasn't just my head any longer. My throat hurt from the tension. *Eddie, Mari, Emi, and so many others. Will the deaths ever end?*

I had thought of my parents so little. *But there was so much that happened. There wasn't time.* The water below me continued its ebb and flow. Did I want to see them? *Yes. No.* I fought back a scream. *I should have thought about them more; I should have missed them more.* A few months had passed, months in which I knew where I had been, what I'd done, and what I'd seen, but they—they didn't know where I'd been. For all they knew, I could be dead. *I do miss them.* I chewed on my lower lip. What could I say to them after all this time? *Do I give them the truth?*

My hand clenched around the hilt of my sword. The sun would soon shine her light across the land. And I knew I would draw attention. I studied the reeds below me. There was a bit of dry ground there. Biting my lip, I debated whether to leave the blade.

Backing up, I took a deep breath. No. It was my last link to the world I had left behind.

"It's not my world," I whispered. "This is."

A warm, toasty aroma filled the air. Coffee. It had been a long time since I had smelled it or tasted it. I closed my eyes and drank it in. *I really am home.*

The slight crunch of wheels driving over loose rock. I jumped, my heart racing. Then the silence of an engine being shut off. My body stiffened. A gray sedan, the same car I had ridden in hundreds of times over the years.

They were here. There had been no time to wait for a response to the text I'd sent. The people I'd received a ride from had let me use a phone. One text. Now I knew the waiting was over.

I let go of the katana's hilt and stepped forward across the dew-dampened grass, away from the lake. The ground was spongy, the lawn perfectly manicured.

I stopped at the edge of the parking lot, where the grass gave way to gravel.

Mom got out first and froze when she caught sight of me. Dad stepped out next and closed the door, the sharp click extra loud in the tense silence. We all stood frozen like statues.

How many months? For the first time, it felt strange. Not once had I given overt thought to which day it was, not until now. *I left on September seventeenth.* It was February when I left Ryujin. *This is more than about time.* My parents didn't move. *Almost five months. How must I look to them?*

My ears rang. I shifted. Black boots encased my feet, light and durable, but the tight pants, the long tunic fitted with a belt—these weren't clothes I'd worn before. I chewed on my lower lip. *And the katana.* There was still no reaction. Nothing. It was as though my parents had turned to stone in front of me.

One foot forward and then another. Neither step was easy, nor were the ones that followed. They watched me approach, but they didn't move, didn't say anything. I raised a hand in greeting, my mouth dry. I looked for something—anything—from them. But there was nothing. *Please. Give me something!*

Dad's hand shot to Mom's wrist, gripping it. He stepped forward, face white, dragging her along with him until they halted right in front of me. She ripped her arm away and hugged me. She squeezed me until it hurt to breathe. She buried her face in the crook of my neck and cried, her sobs achingly loud. I relaxed into her familiar, jasmine-scented embrace.

I'm crying, I realized. Salty tears ran over my lips and dripped into my mom's hair. I clutched her like she was my lifeline, my eyes shut tight. If I loosened my grip, I felt she would disappear forever. The small, old ray of love blossomed within me, blooming until it filled my being, yet bringing with it a pang of guilt that sliced through me like a dagger. I'd not wanted to come home—I'd missed them, but not enough to come home. How could I not have missed her more?

I gasped as strong arms encircled Mom and me, almost lifting us off the ground.

"I don't understand!" Mom cried, her breaths coming in hiccups. "Where were you?"

I flinched. Her accusation rent the air. My parents stepped back, holding me at arm's length as their eyes roved over me.

Where was I? I still didn't know what to say. The answer they wanted, they couldn't have. But what to tell them? I was like a fish puckering its lips, wanting air but failing to attain it—a fish floundering in a dry seabed.

Dad spoke, his voice gruffer than I remembered. Gray hair lined his temples. Had those been there before? He took his wife's arm. "Mel, let's talk about this later." He pulled her away, but his blue eyes didn't leave mine as he said, "Come on."

Mom's gaze flashed across me as she turned, almost unwillingly. Her shoulders stooped, her face pale.

The knot deep within my stomach tightened.

They're older. I was older, too, but not like them. I knew what they saw; I'd been gone for months. But it looked like years had been piled onto them. *It can't have been.* I followed with slow steps. *It's only been a few months.* But what if it wasn't February of the following year, but farther ahead?

Nausea settled in the pit of my stomach.

Mom glanced over her shoulder at me. "But—"

"Mel," Dad interrupted. "We'll talk later. Let's just get Juliet home." His voice cracked when he spoke my name.

Home.

"Juliet," Mom whispered. "Juliet. Are you hungry?" she asked as we sat in the car.

Dad started the engine, his focus on backing out of the small parking lot, but Mom's eyes wouldn't leave me, as though she was afraid I would disappear if she looked away.

I shook my head.

"Something to drink, then? Coffee?"

"No, thank you." I cringed even as I spoke, noticing the way Mom flinched. *So formal.* This was my mother, not some stranger.

But I couldn't ignore the wall that had sprung up between us.

⚘⚘

The music blared over the radio, loud enough to forestall conversation. Mom eventually turned to face the road ahead. She'd always gotten carsick easily.

I tried to ignore the way Mom kept glancing at me in her mirror, as though she were already interrogating me in her head. But I couldn't tell them the truth. Would the truth allay the fears they already had or serve to drive them in deeper? How could they believe me?

I shifted the katana on my hip a little to a more comfortable position. When I glanced up, I saw Mom's eyes narrow. Maybe it was a mistake to bring the sword.

"We're here," Dad said as we pulled into the driveway. It had felt like no time at all. Too early for traffic, our drive had been shortened to about an hour. Even now, the sun's rays were still low over the horizon.

I pressed my forehead against the cool glass window. Our two-story house lay in its familiar ramshackle way. The bright red paint on the door Dad loved so much glared as the sunlight bounced off it. The roses lay pruned and ready for spring, when they would flower in red brilliance.

Red.

So much red. First blood and now—

I swallowed and opened the car door. None of us spoke as we walked up to the door and slipped inside.

"What are you doing?" Mom asked with wide eyes.

I eyed the boot in my hand from where I crouched. Oh. It had never been a practice in our home, at least not at the front door, to take our shoes off. Each of our closets had a shelf for shoes. But in Ryujin, it was customary to exchange outdoor shoes for indoor slippers.

"No matter," Dad insisted, brushing it off. "Let's go in. I could use something to eat."

I slipped the boot back onto my foot and laced it up. Standing, I tried pushing away the strange feeling I had. Both felt natural. Wearing shoes inside, not wearing shoes inside, and yet I found myself liking the habit I'd formed in Ryujin.

"You're wearing different clothes," Mom noted, ignoring Dad.

"Of course she would be," Dad muttered, looking at Mom as though I wasn't still standing there. "It's not yesterday she disappeared."

"I know that!" she exclaimed, tears springing to her eyes. I resisted the urge to lay my hand on her arm. This wasn't going the way I thought it would. *But how did you think this would go?* So many replies ran through my mind, yet they stuck on my tongue like glue.

"Juliet," Mom said, her voice quivering as she strove for control. "Why don't you freshen up? I'll make us some breakfast, and then we can all sit down and talk."

A heaviness settled upon me, a different battle I had still to fight: *Sit down and talk.* I nodded and went upstairs. When I opened the door, I balked. It was the same. Nothing had been moved. Even my basket of clean laundry stood waiting to be folded. It was preserved like a scene out of the past, a memory, a moment of déjà vu. I don't know how long I stood there before a clatter from the kitchen jolted me.

Entering the bathroom, I saw the toiletries I'd left on the counter in a haphazard way, the items I'd decided not to take with me on our vacation. But as I picked up my brush, I realized it had been dusted. Everything had been dusted and cleaned. Mom had never lost hope I'd return.

I dropped the brush, watching it fall as though in slow motion until it clattered against a small glass bowl. It lay there unmoving while I stared and, without touching it, left.

The bedding rustled as I sat on the edge of the bed and fingered the rose stitching on the coverlet. Falling back against the stack of soft white pillows, I stared up at the ceiling. The bed was more comfortable than anything I'd lain on in Ryujin. Pressure built behind my eyes.

"Don't cry," I whispered into the empty room. But the tears came anyway. I cried as I hadn't since Emi had died and Adnan had held me. The tears streamed down my cheeks and onto my bed, soaking the pillow beneath my cheek.

Dragging another pillow to my chest, I clutched it with wild fingers, but a void remained in my heart. I had been kidnapped twice in the past few months, mistreated, and put through the gauntlet. And yet I lived where so many others had died. I was home.

Gasping, I choked on the sobs even as I struggled to hold them back. My breath came in hiccups as I strived for air to enter my lungs.

This is my home, I reminded myself. Then why did it feel so empty?

Fist clenched next to my heart, I lay there, vaguely aware of the unsteady beat hammering inside my chest. Nothing occupied my thoughts. So much pounded against the mental walls I'd put up, but I focused on nothing, on keeping out everything and everyone who wanted a voice. Sometimes, nothing was bliss.

Or maybe it's just the easy way out.

The bedroom that had been my home for two decades now felt like a dream. *I'm home now.* Even though my room had been preserved as though no time had gone by, it had. My job no longer existed, my community of friends was busy with their own lives, and even my hobbies seemed distant. *I need to settle back in.* That meant seeing Cam and figuring out a plan for work.

I fingered my pillow and surveyed my room. Even my things felt like they only belonged to me in a life past.

Get up, Juliet, I reminded myself.

Mom and Dad were waiting for me.

Chapter Three

The fridge and freezer hummed, the low buzz of electricity vibrated, and the warm air blowing through the vents finished off the symphony. It was a far cry from what it had been like in Ryujin. The noise was prevalent here. I found myself missing the quiet.

Mom shifted, and the brown leather couch creaked. Dad tried to ignore it, but stiffened. I licked my lips and stared, unsure of what to say or where to start.

When did we become strangers? My heart thrummed within my chest. These were the two people I had spoken to the most, outside of Cam. It had only been a few months, yet it seemed longer. Dad's graying hair was now a starker contrast in the bright morning light, and Mom appeared weary, age lines showing at the corners of her eyes.

I blinked, and the spell broke.

Dad eased back into the couch. "So where have you been?"

My hands trembled in my lap. I glanced at the cup of coffee sitting on the table in front of me. *I miss the tea back in Ryujin.* My tongue flicked out over my lips. "I—" My mind raced. Dad acted relaxed, but anxiety and nervous energy radiated from Mom as she shifted yet again.

"Well?" he asked when I said nothing.

"I can't say," I whispered. There. It was out.

Mom started, her mouth opening, but Dad laid a hand on her arm. "What do you mean? You can't talk about it?" An unmistakable growl scraped his voice.

My mind was blank. What could I say? "I don't remember." That clicked. *I don't remember.* I picked up my mug, full of steaming brown liquid.

"You don't remember?" Mom asked, lacing her fingers together in her lap. "That's not possible. You have to remember something."

"What's the last thing you remember?" Dad asked.

"Being in the Redwoods with Cam." I shrugged, hoping they couldn't see the slight tremble in my hands. "There's nothing since then—at least, not until yesterday."

"Absolutely nothing?" Dad confirmed.

I shook my head but kept my gaze locked on his. *Show him my sincerity.* "Nothing."

"What happened yesterday?"

Taking a sip of coffee, I considered my next move. Saying I didn't remember the events of the past few months was convenient, but it also could be believable—more believable—than the truth.

"I found myself in the Redwoods." I shrugged, shaking my head and letting my shoulders droop a little. "I hitchhiked to Olympia, used someone's phone to text you, and you know the rest."

Mom snorted. "Who? Who was it with you? Are you sure they didn't have anything to do with it? And what about your clothes? Not to mention the sword!"

"They didn't," I replied. "It was a random person I had never seen before."

"How do you know?" she pressed with a note of hysteria.

I didn't answer, but the tears welling in my eyes did all the work. This was hard—harder than I'd ever imagined. *But how much did you think about it?* The question blared, yet I was the only one who could hear it. I clutched my hands together in my lap. Dad shook his head and sighed. I knew he believed me.

Have I become that good at deception? With just a few sentences, I'd fooled my own parents. Words and tears. I reached up and slid a finger across my cheek. It came away wet. If anything could wreck me, it would be the guilt I now felt. This was nothing in comparison to the guilt I'd felt for putting them through months of my absence. *But it's needed. I can't tell them.*

"Juliet!" Mom almost yelled.

I jumped, the coffee almost sloshing onto my lap.

"Mel." Dad sighed and shifted on the couch, reaching out to lay a hand on Mom's arm.

She jerked away. "Don't *Mel* me," Mom snapped, shooting him a glare. "Our daughter has been gone for *months*, and she returns not knowing anything that's happened during that time?"

The knot in my stomach grew. "Mom?"

Both of my parents remained silent.

"How long have I been gone?" I asked again.

Silence fell again. The thrum of the modern-day world reminded me of where I now sat. Ryujin was no more. Part of me longed for the simplicity again, for the complete quiet that existed there.

"Juliet!"

I looked up at Dad.

"Snap out of it."

"What?"

"Jeffery," Mom interrupted, laying her hand on Dad's arm. "Juliet, what was going on in your mind just now?"

I stared at her. Mom's voice had taken on an eerie sort of calmness to it, though she'd just been shaking with emotion.

"What?" The question escaped before I could take it back. I watched as my parents exchanged another confused glance. "Had you said something?"

"Yes," Mom replied, her voice soft and filled with concern. "Juliet ..."

I found myself waiting as though sitting on pins and needles, holding my breath for the answer. *How long have I been gone?* My heartbeat quickened within my chest. *Thrum, thrum, thrum.*

"You've been gone for almost five months."

My legs uncrossed, and I sat back. *I was right.* It was February here too.

Mom nodded. "It's been a long time, sweetheart. We—" She glanced at Dad. "We didn't think you would be coming back."

My head shook, my hair bouncing from the jerk. That wasn't true. My bedroom had been kept pristine, as though I'd never left. "You didn't lose hope," I murmured. Hearing the timeframe confirmed wrecked me. My foot tapped the ground. I laid my right hand over my injured wrist, thankful for the reminder of Ryujin and my time there, even if it had ended with a broken wrist. "My room is just the same as it was when I left."

Tears streamed down Mom's cheeks, but she didn't make a sound.

Dad cleared his throat. "It's February third. It was September seventeenth when you disappeared in the Redwoods, when you were with Cam ..." He trailed off, his voice cracking. His chin quivered. "So it's been four and a half months, going on five." He took a long gulp of his coffee. "Juliet, it's just ..." He trailed off as his face paled. "It was almost easier to think you were dead than to picture you alive somewhere, with someone, with—" He broke off.

Mom scooted closer to Dad's side. "We couldn't imagine what was being done to you if you were alive."

They didn't know I had been kidnapped. First by Hirose, though I hadn't known it at the time, followed by Tristan, and then by Creulon, though that was purposeful. *But I'd wanted to be taken by his men.* I swallowed. I knew my parents' minds had gone to sex trafficking. *But they aren't far off,* I realized. *While I was never a sex slave, I went through so much, both physically and mentally.* Tears stung my eyes.

"Do you remember something?" Mom asked.

I shook my head.

Dad's jaw tightened. "We'll have to alert the police today."

I jerked. "What?"

Mom's legs crossed at the ankles. "You've been on the missing persons list, Juliet. They scoured the Redwoods for you after you'd been missing for twenty-four hours. We searched everywhere, talked to everyone we could find. Friends and family joined in the hunt for you ..." She inhaled a deep breath. "After a few days, we kept expecting your body to turn up somewhere, but it never did. There was no sign of you."

Almost five months. The timeframe ran through my dazed mind again. I stood up and paced. I hadn't kept track of time there, not until the end, not until I'd seen the cherry blossom trees. *February.* Peering through the clean panes of glass, I watched as gray clouds billowed with a slow wind across the sky. The grass lay green and wet from the gentle rain, which fell from above. I glanced over my shoulder at them. They hadn't moved a muscle.

I sighed and turned. What had the stress done to them?

"We'll try to stave off the questioning until tomorrow," Dad said, his voice gruff. "And we need to find out what the next steps are." He laid a hand on his knee.

"What do you mean?" I asked as I approached.

Mom folded her hands in her lap. "Oh, sweetheart. There's so much." She bit her lip. "We need to figure out what's to be done about you. I'm sure there are tests we need to run."

"What kind of tests?" I interrupted.

"Well," she stated, her foot tapping on the floor. "One is to see if anything has been done to you that you don't remember—"

"What?" I knew where their minds had gone, what they were afraid of. But I hadn't been taken advantage of, no matter how close I had come.

"And two," Mom continued as though she hadn't heard me, "to see if there's anything that can be done to bring back your memories."

I folded my arms across my chest. *Tests.* I strove to push away the feelings of defensiveness that welled up inside of me. I didn't need tests. I knew what had happened to me. I remembered everything. *But how are they to know that?* It was war within me. *But I can't tell them.* My arms fell by my sides.

Mom stood and took my hands. "We'll just take it a day at a time." She smiled, tucking her hair behind her ear. "We'll figure this all out, together, as a family."

Dad got up from the couch. "Cam will want to see you."

Mom nodded, the lines around her eyes deepening. "We need to tell her today as well. She's had a hard time since you disappeared and has dealt with a lot of guilt."

Cam. It had been ages since I'd seen her last, and it probably felt longer for her than it had for me. "It's not her fault," I whispered.

"No, it's not," Dad agreed. "But it doesn't change how much she feels responsible. She's blamed herself ever since that day."

I know how that feels. Pain filled my heart. Ever since Eddie had died, I had carried that guilt with me. *But there isn't anything I can do to change the past. And I was so young.* Ryujin had helped me. It was there that I had learned how to move on and to stop blaming myself. *Now I might be able to help Cam do the same.*

"Juliet?" Mom asked in a plaintive tone as she held up her empty cup. "Could you go fetch more coffee from the kitchen?" Her gaze flitted down, and she froze. "What happened to your wrist?"

It twinged as I glanced down and back up again. "It—" *Wait, I can't tell her the truth. I'm not supposed to remember.* "I don't know." I let fear sift into my voice.

Mom frowned. "Did it break?"

"Mel, she can't remember," Dad broke in, wrapping an arm around her shoulders. "Juliet, why don't you go get the coffee?"

I spun on my heel and left the room, not bothering to remind them it would be more difficult with only one working hand. Out of sight from my parents, I stopped, my back to the wall, and closed my eyes. A moment to breathe.

"Jeffery," Mom whispered, her voice just loud enough for me to hear.

I jerked and turned my head. *You could go. You don't have to listen.* I ignored the warning.

"We need to figure out which hospital we should take her to. She needs help. She can't accept this and just move on. None of us can. I mean, not really. We'll always be wondering, and how can she truly get over having supposedly missed out on half a year of her life?" Mom's voice rose in pitch. "It just can't be like that. I'm sure there's help we can get her."

I imagined Mom leaning toward Dad.

"I'm sure there's some sort of doctor who deals with this," Mom continued. "Aren't there many doctors who can reach into the depths of your mind to unlock lost memories? And I'm pretty sure trauma can cause amnesia, right?"

"Mel," Dad broke in, his voice hoarse. "Mel, don't get carried away. Of course we'll see what we can do, what can be done, but for now, please don't let Juliet see what you're feeling or let her feel any of your doubts. I think the first step is just helping her settle back in—"

Please, I pleaded in silence. *No tests.*

"As though everything is the same? Because it isn't," Mom protested. "It isn't the same, so why pretend otherwise? It's been almost five months, Jeff!"

"Just wait, Mel—wait until we've talked to someone about this. Neither of us has any experience with this sort of thing."

"Jeffery!" Mom snapped. "It's not something we should ever have to deal with. Not only did our daughter go missing, but now claims to not know what happened, where she's been, what she's been doing. She could've been kidnapped by someone, held under lock and key, abused, drugged, used as a sex slave, or any manner of things."

This is why they can never know the truth. My head tilted back. The ceiling was interwoven with tiny curlicues from where it had been painted at some point in time.

"Mel, stop it. Get a hold of yourself. Those thoughts won't help her, not right now. We can't change the past. She is our priority right now, not what she's been through but what she's going through now."

"Oh, Jeff," Mom murmured, her voice breaking.

Air hissed through my teeth as I sucked in a breath, my limbs trembling as I sagged against the wall.

This is so much harder than I expected, I thought as I stepped toward the kitchen. But what did I expect?

⚬⚬⚬

I lay in bed, peering up at the plain white ceiling. This was becoming a habit. When had ceilings become so interesting? With a groan of frustration, I rolled over. I couldn't sleep. Counting, thinking of nice things ... they all distracted me from running over everything that had happened that day. It hadn't even been twenty-four hours since I'd been walking with Adnan and had seen Natsumi. She'd warned me of things to come. She said one day I would understand more than I did now.

I glanced at my bedside table where two knives lay, looking out of place on the dainty piece of white wood. I'd found them when undressing for a shower earlier, one in my boot and one along my forearm. I had forgotten all about them. Now, I stretched out a hand and picked them up, turning them as I felt their familiar weight.

Something creaked in the hall outside my room. I stiffened and moved the knives under my pillow. After a few moments of silence, there was a step, then nothing. Whoever it was had moved on.

Exhaling, I lay back onto my pillow. "I'm home," I reminded myself in a whisper. My head swam. On the wall hung a framed drawing of our family tree Mom had created years ago. The elaborate strokes of ink portraying the extensiveness of the tree, down to the very roots below the ground. *Roots.* A few months ago, I'd traveled to another world through roots, and now—now I'd returned to my roots.

⚜ ⚜

A sharp bang clashed through the air. I jerked awake and leapt out of bed. The door was open, and a small silhouette stood there. I rubbed my eyes. Mom's blurred figure sharpened as I focused.

"Juliet." Mom hesitated on the threshold. "I didn't mean to open the door with that much force ..." She eyed my hand as her voice trailed off. She stared at my right hand.

The dagger.

"Oh," I said as I thrust it behind my back. "It's okay."

Mom stepped back. "Dinner is ready."

"Dinner," I echoed.

She nodded. "Yes, I made your favorite. Dad's already down there."

Is her formality as obvious to her as it is to me? It was then that I smelled the savory aroma of enchiladas with all its spices and comforting warmth wafting into my room. I felt myself relax a fraction more.

"Enchiladas!" The joy bubbling up within me pushed away the formality surrounding our conversation.

Mom's face brightened, her shoulders falling a little from their tense position. "Better come before Dad eats it all," she called as she walked away.

I paused to tuck both daggers underneath my mattress. Mom knew I had one now. She'd seen how I'd reacted. I glanced once more at my bed before turning. *She won't forget that.*

CHAPTER FOUR

The floor creaked as I stepped off the stairs and headed toward the living room. Portraits hung along the wall in a collage of black frames, showcasing the life I'd had.

I stopped in my tracks. Silence hung in a heavy stillness throughout the hallway. There was a gold-edged portrait next to mine. In it, a brown-haired, freckle-faced boy stared back at me, his eyes mischievous and glinting. I sucked in a breath. *Will his death ever stop hurting?*

Throughout the house, heat began blowing through the vents with a throbbing huff of air. In the next frame, Eddie was a little older, a little closer to the day he would no longer be alive. For the first time, I was able to look at these portraits without the heaviness of guilt weighing me down. *I'll never stop missing you.*

Blinking back tears, I moved on to the next one.

"Juliet?"

I jumped up to see Mom standing at the end of the hallway, her forehead creased.

"Honey, the police are here."

I sniffed and stood a little straighter. "What?"

She nodded and forced her face to relax. "It's all right. Dinner will just have to wait a little while. Come on."

I nodded and glanced once more at the photo. Looking away, I drew in a deep, shuddering breath and squared my shoulders. The police—that didn't take long.

I continued down the hallway. Passing the corridor that led to the kitchen, a waft of savory spices filled the air. My stomach rumbled.

A few more steps, and I entered our large and spacious living room. *The same room I have spent countless hours in over my lifetime.*

"Juliet," Dad began in his distinctive monotone. "These are detectives Brockwell and Anderson."

Deep breaths. I forced the scowl from my face as I approached. "Hello."

The detectives eyed me for a moment before they both nodded.

"Juliet Barrows," Detective Anderson replied before looking at Mom and Dad. "We have some questions for you." His gaze flicked down to the notebook he held in his hands.

"Why don't we sit?" Detective Brockwell suggested. Without waiting, he sat down on the couch. It rustled under his weight as he settled. His thin lips appeared even thinner as he concentrated on me.

I took a seat across from them, listening as Mom and Dad shifted their weight behind me.

Anderson leaned forward. "Tell us, please, what happened."

"I don't know."

"What. Do. You. Mean. You. Don't. Know?" Brockwell asked.

"I don't know," I repeated. "I don't remember anything after Cam and I separated until I woke up yesterday."

"All right, then," Anderson replied with a sigh. "How did you and Cam get separated?"

I squinted as though trying to remember. "Cam had to pee, so she went off, and I kept walking." *Make them feel it.* Eyes wide, I continued, "I didn't go far, but somehow Cam got lost. We called back and forth, like a Marco Polo game, and then ..."

"And then?" Brockwell exclaimed, leaning forward. "What happened then?"

I shrugged and raised my hands in the air. "Nothing. I don't remember anything after that."

Both detectives relaxed back into the couch. Anderson peeked at his phone, then at his blank pad of paper. He flipped back a page before setting it back in his pocket.

"Well," Brockwell said, patting down his tie, "it correlates with Cam's description of the events."

Of course it does. I glanced back and forth between the two men. *That part is the truth.*

Anderson laid a bulky arm over his chest and reached up to stroke the stubble on his chin. "What happened after that?"

I tapped my fingers against my knee. "I don't remember."

"When *do* you remember?" Anderson asked.

Brockwell spoke before I could. "Let me guess, it was yesterday?"

I nodded, trying to hide how my heart rate rose. Suspicion shone in the way the detective's head tilted to the side and in how his bushy eyebrows drew together. Yet he gestured for me to continue.

I drew in a deep breath and gathered my thoughts. "I woke up still in the Redwoods." As I spoke, I let confusion seep into my tone. "I wasn't sure what was going on, what was happening, for a bit. But I remembered being there with Cam—" I hesitated as my friend's petite figure and thick brown hair surged into my thoughts. I shook my head. "I could tell it was different than when I remembered being there with Cam."

"How so?" Anderson asked, tapping his pen on his thigh.

"The temperature was a lot colder. At first, I didn't do anything, but then I realized I had to find a way out of there. It was too cold." I shivered at the memory of finding myself back in my world, and without Adnan.

"Do you remember something else?" Brockwell asked, stilling.

"No." I couldn't tell if he believed me or not. *Does it really matter in the end?*

"All right," he replied, the couch creaking as he shifted his weight. "I gather you walked until you came across someone?"

"I headed south. I knew if I was anywhere near the spot I'd been hiking with Cam, then there would be a road somewhere south of me." My foot tapped on the wood floor. "And there was. I hitchhiked to Olympia, where I texted my parents. I think you know the rest."

Mom stepped forward and tucked her hair behind one ear as she spoke. "That was early this morning."

Brockwell glanced at his partner. "Well, I suppose there isn't much else we can ask you, given you don't remember anything." He kept his voice even, but the nagging feeling that he suspected me hadn't left.

I gave a wan smile. "I wish I could remember," I murmured. "But I don't."

Anderson stood up. "I'm sorry. Perhaps you will. Give it time." He surveyed my parents. "It would be best if you took her to the hospital to be checked out. There are tests that should be run."

I stood as well. "But—"

"You're right," Mom agreed, ignoring me. "We'll do that."

"But we'll give Juliet a little time to settle in first," Dad said, putting his arm around Mom.

Brockwell shifted his weight, the couch creaking. "There was no one else with you in the forest?"

Adnan flashed into my mind. It was such a clear image of him. His clothes in shades of browns and dark greens. His cloak pulled tight around him, cowl dropping down to reveal a face framed by shaggy brown hair and stubble on his cheeks and chin ...

An ache grew deep within, so real that it physically hurt. *He's not here.* My hand clenched. "No, it was just me. There was no one else."

"You're sure?" Brockwell pressed. "There was no one else?"

"I'm *sure*," I repeated. *But I wish there had been. Where are you?*

"Is there something wrong, Detective?" Mom asked, wringing her hands. "Do you think she wasn't alone?"

"No, of course not, Mrs. Barrows." Anderson shot a quick glare at his partner. "We'll be going now, but we'll be in touch if we have any more questions."

Brockwell stood. "And if you *do* remember something, please let us know."

Mom nodded and came to stand beside me.

"Thanks," Dad said, leading the way to the front door. The detectives' footsteps clicked against the wood floor as they followed him. I had a feeling this wasn't the last I'd see of Anderson and Brockwell. My heart hammered inside my chest.

The door closed with a soft thud. My hands trembled. The spicy smells wafting from the kitchen reminded me of home, but my stomach clenched. Food was the last thing I wanted right now. I fought to keep my emotions under control. *Adnan should be here.* He'd know what to do, how to handle all of this. I sighed. He'd know what I'd need to hear. *And I miss him.*

"Come on, honey." Mom stood, waiting. Her eyes were loving, but hurt shone there. *She cares. She loves me. I've been missing for almost five months, which has seemed like a lifetime to her.*

I stood and gave her a hug, her familiar jasmine perfume surrounding me. Tears sprang to my eyes. She clutched me tighter, not wanting to let me go. My chin trembled as I fought to keep from crying. Jasmine reminded me of Ryujin.

"I forgot you always loved this scent, Mom," I whispered, letting go of her.

Mom sniffled and reached up to stroke my cheek as though I were a little girl again. "I can't seem to switch to anything else," she admitted, but her eyebrows drew together. "Does it mean something to you?"

I nodded and took another deep breath. The scent washed over me. My breath caught in my chest. "It's just home," I replied. *Home here or there?* My body swayed, and I backed up a step. "I need a moment."

"Juliet—"

"Go on and eat without me," I blurted as I fled, my feet barely clinging to my slippers as I made my way back to the safety of my room.

The wood floor creaked and groaned under my weight, the sounds familiar but not comforting. My chest hurt. My hands shook as I closed the door behind me and leaned against it.

My hands clenched into fists. I'd been able to smell Adnan through the portal, feel him ... but I sank down onto the floor, my back to the door. *Did I imagine it all?* Had I wanted him to come so badly that I had imagined him doing so?

Tears slid down my cheeks, faster and faster. I cradled my head on my arms as I cried. My throat ached from the pressure of keeping my sobs quiet. My parents couldn't know. *They must not know.* Secrets upon secrets.

"There's no one to talk to," I whispered. *Not here.*

As the tears slowed and dried up, like a dam blocking a river's rushing current, I stood. A few steps, and I was at the window. Here, I gazed out at an atypical Pacific Northwest winter afternoon. It was beautiful, peaceful, and bright. The unusual occurrence of sunshine chased away the depressing gray. The backyard was green and perfectly manicured, thanks to my dad. The houses reminded me of all the people who lived around us. And the paved street to the left, with its metal streetlights, reminded me of the world I was from—the world I was *in*.

Ryujin was the past. *My world is the present, with or without Adnan.* I closed my eyes and drew in a deep breath. Musty earth and the scent of rain.

"I won't forget you," I whispered, clasping my arms about me. I watched as the sun continued its slow descent below the horizon. The rays shot across the sky with a brilliance of pink. I should have been happy to be home, to be with my parents, to see Cam. But no matter how much I told myself that, I felt like something was missing. I shook my head. *Adnan wouldn't want this to hurt so much. He would tell me to keep going, no matter what.*

I drew the shades down. "Stay strong, Juliet," I whispered to the dark room.

Adnan had said that to me. Kin had spoken those words. Now they floated in the air, vibrant, reaching for me but never quite arriving.

My jaw clenched. I was home.

Chapter Five

The sun from the day before had gone, hidden behind the clouds. The gray dreariness was back. It fed into my soul, leaving me unsettled and uncertain. The moment I woke up, I knew what I needed to do. *Who* I needed to see. It was the first step in beginning to settle back into my life.

I felt certain my parents wouldn't have let me leave if I had asked. So I didn't ask them. Dressing and slipping my shoes on was the easy part. Even leaving my room and quietly closing the door was easy.

Five months ago, I wouldn't have dared sneak out of the house. I wouldn't have given it a thought. But things were different now—I was different. It was easy to avoid the stairs that creaked. Downstairs, I crept along the hallway toward the kitchen. The nightmares I had dealt with throughout the night still hovered on the fringes of my mind as I hesitated. *Mom.* I couldn't let her see me. Dishes clattered in the kitchen as she cleaned. Taking a couple of steps forward, I paused in front of the closed office door. I knew Dad would be inside, surrounded by paperwork. He had never been the most organized accountant. A small grin flickered over my lips as I pictured him.

Silence fell. I heard footsteps approaching. Slipping back down the hallway to the bathroom, I hid inside and peered around the open doorway. Mom came out of the kitchen with a mug in one hand and entered the living room.

Oh, by the—

I bit back a groan. The living room was in perfect line of sight of both the front door and the archway into the kitchen, where the door to the backyard was. There wouldn't be any slipping past her. My heart raced as I tried to figure out another way. *Of course.* I headed back upstairs with a grin and closed my bedroom door with a soft click. The adrenaline boost rejuvenated me. *I'm not so scared anymore.*

I couldn't keep a little bounce out of my walk as I strode across to the wide window. Something like this would have been unimaginable before Ryujin. I swung the latch and winced as it clicked louder than I had expected. But there was no sound in the hallway outside. With careful, slow movements, I lifted the screen out of its setting and leaned down to set it against the outside wall of the house. Sticking my head out, I looked at the roof of the covered porch just a few feet below me. I glanced down at my wrist. It ached worse at the thought. I blew out the breath I had been holding.

Swinging one leg over the sill, I balanced for a moment before gripping it with my good hand and swinging my other leg over so that both legs dangled over the covered porch. *You can do this.*

I scooted off the windowsill, letting my one good hand slow my fall before I let go and dropped onto the roof. My ankles jarred on impact. Taking another deep breath, I rose from my crouch and grinned. Now for the same thing again. Within a minute, I was on the ground. *There.*

I wiped my hands on the back of my pants as I strode along the yard to the white fence. Gripping the top with both hands, I jumped and heaved myself up so I could swing one leg over, then the other. Dropping to the ground, I stood and looked up to see a strange woman watching me with wide eyes from where she stood on the sidewalk.

I inclined my head and moved past her. The wind cut through the layers I wore. I buried my hands in my pockets, wishing I had grabbed a heavier jacket. It was a couple miles to Cam's house, and I remembered the way like the back of my hand.

Yet even through the biting air, energy rushed through me. I was outside again. The fresh air surrounded me, the quiet stillness—until a car blew past me with a dull roar. *It's not like Ryujin,* I reminded myself. Everything was louder here. The cars, the faint electrical current from the power lines, the machines, everything. I had been gone less than five months, and already my world felt foreign.

My steps bounced as I strode. I wished there was someone I could talk to about it, to voice my thoughts ... but there was no one. *It used to be Cam.* I felt a surge of nervousness at the thought of seeing her again. I missed her. But no matter how close we were ...

"It'll be just like it used to be," I whispered.

But the voice in my head knew the truth: *No, it won't, Juliet. Because you can't tell her anything.*

Shadows from the awning hid me within their dark depths. I stood still, standing across the street from Cam's house. Her beat-up old bug was outside, so I knew she must be home. There was a slight movement in one of the upper windows—maybe it was just a breeze, but it was Cam's room. I'd spent countless hours there, doing homework, talking, having sleepovers ...

I bit my lip. *She's so close.*

"Hey, you need something?"

I started at the sound of the man's voice. Turning my head, I saw an older man sitting on his porch, a glass of orange juice in one hand and a newspaper in his lap.

"No."

"Then why are you standing in my yard, next to *my* house? And what interests you about the house across the street?" He raised one eyebrow.

I remembered an old woman sitting on her porch in a small coastal town. She had given me advice. "I'm sorry," I said as I moved forward to the sidewalk. "I'm just trying to make a decision."

"Humph. Really? What sort of decision takes that long to make? Life is too short to dilly-dally over choices. You either go forward or go back, and that's the way of it. You youngsters these days are always waiting for some sign or someone to tell you what to do." He shook his head and took a swallow of juice. "You know that sometimes you'll be given the answer by just going after something? Go after it, and if it's meant to be, it will be—and if it's not, well, then you have your answer."

I grinned. "That's actually pretty wise." *He's not the only one to sit on a porch and lay it out to me.*

"Well, of course it is. I'd better have gained some wisdom over the years; otherwise, that would be very sad indeed. You just remember that. Gain experience, gain wisdom. You won't always make the right choices, but if you learn from your mistakes and those of others, you'll be better off. " He shrugged and picked up his newspaper.

The grass below my feet felt spongy as I shifted my stance. "You know," I began, my voice measured. "I met an old woman on her porch one time. She gave me some advice as well."

The man cocked his head to the side. "Of course she did. We old folk often have at least a little to give. Now, have you made your decision yet?"

I grinned. "Yes."

"Good, now get a move on, then. You're making me nervous with your lurking."

I nodded and took a hesitant step, then another. With each one, my stride grew faster and more confident. I stopped in front of the red door and knocked. Three times my knuckles rapped against the wood.

A few moments of silence passed before Cam's face appeared in the narrow window alongside the door. Her eyes widened in recognition. Her jaw dropped. I raised a hand. Her head popped back out of view and then the door opened.

"Juliet." She stood there, staring at me, her complexion paler than usual.

"Hey," I said. Warmth spread over me at the sight of my best friend. I took her in—her small figure, her thick brown hair in a braid hanging over her shoulder, and her soft brown eyes. Shock waged a war within the depths of those eyes, in the quiver of her chin, and in her nervous fingers playing with her shirt hem.

"Juliet," she murmured again. "What—how—" She peered over my shoulder before stepping aside. "Why don't you come in."

I cringed at the formality of her tone, but I nodded and followed her inside.

"Do you want coffee?" Cam asked as she led the way down the hallway.

"Do you have tea?"

"Tea ..." she muttered, glancing at me with a raised eyebrow. "You used to always want coffee if there was a choice."

I shrugged my shoulders. "Tea has grown on me." I glanced about the room, noting the house seemed quiet. "Are you alone?"

"Yes. I only have one roommate now, and she's at work. Anyway, she won't be back for some time, so we—we can talk." Cam set the kettle on the stove with a sharp clatter. She leaned her back against the counter and crossed her arms over her chest. "So?"

I took off my wet jacket and sat on a barstool. "I don't know what to tell you."

Cam shook her head. "Yes, you do."

No. She wouldn't understand. She couldn't. Could she? She had been there for me when Eddie died. She had been there all the times we had imagined adventures as children, but the one that really mattered, she hadn't. She wasn't there in Ryujin. *She didn't come with me.*

Air filled my lungs as I inhaled. "I—"

The teapot's shrill whistle filled the room.

I watched as Cam poured the steaming tea and set a mug in front of me. The water swirled with a faint brown hue as it saturated the sachet. My mind focused in tunnel vision. *Sachet. Kin. Herbs.* Kin had given me herbs to help me sleep while I was in Creulon's mountain fortress. And Saya—Saya had used them to help us rescue the townsfolk from Umi no Machi. I swallowed and shoved it all to the back of my mind.

Clothing rustled as Cam took a seat on the barstool next to me. "So?" she asked, angling toward me.

"I don't remember." I wrapped my cold hands around the warm ceramic. The heat seeped through the bandage around my left wrist.

Her eyes narrowed. "Your mom told me she thinks you broke your wrist."

I nodded.

"You *really* don't remember?"

I fought to keep my voice level. Keeping the truth from her was harder than keeping it from my parents. *Why?* The question hit me like a thunderbolt. Cam sipped at her drink, lost in thought. *Because Cam was there for me in the way my parents weren't after Eddie's death.* A soft clatter brought me back to the present. Cam had set her mug down. I took a sip of the hot liquid. It wasn't the same, but it still reminded me of Ryujin.

"Juliet? Do you remember?"

The past months had to stay a secret. It would be easier that way. "No."

Cam's eyes widened. "I thought we always told each other the truth."

"Cam, I—"

She leaned away from me, her eyes glistening.

"I wish I could tell you more, but I can't. I don't remember."

There was no shock in the look she gave me.

"You already knew," I stated. "My parents told you."

"Yes, but I don't believe it," Cam replied. "I don't know why you're keeping this a secret. You can tell me. You can tell me anything."

I winced at her sharp undertone.

"I don't know what was so terrible you can't bring yourself to tell anyone, at least not yet, and so you're pushing it down as deep as you can, or—or if you regret something, but you—or you—oh, I don't know!" Cam's voice shook. "You've done it before, you know," she began again, quieter now. "When Eddie's accident happened. You pushed it all down. It took you a long time before you could talk to me about it, but it's always been hard for you." Pain edged her voice.

My eyes widened. *She's right.* I could almost hear my own heartbeat as everything drifted away and I became lost in my thoughts. *But it's not just about Eddie, about me ... It's about her. She's hurting.*

Time felt like it began to slow, and my vision grew hazy.

Can I tell her? She could be someone to talk to, to process with. Adnan knew I'd needed someone, and I did, just like I needed someone now. Sense and reason battled within me. She wouldn't understand. Even if she tried, would she believe me or cast me off as a deluded, crazy person?

No one here will understand, even if they do believe me. They can't understand.

My eyes misted.

"Juliet?" Cam asked, laying a small hand on my arm. "Talk to me, please?"

"What?"

"You're going through something. I can see the war you're fighting. Tell me. I'm here."

"It's nothing," I snapped, yet I felt as if only a thread separated me from revealing everything to her.

Cam sighed and withdrew her hand. "Okay. I don't know your reasoning, Juliet, but I'm here whenever you're ready to talk." She took a sip of her tea.

A low chuckle escaped me, the sound strained and cutting through the silence like a knife. "I don't know, Cam," I said, tucking the hair that had fallen from my bun back behind my ear. "I don't know if I ever can. What if I never remember?" The hope that had begun shining in her eyes as I spoke vanished with my question. *This is too hard.* I stood up and nodded to her. "I love you, Cam, and I wouldn't ever do anything to jeopardize our friendship. I hope you know that. Goodbye."

"But it's my fault! It's my fault. It's my fault." Cam's voice rent the air, wracked with grief. I turned around, frozen, watching as tears spilled down her bronzed cheeks. Her hands waved. "You don't know how it's been! You can't know! Because you've been gone for so long, *Juliet*! I have had to live each day as though nothing had happened, as though that day in the Redwoods had never *happened*."

Who asked her to pretend? Realizing my lips had parted, I closed them. *Is this how she chose to grieve?*

Cam's tone deepened as it lowered. "Can you even begin to imagine how that was?" Her hands clenched into fists in her lap.

I can, Cam. I know how it feels. I have so much blood on my hands.

"I had to go to work, spend time with family and friends, and continue living. And yet day and night, I never stopped grieving. I never stopped wondering where you were or what you were doing." Her voice rose. "I never stopped wondering if you were dead! For all I knew, you were." Cam shook her head, sending teardrops flying. Mid-sob, she choked out, "But I never stopped having hope."

I sucked in a breath. The kitchen felt stifling, warm—a feverish toll overtaking my body. I rose to open the window. A figure shone in the glass. I winced. *It's just Cam.* Sighing with relief, I finished raising the window and sat back down. Already, the cold air rushed into the room, fighting against the tension palpitating throughout.

Cam shook her head with a slow motion, her chin quivering. "I've missed you so much."

I fought to keep my own grief from spilling over. Had I ever thought about what she might have been going through? I couldn't remember. "Cam," I began. "It wasn't your fault."

Cam sniffled, the sound loud in the small kitchen.

"I went through a portal," I whispered.

There. One of my secrets was out.

Cam set down her mug. "What?"

No going back now. My chest hurt. "I went through a portal to another world." I took another sip of the rapidly cooling tea.

"Juliet—"

I raised a hand. "No, let me finish. It took me a while to realize what was even happening. But it was another *world*, Cam. So much happened there." I closed my eyes. "I am not the same person I was." I looked at Cam. *And I won't ever be her again.* I had changed and grown, and I had realized how much I still had to learn. "This world is big, the universe is big, but I didn't realize how much," I said, hardly hearing my own voice. "We haven't even begun to scrape the surface." I rose and paced back and forth, my mind racing. *There are other countries in that world. It's not just Ryujin.*

"Juliet."

Cam's voice brought me back. I stopped pacing and stilled, half-forgetting I still held a mug of tea in one hand.

"It's not possible."

"It is!" Raindrops pinged against me as an extra gust blew into the room. I turned around and slid the window closed. The room felt so quiet.

"So, another world, huh?"

I shrugged.

"I see why you've been pretending you don't remember anything."

I stepped forward. "Do you believe me?"

Cam sighed. "I don't know, Juliet. It's far-fetched." She twirled a lock of her thick hair.

My fingers drummed on the tabletop. *That's it.* I stood up. "I can show you my scars."

"What?"

"My wrist was broken, but you already know that. It happened a few days ago after I jumped off the parapet of a fortress, trying to escape Tris—someone."

Cam's eyes widened, disbelief shining within their depths. But I plunged ahead anyway.

"And this"—I lifted my shirt to expose my torso—"is where a man who kidnapped me slid a knife along my ribs and broke a few of them. That was soon after I arrived." *And now one of those two men is going to be emperor.*

Cam's mouth opened and closed. "How do I know you're not just making that up?"

"Why would I?"

She shook her head. "It's crazy, but suppose I do believe you—what's next?"

"Mom and Dad want me to go get checked out at the hospital."

"Makes sense."

I crossed my arms over my chest. "It's harder than I thought it would be, Cam. All of it. Coming back hasn't been quite what I expected."

"Just answer me this," she said. "Did you try to return sooner? Was it your choice to remain there as long as you did?"

What's the answer to that? I sat back down in the chair. "I did try, Cam. I tried a couple of times. It's complicated, but part of it was my choice, and part of it wasn't. I can't really explain unless I tell you everything."

Cam nodded and scooted to the edge of the chair. "It's not that I don't want to hear more—I do—but this is a lot to take in." She pushed her chair back and stood. "I think I need to try to wrap my head around all of this. You're right. It's not easy, is it?" She walked to the door. "I love you. We've been friends for so long ... I know our friendship will survive even this." Her voice quieted. "But I think you should go back home. I need time to process this, and you—you should go back before your parents worry."

"How did you know I snuck out?"

Her eyes rolled. "Because there is no way they would have let you go so soon. They always had a tight clutch on you, and it'll be worse now."

I nodded, chewing on my lower lip. The air settled on me with a heavy weight. Should I have even told her anything? But my story was out, whether it was a good thing or not. I watched as Cam turned and left, listening as her footsteps faded up the stairs on the way to her room.

I let myself out and broke into a run. The nervous energy in my body needed release. The rain had stopped, leaving a bleak, gray emptiness in its place. The streets were a familiar maze of paths, almost like riding a bike again after a long time or picking up an old language. The breeze whipped my hair, and my cheeks stung from the bite of winter. My heart beat faster as it pumped hot blood through my veins. A sense of euphoria filled me, pushing back the pain and fear hiding below the surface. After a little distance, I slowed to a pace I could better maintain.

My feet had eaten up the couple miles back to the house before I stopped, panting for breath, my chest aching. I dropped into a stretch, moving from one form into another, using the techniques I had practiced time and time again under the scrutiny of Sensei. Memories of the training cavern filled my mind. I had watched the other men train, but Sensei hadn't let them work with me—and that was when I'd suspected it was because they were following Tristan's orders. The night I trained alone rose to the surface.

I'd almost kissed him. Tristan's shirtless body, his handsome face with its blue eyes and blond hair ... he had flirted with me, taunted me. I gritted my teeth and continued through the exercises. He had manipulated me. Used me. I relished the control I had over my body, the awareness of the ache in my muscles, and the fatigue drawing its veil over my senses. I sucked in a breath.

He has a secret. Don't listen to him. Adnan's tall, strong figure pushed Tristan out of the way.

Tristan was full of lies, I agreed as I entered my house.

Inside, I froze at the sight of my mom waiting for me with a long wooden spoon in one hand and the other propped on her wide hips. A younger version of her flashed through my mind, a glimpse of a time I'd displeased her. Now, I was faced with a mother whose eyes were creased at the corners from constant worry, a mother who had lines in her face she hadn't had five months ago, a mother who now regarded me with such love and such heartbrokenness it stirred up an ache in my own heart. A string seemed to be attached between the two of us, trying to draw us ever closer, even while something invisible threatened to stretch it so thin it would snap.

There was no need for secrecy anymore. I'd visited Cam, and Mom knew I'd been gone. I closed the door behind me.

"Juliet?" Mom said, her tone icy. "Juliet! I've been worried sick!" She ran forward, grabbed my upper arms, and almost shook me as she scanned me from head to toe. "Are you all right? Where *were* you?"

Dad entered the room and regarded the two of us.

"Mom, I'm fine," I protested. "See? Not a scratch."

"You—you—" she blustered, looking from me to Dad. "I don't even understand how you left!" Mom said, letting go of me. "I was sitting in the living room. How did you get out?" Her foot tapped a quick beat on the floor.

She doesn't want to know. "You don't want to know where I even was?" I replied, hoping to divert her attention.

She let go of my arms and backed up. "How did you leave without my noticing? I was sitting where I could see both the front and back door."

"To make sure I couldn't leave?"

"Juliet." Mom's voice took a plaintive edge. "It's not like that."

I stopped with one foot on the bottom step. "Isn't it?"

"Juliet." Dad's voice cut into the air like a knife. "Answer your mother: How did you get out?"

I realized I didn't want to say. Something was keeping me back, but I wasn't sure what it was.

Dad crossed his arms. "And where were you?"

I swallowed.

I hadn't missed this—the questioning, the drive to keep me close as though I were a child. The realization hit me like a thunderbolt. I took a deep breath and focused on softening my tone. "Mom, Dad, can we sit down?"

Mom's eyebrows creased. Her lips parted, closed, and she nodded. "Yes, we do need to talk. I think we need to talk about what you're going to do now that you are home. You don't have a job anymore. Maybe the coffee shop would rehire you ..."

What? A job was part of the plan, of needing to resume my life, but why now? *Why the accusatorial tone?* I led the way to the couch. The room felt silent and oppressive as I watched my parents sit down across from me.

Mom squeezed Dad's hand. "We also think you should see a doctor and get checked out, just to make sure everything is fine."

"No!" I bit my lip. "No," I said a little quieter. "I don't need a doctor. I'm fine. But I do want to know something. How long am I on house arrest for?"

"Juliet, you're not on—"

"Until we think you're ready," Dad interrupted.

"Jeffery!" Mom snapped.

"Mel, you know as well as I do that she's not a little girl and hasn't been for some time. She's not fragile." Dad's shoulders rose and fell before he exhaled through clenched teeth. His large blue eyes, so like my own, were dark with anger. "Why, Juliet? Why did you have to go and leave us?"

This again. The walls enclosing the large room seemed to shrink. "Do you think I chose to do it?" A pang of guilt shot through me. *Hadn't I? I chose to leave Umi no Machi.*

"Then what was it?" Dad sighed, his aged blue eyes weary.

"I didn't intend to leave."

"Were you forced? Were you kidnapped? What *happened*?"

I ignored the tear sliding down Mom's cheek, my voice rising. "Dad, how could I know if I don't remember?" My face warmed. Everything happens for a reason, but I was struggling to continue thinking that pretending to be an amnesiac was the best choice.

My parents sat back.

"And I think it's time we talk about something else."

Dad waved a hand through the air.

"As you both know, I'm an adult." I ignored the hardening of the lines around Mom's eyes. "I don't think I should need permission to leave the house, or to be accountable for whatever I do and wherever I go."

"Juliet—"

"I'm not saying I don't appreciate that you care," I continued, keeping my voice even. "I know it's been harder since ..." I took a deep breath. "Since Eddie died. And—"

"*What?*" Dad and Mom exchanged glances before leaning forward.

"What are you talking about?" Dad asked.

I resisted the urge to roll my eyes. *Why do they have to make this even harder than it already is?* I tucked my hands under my thighs. "I know you both have been more protective since Eddie died, and I don't blame you, but—"

"Juliet, Eddie isn't dead."

Fighting for a breath, I felt as though the air had all been sucked out of the room. "What?"

Mom scooted to the edge of the couch. "Are you all right, honey?"

Sounds became distant as I fought against tunnel vision. My heart pounded in my chest.

"What do you mean?" I managed, my hands shaking.

Dad put a hand on Mom's leg to still her. "Eddie isn't dead, Juliet. Why did you think he was?"

"But he—he died, eleven years ago."

Mom shook her head.

"He drowned," I murmured, my own voice distant to my ears. "I grabbed him, but he was limp. And I slipped with the next wave. I couldn't hold on to him." Tears streamed down my cheeks. "I let go," I whispered. "I watched the next wave take him." *He was gone,* I thought, remembering. My hands clenched in my lap. "He was gone," I said out loud, my voice breaking.

The room was silent.

A half-sob forced its way out of me. I glanced up at Mom and Dad, taking in their pale faces, their eyes wide, their bodies frozen. *This is real.* I collapsed forward, my face hidden behind my hands as I cried. I felt movement as two forms rustled, settling in on either side of me. A hand rubbed my upper back in slow circles, something that hadn't been done since I was a small child.

I cried harder.

All the pain that had been hidden deep within from my parents for so many years had come flooding to the surface. Eleven years of guilt and heart-wrenching pain had surfaced.

"Juliet, honey." Mom's voice was gentle. "It's all right. Your brother *isn't* dead. He's alive and well."

"At least he was the last time we heard from him," Dad muttered over my head.

I shook my head. "What are you talking about?" I raised my head and dried my face on my sleeves, striving to control my crying, to slow it down. My voice shook. "I don't understand why you're saying these things. Eddie is dead. You both were there."

"No, Juliet." Mom frowned. "He survived. I remember the time you were talking about. Eleven years ago, we went to the beach. You and your brother were swimming in the waves." Mom continued to rub slow circles over my back.

"But Juliet, when the waves sucked him under, he came back up. *You* grabbed him. He was scared, but he was fine, Juliet."

I moved my head from side to side as that day at the beach flew past my mind's eye in bright flashes. "No, no, no," I muttered under my breath.

"Yes, Juliet. Here, look!" Mom stood and pulled me up with her. "Come here." She led me into the hallway, Dad's heavier footsteps following us. "Look!" She stopped me in front of the portraits hanging the length of the wall.

It was him.

Eddie. Eddie. Eddie. One after the other. They didn't stop that summer at the beach. He grew. *I grew.* He was in so many of them. Getting facial hair, his jawline growing stronger, more masculine, his shoulders broadening ... *Taller than me.*

I stopped moving. The picture I stood in front of had to have been from the past year. I looked the same. Eddie had his arm around my shoulders, his grin still just as goofy. *He's so handsome.* My breath caught. Mom had interrupted me last time. *I didn't see these!*

"What is this?" I asked, unable to look away.

"It's your brother, Juliet," Mom whispered, her own voice breaking. "I think it's time we take you to the doctor."

I hardly heard her. "Where is he?"

"He's overseas," Dad answered, rubbing the scruff on his cheeks. "He joined the Marine Corps the moment he turned eighteen. Now he's recon."

"Where is he right now?"

Dad shook his head. "I don't know. He's not allowed to tell us much, and we don't often get to talk to him, but last I heard, he was doing well."

"Does he know?" My question hung in the air.

"No," Mom replied. "Not yet. We sent an email, but we haven't received a reply from him yet."

He's alive. Each thought swirled through my brain like a leaf on rippling water. *How is this possible?* I reached forward and traced Eddie's face with my finger. These pictures were real. I blinked and swayed.

"I need some time." I turned and fled to my room, my head throbbing. No echoes of footsteps followed me. I closed the door behind me. The walls seemed to close in about me. I paced the room, treading a familiar, well-worn path.

Outside of the room, I was watched. My parents saw my every move. Neither was able to hide the concern written across their faces. I groaned. The lessons I had learned, or thought I had learned, felt out of reach. I used to convince myself that I could get over the past, get over the things I had seen and experienced.

My breathing became fast and shallow. I sat down at my desk, barely sitting before I was up and moving again. No caffeine had entered my system, yet I felt as jittery. I hadn't felt this fire since I had seen the horrors done in Mari's village, since I had realized how lost I was and that I needed to do something about it. My skin felt hot. I strode to the window and opened it to let in a cold breeze.

Rain dripped off the leaves of the evergreens, falling between the bare branches of the deciduous trees. The ground was wet. The air smelled of fresh pines, clean water, and the brisk scent of fresh air. I closed my eyes and breathed in deep.

Eddie is alive.

My brain hurt as I fought through the past eleven years of him being gone and now being alive. I pressed my fingers into my temples. Adnan, Saya, being in Ryujin—it had all helped me stop carrying the heavy guilt from his death. But now he was alive.

"What is going on?" I murmured. Soon he'd know I was back ... yet how—

Pain pulsed through my head. I stumbled away from the window and curled up on the floor.

Chapter Six

A cool breeze swept over my body. I shivered and stirred, raising myself on one elbow. My quilts lay bunched to either side of me, draping over the bed onto the floor. Running a hand through my hair, I felt the damp strands stay in place. With a soft sigh, I sat up and shivered again.

The window was still open.

Eddie is alive.

My chin quivered.

Something hit the glass. A sharp pang rent the air. I jumped to my feet, my pulse rapid. Running to the window, I saw the small form of a brown bird beating its wings from where it had fallen onto the covered porch.

With a sharp breath, I squared my shoulders and entered my small bathroom. I turned the knob in the shower, and with a small squeak, water flew out of the spout with a hiss. I watched it fall before reaching out a finger. It was cold. Dropping my clothes on the floor, I stepped in, goosebumps breaking out over my skin. Closing my eyes, I tilted my head back and gritted my teeth. The water washed away the sweat from my nap.

Reaching back, I turned the temperature warmer. As the water turned from cold to hot, I felt myself begin to relax. I opened my eyes. Glass surrounded me. The water ran down it in rivulets. *Water. Blood.*

Emi. Emi, dead on the ground. Tristan, killing so many—

But he'd lost. I had trusted him, but I had just been a puppet on a string. My jaw clenched. *A stupid puppet.*

I turned off the water and squeezed what I could of it out of my hair. Reaching down, I picked up the length of bandage and rewrapped my aching wrist. I knew I needed to see a doctor, make sure the break was set properly and healing well, even though Adnan had set it.

But he wasn't here now. *And Eddie's alive.* I shook my head and tied my robe before walking to the mirror. I wiped condensation off the mirror, my reflection looking back at me. Clutching the sink's rim, I took in the puffy eyes and dark circles, the thin face looking back at me. It was no longer just me. Emi smiled. I bit back a startled cry, and my hand slipped. She was gone. I searched the mirror and the bathroom, but Emi wasn't there.

My hands trembled. "You can't forget the past, Juliet," I whispered. "But you do have to find the strength to continue on." Straightening my back and shoulders, I watched as my head edged up ever so higher. Emi and Mari, along with countless others, hadn't given up their lives so I could give up mine.

I'll never forget you.

A footstep sounded in my room. I turned from the mirror and saw Mom sitting on the bed. "Mom." I hesitated before going to my dresser. "Is there something you want?"

She shifted on the bed. "I heard the shower. What are *you* doing?"

I shrugged. "Rewrapping this." I brought my injured wrist to my chest.

Mom's eyes slanted, and her lips narrowed as she shot me a pitying look. "We need to get you to the doctor."

For what reason? My wrist or something else? I stiffened and turned back to the wardrobe. Tightening my robe around my waist, I opened the door and stared at the clothes inside.

"How are you doing?"

I let my hands fall to my sides. "All right." *That's a lie.* The thought swept through my mind. *Lies. Lies. Lies.* Eddie pushed his way into my thoughts. *No.* I shook my head, my hair flying through the air. *Get out.* I couldn't think about him. My brain hurt trying to make sense of it all. *How can he be alive?*

"Juliet?"

I stilled. Everything from the past eleven years ... I questioned it all now. *No.* I knew what I remembered. It was real. *They're not a figment of my imagination, nor is this a dream.*

"Come here, honey."

Slowly, I approached my mom and sat next to her on the bed. She pulled me into her, and I slid into her grasp, resting my head on her shoulder. The warmth and security of her supple body enfolded me, bringing back warm reminders of the countless times she had held me like that.

"Juliet."

I reached up a hand to push my hair out of my face. When it came away damp, I realized I had begun crying.

"I'll always love you." Mom's hushed whisper fell like a caress over me. "It doesn't matter if you can't remember ..." Her chest rose and fell next to me. "Whatever happened in the past few months doesn't change how much I care for you or the love I have for you."

The past few months, or the past eleven years? Tears slid down my cheeks faster. *Eddie is now alive.*

"I hope you remember one day," Mom continued, giving me a slight squeeze. "And maybe your amnesia has something to do with you thinking Eddie died."

Guilt gnawed at me. But there was nothing that would explain my disappearance that she would believe. "I love you too."

Mom tightened her grip. "Just remember, I'm always here if you need to talk. I don't need the truth to still love and trust you."

Trust. I wanted her to trust me, and I believed that she meant it—to an extent—but I also knew that the past made me doubt how much she would actually go through with such a promise. I sniffed.

The rain pinged against the glass. It was a gray day. I laid my hands under my thighs. The window screen was still not back in place.

Jasmine wafted through the air. Emi's face drifted into view again, and my heart sang with pain. The air felt heavy as it surrounded me with a quiet silence. I glanced at Mom. *She can't ever know. The jasmine ...* My eyes glistened with tears as I remembered Ryujin.

Tristan's arm fell, and red burst forth—I closed my eyes and opened them again, clutching my quilt. *Adnan is out there somewhere—maybe not in this world, but he's alive.* And I knew what he would tell me. I had to keep moving forward. There was no running away, not anymore.

Emi haunted my every thought, threatening to break down the hastily built walls I had constructed in my mind. I stood at the window. Tears ran down the panes of glass as the rain thrummed with a dull ping. The lights in my room were off. *No glare.* I focused on my breathing—smooth, deep, drawing the air into my lungs before expelling. The window wasn't a mirror. I couldn't see Emi here. It had been hours since I had seen her reflection in my bathroom, yet every time I neared a mirror ...

I couldn't lose control.

My room felt like a prison, and yet I knew it wasn't. *The mind can play tricks.* I reminded myself of that over and over, yet I couldn't help the antsy feeling stealing over me. *It has before, and it can again.* A shaft of moonlight broke through the clouds and streamed into the bedroom. I glanced toward where my two knives lay hidden under my bed. My fingers clenched and unclenched. My sword was in my closet. *I'm in no prison.* There were no chains here. There wasn't anyone threatening to imprison me if I didn't obey. My chest rose and fell. *I'm safe here.*

I returned my attention to the window. A man walked his shaggy dog down the sidewalk, clutching an umbrella in one hand to ward off the never-ending wet. *Tourist.*

My fingers tapped an unknown rhythm on the windowsill. My parents knew about the sword and knives, but they hadn't asked questions—not that I wanted them.

The man with the dog went out of sight around the bend in the road. It had always been a quiet neighborhood. A car pulled into view, its headlights bright in the coming darkness, the sound lost amidst the dull droning of the gentle rain. *Wait. I know that car,* I thought as it pulled into the driveway.

I ran my fingers through my hair and pulled it back into a messy low bun. Taking a deep breath and straightening my shoulders, I left the room.

I ignored the photographs lining the wall as I strode down the hallway. A knock thumped against the front door. Voices filtered through the quiet as I rounded the corner into the living room, and both figures turned to face me. Mom—aging, plump, her brown eyes creased with concern. Cam—young, petite, her face paling even as she took me in.

"Juliet," Mom murmured when nothing was said. "Cam's here." She glanced back and forth between us.

But why? Hopeful, I waited, wondering.

"Hi, Juliet," she greeted, removing her jacket. Mom took it and left, muttering something about hanging it to dry. Neither of us spoke as she walked away.

Does she want to talk about this morning? I stuck my hands in the back pockets of my jeans. "No work?"

Cam shook her head. "I took the day off. Can we talk?"

I nodded and led the way back to my room. Cam's soft footsteps followed me. *Just like in the woods—first Adnan, then Cam.* He had also wanted to talk after I told him the truth about who I was, where I'd come from. Grief threatened to expose my façade. I took a deep breath and closed my bedroom door behind us.

Cam walked over to the lamp and turned it on. Angling my chair away from the window, afraid of what I might see there, I watched as my friend sat on the edge of the bed.

"This morning was ..." she trailed off, then started as the door opened.

"Here is some coffee," Mom said as she walked through with two mugs.

"Thanks, Mel." Cam beamed.

"Thanks," I murmured, taking my own mug. Steam rose from the coffee in a soothing swirl. The smell was still so reminiscent of home, of my old job, of what I'd drank weekend mornings with my parents. And yet I missed the rice tea in Ryujin.

The door closed again.

Cam wrapped her hands around her mug. "Juliet, it's been four and a half months."

I took a sip of the hot liquid. *How many times are we going to circle back to this? It's been a while. I got it!* It wasn't just a long time for my parents and Cam, but for me too.

"I can't say we haven't both changed in that time. I can't begin to imagine how it's been for you, and I know my life hasn't been nearly as crazy"—Cam licked her lips—"but it hasn't been easy. I have lived every day not understanding exactly what happened."

"It wasn't your fault, Cam. There wasn't anything you could have done."

Cam's hands trembled. "It *is* my fault."

"No, it isn't," I reassured, setting my coffee to the side. "But I do know how easy it is to dismiss."

Cam's eyes widened, and I realized she was peering over my shoulder. "Where's the screen?"

"I, uh, removed it."

"Why?"

"When I snuck out to see you this morning."

Cam nodded. "Just like old times?"

"Probably worse," I replied with a slight grin.

Cam's face darkened. "You're probably right." She took her mug and drank. Her lips pursed. "It's not the hottest."

"I can warm it up for you," I offered.

She shook her head. "No, that's okay. Coffee is good whether hot or cold."

Forcing myself to nod in reply, I sipped, regarding her over the rim. "Eddie is a Marine," I said, breaking the silence.

"Uh, yes, what about it?" Cam asked, her nose wrinkling. "It's not like you're that close anyway ... or, at least, you two have had an off-and-on close relationship for a while. But yes, I get that you haven't talked to him in a few months."

I haven't talked to him because he's been dead for eleven years, I wanted to say. Instead, I forced it down. "Cam, I haven't talked to him because—" *Because what?* The ache grew worse. I glanced down at my clasped hands, at the bandage, reminding me that it had all happened, that it had all been real. *Even Eddie's death was real.* "Because I didn't know he was alive until today."

"*What?*"

"Yeah."

"You thought he was dead?"

I nodded.

Cam stood up and paced the floor. She laughed. "Are you sure you're not an amnesiac?"

I flinched. Her question stung.

"Juliet, you're like a sister to me. But this changes things, doesn't it?"

I stood as well. "What do you mean?"

"First, you told me this crazy story—one that I was inclined to believe—but now?" She threw her hands up in the air. "Now I'm beginning to think maybe it's not so believable. How can you forget your *brother* is alive?"

I stepped back.

"I think you should get checked out." She didn't avert her gaze. "It would be best."

My arms crossed over my chest. "Anything else?"

She sighed. "No." Walking to the door, she laid her hand on the knob. "I should go. You have a lot going on and a lot to think about ... and I know it must be difficult." Cam reached out and touched my shoulder. "I'll see you later. I really hope you get the answers you need."

"What answers?" But my question was spoken to an empty room. Cam was gone, already receding down the hallway. The faint murmur of voices reached me as Mom spoke with her, and then the front door closed.

I bit my lip. *Why did Cam even come?*

I leaned back in my chair, my mind whirring. Standing, I strode across the floor to my bed. Crouching down, I pulled my two knives out from under the mattress, noting their familiar weight. The one I used to keep in my right boot was long and slim; the other, which I'd worn in a sheath on my left forearm, was shorter but still slender. Both had come with me through the portal, reminders of the world I had lived in for a few short months, in case I ever doubted. *Why couldn't Adnan come through with me? Why objects and not people?*

With slow movements, I began the techniques Sensei had taught me, techniques I remembered with ease. But just like in Ryujin, I had to concentrate on fluidity, on the knives becoming an extension of myself.

Hirose had given these to me. I raised the shorter knife as though to block a sword strike, counterbalancing it with the slimmer one. *Adnan would have helped me continue learning.* I swung in a slow circle, making as though to stab an invisible opponent. Adnan would tell me to learn from my past, but to move on.

My breathing heavy, I stopped. My mind threatened to split between two gulfs—one being lost to the past and the other fighting to stay in the present. *Why do I feel like it's a losing battle?* With a grunt, I threw the shorter knife. The hilt bounced off the closed bathroom door with a thud and fell to the floor. I walked over and picked it up.

A footstep sounded outside my door. Whoever it was moved on. I glanced down at the knives I held. *Put them away.* With slow steps, I walked over to the vent in my floor and hid the knives inside. *Focus.* Right now, I just needed to figure out the next steps in my life.

My eyes roved over the desk and caught on the laptop that sat there. I sat down and ran my fingers over the slick metal. The lid opened with a slight click. It had been so long, yet my fingers typed out the password as though it had been yesterday. Light clicks sounded as I tapped each key.

Juliet Barrows—missing—Washington.

I let my finger hover over the "Enter" button before pressing down. I waited the second or so for the search results to load. Link after link popped up, my face plastered all over them. Pages of articles, videos, and reports from various news websites chronicling my disappearance, the futile search, and that I had been found. There was no reason. The reporters ate up the amnesia story, which added to the drama.

I kept scrolling. As the days passed after September 17th, so did my story. There were updates at first, testimonials from loved ones, but then my story faded just like I knew all the others out there did.

I remembered the photo of me that every article showed. The week before I had graduated with my bachelor's degree, I was thinking about beginning my career … That face was full of energy, excited, ready to start the next phase. But it had only been a few months ago. College didn't matter the same way anymore.

With a sharp click, all the tabs closed. It felt like I'd read someone else's story, quotes from other parents, grief from another's family. A sour taste filled my mouth. My parents' desperation to find their missing daughter had leaked onto the pages.

Where is the normalcy we used to have? I shook my head. Even before Ryujin, we hadn't had that since before Eddie died. *Eddie.* My breath caught. He hadn't been part of my life since that fateful day when the ocean had claimed his life. *Yet he's alive.* I leaned back into my chair. Part of me believed it—how could I not?—but another part needed to see him for myself.

"I don't understand," I whispered.

"Juliet!" Mom called, her voice distant. The following words were indistinguishable. It was probably time for dinner. Yet dinner wasn't a normal thing, not anymore. Our lives had changed.

I needed to be fully present, and helping to bring back a sense of normalcy to this family was key. *I'm here now.* Ryujin was now part of my past, and I may never return there.

I took a deep breath and straightened my posture. *It's not the lion's den; it's just my family.*

CHAPTER SEVEN

S ilver and gleaming, the phone sat in front of me. I sat waiting for it to ring, waiting for the unknown number to pop up on the screen. The military was allowing Eddie a phone call, given the circumstances. *Given that I've come back.* My fingers tapped against the desk's surface. The tapping increased as I thought back over the events of the past day. Just yesterday, I'd found out Eddie was still alive. *But that isn't the only weird thing that's happened.* I chewed on my lower lip as I concentrated. Mom and Dad were acting odd. Taking a deep breath, I shrugged. The entire experience wasn't something that happened to every family. *Not that we haven't already been through a lot ...*

The phone rang.

I gulped and licked my lips before picking up the phone.

"Juliet?" The voice was deep.

"Eddie?"

A low chuckle came over the phone. "Hey, it's good to hear your voice. I don't have long, but I'm glad they're letting us have this call."

I listened to him speak. He sounded different. When he was a boy, he'd been mischievous, always with a note of laughter in his voice, as though everything was one big joke. But now he sounded serious, like a deep thinker.

"How are you doing, Jules?"

Taking a deep breath, I had to force myself to speak. "I'm a little over-whelmed." Everything went through my head, but it was so hard to figure out what to say. And how could I ask him why he was alive when he had been dead?

Eddie sighed on the other side, as though also trying to figure out what to say. "So, Dad said in his email that you haven't been to the doctor yet?"

Seriously? You too? "Um, no, I haven't."

"Ah."

There was a moment of silence in which the wind rattled against the window outside my room.

"Jules, you really should listen to Mom and Dad. They just want to take care of you, and if they think you should go in, then you should go. All right?"

I bit back a groan. This was not how I wanted this conversation to go. My first time talking to my long-dead brother—now not dead—and he was trying to convince me to listen to my parents.

"Hey," he continued. "I know it's not ideal; none of it is. You didn't choose any of this. I can't imagine how confused you are or how hard it's been the past few months ... but the reality is that it's what's happening, and—" He hesitated.

My lips parted to speak.

"And it's just the way it is," Eddie finished. "I love you, Jules. I wish I could be there to support you, to help you through all of this, but I can't. Soon, I'll be home, but I can't say we'll have another phone conversation before then."

"Eddie, I—"

"One more thing. You'll email, won't you?"

I nodded, even though I knew he couldn't see me. "Yes, I will."

"Good."

Tears stung my eyes. I didn't know this Eddie. He had been a little boy, not a grown man.

"Hey," Eddie said, his voice sounding lighter. "Do you remember that time we all went to the beach?"

My heart skipped a beat.

"All I wanted to do was build sand trees—"

I wracked my brain.

"—and you wanted to build an actual castle? I thought it would be possible to build these huge trees in the sand, but instead they just turned into lumps of squiggly messes, almost like upside-down trees." He laughed.

Roots. The memory slowly swam back into my mind. *It was the year before Eddie died.*

"Anyways," Eddie continued. "Mom and Dad got so tired of our bickering that they told you to just help me anyway. But you argued that it wouldn't work, and obviously, it wasn't working. You were so stubborn."

"I remember," I whispered.

"You were like that weird sand pile of roots that I'd made. You're still like that, you know. So stubborn. Oftentimes, it is a good thing. But this time—this time, Juliet, you need to listen to Mom and Dad and let them help you."

I fought for control over my erratic emotions. Sucking in a breath of air, I forced my tone to remain even. "I love you, Eddie. I've missed you so much. More than you can know."

Eddie laughed again, but this time there was an incredulous note. "All right, Jules. I've got to go, but just remember I love you too. Email me, okay?"

"All right."

"Bye."

With a click, the other line ended. My first phone call with my brother—my brother who was supposed to be dead and yet somehow was alive. Silent tears rolled down my cheeks.

The door opened and Mom stuck her head through. I rushed to dry my cheeks.

Mom's face wrinkled in concern. "Hey, let's go out."

"Out?" I echoed.

"Come on." She pushed the door the rest of the way open. "It might help."

I grabbed my boots and coat and followed her out to the car. Part of me didn't want to go anywhere. My bedroom was a place to hide, a place where I didn't have to guard my emotions. And yet I felt some excitement and relief. This was normal. This was something we used to do.

Violin music played over the radio as I watched our house fade into the background. Just as the neighborhood flashed past, a little part of me slipped free as my mind wandered into oblivion.

I jerked as the car stopped.

Mom grabbed her purse and opened her door. "I'm going to run in and grab us some coffee. Might be easier if you stay here?"

I stared at the coffee shop she'd parked in front of. *My old workplace.* It felt like so long ago. I nodded. Facing my old coworkers wasn't something I was ready to do. Mom got out of the car.

Water gleamed on the glass. I lifted my fingers and traced a line down the pane. A man stood at the corner of the shop. My heartbeat raced even as my body seemed to freeze, and I leaned closer until my forehead touched the cool glass. He turned and stared at me. My heart caught in my chest. *Adnan.* I fumbled for the door handle. But it wouldn't open—locked. I flicked the lock and opened the door. A long, shrill screech filled the air as the car alarm blared. I half-jumped, half-fell out of the car.

"Juliet!" Mom called, her body half out of the coffee shop door. "What are you doing?" Her hand scrabbled in her purse for the keys.

My eyes flicked past her to the corner—but it was empty. Adnan wasn't there. No one stood there. The alarm stopped, and all was quiet. I squinted at the spot, but it remained empty. *No.* He had been there.

"Juliet?"

"I'm all right," I managed. "I thought I saw someone." The air felt stifling and silent now. I'd seen him.

Mom frowned but ducked back into the shop. I waited, standing next to the car, alone with my thoughts and questions.

It wasn't long before she headed back out with two cups and a brown paper bag.

"Who?" Mom asked, setting her coffee inside the car. She peered at me over the rim.

"Someone I know."

She rolled her eyes. "*Who?*"

"Shizukana."

Mom snorted. "Sheezoocan? Now, who has a name like that?"

"Shizukana, and it's not his real name," I protested, my first sight of him in Umi no Machi slipping into my mind: the way he'd bandaged my hand, him following Saya and me, our travels in Ryujin ... But there was no sign of him now. *Maybe my mind was playing tricks.*

With a heavy sigh, I slid into the passenger seat.

Mom handed me a brown paper sack. "Where do you know him from?"

"It's been a while."

Mom watched me take the scone out of the bag, but chose not to ask more questions. "Eat. It'll help you feel better."

I took a bite of the moist scone, the flakiness filling my palate with flavors of strawberries and cream. It was good. Really good.

Mom backed the car up. "I know you don't want to believe it, Juliet, but you know you're having a hard time."

The scone turned dry. I swallowed and almost choked. *She's wrong. Infiltrating Creulon's court was hard, seeing Mari's dead body was hard, watching Emi die …* My chin quivered. *Those were hard.*

I took a sip of coffee. The faint taste of dark chocolate slid over my tongue.

⚜

Terror held me within her grasp, vivid and striking as it radiated in the pounding of my heart, loud to my own ears. My body stilled like the calm before a storm. My head filled with a dull buzz as I fought against the fear threatening to overtake me. I slid to the edge of my bed, my blankets thrown back, my body again drenched in cold sweat.

This night was different. I couldn't remember my dreams. There was nothing tangible for me to hold on to, only the feelings they left me with. And somehow that was worse. I ran a hand through my long hair before holding my head in my hands. It had only been one day since I'd seen Emi looking at me in the mirror.

And not even a week since I've been back. I sighed and stood. Bright light of early morning streamed through the window, whose shades were open to let it through. I raised my chin, welcoming the light to fight back the darkness entrapping my mind. My hands trembled.

A light knock sounded on the door. "Juliet, breakfast is about ready if you're hungry."

"All right, I'll be there in a moment," I called back. It was then that I smelled the aroma of bacon. My stomach grumbled.

After dressing, I examined my left hand. It was pale and a little limp-looking, but I knew that was just because it was injured. Yet it hurt worse this morning. Had I been clenching my hand during the night without realizing? With a grimace, I wrapped the bandage around my forearm and wrist. It wouldn't be surprising if I'd done something while having those nightmares. A heavy sigh escaped my lips.

I left my room.

The savory smell of bacon was stronger in the hallway. I glanced at the portraits in the hall. Eddie's face stared back at me, his jaw strong and sure, his face aged, but still young, still full of life. I focused on breathing, calming until I could continue with a modicum of control.

The kitchen was brightly lit. The overhead lights shone down on Mom as she bustled around, laying plates of bacon, eggs, hash browns, and toasted English muffins with butter and jam on the table. My lips parted, but Mom spoke first. "Juliet, I almost sent your dad to fetch you."

My eyebrows rose as I sat down. *Sent Dad to fetch me?* The chair creaked as it settled under my weight. "Looks delicious."

"Morning," Dad greeted as he walked through the door.

"Morning, Dad." Relaxation stole over me as I watched him sit and pour a fresh, hot cup of coffee. He grunted in appreciation as he took a sip. Mom bustled around, muttering to herself before sitting and pouring herself a cup.

"So, Juliet," Dad said as he filled his plate. "Have you given any more thought to a job?"

Not this again. My fists clenched.

"I know I can afford for you to live here rent-free, but you aren't a little girl anymore." Dad returned his attention to the newspaper folded neatly on the table next to his plate. He scanned the page as if he'd forgotten what he'd said.

"Juliet," Mom added. "I agree with your dad. I know that you've been through a lot—"

The dam broke. "A lot?" I burst out. "What?"

Dad looked up then. "Now, there's no reason to get irritated. You've been given much more grace from us than most parents probably would."

"You've kept yourself busy," Mom explained around a bite of egg. "But you know what I say about idleness." She smirked and winked at me.

"Mom," I said, trying to restrain myself. I chose each word as though a snake would bite if I made the wrong move. "You tend to spend most of your days in the garden, or shopping, or having friends over for coffee and sweets—"

"How dare you!" Mom snapped. "That's disrespectful and not how I—*we've*—raised you." Her face hardened. "Jeffery!"

"Yes?" Dad asked while chewing.

Mom swept a hand out. "Would you like to say something?"

"You're doing just fine, Mel." He returned his attention to his newspaper and shoved a piece of bacon between his teeth.

"Dad!" I blurted. "You always have something to say. Why aren't you part of this conversation?"

"Juliet, what has gotten into you?" Mom said before Dad could do more than glance up. "I like to pride myself on being one of the busiest women we know, and thought to teach you those same ideals, though why you decided to quit your job, I still don't know."

My mind raced. "Mom, Dad," I began in a quiet voice. "I do plan on getting a job. I just don't understand this urgency, this pressure that you both are putting on me."

Mom stood up, her chair skittering backward. "What's gotten into *you*?" Her face reddened just as her knuckles whitened from gripping the tablecloth so tightly.

I reeled back at her visible fury, her eyes flashing fire as she inhaled and sat back in her chair.

"We'll speak of this later. But this won't be the last conversation, Juliet."

I threw my napkin down on the table. It was better than my impulse to punch something. "Fine, you want me to start my life just a few days after coming back, then I'll do it. Whatever you want." I stepped back from the table. "But neither of you are acting like the parents I know, the parents I remember, the parents who have spent the last few days trying to heal what has happened to our family." I took a deep breath, ignoring their raised eyebrows and wide eyes. My voice lowered. "You ask what's the matter with me? Well, I want to know what's the matter with the two of you." I bit my lip. *Who are you?* I wanted to ask, but chose to refrain.

"Juliet," Dad bit out. "Mel!" He sent a beseeching look to Mom.

"What do you mean?" Mom's voice was like ice as she pushed her plate forward on the table so she could rest her forearms on its surface. "All we want is for healing, for us to *move on*, Juliet." Mom's chair rocked back as she stood. "Are you feeling all right?"

I chuckled. *This can't be happening.* "Mom." It took all my focus to keep my voice even. "I *do* want us to move on as well. I'm sorry I don't remember what happened. I'm sorry it's been so hard for you both. I am sorry." My voice cracked.

"Mel." Dad cocked an eyebrow as he stroked his jaw. "Maybe we should talk more when emotions have calmed down."

Mom stilled. "Yes, you're right."

I shrank back. "I think I'll go to my room for a little while." With that, I rushed out of the room, silent tears sliding down my cheeks. Inside the safety of my room, the door closed and locked behind me, I crumpled to the floor. Confusion and anger swept over me in even waves. I cried until I could have wept from pure exhaustion.

With the tears spent, I struggled to stand, weary and unsteady. With slow steps, I walked into the bathroom and leaned against the sink. My cheeks were puffy and swollen, my eyes dark.

Is this me? I splashed cold water on my face and dried it with a soft towel. *What is happening?* My parents were my parents, and yet not the parents I remember. *Are these the consequences of my having gone to Ryujin?* I sucked in air. My image stared back at me through the clean reflective glass. *Am I also me and yet not me?* I wasn't the same girl who had left.

CHAPTER EIGHT

Time slipped by, bringing with it another shower. The rain pinged against the window, heralding a soft knock, which brought me back into the present. My feet made little noise on the floor as I walked over and unlocked the door. It opened to reveal Mom standing there, her face somehow harder than I remembered.

"Can I come in?"

I nodded and sat up from where I had been lying on my bed.

Mom sat down next to me, wringing her hands in her lap—something I'd never seen her do before. "Juliet, do you remember what happened earlier?" The scent of jasmine filled the air.

"How could I forget?" I asked, a laugh forcing its way out. I choked it down at the concerned frown that crossed Mom's face.

"How do you feel now?" She reached out a hand but withdrew it.

"Confused," I answered with a shrug. "You and Dad aren't joking, are you?" I knew the answer before Mom spoke.

"No, we weren't." Her pallor worsened. "We think it would be best to resume life like normal, as soon as possible."

"But, Mom, I *was* gone. That can't just be erased."

She stood and crossed her arms. "No, you're right. It can't, but we can put our best foot forward. Do you disagree?"

"No. I've already thought about a job, and I've spoken to Cam—twice. I'm trying to help—"

"I'm going to take you to see a doctor." Her face hardened. "I should have made an appointment already."

"I don't need a doctor." *Or do I?* If it would help my parents, and maybe even my sleep, then it would be worth it.

"You're going to see someone, and that's that." She took a breath. "But don't worry." She left the room.

I stood up and crossed the room to my desk. My laptop felt smooth and cool in my grasp. I opened my email. *E. Eddie.* I don't know if I'd ever get used to seeing Eddie's name in my contacts or typing out a message to him.

Eddie,

I hope this finds you well. I wish I could see you. There is so much to talk about, so much—

My fingers stopped tapping as I thought.

—to tell you.

I had a strange conversation with Mom and Dad ... well, all morning it's been a little strange. I'm wondering if maybe the stress and tension of the past few months has just gotten to them—to all of us.

When you get this, please reply.

Love, Juliet

I hit send and closed my email. The screen was bright. My fingers tensed a moment before my index finger moved, opening a search engine: "Eddie Barrows. Death."

Nothing.

Not one article, not one video, nothing to state that he had died. A numbness fell over me like a cold body of water had encased me. My world was closing in around me. My parents were not the parents I remembered, I wasn't the daughter they remembered, and Eddie was alive.

My life couldn't be erased.

I slammed the lid of my computer down and paced the room. It was suffocating. The walls enclosed around me, and the quiet was too much. I grabbed a jacket and left through the window. I left our yard and strode down the empty sidewalk. It was cold, and it was dreary and darkening quickly. But unlike Ryujin, there were streetlamps here. It was never going to be dark like it was there. The distant sound of a car grew closer and then faded again as it went down a different street.

I drew my jacket tighter around me to ward off the chill. At least back in Ryujin, everything made sense. Everything was simpler. I grunted. No, it wasn't simple even there. *But at least I didn't have people telling me I'd made it all up, or that I just didn't remember.*

I rapped my knuckles on the door. The sharp rap rang through the air on the quiet street. After a few moments of silence, I raised my hand and knocked again.

A light shone around the edges of some curtains as a switch was flicked on. The door opened. "Juliet!" Cam stepped aside to let me in. "What are you doing here?"

"We need to talk." I led the way into her kitchen and sat down at the table, my knees bouncing with nervous energy.

Cam nodded. She sat down, her pajamas loose and cozy, her ankles crossed as she leaned back in her chair.

"Something is off with my mom and dad."

"Oh?" Cam replied. Her lips pursed. "Isn't that normal?" She laughed, her eyes crinkling.

"No, it's more than that. I don't know what happened. Everything was fine yesterday, but this morning they changed. They're not the same people. They're different. It's like they took on the roles of other people and they're all in." I stood up and paced the floor. "I don't understand what's going on."

Cam examined her fingernails. "So?"

"Cam!" I slapped my hand down on the table, wincing at the sting that spread across my hand and wrist.

"No need to be so snappish," Cam muttered, turning her attention from her nails to me. "What's eating at you?"

I groaned. "I just told you!"

"Not really ..." Cam replied, trailing off. "I mean, you said they're different, acting different, blah blah blah."

"They're not being patient!"

"Like normal," Cam inserted.

"Mom wants me to see a doctor—"

"Which you already knew."

I gritted my teeth. "Cam!"

"No need to snap," Cam reminded me. "I'm just stating the facts. They are right, so I don't quite get why you're so annoyed." She flicked her dark hair over her shoulder.

Why am I so upset? It was going to be hard. It became harder when I began playing the role of an amnesiac. Of course it wouldn't be left at that.

"Juliet, you already know I agree. I think you should see a doctor, given ... everything."

"This *is* serious!" I snapped, making to sit back down across from Cam. The sudden movement sent the chair falling to the floor. Its loud clang reverberated through the small room.

"You don't say?" Cam said, her voice almost a low drawl.

"Cam!"

"By the way, I do prefer Camila."

"What?"

"Camila," she said. "That's what I prefer. I've never had to remind you before ..." She leaned forward and peered at me. "I think maybe it's time for you to go home, Juliet. Do you want me to take you?"

"Why are you acting this way?"

She yawned. "What way?"

"You're more snappish and devil-may-care."

She shrugged and flipped her dark braid over her shoulder. "I think you're the one being dramatic and emotional, not me." She waved. "Do you want me to give you a ride?"

"No, I can walk," I ground out, trying to suppress the anger building within me.

"Well, I have nothing to say beyond what I've already told you. I think you should obey your parents, and yeah."

My brain whirled. "Are you upset with me?"

Cam's thick brows rose. "What? I know you're having some weird amnesia syndrome problem, but no, I'm not upset with you."

"You know," I said, taking a step back, "I think I should leave. I need some fresh air."

Cam nodded and raised a hand in a languid farewell. It took all I had not to run to the front door and slip through and then keep running until I could escape whatever new horror I had entered. *But this is my home.*

I tilted my head back, gazing up at the blackness of the heavens as I walked. Stars glittered faintly, nowhere near as brilliant as the ones I'd seen in Ryujin. They twinkled, struggling against the brightness of the lights around me. A soft smile caressed my face as I relished in the cool night air on my skin. I sighed and continued down the sidewalk, beginning the trek back home.

Home. I gritted my teeth. *Why is it hard to think of it as home?* An ache throbbed in my temples. Even my ears buzzed, as though warning me not all was as it should be. I lost myself in thoughts and the past. A vague awareness surrounded me as to other people from time to time, or the houses around me, some loud, some quiet.

"Argh!" I half-yelled into the empty air. It had always been difficult since Eddie died. *But not like this.* I clenched my teeth. My shoes slapped against the pavement. I didn't want to go home, but I had nowhere else to go.

Tears pricked at my eyes, catching on my lashes before falling down my cold cheeks. I picked up a stick that lay across my path. Bending it between my chilled fingers, I watched and listened as it snapped in half. Again and again, until there was nothing else left to break. The pieces lay in a winding path behind me. My chest ached. *Nothing else to break.* I fought back a sob. My chest grew tight, like a shard of glass had pierced it. The wood lay behind me, but my heart still beat within me, a sally of drums warning me that my soul had splintered.

"I'm broken," I whispered to the quiet evening. *And I don't know how to put the pieces back together.*

⚬⚬⚬ ⚬⚬⚬

The house was so quiet. There was no sign they'd noticed I'd disappeared again. It was easy to slip back upstairs to my room. As I passed the door to my parents' bedroom, I could hear faint sounds from the TV.

Inside the familiar warmth of my room, I sat on my bed and leaned back against the soft give of my pillows. Part of me wished I could fall asleep, my troubles forgotten, at least for a few hours, yet sleep always brought a set of its own. I couldn't tell what was worse—living my life in wakefulness or in terror-filled sleep.

Ryujin would never leave me. And now my own world wouldn't help me heal.

The white candle on my side table caught my eye. Earlier I had grabbed it from a bookcase downstairs. I leaned over and grabbed the matchbox. With a sharp strike, fire flared, and I lit the candle sitting there. The soft, warm glow drew me farther into the memories swimming in my mind. I rocked back and forth, trying to get warm. There was something comforting about the candle-light. It reminded me of Ryujin, a world where I had been in such danger, had done things I'd never have imagined, seen things I wished I could forget—and yet it wasn't turned upside down like my home had.

"I have electricity," I whispered, looking at the ceiling. "I have everything I've grown up with—the people, the places, my parents, Eddie, Cam ... This is my home." My chest felt heavy. The weight was inescapable.

I drew the blanket up to my chin and twisted onto my side. My home was always a place of refuge, of belonging. *It still is.* The thought repeated itself. *It still is.*

Chapter Nine

My head tilted back as I enjoyed the warmth from the sun on my face. There had been a break in the clouds, a pause from the morning rain, and so I'd escaped to the backyard from the stifling intensity of my bedroom. I felt alone, even though I wasn't. Dad remained holed up in his office, and Mom kept herself busy. Even with my bedroom door shut, I had felt like she was watching me.

I closed my eyes, my head buzzing a little. I listened to the birds singing, coming out of hiding now that the rain had stopped and sunshine greeted them. *That's what I am. A bird learning its freedom.*

I opened my eyes. The hairs on my arms stood on end. I stiffened. Something had changed in the air. I felt eyes on me. Scanning the yard, I saw that I was alone. There was only me. I stood, each breath coming in and out as though in slow motion. The birdsong faded away until I heard nothing but my own beating heart. I took a slow step, then another. Each one brought me closer to the corner of the house. A slight movement, and someone stepped out from where the backyard opened to the front of the house.

I froze. Time stilled. I knew that man.

My heart skipped a beat.

He stood there, his tall figure straight, his arms hanging by his sides, so still he could have been a statue. But his eyes roved over me, his dark green eyes shining with emotion.

Adnan.

The war deep inside grew harder to ignore.

I raised my hand, reaching out to him without thinking. *Wait.* I drew my hand back and watched as his jaw tightened. "You're real?" I whispered, taking a hesitant step forward. "Adnan?" My voice broke. I trembled, my mind struggling to form coherent thoughts.

He approached me, each stride sure. "Juliet."

I sucked in a breath as I heard my name spoken in his deep voice. My mind broke free of its daze. I ran forward, crossing the remaining distance, my heart beating erratically. He opened his arms, and I fell into his strong embrace. I clung to him, afraid he would disappear, afraid it had all been a dream and would soon turn into a nightmare. Fear raged rampant through me, so potent that I didn't even mind the pulsing ache of my wrist as I gripped him.

He felt solid and warm.

But what if he's just smoke? What if he disappears? I breathed in the scent of rain and musty earth.

"Juliet," Adnan murmured, disentangling himself from me. He stepped back a pace but kept his hands on my forearms. His gaze captured my own. "Juliet, I almost can't believe I found you."

Tears filled my eyes. A half-sob, half-laugh escaped my lips. "You disappeared!" I exclaimed. "I knew you were there. I felt you come through the portal, but when I got here, you weren't with me. And the other day, I thought I saw you at the coffee shop—" Another dagger of fear drove into my heart. "You're a phantom, a figment of my imagination—" My voice broke and tears pricked my eyes. "I'm talking to myself."

Adnan tightened his grip. "No, I'm not. I'm as real as you are."

I leaned closer, wanting to feel his warmth again, but he kept me at arm's length.

"I was there. I'm *not* a phantom. You know I'm not. You know what is true." He tapped a finger against my heart. Reaching up, he laid his calloused hands over the sides of my face and leaned forward. "Look at me."

I stared into his familiar green eyes, which were stormy with feeling. "How did you know I live here?"

"By research." He grinned. "And at the coffee shop, you weren't alone. It wasn't the right time."

"So it *was* you there that day ..." I trailed off, and felt myself begin to relax as his right hand fingered my hair.

"I'm sorry I wasn't there for you," he whispered, leaning his head down.

Drops of sunshine turned into rays on my soul. "You're here now, you can stay—"

"Juliet—"

"No, wait, let me finish." I reached up to take his hands in mine. "You're here now, and we can figure it all out. But I don't think I ever gave up on seeing you, not really."

"You never do," Adnan admitted with a twinkle. His thumbs rubbed slow circles on the backs of my hands.

"I thought you hadn't come with me after all, though." I sighed.

"I was in a different part of the country."

"What?"

"We arrived at two different portal locations, Juliet." He shrugged.

"You did follow me ..."

Adnan's features softened. "I'd follow you anywhere." It was spoken so hushed I almost wasn't sure I'd heard him.

A warmth bloomed within my chest, and my heartbeat quickened. I couldn't help the grin breaking out across my face. His eyes lightened as he watched me.

But my smile soon faded. "But why didn't you arrive with me? Why somewhere else? I arrived at the same portal I'd used before, but you were with me when we fell through the tree, so you should've been there with me."

Adnan slipped his hands out of my grip and ran his hands through his hair. "Because I had to arrive back at my own portal."

His own portal ...

"What?" I breathed.

He turned away, but not before I saw his eyes close, as though in pain. I stepped forward and laid my hand on his shoulder, part of me afraid he'd brush me away, but he didn't.

He turned to face me again. "Remember when I told you about that boy who had come from here, someone whom I'd met a long time ago?" His voice was halting. "The boy I knew?"

I nodded.

"That boy is me. I was speaking of myself."

I gasped. "It's you. You're from my world." My jaw dropped. I should have known.

Adnan nodded. "I didn't mean to keep another secret from you. I was going to tell you, I just—just wasn't ready yet. I'm sorry, Juliet. It was a long time ago." He took my hands in his, his touch gentle. "That day, I opened so much of myself to you. I hadn't ever done that. At least, not since I first arrived on Ryujin's world." He laughed. "I'm not even from this country; my family was just vacationing here. We'd never seen the United States of America before." The way he enunciated it sounded foreign.

He's from my world. I shook my head, still trying to come to grips with it all. "Where? Where are you really from then?"

"Saudi Arabia."

"Saudi Arabia," I repeated.

"My native language is Farsi. When I was eight, I went through a portal, unexpectedly"—Adnan grimaced as he continued—"and the country I found myself in was not Ryujin."

I shivered as a breeze picked up.

"Here," Adnan said, leading me to the back porch. He pulled me down onto the couch beside him and took the blanket dangling over the back. Draping it over me, he angled himself to face me. "I was eight, Juliet, when I found myself in a strange world, a strange country, a different time—without my parents, my siblings ... without anyone I loved or trusted." He paused.

"What did you do?" I whispered, twirling a lock of hair.

Adnan started. "I was taken in by an innkeeper and his wife. They could've sold me, you know, but instead they took me in as the son they'd never had."

I reeled, processing what he'd just said. "Sold you?"

He nodded. "Yes. I grew up in the group of smaller countries the northern raiders are from."

The northern raiders—Umi no Machi—they are his people. I felt hot, my head beginning to ache as I processed. "You're one of them."

"No," he bit out. "No," he repeated more gently. "I'm not. My parents, though, are stern but kind. I haven't been back in a very long time."

My foot tapped the ground. "How long were you in that world?"

"Many, many years. Long enough that I stopped searching for a way back."

"How long?" I asked again.

He sighed. "Almost twenty years? Maybe eighteen now?"

"So you're twenty-six?"

He shrugged. "I guess so. Though I never kept track of my age."

"You're younger than I thought," I muttered. *At least our age gap is closer than I expected.*

He raised an eyebrow. "What?"

"I thought you'd be older." I shrugged and slipped my feet onto the edge of the couch. "So, Adnan ... ?" I studied him. If he trimmed his hair and beard, he would appear younger, I realized.

Adnan nodded. "Is my birth name, like I told you before."

I chewed on the inside of my cheek. Adnan shook himself and leaned closer so that our legs brushed.

"Did you find your family?" I asked.

"I've only been here for a week," he reminded me. "Same as you."

I grinned. "Right. Time has felt weird. Has it only been that long?"

His brows drew together, but all he did was nod.

"You'll look for your parents?"

He shook his head. "No."

I raised my chin. "Why not?"

"It's been a long time, Juliet. So no, I don't plan on looking for them."

"But—" I hesitated. "They're your family."

"By blood, yes."

"Maybe you should look for them."

Adnan leaned against the back of the couch and regarded me. "I needed to find you, not them, Juliet."

I shivered. *Don't overthink it.* But the warm feeling was back.

"Juliet, we can't stay here."

My jaw dropped. "What?"

"Something is wrong here. We can't stay. This isn't the same world we left."

"Yes, it is!" I protested. "This is my world, my home. My *family* is here!"

"Is that everything to you?" He crossed his arms.

Irritation flickered over me like a tidal wave. "This is my *home*, Adnan. It may not be yours, but it is mine," I snapped.

He flinched, but I was too angry to feel any remorse. "Juliet, something is different here. It's dark, oppressive, and the people are equally so."

I stiffened. Deep down, his words resonated. *No.* I pushed the doubts away.

"Come with me, Juliet." Adnan took my hand, relaxing when I didn't pull away. "This world isn't right."

"This is my family," I protested again. "Everything I've been doing—"

"Is not for them," he finished. "It's for you, and yet you're trying to fix everything the wrong way."

My lips opened and closed. "I'm just trying to bring a sense of normalcy back," I whispered, pulling my hand out of his. "I'm trying to do what my parents want me to do."

"Does that mean it's right for you?"

I frowned. "They're my family ..." But my voice was losing its urgency.

"I want you with me. Will you come?"

My heart thumped. "You're leaving?"

Adnan nodded once. "Yes. I'll try, at least. Find the portal again."

No, no, no. All sounds ceased. It was just the two of us sitting there.

"But I—"

"I can't live without you," he burst out. "I want you with me."

I halted, startled. Everything came into focus and yet blurred all at the same time. "What?" I asked. My body had frozen in place, but the wind sent my hair rippling across my cheeks. I could feel the sharp bite of the breeze, hear the distant chirping of birds, the buzzing of a fly as it flew too close to my ear.

"I can't live ... without you. I love you." His tone was clearer now, stronger, as though once said it was the easiest thing in the world to say it again. "It took me a while to realize it, or once I did, to admit it ..." He chuckled. "But why do you think I followed you here? This wasn't the first time, either. I've been following you since the day you left Umi no Machi." He brushed his hair from his eyes, holding it there as the wind tried to blow it back. "I know it clear as day, Juliet."

A light turned on. I breathed in, feeling lighter than air. *I love him.* It was then that I knew I felt the same: I couldn't live without him either. Joy blossomed. *He loves me.*

Adnan leaned closer, his grip on my hand tightening. "Will you come with me?"

And just like that, the light went out.

"Go with you? Go where? Back to Ryujin?" I knew, with a sinking pit in my stomach, the answer even as I asked.

"Yes," he confirmed.

"I can't; my family is here. My home is here. They're my parents—"

"It isn't safe for you here." He lowered his hand as the breeze disappeared as fast as the warmth within me.

"How do you know that?"

Adnan's face darkened.

"Why do you think that?" I pressed.

"Juliet, you don't have a choice. You'll be a husk of your former self if you stay here."

"*What?*" So many half-thoughts ran through my mind. My hands shook as I clenched them into fists at my sides.

"Come with me," Adnan said.

I glanced over my shoulder, taking in the pristine cool blue of my home. *This* is *my home.* I faced him and opened my eyes. "I can't," I whispered. "I have to stay. I have to help them. You're right; something is wrong."

"Juliet, don't you realize—?" Adnan groaned in frustration. "*They* can't be helped. It's not just them; it's everyone in this godforsaken place. You have been here. I've been out there." He made a sweeping gesture with his arm. "Something isn't right. You have to admit that."

I lowered my gaze to his boots—the same, familiar boots he'd always worn. "Maybe—"

"No," Adnan said, his hands clenching into fists in his lap. "I'm leaving tonight."

Rain began to drizzle from the sky. The silence felt like it pressed in from all sides as he waited for my answer.

I wanted to be with him, but this was all wrong. Against all odds, he'd come back for me once again—because he loved me. And I loved him. *But this is my family.* I bit my lip. *This is where I belong.*

"I'm not leaving." I couldn't look at him.

"Fine," he replied without a hint of emotion. I glanced up. His face had become a mask I knew all too well. My heart splintered. "I can't force you, nor do I wish to. You're on your own, Juliet." He stood and regarded me. "I wish things were different. You—" He bit off whatever he was going to say.

I closed my eyes against the pain he tried to hide.

He stepped off the porch. "Goodbye."

Tears stung my eyes. "Wait." Shaking my head, I stood and watched as the rain fell onto his skin and slid down into the beard hiding the lower half of his face. "I wish things were different too. I hope you understand."

"You're going down a dark path, Juliet. I just hope you realize it before you live to regret it." He swept an arm out. "This isn't your home, no matter how many times you keep telling yourself that." He turned and walked away. He was gone.

Tears coursed down my cheeks as I fell to my knees. Burying my face in my arms, I cried. A haze fell over me. My chest ached. All I could see was Adnan's figure turning away from me, disappearing once again, leaving me.

But this time, it was my fault.

This time, I had let him go.

I rocked from side to side, my sobs giving way to soft, choking cries. Somewhere inside the house, a door slammed, reminding me that my parents were so close. I sniffed and wiped my nose on my sleeve. Part of me had left with Adnan. An emptiness lay inside, the gulf so great I wasn't sure how I would begin to heal it.

I bit back another wrenching sob, struggling to regain control of myself. Standing, I wiped my face on the hem of my shirt and squared my shoulders. I had made my decision. There was no going back. I stepped into the house. But now my heart warred with itself again. The choice I'd made no longer felt easy ... or right.

Chapter Ten

I gritted my teeth as I pushed my body to its limit. The stretch deepened until the tendons, the skin, and the muscles burned with a ferocity ready to rend them asunder. I breathed, deepening the stretch with each exhale. A sigh escaped my lips as I uncurled and tilted my head to look at the sky.

It was a beautiful day, a rare one where the startling blue of the skies shone in stark contrast to the usual gray. Even the birds chattered, like they knew spring was approaching. Releasing the stretch, I twirled in a slow circle as I swept the backyard, whose tall fences separated me from the rest of the world. It was a morning in which I could hear the laughter of children as moms got them out of the house for a change.

I drank some water and eased down into downward dog. I closed my eyes. *Last night.* Last night had been difficult. Adnan haunted my thoughts. I exhaled. I had taken melatonin to sleep. The bottle was easy to find, almost full in the medicine cabinet. I had only ever used it while traveling ... and after Eddie died. *Or didn't die.* I moved into a planking position.

When the melatonin hadn't kicked in fast enough last night, I'd taken Benadryl. I could still see the pills in the palm of my hand. But they'd done their job; they'd knocked me out. I stood and breathed in. Unlike last night, my hands no longer trembled. Not now. Air whistled past my teeth as it left my lungs. I couldn't stop thinking about Adnan.

A sharp clang split the air. I whirled around, my body tensing, my arms rising as I sank back and down into a defensive stance.

Mom stared at me, her hands full of tools. "You're not listening to me."

Why is she gardening? It's the middle of winter. I fought to keep my boiling emotions below the surface. *Remain in control.* The children continued to laugh in the background as they played. I gritted my teeth. "Mom, I've been trying to do as you asked."

Mom set the spade and other gardening implements down. "Juliet, do you remember anything yet?"

"No, Mom."

"Are you sure?"

I knelt down, tying a loose shoelace. "I am sure."

"I'm sorry to hear that," Mom murmured. The grass rustled as she walked closer. "I—we've—found someone."

I finished tying my shoes and stood. "What?"

"A doctor."

I shook my head. "No, Mom."

"Yes." Her shoulders drooped.

Was that regret? I crossed my arms, ignoring the ache in my wrist. "Maybe that would be best. But I don't need a therapist."

Mom's stormy eyes darkened. "You live in a fantasy. A fantasy in your mind, where you don't even remember your brother." She gulped and eased her shoulders down. "You've been unwell, Juliet." She tugged her garden gloves farther up her wrist. "But we'll help you feel better. There are people who can help you."

I said nothing, but inside, my soul crumpled a little.

Her voice hardened. "You are confused, but we will set things straight. It will take time, but we'll get there. *You'll* get there." She crouched down to pick up the garden tools. "You'll see." She turned and walked away, calling over her shoulder, "Tomorrow is your first appointment."

I watched her round the corner of the house. Tomorrow. My jaw locked. Tomorrow was my first appointment. I stepped toward the house. Mom had said "first." This wouldn't be a "one and done."

Reality wants to play tricks on me.

⊱ ⊰

I entered my room. Dad raised a hand in greeting from where he sat on the bed. I hesitated.

"Your mother wants me to speak with you," he said with a shrug.

I nodded, watching as his lips moved uncertainly without speaking and his hand played with his pant leg. He was different. He'd changed. So had Mom. *Do I even know them anymore?* I sat down at my desk and swiveled my chair to face him.

Dad grimaced and rubbed at the rough stubble on his jaw. "Do you have something you want to say?"

That's what he came up with?

I shook my head, knowing I wasn't making this easy on him.

"Hmm. She told you she—we—made the appointment for tomorrow?"

I nodded.

"You shouldn't worry. It's for the best." Dad hesitated and took a deep breath. "He's one of the best. We'll figure this out. You're unwell, Juliet, but we love you, no matter what's wrong. We'll get through this, all of us together."

I gripped the sides of my chair. "Dad, I—"

"What?"

My lips parted. "I love you too."

Dad's lips parted, his yellowed teeth peering from between them.

I picked up my glass. My fingers trembled.

"Good. Well, then." Dad slapped his legs with the palms of his hands.

I gripped the glass so hard I feared it would shatter. A deep hole yawned inside my chest.

Dad stood and strode to the door, his footsteps soft but sure. He turned and raised a hand.

I closed my eyes. *Like Adnan. Adnan walked quietly, effortlessly.* The hole deepened. I struggled to hang on to reality. I laid the glass down on the desk, knowing in another few moments it might have splintered, just as my heart threatened to do.

Don't worry. Everyone told me not to worry. *Yet they all agree I need help.* I stood and went to the window. Shadows lay on the grass, thrown by the lights on the house. *It feels like a lifetime.* This was my childhood home. *My home, and I'll fight for it.*

I leaned my forehead against the cool glass. I yawned, my entire body feeling tired. Exhaustion pulled at my mind, a grasping, hungry touch. I slipped under my feather comforter and curled up on my side into the soft mattress.

I forced myself to relax my jaw. *Relax,* I told myself. With my eyes closed, my heart rate stilling, I tried to focus on nothing. It wasn't a white canvas before my eyes but a black one. An empty void. Every time a memory tried to force its way to the surface, or a thought drift through a crack in the walls, I pushed them back, farther in, farther down. All was quiet. No. A distant fan blew from the kitchen. A curl of hair whispered against my cheek.

It's never quiet here.

I groaned and rolled to my other side.

There's always something—some small sound.

I sat up with a jerk. The sleep I wanted wasn't coming. My comforter fell to the side as I slipped out of bed and down the hall. In the kitchen, I hesitated, listening. It was empty. There was no sign of Mom.

I opened the medicine cabinet in the pantry and picked up the bottle of melatonin.

"Juliet?" The voice was quiet and yet accusatory.

My body jerked, the bottle almost slipping out of my hands. The pills inside rattled.

Mom folded her arms, her head tilted to one side. "Juliet, what are you doing?"

"Just taking some of this to help me sleep." I lifted the small, white bottle to show her.

"I know that isn't all." Mom stepped forward and took it from me, her weary voice matching her drooping shoulders. "Why the Benadryl too?"

I clenched my teeth together.

"I know you took them last night. The bottles weren't in the same place I had them."

"They were—"

"No." Mom sighed and pointed at the shelf behind me. "You faced them the wrong way, Juliet. Why are you taking these?" she asked, holding up the offending pills.

"To help me sleep," I whispered, fighting a wave of defensiveness. "There's no problem with melatonin."

Mom's face paled a few shades. "You can't sleep?" she spat. "*You!* You can't sleep? What about me? Am I taking the pills to help with the stress you're putting me through? No! I'm going to hide the pills where you can't find them." She took a deep breath. "Juliet, just go back to bed."

I watched with wide eyes as she set the bottle down on the shelf with a sharp clatter. "Mom!"

"No, in this case, there is a danger. You don't know how dangerous you are to yourself."

"Mom, it's just melatonin!"

She grabbed the melatonin and the Benadryl. "We're done talking!" she snapped and spun on her heel.

I was left alone in the kitchen. The melatonin I'd come for was gone. And all I had succeeded in doing was making my mom even more paranoid than she already was. I threw my head back. *Haven't I already been through enough?* I felt tears prick my eyes as rage blew in to mix with the sorrow. *I have seen so much. I have done things I don't want to remember.*

A candle flickered on the kitchen counter. The flame was so small. Once, I'd felt a flame flicker inside of me, an ember that had fanned into a fire. I sucked in air like it was going to be my last breath. *That flame is gone.*

CHAPTER ELEVEN

Muted footsteps strode up and down the corridor outside. My fingers drummed on my thigh—*tap, tap, tap*—as my eyes followed Mom's figure. She paced the floor. Three steps, turn; three steps, and repeat. The room was white, the walls bare. Yet I felt a sort of sickness threatening to ooze out of the clean walls, floor, chairs, mirror, and flat table. A single white paper covered the table's surface, ready for the next patient. I sniffed, crinkling my nose at the clean scent filling my nostrils. Clorox. Bleach. The room was pristine.

Footsteps halted outside the door. The handle turned. A small woman came in, a careful smile on her pale face that didn't reach her eyes. I watched as she walked past Mom, who came next to me and sat before the monitor. The chair creaked as the woman settled.

Breathe.

"Hello," the woman said, already typing on the keyboard, little clicks sounding under the flurry of her fingers. "Can you state your name and date of birth?"

I nodded. My lips parted. "Juliet Barrows. February nineteenth, two thousand and one."

The woman nodded. "Very well." She glanced from the monitor to Mom. "You must be Mel?"

Mom nodded. "Yes."

"I'm Marjorie, a nurse assistant here. I think we covered everything over the phone, though. Is there anything you would like to add?"

"Yes, I—"

"No," Mom interrupted, leaning forward over the counter. "There is nothing."

Marjorie nodded and surveyed me. "Very well."

Shouldn't she be listening to me? Not my mom?

My jaw clenched. "Wait a moment."

Both women focused on me.

"I don't even know why I am here." *Yes, you do.* The protest screamed in my mind. *But I shouldn't be here.*

"It's all right." Marjorie shot me a pitying look as she cocked her head to the side. "But we'll get it all figured out. Now, as I'm sure you're aware ..." She paused and glanced at her monitor again before turning to face us. "We'll be doing a full physical, some bloodwork, a couple small tests, maybe a screening or two"—she waved a hand in the air—"but nothing you haven't done before, I'm sure." She watched me like a wolf about to pounce on her prey.

Something is off. My arms crossed over my chest and my foot tapped the floor.

"Feel free to ask questions whenever you would like, and we will do our best to provide you with answers. If you're uncomfortable at any time, please let us know."

Questions? I wanted to know why this nurse seemed to look at my mom as my authority. My shoulders relaxed. "I'm uncomfortable now."

Marjorie chuckled. "Very funny." She handed me a clipboard with a page covered in small black print. "You've done most of the preliminary paperwork, so the last thing is for you to just go over this."

I took the clipboard and let my eyes adjust to the print and the boxes beside each paragraph. "A depression screening?"

Marjorie nodded. "It's done at every appointment, no matter what the appointment is for. It should only take a few moments. Here's a pen."

I took the offered pen and scanned the familiar questions. Ten of them, each with multiple choice answers. I'd never hesitated before. But this time, I had to reread the first questions a couple of times.

"Juliet," Mom whispered. "Go ahead. Fill it out. You've done this before."

But things have changed, I wanted to say. The room grew smaller. A set of footsteps approached and faded beyond the door. The crisp paper crackled as I fingered it with my left hand while rolling the pen between the fingers of my right.

Little interest or pleasure in doing things?

Feeling down, depressed, or hopeless?

Trouble falling or staying asleep, or sleeping too much?

Feeling tired or having little energy?

Poor appetite or overeating?

Feeling bad about yourself—or that you are a failure or have let yourself or your family down?

Trouble concentrating on things, such as reading the newspaper or watching television?

Moving or speaking so slowly that other people have noticed? Or the opposite extreme?

Thoughts that you would be better off dead, or of hurting yourself?

If you checked off any problems, how difficult have these problems made it for you at work, home, or with other people?

"Is everything all right?" Mom's voice broke into my thoughts. I shook myself and set the pen to paper, watching the black ink ooze out into the shape of an *X*, marking the first question, *Nearly every day.* Then on to the next question, so absorbed it seemed as if I was alone in the room.

Am I a failure? I tapped the pen from finger to finger. *No, wrong question. Do I feel like I'm a failure?* The pen stilled. *Yes.* I marked the box for "nearly every day." But I could make things better, especially if they were my fault to begin with.

Last question ... *extremely difficult.*

The paper rustled as I slid it across the smooth desk to the nurse. She grinned, her dark eyes appearing rounder and more luminous as the bright light from the ceiling fell upon them. I stiffened. Why did that seem so familiar?

"Is something wrong?" Marjorie asked.

Saya. Her eyes reminded me of Saya's. I shook my head. "No, nothing."

"All right, then. I will let the doctor know you are ready. He'll be in shortly."

"Thank you," Mom replied, turning to an empty chair. "What did you see?" Mom asked.

I glanced up. "What?"

"The nurse, have you seen her before?"

"No," I said, my foot stilling.

Mom's lips pursed, and her hands twitched where she held them in her lap.

I watched as she peered up at the clock on the wall. One of the hands ticked. Another minute had passed. Mom used to always be so still, so patient …

Three raps sounded on the door. It opened and a man came in, his white coat pristine over wrinkle-free scrubs. His face was pale, as though it hardly saw the light of day. He shifted a clipboard to his other hand and closed the door behind him.

"Hello, I'm Doctor Tamini." He shrugged his narrow shoulders. "So, Juliet, before we begin, do you have any questions for me?"

"You're not my regular doctor."

Tamini glanced between Mom and me. "No, I am not, but I am now your new primary. Did the nurse explain everything that would be included in today's exam?"

"For the most part," I answered. My gaze caught on a blemish in the wall opposite to me, a small spot, almost unnoticeable, yet stained darker than the cream-colored paint. *Blood?* The dark red filled my vision, oozing out of the dark corner of my mind. Rivulets ran over my thoughts.

"Juliet?"

I glanced up to see Mom and the doctor watching me. "Yes?"

"Doctor Tamini asked you a question," Mom said, her look sharper than knives. "Could you switch chairs to sit next to his desk?"

I obeyed, holding out my arm as the doctor took my blood pressure. His eyes were concentrated on the dial, and as the pressure on my arm increased, I frowned and squinted. "Almost done," Tamini said as I twitched in my seat, the pressure intensifying. "There."

No spot on the wall.

"Juliet?" Mom leaned forward out of her seat. "Is everything all right?"

"Fine," I mumbled, swallowing past the sudden lump in my throat. "Everything is fine." I looked again, but there was still no sign of the blemish I'd seen.

"Great!" Tamini said, overdoing the brightness in his tone. "Why don't you come take a seat on the table so I can do a quick visual exam?"

The paper on the table crunched as I sat down, my legs dangling over the edge. I stiffened as Tamini came and stood in front of me, a light in his right hand and some kind of tool in his left.

"This won't take long," he said, smiling.

"What are you doing?"

"I'll explain as we go. Just try to relax and take a deep breath."

⁂

An hour passed. Then another. I fought back a yawn. The visual exam had gone by without hesitation, and then the screenings. After that, a nurse had come in for a physical. Now, Doctor Tamini approached me with yet another tray of needles.

"What is this for?" I asked, leaning back. My back hurt from sitting on the table for so long.

"We're going to run a couple more tests, one for your blood count and also one for a complete metabolic panel. These are necessary for a thorough test." His voice was methodical as though he'd explained this a thousand times before.

"Has this happened before?" I asked, trying hard not to veer away from the needles in front of me.

"What?" Tamini swabbed at the inside of my arm.

"Has anyone else said they couldn't remember months of their life?"

"Not in this way, no." He stabbed the needle into my skin. I flinched at the sharp prick. "We're almost done," Tamini said, switching tubes as the first one quickly filled up with bright red blood. "All right. All done." With deft movements, he wrapped my arm and scooted his chair back across the floor. "Are you currently working?"

I shook my head.

"When was the last time you did?"

"Almost exactly five months ago," Mom answered, leaving me sitting there with my mouth still open to answer.

Tamini marked something on a clipboard. "And I'm assuming you're still settling in since you found yourself in the Redwoods, I believe it was?"

I glanced at Mom, hesitating. She hadn't turned from the doctor, frozen, her hands twitching in her lap. "Correct, and yes, it was the Redwoods," I said after several long moments.

Tamini tapped his pen against the clipboard. "Alright." The pen continued to tap. "Any medications?"

"None."

"Well," Mom said, "that's not exactly true ... Juliet?"

"I took melatonin and Benadryl once recently," I admitted.

Tamini raised an eyebrow. "Why melatonin?"

"I've been having trouble sleeping."

He made a note. "I see. For how long?"

I hesitated again. "A few days."

"And Benadryl?" he asked.

"To help knock me out," I explained, unnerved by his constant rustling of pen against paper.

Tamini nodded. "Interesting. Okay, and what about relationships? Are you seeing anyone?"

Adnan. I stiffened. "No." *He's not here.*

Tamini leaned forward. "No one?"

"No one," I echoed.

"When was the last time you were in a relationship with someone?"

Tristan flashed through my mind. His bright blond hair, sparkling eyes, ready smile, and then the darkness—we were engaged—but not ...

"It's been a little while," I answered.

The doctor peered at Mom but returned his attention to me. "Do you have any knowledge of being sexually active during those months?"

No. My heart beat faster.

"And there is no one in your life now?"

Adnan. But I had said goodbye to him. He was gone.

"Juliet?"

"No," I breathed, seeing Adnan's tall, strong figure in my mind.

"But then again, you wouldn't remember, would you?" the doctor asked, scooting his chair a little closer.

"I have not—none that I am aware of." *What does this mean now?* A pit grew in my stomach. *What exams are next?*

"Juliet," Tamini began. "You don't look well."

My breaths came in short and fast as the air became stifling. My eyes flitted around the small room, the bare furnishings, the plain walls. It was too small—

"Juliet?"

Forcing my heart rate to slow and my body to still, I felt my body relax. "I'm fine. Do you have any more questions?" I didn't recognize the overly bright tone that came out of me.

"Have you had any recent surgeries?"

"She's never had a complicated surgery," Mom put in. "She's been healthy her whole life, and she never even gets sick."

"There is one last test I want to do," Tamini said.

"What test?"

Tamini laid the pen on the desk. "Is there any chance you could be pregnant?"

"What?" I exclaimed, ignoring the gasp that came from Mom. Glancing at her, I saw her eyes widen, a look of disbelief on her face. "No! Of course not."

"Just routine, to double-check nothing has happened. Do you mind if we conduct a test to ascertain—"

"No, there's no chance I've been or am pregnant. *None.*"

"How do you know?"

I reeled back in my chair. "Because it's impossible, that's how."

A muscle pulsed in the doctor's jaw. "You and your mom claim that you don't remember anything. So that is how it *is* possible. You don't remember what has happened, what could have happened—"

"Doctor," Mom protested, lifting a limp hand into the air.

"That may be true," I replied. "Fine, I'll take the pregnancy test. But it'll be negative."

Tamini sat back in his chair and stroked his clean-shaven jaw. "Very well. To ease your mind, it is very usual to conduct this test anytime a female has had a lapse and is not sure of what may or may not have happened to her. You would not be the only person to have had this done, and even if the results were positive, there are steps we could take, and we might be able to start piecing together why there are things you don't remember."

I crossed my legs. "Anything else?"

"Would you like to hear the results I have so far? Some of them I won't have for a couple days, but I can at least tell you a few things. If not, I recommend making another appointment for next week so I can explain it in full."

I don't want to come back. "Go ahead."

Tamini straightened the papers on his clipboard. "Well, first off, the results for your depression screening. I would like to advise you to see a therapist and a neurologist. We'll have a list of possibilities drawn up for you to take with you. I think it would be very beneficial for you to begin seeing someone." He glanced at me but turned away as though he couldn't bear to maintain eye contact. His foot tapped on the ground.

"Juliet," Mom whispered in my ear. "Try not to look like you're about to murder someone."

I swallowed, forcing myself to relax.

"Just one more thing …" the doctor added. "You said you haven't had any surgeries in the past year or so, but what about injuries?"

The ready answer of *yes* hovered on my lips, but I caught myself in time. "No." I shook my head. "Not that I can remember."

"Well, your wrist seems to be causing you pain." He glanced down at my right wrist, and I had to resist the urge to jerk it out of sight. "And," he continued, "I think you may be recovering from some broken ribs as well. Your side is tender and slightly swollen, though there aren't any marks left that I could discern, so my guess would be that happened at least a couple of months ago, but no longer than three or four. There is also some scarring over the area." He consulted his clipboard. "There are also some light scars on your palm that I believe will fade with time, and already appear to be doing so, but I believe they are from a more recent occurrence. Because of your injuries, I also prescribed you to see a physical therapist to make sure the healing process is a smooth one. And I think X-rays should be taken of your wrist and ribs. If you have time today, I would like to go ahead and send an order down to the labs for those to be done."

"Yes, the wrist." I winced. "I think it was broken, but I don't know how." *Adnan set the break. He took care of me, just like he had after my rib injury.* It hurt to breathe. "That's fine," I managed to say.

Tamini steepled his long fingers together. "All right, well, I'm sure as the rest of the results come in we'll have more answers, and it will definitely help as you begin your appointments with a physical therapist and psychological therapist." Tamini stood up and walked to the door. "The nurse will be in soon with the paperwork and the urine test, and then you both are free to go."

I sat unseeing as Tamini left, and the room grew silent once more. A hand pressed into my forearm, and I jumped.

"Juliet?" Mom asked, scooting closer. "We'll figure this out, okay? We'll help you get better. Maybe the therapist has ideas about why you've been so different and—and distant the last few days."

"The last few days?" I echoed, standing up.

"We're taking steps needed to figure it out. And don't worry about the appointments. I'll take care of all the details."

Sure, you will.

I watched as Mom turned her attention to the door. My gaze flitted to the wall. The pristine, white wall. No mark, no spot, no blemish of any kind. My breath caught. There was no sign of the drops of blood I had seen.

Chapter Twelve

The drive home was as quiet as it could be. From time to time, I felt Mom's scrutinizing eyes on me. But I didn't look away from the window while the houses on the quiet streets rolled by. It was turning out to be a gray, dreary day. Spring felt so far away.

We wound our way down a road flanking the harbor. Sailboats drifted on the water, tied to various docks. Few were out on the water on a day like this.

Mom turned into our neighborhood. The same man who had walked his dog a couple of days prior meandered down the sidewalk with his retriever. There was no umbrella this time. I watched as we passed. He didn't look up.

The car slowed to a stop before the engine turned off with a soft purr.

As we got out of the car, the front door opened. Dad stood there, silhouetted by a little light shining from a lamp behind him. "Eddie called."

I froze. *Eddie. My brother.* A drizzle of rain began to fall.

"He did?" Mom asked, stepping forward. "Can he talk?"

Dad shook his head. "No, he had to get off. He couldn't wait for you to come back. He wanted to speak with *you*."

I swallowed. "Did he say anything?"

"He said he'll reply to your email and that he'll call again when he can, but he's not sure when he will be able to again."

A pang of sadness ripped through me. I'd wanted to hear his voice again. I shifted, impatient, my fingers itching to open my laptop and check my email.

"I'll work on dinner," Mom muttered, entering the house. "Juliet?"

I closed the door behind me. "Yes?"

Mom hesitated, but her fingers clutched at her coat. "Never mind."

"How did the appointment go?" Dad asked, halting me in my footsteps once again.

"Juliet had the X-rays done today. Her wrist *was* broken, but was set at some point. Doctor says it's healing nicely."

"Okay." Dad's lips pursed. "Anything else?"

"I'll tell you later." Mom frowned and shot Dad a look that said much more than that.

I winced. "I'll be in my room."

I took off my shoes and slipped down the hallway. The family portraits watched me pass in silence. Alone in my room, I listened as the rain pattered against the window. Air hissed through my teeth as I sucked in a breath. My laptop lay on my desk, waiting. The metal was cool to the touch as I slid my fingers along it until they landed in the groove. With a soft click, the lid opened.

My email was up on the screen. I waited as it refreshed. There, a new message. My heart pounded within my chest—a rhythmic thumping, loud in my own ears. I opened the email.

Hey Jules—

Jules? I twirled a lock of hair between my fingers. Right. Eddie had called me that on the phone—a pet name. An endearment I wasn't familiar with, one that he'd evidently called me for years. *But I don't remember this.* A queasy feeling washed over me. I continued reading.

I tried calling you, but you were at the doctor's according to Dad. I wish we'd had the chance to talk. I'll try again when I can, but I don't know when that will be. Email is easier to make happen, though, so please respond as soon as you can, and I'll check it soon.

I took a deep breath. This was Eddie who'd emailed me. My brother. *The brother who died.* I shook my head. *No. He didn't die.* My temples throbbed. *He did ... no, he didn't, Juliet,* I told myself. *He didn't.*

Jules, I don't know what's happening.

I sucked in air, my eyes flying as I scanned the email.

I hope the doctors can provide you with answers. I wish I could be there with you. I wish I could tell you what you want to hear, but I can't.

I don't know why you don't remember. I can't imagine how hard the not knowing is. I hope the doctors help you figure it all out. I'll talk to you soon. I love you.

-Eddie

I knew where I was and where I had been. *Ryujin.* I sat back in my chair and closed the laptop. *He spoke with Dad.* I'd never mentioned the doctor or the exact timeline of being in Ryujin.

What if … ? The thought remained unfinished, but it was too late. A sliver of doubt wormed its way into my mind. I wrapped my arms around myself. I remembered Adnan's strong arms around me, holding me. He had been here, and I'd let him go. My family didn't know what I'd seen, what I'd done, where I'd been. They couldn't know. Especially not now. Cam had proved that. She didn't believe me. *Why would my parents?*

A gust of wind blew against the window, rattling the glass. I stood up, knocking my chair back in my haste. I stood at my window much like how I used to do in Creulon's fortress. It would be easier to believe that it all had never happened. Time slipped by. I was a girl torn between two worlds, two lives.

When the knock on the door came, I wasn't sure how long I'd been standing there. I tucked my hair behind my ear and steeled myself. "Come in."

The door opened, and Mom paused on the threshold. "Did you get some sleep?"

I shook my head.

"I'd hoped you might have. Cam will be here any moment. She's joining us for dinner."

One long, slow blink. "Cam is coming?" I echoed, feeling the confusion radiate from my face.

"Yes." Mom's eyes were like hardened stone.

"What's wrong?" The question slipped past my lips before I could stop it.

Mom's face softened the slightest bit. "I wish things weren't like this."

For a moment, I saw how Mom used to be, with her warmth and sincerity. "Me too," I whispered. I wanted my old life back. *But it wasn't easy, even then.* I pushed those thoughts away as Mom stepped back.

A knock rang out. I could have sighed with relief.

"You know, Juliet," Mom said, "things haven't changed for us. Just for you and, through you, us. But this isn't about us. It's about you. And I hope one day you'll remember who you are and, for that matter, who we are."

Biting my lip, I froze, my heartbeat slow and steady. "And if I don't?"

Her voice deepened. "Then I—I just don't know."

A pang filled my soul, and I sucked in a breath.

"You should put on some makeup," Mom noted, peering at my face. "You have dark circles under your eyes, and you look pale and worn. I would almost tell you to cut back on your daily schedule, except that you don't really have one beyond your backyard workouts, and I'm guessing no matter how many times I tell you, you're not going to stop those." She shook her head, and again the familiar scent of jasmine wafted through the air.

Memories of training with Sensei in Ryujin jabbed my mind like a needle. My shoulders drooped.

Mom's lips parted as she sighed. "All right, I guess you'll have to just figure things out, then. Try to act normal, okay? I want Cam to think we're recovering, and things are being figured out, because they are. Your first appointment with the therapist is tomorrow, and the physical therapist is in two days."

Tomorrow. Two days. An invisible weight settled on my shoulders. I pushed it away. "So fast?" I asked.

"Yes. I went through the list, and these therapists had cancellations and were able to get you in quickly."

The knock sounded again.

"Jeffery, the door!" Mom yelled. She shook her head. "That man."

Forcing my body to relax, I took a deep breath. "I love you, Mom," I murmured. *I do love you.* But I loved how I remembered her.

Mom's shoulders tightened. "Just put on a little makeup, okay, Juliet? But hurry up." She turned and left, her footsteps fading away in the carpeted hallway.

Still and silent, I remained standing there, lost in a haze. Even the scents from dinner cooking faded away. My vision lost focus, and my mind slowed into a beat that matched the calm one of my heart. A distant voice echoed Mom's instructions, but I ignored them.

It wasn't until I heard my name that I jolted out of the state I was held in. I dragged myself to the bathroom to apply the requested makeup.

The only way I knew how to fight this was to make everything seem normal, to try to fall back into my normal routines, to live the life I'd lived before. *Or the life my parents want me to live.* I needed that life back. If I did what my parents wanted, if I lived the way they wanted, and dropped anything related to my disappearance, then my life could become normal again. We could be happy.

I stood in the archway. Dad sat at the head of the dining table, his fingers drumming on the dark wood as he read the book in his other hand. The bright light reflected off the cream walls and green accented cabinets. Mom set a dish on the table, her eyes flitting over everything to make sure it was all there. She chatted with Cam, who peered at her fingernails and nodded in time to Mom's chatter. Something wasn't right. She slumped in her chair, as if this was the last place she wanted to be.

As if she knew I was watching, she froze and glanced up. Her eyes brightened a little, driving away the dullness for a moment before it settled back over her features like a thick blanket. She nodded. "Hey."

"Aw, there you are." Mom pointed to the table. "Take a seat. Dinner is ready."

Dad set his book to the side. My hand twitched as I took my seat and laid a napkin across my lap.

"Hey, Cam." I stabbed a potato with my fork.

"How's it going?" she asked, barely looking up from her plate.

"All right, you?"

"Just work as usual, and roommates are a pain as usual."

My eyebrows rose, and my hand halted with the fork halfway to my lips. "I thought you liked your roommates."

Mom kicked my foot.

"Ha-ha," Cam chuckled dryly. "Very funny." She rolled her eyes. "By the way, you look good, girl. Your mom told me you've been working out, but man, it shows." She nodded again. "Keep it up."

Who is she? I lifted a bite to my lips and began to chew. A vague recognition of roast chicken flittered through my thoughts.

Cam tapped her fork on her plate. "I can see what you're trying to hide behind that makeup." She waved a hand through the air.

Out of the corner of my eye, I watched Mom stiffen.

"You're not one for late nights," Cam said. "But you've looked like you've had more than the odd one here and there. Why'd you decide to leave me out of the fun?"

"Cam, I was just at your place a couple of nights ago," I muttered. I glanced at Dad, who was engrossed back in his book, oblivious to what was happening at the table.

"Very funny," Cam drawled with another eyeroll.

I swallowed, no longer hungry. My stomach rolled as a wave of queasiness washed over me.

"You doing better now?" Cam asked, eyeing me.

"Uh—"

Another kick.

"Yes, much better. I'm getting help—"

"She's doing so much better!" Mom interrupted, shooting me a glare. "Now, Cam ..."

I twirled my fork around on my plate as Mom's voice lowered into a droning buzz in the background. I didn't find the answers I sought on my plate. *All I do is pretend Ryujin never happened.*

My hand traced my rib cage. It felt as though it throbbed with just the memory of my broken ribs—of Hirose's sidekick slashing me with his knife. I sucked in a breath. It had all been real. The doctor had seen my wounds. They were there. The knives and katana were upstairs. *Stop.*

The rest of the meal passed by in a blur. Mom expertly kept Cam in conversation, not giving us room to speak anymore. In a way, I was glad for the silence. For not having to pretend everything was fine.

When it came time, I walked Cam to the door and bade her farewell. I closed the door behind her. Squaring my shoulders, I turned off the front room lamps and headed back to the kitchen. Voices filtered into the hallway. I hesitated and crept to the archway. Out of sight, I waited, my body pressed against the wall as

I listened. My muscles tightened as I fought the urge to just walk away, to not eavesdrop, but I needed to hear this.

"Mel," Dad murmured with his deep voice. "You said she'd be fine."

"Yes, I did say that, but I just don't know. Jeffery, I'm not sure she'll ever recover."

"Well," Dad replied, with a bit of a "devil-may-care" tone. "We'll just see what the therapists have to say and what progress Juliet makes."

Mom said nothing.

"What if she doesn't recover?" Dad asked.

There was a pause as I waited with bated breath for Mom to answer.

"Then our lives will change drastically."

My hands clenched into fists as my muscles tensed, but I didn't move. Hot tears fell from my eyes. They rolled down my cheeks, unhindered.

"All right, Mel."

A small sob worked its way up within me. I clamped a hand over my mouth and reeled on the back of my heels. My feet ate up the ground as I ran to my room.

"It's not me," I whispered into the quiet air. "It's them. It's them." I sighed and ran my fingers through my hair.

I'm doing my best. I'm doing what they want.

Yet the doubts crept in, faster and faster.

⁂

A shrill scream ripped through the room, and I leapt out of bed. The echo of that cry seemed to bounce off the walls. My heart pounded, my breaths coming in rapid gasps as I peered around the dark room.

Empty.

An ache filled my chest from my rapid heartbeat.

Footsteps pounded down the hallway. My door flung open, the whites of Mom's eyes appearing even lighter in the dim room. Dad peered over her shoulder.

"Juliet?" she asked, taking a hesitant step forward. "Juliet, turn on the lamp, please."

I remained frozen, the faces of the dead floating unbidden before my eyes, so real I was afraid they stood there in front of me. Mom's voice attempted to penetrate the fog enveloping me, but it was too thick.

It was so dark my heart cried for relief. Then the lamp flickered on, and light flooded my bedroom.

I watched those I loved and cared for, those I had hurt, drift away, leaving only glimpses in their wake.

"Juliet, what are you … ?" She trailed off, her lips moving but no sound escaping them.

I followed her gaze down to the knife clenched in my hand, whose knuckles were white from gripping the hilt. *The knives.* I'd forgotten I had taken them out of the vent. *And I never put them back.* I stiffened and tucked it behind my back, hoping they wouldn't see the other one on my bedside table. Closing my eyes, I saw Adnan standing before me, his rare, but soft smile sad and encouraging. *Let go of them, Juliet. You cannot forget the past, but you also cannot fear it if you are to live on.* He faded, but his words didn't. They remained as a whisper in my mind.

I opened my eyes. "I'm sorry," I whispered, my voice hoarse. "I heard someone scream."

Mom shook her head. "That was you."

What? My heartbeat slowed, but my hands shook as the adrenaline eased away. *No.*

"You are lost, Juliet. Please, please, *please* leave whatever this is behind and come back to us." Mom hugged herself, and Dad laid a hand on her shoulder. "You're getting worse. I should've seen the signs sooner. I should've known!" Her voice broke, and she swallowed back a half-suppressed sob.

This is a trial. I tugged on my shirt. The room felt hot. *But it is not of my making.*

Mom turned and whispered something to Dad, who left. She sighed and regarded me with tired eyes. "Dad is calling the two detectives who were here last time."

"Mom—"

"No, Juliet." Mom held up a hand. "This has taken a turn for the worse. We'll still go see the therapist later this morning, but I—" She hesitated. "Get rid of the knives, Juliet."

I resisted glancing at the other knife as I nodded. She didn't need to know that their familiar weight was what kept me anchored.

"Where did you get them?"

I didn't answer.

"It doesn't matter," Mom said with another sigh. "I just want them gone. I won't tell the detectives, but you'd better get rid of them by the time they get here."

"Why not tell them?" Dad asked, coming back in.

"Because!" Mom snapped, sucking in a breath. "Because," she repeated in a gentler tone, showing a visible effort to pull herself together, "our family doesn't need this. We don't need the scrutiny, or the gossip. We'll be fine. Juliet is going to get better, and we'll be fine."

More hung in the air, unsaid. *We don't need anyone thinking our daughter is even crazier than she is.* My hands trembled.

"All right," Dad muttered. "Juliet, get rid of the knives. Mel, let's go back to bed and get some sleep." He yawned and rubbed his face.

And they were gone.

After their steps receded down the hallway, silence filled my room. But I could still hear Mom's voice in my head. *They think I'm out of my mind.* My eyes drilled a hole into the now-empty doorway. *I'm not crazy.* I took a deep, shuddering breath as I walked forward and closed the door.

Hide them. I picked up the other knife. Ignoring the pulsing throb of my wrist, I strode forward and halted in front of the floor vent. I pried it up and set them inside.

Sitting back on my heels, I laid the cover back down. With a grunt, I stood and turned off the lamp. The room fell into darkness once again, barely lit by the dim shaft of moonlight coming through the window. I could still see the faces at the edges of my consciousness. Adnan no longer smiled, but I wanted him to. With all my soul, I wanted to see his face. I wanted to feel his arms around me. *I want him here.*

Something wet slid down my cheeks. I reached a trembling hand up and touched my fingertips to my cheeks. The cooling warmth of tears left their soft touch on my skin. *I need to act normal. Then everything will be better.*

My hands clenched into fists as they hung at my sides. *This is my home.* My family and friends were different, but our lives had also changed the moment I went through the portal to Ryujin, and then again when I'd returned home.

It'll just take time.

Chapter Thirteen

Endless evergreens flashed by in a blurred green haze. A dull roaring filled my ears as the air whipped through the cracked window into the car. I could feel more than see the strands of my hair swirling above my head as I played with a grainy bit of leather coming away from the seat. The night had left its mark upon me. While it wasn't the first night I had had nightmares, there was something different this time. They'd left me with a sort of hollowness inside, a gray dreariness that I couldn't seem to shake. Winter had hold of me, both inside and out.

"Here." Mom handed me a bottle of water. "Take these."

I held out my hand and felt something small and light touch my skin. Three white pills. "Mom?"

"Take them!" she snapped. Her eyes flashed with anger. "They were prescribed to help you with your depression and all the other things going on."

"But Mom—"

"Juliet." Her voice was like ice. "I picked them up for you. If you had wanted to say something against this, then it should have been done before."

I inhaled. "I forgot. Do you even know what's in them? What the possible side effects are?"

"No, but it doesn't really matter. The doctor says they'll help you." She tucked her brown hair behind her ears and readjusted her hands on the steering wheel.

Everyone thought something was wrong with me. *Everyone except me.* I clenched my fingers over the pills, hiding them from sight. *Because I chose to play the amnesiac.*

"Juliet," Mom spoke, softer now. "Please just take them. We'll try whatever might help. Any risk is better than living this life."

Because you don't want a daughter who is mentally ill. The thought crept in before I could stop it. *It's not true.*

"Juliet."

I opened my fingers, revealing the plain white pills. They appeared so nondescript, yet fear tightened its hold in my stomach. "Mom, I don't need these."

"Yes, you do!" Her face reddened. "You do! Please, just take them. Trust me, trust your dad."

"I'll be better without them," I whispered, my hand shaking.

"No, you won't." Mom slammed on the brakes.

I almost dropped the pills as my body shot forward.

"Sorry," she muttered, waiting for the car in front of us to finish its turn. The vehicle rumbled on again, and the air began to hiss through the crack in the window. "I won't say it again, Juliet. Take them."

There was no pleading in Mom's voice. It was an order. A threat hid behind her voice.

I lifted the pills to my lips with trembling fingers. They went down so easy, and yet when I turned to face the window, I felt silent tears roll down my cheeks.

"Thank you. Don't forget what the doctors said."

I listened, my breathing even, but the tears didn't stop.

"You have severe depression, anxiety … the classification is PTSD. None of us knows why, because you can't remember what happened during the time you were missing."

Unless you don't know everything. I bit back a sob.

"Hopefully these medications will help. And the therapists will help you deal with the PTSD as well. We'll get through this, Juliet."

"You mean the drugs," I muttered, turning to look at her.

"Drugs, medications, whatever," Mom hissed, her eyes narrowed as she focused on the road. "Twice a day, morning and night. We'll make you better, hon."

Hon. A term of endearment. She was my mother. *I need to trust her.* Yet why did she seem like a viper, so soft on the outside, so gorgeous, and yet hiding something terrifying within?

Mom kept her eyes glued to the road. "I liked your therapist, and your neurologist seems nice."

"Hm-mm," I murmured, staring out the window.

"I know it's just been the initial appointments, but they are here to help you."

The car slowed as we entered our neighborhood. I leaned my head on the palm of my hand.

"Do you feel any different?" Mom asked, glancing over at me. "Feel any-thing?"

"No." *Was that even true?* I did feel off. But I couldn't tell whether that was the drugs already taking effect or if it was me struggling with everything that was happening. I tapped my fingers on the seat. Maybe the pills would help.

"What are the pills?" I asked, my fingers stilling.

"Don't worry about that."

"Mom, what are they?"

She shrugged her shoulders. "We can check the paperwork when we get home if you'd like. I don't remember off the top of my head."

"And you and Dad are fine with all of this?"

"Yes. We are doing what we know is best for you. Don't fuss. All will be made right in time." She pulled into the driveway and turned the engine off. "Why don't you go get some sleep? I have a feeling you'll need it." She took a bottle out of her purse and handed me another two pills. "Here, these will help with that. Doctor's orders. Don't worry, these are just some sleep meds to help you catch up on sleep, rather than taking Benadryl."

"Why not melatonin?"

"Because these are stronger and will help more in the short term."

I took them and swallowed them down with the barest feeling of hesitation this time. Mom followed me inside and took my coat.

"I'll hang this," she said, already turning to the closet. "Go rest."

I nodded. With stumbling footsteps, I walked down the hallway. It seemed to bend and curve. I yawned. Even my door felt harder to open. Inside, I swayed as I neared my bed. Each step brought me closer and yet farther all at the same time. I collapsed on top of my comforter and closed my eyes, the lids heavy. Black filled my vision, and my thoughts blurred out of existence.

"You're right, Mom." I leaned forward, sliding on the smooth leather. "I'm beginning to remember. Somehow, I'd imagined myself elsewhere for months. But I'm choosing to forget those waking dreams." I took her hand. "I will get better. I am getting better."

Mom's lips curved upward. A wave of happiness and relief washed over me. I relaxed back in my chair and looked out the car window. The sun shone, the skies a pale blue. Everything was going to be fine; I was going to be fine.

"Mom?" I asked. When no answer came, I glanced over to see her chair empty as if she'd never sat there. The driver's seat was empty. "Mom?"

A shadow fell across me, and I turned to see that the sun had disappeared and the sky had turned gray. The world had fallen silent; not even the tick of a clock or the hum of appliances stirred the quietness.

The ceiling glared down at me from above, its grains bumpy and uneven. My fingers moved, bunching around the quilt beneath my body. A low whirring sounded in the background from a rotating fan in the corner, its blades slow and methodical. I tried to move, but my body obeyed my commands in a sluggish and slow manner as euphoria filled my senses.

I'm in bed.

The mattress rustled as I rolled over, cradling my cheek on my arm. A soft sigh escaped my lips and, if possible, I sank farther into the soft feather bedding. *I didn't have any night terrors,* I thought. My body began to stiffen as I realized that wasn't right, but why wasn't it? I sat up, leaning against the headboard, and rested my laced hands across my drawn-up knees. The room was cold.

Something is wrong.

I wanted to scream at myself, but I didn't know why. Pressure built in my temples, and I put my hands to the sides of my head to ease the numbing pain.

"Everything is all right," I whispered in a sing-song voice. "It must have been in my mind. There isn't anything wrong." I took a shuddering breath and slid off the bed, my bare feet hitting the carpet with a soft thud. With muffled footsteps, I slipped down the hallway to my parents' room and peered through the cracked doorway. A sliver of moonlight made its way through the slit in the curtains and fell across their bed, revealing their two forms under a thin sheet. Dad's soft snores filtered through the air as his chest rose and fell. *This is normal.* They were where they were supposed to be at this time of night.

I moved down the stairs and into the kitchen. I flicked the switch, letting my eyes adjust as light filled the small space. I remembered nothing from while I slept. I jerked as the realization hit me. *But why would I expect the nightmares?* My lips pursed as I paused, not moving, trying to think.

"Juliet?" Mom stood in the entryway.

"Hey," I greeted, my voice croaking. *Mom's here. Something …*

"What are you doing?"

"I—I don't know." I stumbled to a stop, unsure of how to even express my confusion. *Something isn't right.*

"Come on, come lie down. It's early, but you haven't been sleeping well lately, so you should get some more rest."

My movements were like a robot's as I followed her, and my stomach growled. "But I'm hungry."

"I'll make a hearty breakfast," Mom said, her voice soothing. She helped me into bed and tucked the blankets around me. "You're not too warm?"

Too warm? I shook my head.

"Here," she said. "Take these. They'll help you feel better."

I sat up a little and took the pills. "What are they?" Somehow, they reminded me of something that … felt familiar. "I've taken these before."

"No, just something similar." Mom patted my leg. "Now go on. Here's some water. They'll help you."

I placed them on my tongue and drank a little water. They slid down my throat with ease.

"Now go to sleep," Mom crooned. "Good night, Juliet."

The light flickered off, and sleep began to claim me. *Good night, Mom.* But I didn't speak. My lips didn't want to voice the slow thoughts in my head.

"How is she doing?"

I heard the voice as though through a distant tunnel.

"Better," a soft voice answered. *Mom.*

"Good," a deeper voice replied in hushed tones. *Dad.*

"She'll sleep awhile."

The voices faded. My thoughts moved in slow, foggy circles. Mom's voice, Dad's voice, going 'round and 'round, a comforting, soothing lullaby that seeped through my thoughts.

I swallowed. My body felt heavy. I couldn't move. *I don't need to move.* Clinics, doctors, and therapists flitted in and out of my mind like the slow eddy of the tide. It became harder to think. *Everything is all right.* It was the last thought before sleep claimed me.

❧ ❧

I twirled my fork between my fingers, watching the silver tines slide into a blur. The food on my plate didn't look appetizing.

"Stop playing with your food and eat, Juliet," Mom ordered.

I stopped twirling the fork and scooped up some eggs. My nose wrinkled.

"How are you feeling this morning?"

I set the fork down and crossed my arms. "I don't know ... weird."

"Weird?" Mom asked. "Weird, how?"

I tapped my temple. "My mind—it's fuzzy, hazy almost. I must just be tired."

Mom set three white pills on the table next to my plate. I held them up to the light and regarded their familiar smooth shapes.

"Go ahead and take them," Mom urged. "Your doctors said we should start seeing results soon."

"Results?" I lifted them toward my lips. *Results, doctors—Adnan.* I gasped for air. "Mom, I don't feel right," I gasped out. Pain lanced through my left wrist, its tendrils shooting up my arm. I yelped and clutched it to my chest.

"Oh, I'm so sorry. I forgot to rewrap your wrist after you showered this morning. And now you've gone and made it worse. Sit still, Juliet."

I hurt my wrist. Back at the castle ... Tristan. Mom bent down to take my wrist in her soft hands. *I'm back home. It's only been a few days ...* I struggled to breathe.

"Mom," I began. "The pills—"

"Just take the medicine," Mom urged as she wrapped my wrist with a firm grip.

"No," I whispered, pulling away. "I can't. You're making me forget who I am."

"No, we're not." Mom finished wrapping my wrist, and the aching began to abate. "Just take them." She handed me a glass of water and nodded in encouragement.

"Mom, I can't." A weakness filled my mind and body. Every action I fought for. I licked my lips. The three harmless-looking pills lay there, waiting.

"Jeffery," Mom said, sighing in relief as Dad walked into the room. "I need your help. Juliet needs to take her medicine."

"Dad, no!" I pleaded as he neared.

"Sorry, Juliet, doctor's orders. Take them."

I shook my head.

"All right, then, I'm sorry, but this is the only choice." He laid a heavy hand on my shoulder. "Open." He held the pills in his other hand up to my lips.

Tears sprang to my eyes. "No."

Mom's hands shot forward. She gripped my jaw and pried it open. I winced.

"There now," she murmured. "These *will* help you, Juliet. We'll get our lives back the way they used to be."

She stuffed the pills between my lips. Dad tilted my head back, and Mom poured water down my throat. I spluttered and swallowed the pills.

"We want you better." She sat down and took my hand. "Now, why don't you go sit down on the couch? You should be taking it easy until you're off the meds, doctor's orders. No, I'll take you upstairs to your room. You'll be most comfortable there anyway." Standing, she led me out of the kitchen as though I were a small child again. Tears pricked my eyes as I followed her to my room. I had no energy left to fight. My limbs felt heavier as we drew closer to my room.

Inside, she gestured to my desk chair. "Sit there. I have a lot to do downstairs, so just rest and enjoy some peace and quiet."

I sat down and listened as her footsteps left the room and receded down the hallway. My thoughts grew muddled, distant—

This has happened before. Closing my eyes, I shook my head. *When? How?* It was right there, at the edge of my grasp, but I couldn't reach it. I opened my eyes and peered through the window down into the street, fighting the waves of exhaustion beginning to roll over me. A figure appeared, tall and walking with slow strides. A man's figure. He was familiar somehow. I found myself leaning forward as I peered through the window. *The Unknown.* The thought slid into my thoughts. I stiffened. *Adnan.* I knew that man. *He came back.* I stood, and my chair fell backward onto the floor. *Run.* But my feet wouldn't carry me fast enough. It was like wading through water.

"Juliet!" Mom yelled as I made my way past the kitchen. I ignored her and flung open the front door.

"Juliet!" she yelled again.

My heart pounded within my chest and adrenaline pumped through my veins, setting my blood on fire and driving back the fog filling my mind and body.

I froze on the sidewalk. There was no one there. Not a soul was in sight. My body felt pulled between a state of make-believe calmness and panic. Mom had followed me, her heavy breathing the only sound I heard other than the pounding of my heart.

"Juliet," she exclaimed, not bothering to hide her frustration. "Come home. What are you doing?" she hissed.

I gasped for air. *He's not here. But I'd seen him!* I stopped. Pain curled, aching and sordid fingers around my heart. Hope dwindled, replaced by bitter confusion and anger. *He's not here.*

"Juliet, come home."

"He's not here."

"Who?" Mom demanded, pulling me around to face her.

I didn't realize I'd spoken out loud.

"Juliet, come home. Your mind is not separating reality. You know this. Come on." She tugged me toward her, and I followed.

I'm not mad. I remember.

I ignored the pain from the gravel biting into the soles of my bare feet. But had I imagined him being here? Something was wrong with me. I didn't feel right. The fog grew denser. *Where is he?*

I lifted my hand to tuck my hair behind my ear and felt a twang of pain. My wrist. I'd hurt it escaping from Tristan. It was real. It had all been real. *But Adnan isn't here.* I didn't bother to hide the salty tears that sprang to my eyes. He left, and he wasn't coming back.

CHAPTER FOURTEEN

When the knock sounded on the door, I was sitting on the couch. Mom came out of the kitchen, drying her hands on a towel.

"Jeffery!" she called out as she went to the door and opened it. "Hello, detectives, come on in."

Stiffening, I sat up and swung my legs over the side of the couch. Dad came into the room at the same time as Mom closed the door. He greeted Anderson and Brockwell.

I licked my lips, another chill settling over me.

"Juliet Barrows, we have already spoken with your parents. While we cannot enforce house arrest, we do strongly encourage you to stay indoors unless you're supervised."

I stood, feeling lightheaded as I faced the four of them. *House arrest?* Since I'd returned, it'd felt almost like that, but using the term brought it all into reality in a harsh way.

"Juliet?" Mom asked, tucking her hand into Dad's.

"Why?" It was the only question I could think to ask right now. My thoughts were muddled.

"Given your amnesia," Anderson began, "there is concern about the months you were gone and whether you will remember or not." He rested his hands on his utility belt. "But given your activity recently, there is also some cause to believe you could be a danger to yourself." He glanced between my parents and me. "Especially given the medications you're on."

Amnesia. House arrest. Meds. I shook my head. *This is wrong.*

"You can't do this," I managed, taking a step forward. "You have no right, nor do you," I said, addressing my parents.

They exchanged a look.

"Juliet, can you come with me?" Mom asked.

My legs moved like a robot as I followed my mother down the hallway to my room. *What was that?*

Inside, Mom closed the door and turned to face me. "Give them to me."

"What?"

"Give them to me," she hissed, holding out her hands.

The knives.

My lips parted. "No."

"Now, Juliet."

"And if I don't?" I asked, feeling eerily calm even as I challenged the woman who had raised me, who had always been the one to whom I tended to defer.

"Do you really want to test me?" She waited, watching for my reaction. Her brown hair hung loose from the tie behind her neck.

I'm not the one who is insane.

I took a deep breath. "No."

"Fine," she snapped, her attention catching somewhere behind me, and I turned to look. Something hard landed on my cheek, the force of the blow sending my head to the side. I backed up, my eyes tearing up, my skin stinging. Mom stepped back, glancing between her hand and my face. She'd slapped me. "Now, Juliet." She held out the same hand again.

"Mom," I choked out, struggling to come to grips with the shock radiating in waves through my mind.

"How many more therapists do you want to see, Juliet?" she asked, her eyes flashing fire. "Who are they going to believe, you or me?"

My mother had never looked more terrifying.

I reached down and took my two knives, one from my waist and the other from my right boot. I handed them to her.

She gave one back to me. "Go to the bathroom. Take this with you." She nodded without taking her eyes off me. "Then we'll speak with the detectives."

I turned, feeling wooden. *This isn't right.*

A thud lanced through the air. A scream followed. I spun on my heels.

"Help!" Mom shouted. *Thud!* She drove one of my knives into the frame around the door. She backed away as footsteps pounded down the hallway. The door flew open, Dad and the two detectives pressing their way into the room.

"She attacked me!" she sobbed, tears sliding down her cheeks. "Jeffery, she *attacked* me!" Mom flew into Dad's arms.

The room suffocated me, and my chest hurt from an unseen pressure.

"Give us the knife, Juliet," one of the detectives said as he advanced a slow step.

I didn't move.

"Juliet." He gave me an encouraging nod. He reached out and took it from my limp grasp.

The world spun. Noises weren't filtering in the same way anymore. Mom spoke to the detective, gesturing to me, but I couldn't hear her.

"I didn't do this." It took me a moment to realize I had spoken. "I didn't do this!" I repeated, stronger this time.

A heavy hand descended on my shoulder. "Steady there."

Mom wrung her hands. "First it was the self-harm, and now this!"

"What self-harm?" the detective asked, frowning.

"Look at her wrist. It's still healing from when she broke it. She tried jumping off the roof," Mom explained. "And then her rib cage has a scar from when she cut herself."

"Why didn't we know about this?"

Mom cried harder, her arms going up to cradle her face.

Dad tightened his hold. "We were hoping the medications would help."

Mom lowered her arms to reveal wet cheeks and red eyes. "She needs help."

"No, I don't." I strained against the hold the large man had on me. "It's not me—it's them!" As soon as I finished speaking, I wished I hadn't.

The detective sighed and turned to my parents. "What would you like to do?"

Mom cried harder.

This is all an act, I realized. *They planned this. This is what they wanted all along. I'm to be a prisoner in my own home, under the control of my parents.* The ache that filled me then was nothing like I had experienced before. *They betrayed me.*

"We need to stay the course," Mom said around her tears. "We'll have to watch her carefully, and I need to alert her doctor as to what's happened."

No, no, no. The figures blurred before me. *This can't be happening.*

⁂

When I awoke, a clock ticked in the background. With every second, the sound mirrored my rapid pulse. I took in a ragged breath and sat up. Lifting my hand, I brushed back wet hair from my forehead. My eyes roved the dark room. *No clock.* The ticking faded. *It was just in my mind.* I picked up my phone and glanced at the screen. It was just after midnight.

Something felt wrong with my left hand. It was wrapped. *I injured it ... it had broken ...* My eyes narrowed. *Not that long ago.* I reached over to turn on the lamp. *Not a candle or a lantern.* My shoulders stiffened. *Why can't I remember?* I rubbed my eyes. *Amnesiac. Pills.* The thoughts swooped and soared through my mind in slow motion. *Therapists. Doctors. Appointments.*

With a little click, a gentle glow of light from my lamp filled the corner of the room, settling over me like a warm blanket. I glanced at the window. It was open—I felt the cool breeze rushing through—but I knew I was in a cage, one I had made with my own mind. My forehead creased. The things I saw in my mind haunted my thoughts and movements. The people in them felt familiar. It was like watching a movie with myself in it.

I barely kept myself in control, away from the wild panic and fear residing just under the surface. *It's too much.* Stillness filled the room around me, and it was too quiet—not enough distraction for my ramshackle mind. Flashes of recollections flooded me, terror that seemed so real, yet I told myself repeatedly they were just dreams. So many faces, but some of them—I knew their names, I could hear their voices in my ears, feel their touch ... Saya with her quiet care, Mari with her blue dress, Emi with her lack of childlike innocence, Tristan with his gleaming smile, and Adnan ... Adnan with his grizzled handsomeness and *love.*

I rubbed my fingers together and snapped them, the sharp click cracking through the room like a gunshot. They were just nightmares, nightmares of blood and bone, laughs and cries brought about by the sleeping pills. *The pills.*

I gasped as something sharp ricocheted in my temples. They were *making* me into an amnesiac. They were helping me to forget, not to remember. *But why?*

My clothes clung like a second skin from cold sweat, damp enough that they sent a chill through my body. There wasn't a sound to be heard in the rest of the house. I was almost afraid to move, afraid the slightest noise would send Mom in here like a hurricane. I knew something like this had happened before—her coming in, forcing more of the meds on me—but then I couldn't remember much more. She *said* I would remember, that they would help. *But they aren't helping. Or are they?*

Mom's voice slipped into my thoughts. She said something was wrong with my mind.

House arrest. The realization fell before my mind's eye and hovered there. My breathing quickened. The detectives, Mom's set up—it all came trickling back in. A pulsing ache grew behind my temples. They must have forced me to take more medications.

I stood up and made my way into the bathroom and turned the light on. The mirror reflected my figure. I grasped the side of the sink with my right hand. The porcelain was cold. I froze, still and silent, as I stared at a face not my own. My breath caught in my lungs. The woman before me stood still, her blue eyes wide and puffy, surrounded by dark circles. The face was thinner, narrower than I remembered.

A buzzing filled my ears. *I knew her.* My heart raced, and I struggled for air. *I know her.* Black clouded my vision. *It's me, and not me.*

I stepped back and teetered as my foot caught on something. Losing my balance, my arms flailed as I fell backward.

Everything went black.

⁓⁓⁂⁓⁓

Bright sunlight streamed into the bathroom. It glared against the backs of my eyelids. I groaned and shifted away from the cold tiles. Opening my eyes, I sat up and leaned against the wall. My head throbbed, my temples ached, and my wrist flared in pain. Cradling it to my chest, I took a deep breath. I'd fallen. How long had I been out? With shaky legs, I stood.

My bedroom door opened. I turned away from the mirror and its distorted view.

Mom approached the bathroom but stopped short when she saw me. "Are you all right?" Her forehead creased. "You look exhausted. The sleeping meds are supposed to help with that."

"Mom," I began, hearing the tremor in my own voice. "I'm forgetting things. I don't feel myself."

"What do you mean?" Confusion radiated from her narrowed eyes and pursed lips.

"The medications are supposed to help, aren't they?"

"Oh, Juliet, yes. They're supposed to help you heal and recover."

"But I'm forgetting more," I whispered.

"Oh, honey, it will all work out in the end. Just keep taking them." She shot me a small grin and left. As her footsteps faded, I frowned in concentration. No, there was something there. Closing my eyes, I remembered the events of the last few days. *Adnan. He left me. No, I forced him.*

My fingers lifted to touch my cheeks. They were wet.

Chapter Fifteen

I had finished eating. The remnants of mashed potatoes, roast chicken, and vegetables still lay on their respective plates. Dad burped and leaned back in his chair with a hand over his belly. "That was delicious, Mel." He grinned and took his glass.

Mom turned her attention to me. "Juliet?"

The three pills waited on the table next to my plate. I should've taken them with my food, but I'd hesitated. The glass of water Mom had refilled also lay there, untouched.

"Juliet? You should go ahead and take them."

I nodded, watching as Mom's attention returned to Dad, who spoke to her about his day. *They aren't helping me. This isn't working.* With slow movements, I tucked the pills into my napkin and folded it. It was like any other dirty napkin, needing to be thrown away after a meal. *Just pretend to take them.* I drank my water and stood up, my plate in my hands.

"Oh, I can take that, Juliet," Mom said, scooting her chair back.

"It's all right, I—"

Mom stood and took the plate out of my hands. "What's wrong?" she asked, her head slanting to the side. "You look a little weird."

"Nothing," I breathed. "Just feeling tired." I yawned even as I spoke. It wasn't a complete lie, but my shoulders fell. I was sick of all the lies.

"Go to bed. I'll take care of the dishes." She held my plate in her hands, my napkin sitting there with the pills hidden within. But I turned, feeling her eyes boring into my back as I left the kitchen. Flexing my injured wrist, I winced. It was so itchy.

I closed the door behind me. The room felt stuffy and warm, so I opened the window to let in the fresh, cold air. The stars were small and weak from all the city lights. Not like they had been in Ryujin. The brilliance of the night sky wasn't to be seen here. Here, all the streetlamps were on, windows shone light from within the houses, and even the porch lights were on. Here, the darkness was beaten back.

My hands trembled. Taking a shuddering breath, I unwrapped my wrist and rubbed it gently with my other hand. I fought the tears welling up in my eyes. Stepping forward, I drew the curtains closed but left the window open. *Come back, Adnan.* I sat on the edge of the bed. *Come back to me.* It had only been days since I'd seen him, and yet it felt like an eternity had passed. *How long has it been?* The pills were changing me. *Just pretend.* Why hadn't I pretended to take them before? Why did I just take them?

A yawn threatened to split my jaw wide open. I shifted in bed and heard something clink against the wall before landing on the floor. Reaching an arm down, I grunted as I stretched my fingers as far as they could go. Something hard and slim met my grip. Pulling it up, I turned on the light and looked at what I held: a picture of Eddie and me.

I traced the smooth glass. He hadn't been in the past eleven years of my life, but I had been in his. A small hook stuck out of the wall, where the picture had fallen. *I'm just pretending to be someone I'm not.*

"The pretender," I whispered. Tristan had been the pretender, but what was I doing even now? Had Natsumi's warning to me when I arrived in Umi no Machi meant something more? I shook my head. Natsumi had said all would be revealed in time, that I would have answers … but if that were true, where were they? *Maybe I won't find them here.*

I reached up and hung the picture back in its place. Maybe this wasn't where I belonged after all.

What if I was the pretender?

✺✺✺✺✺ ✺✺✺✺✺

It had now been more than twenty-four hours since my last dose. Dawn hadn't yet finished stretching her fingers over the land, chasing away the shadows of the night. The morning light was dim. On my nightstand lay three small pills. I sat up. At some point, Mom had come in and set them there.

Does she know? I swallowed. I picked them up. What if she'd figured it out? My hands trembled. This morning, I had woken up with more clarity than I had in days, but also more pain. My wrist ached. The drugs had been dulling every sense.

I pulled the covers up. My room was cold. Adnan had been on the fringes of my mind, haunting me as I slept, but he hadn't said anything. He didn't have to. I stood and walked into the bathroom. He'd tried to warn me. Turning on the light, I lifted the toilet seat lid and let the pills slip out of my fingers. They splashed into the water and sank. I flushed, watching as they swooshed out of sight.

"I can't stay here," I whispered. Flexing my wrist and fingers, I grimaced at the twinges of pain. It was healing, but not fast enough. I bit my lip as I rewrapped my wrist and dressed.

Stepping into the hallway, I froze as I saw Mom walking down toward me. "Morning! You seem so much more like yourself. No more strange sightings of people you think you know?"

Adnan.

"Your dad had to go into the office today, so it's just you and me. At one-thirty, we need to leave for your appointment, so be ready."

Which appointment? I realized she was waiting for a response. "Okay, which appointment?"

"This one is with the psychologist, and the next scheduled one is with the neurologist. Anyways, breakfast is in the kitchen if you're hungry." Her eyes were brown, unlike mine, but we shared the same shape, and I couldn't see any of the heartfelt love that used to fill them. They were empty husks, but they were still her eyes.

A pit formed in my stomach. "I'm not hungry, but thanks," I whispered, forcing myself to speak.

"Why don't you go outside and get some fresh air? Your doctor said you should be spending time out there every day. Also, I know you've been having a hard time with the drowsiness in the medicine, but that should begin to wear off as your body gets used to it ..." Mom frowned. "Then again, the doctor said we'll probably have to give you a stronger dose as your body grows accustomed to it, so maybe not—"

"I know, Mom. I was there."

"Yes, yes, so you were." Mom grinned. "Oh, and if you do go into the backyard, you can rest easy. I had a camera installed."

My eyes shot to her face. "What?"

"A camera," she repeated. "I had a camera installed in the backyard. When you said you thought you saw someone that day in the parking lot, and then also that day when you went dashing down the street, I thought it best to have a camera installed. The doctor said it might make you feel safer, more secure."

"I don't need to be watched—"

"No, no, hon. It's not for you. It's just to make you feel safer. Besides, yesterday was a good day."

Because I had stopped taking the medication. Because I had kept to myself. Because I had acted exactly how my parents wanted me to. My heart quickened in my chest.

"Juliet!"

I jumped.

"I'm talking to you. You don't need to hunt for a job anymore. I have good news. It seems your old job might be available—"

"What do you mean?"

"Well, I gave them a call, and they said you should stop by sometime soon. I told them you would."

I resisted the urge to shake my head. *It's another step in normalizing our lives. I need to be working.* "Thanks, Mom." I forced myself to turn away when I felt I'd crack from the pressure. *She's not the same person.*

She walked into Dad's office and closed the door behind her. My thoughts were clearer now. I curled my hands into fists at my sides. Adnan was right. I had been the one to drive him away; I had chosen to sink down, to not be strong enough.

I sucked in a breath. *Maybe I do need fresh air.* I walked through the kitchen and out through the back door, which closed behind me with a soft *click*. I sat in one of the chairs on the covered porch. The air smelled musty, the cold breeze carrying with it the scents of rotting leaves, wet earth, and old rain. Searching,

I saw the camera, which was attached to the corner of the porch, but it was above my head. I relaxed as I realized I wasn't in view. It couldn't cover the whole backyard.

Cold air rushed into my lungs as I breathed. Eyes closed, I stiffened as the temperature seemed to warm, as a soft glow of heat surrounded my body like that of a warm, fuzzy blanket. The air stilled and all sounds ceased; the bird in the distance stopped chirping, a humming engine silenced, and all else faded until there was nothing.

And I knew I wasn't alone.

My eyes snapped open.

"Hello, Juliet."

Before she'd even stopped speaking, I froze. It couldn't be.

"Yes, it can. Or should I say, I can."

I turned my head. She stood just a couple yards away from me, under the roof, on the other side of the opposite chair. "Natsumi," I murmured. I glanced at the back door, but the curtain hung still. Mom wasn't watching. "Am I imagining you being here?"

Natsumi bowed her head in greeting. "Oh, you of little faith." She sighed. "You know, it wasn't so long ago that you embraced that you were in a different world. Reality defied logic. Why do you second-guess that I am truly here?" She spread her arms out. "Why do you suppose I'm here, Juliet?"

I stopped gaping. "I don't know. How did you find me?"

Natsumi sat in the chair across from me and crossed her legs. Her slim legs were encased in dark blue pants, and a long coat fell mid-thigh, a black that matched her laced boots. She always managed to fit in yet also stand out wherever she was.

"I was not looking for you," she remarked, leaning back, "but the fact that I am here means I am meant to be here, in this moment, with you."

A chill slithered so deep inside me that even the warmth in the air couldn't reach it. "What are you?"

She chuckled. "*Who* am I, do you mean?" One delicate eyebrow rose. "I am Natsumi."

"Is your name really Natsumi?"

She laughed again, a crystal-clear note that sounded like the tinkling of delicate bells. "It depends on who you ask."

I leaned forward, my hands clasped in my lap. "Like Adnan, then."

"Oh, I am not an assassin." She shook her head. "But I have been known by many names over the years."

My eyes widened. "What?"

"I have been alive longer than I look." Natsumi tapped her cheek. "Yes, I know I look, what, a few years older than you? But I have existed longer than you think."

I gritted my teeth. "I'm growing tired of the word games. First with Adnan, and now with you."

Natsumi's eyes grew more serious as they darkened in hue. "I saw a vision of you and knew I needed to be here. So here I am." She drummed her slender fingers on the chair's arm. "Now, why don't you ask me a question?"

The portal brought her. Why? I sucked in a breath. "Why me? Why has all this happened to me?"

Her eyes widened, and her shoulders rose in a delicate shrug. "Why does anything happen to anyone?"

I bit my lip. My frustration grew.

"Juliet," she continued, reaching up to smooth her already-perfect hair, "things are not perfect for anyone. Not a single person in any world has everything happen exactly the way they want. They might try to control everything, but the crux of the matter is, none of us can control everything."

"None of us?" I echoed, gripping my thigh with my right hand. "And you're part of that equation?"

"No mortal can know the future," she replied. "I—"

"But you're a seer," I challenged, my voice rising an octave.

"I am. Do I know all? No. Can I? No."

"You know more than you let on."

"Perhaps. But again, this is not about me; this is about you. You are responsible for yourself, no one else. You seem to be lost," she mused, regarding me. "Have you given up on hope?"

Don't answer. She always has questions and never answers.

"Juliet, nothing is ever lost when you have hope. Pursue hope until the end."

Hope. It was there, deep inside, but it was but an ember. Adnan had gone. I had stayed. What was next? My foot began to tap a nervous rhythm on the floor as I remembered the ache of Adnan's absence, the weariness of hiding, the pain of living the way I had been with my parents. "What am I supposed to do?"

Natsumi straightened in her chair. It creaked. "I think you know." She stood up. "Have faith, Juliet." She backed away from the porch, standing in the spring-green grass. "Besides, it's not my place to tell you what to do. You have to make that decision for yourself. Do you ever look in the mirror?"

But I do know. I blinked and knew, in that millisecond before I opened my eyes again, that she would be gone. The temperature had dropped, and light rain cascaded on the grass from the gray skies above. The world seemed bleak now, but deep down, I knew she had been right. I did know what to do, more so now than I had even the day before.

I stood and stepped down into the yard. It was time. The cold, wet rain splashing onto me ran down my neck in thousands of tiny rivulets until they were lost in the dampness of my jacket. I tilted my face up to meet the water's kiss.

"Juliet! What do you think you're doing? Do you want to catch a cold? Come in!"

Water dripped off my hair as I turned to face my mother. The spell had broken. "I'm going to my room," I murmured, making to pass her by.

"Don't forget about your appointment." Mom's lips curved up, but it wasn't warm.

Throat dry, I felt her eyes on me as I made my way out of the kitchen. In my room, I closed the door and turned around. My gaze flickered over the water on the windowsill. It had fallen through the open window, leaving the wood soaked and the carpet damp.

My fingers trembled as I closed it with a light click. The drops sliding down the glass reminded me of tears, and I could have almost sworn someone stared back at me, but when I looked again, there was nothing but the rain pattering against the panes and the gray, bleary sky looking down on the empty yard.

I sat down at my desk and opened my laptop. Opening my email, I gaped for a moment at the cursor flashing on the screen. *You know what to say.* The keys clicked as my fingers flew over them.

Eddie,

I wish I could have seen you … but I just wanted you to know that I love you. Please stay safe. Hurry home to Mom and Dad. They'll need you. It's been rough here, as I know you know. I've missed you for a very long time, longer than you know. I can still hear your laugh, and not a day goes by that I don't think of you.

I am, and will always be, your sister.

Love you.

Juliet

I sighed and closed my laptop. It was time. I drew myself up, my shoulders straightening as a plan worked its way through my mind. My home was with Adnan, and he had left. He had been right. Something was wrong here. It wasn't the same world I'd left, and I'd known that. I hadn't wanted to accept it.

"This isn't my home, not anymore." The moment I spoke, I felt like the world had been lifted off my shoulders. My soul felt lighter. I straightened and grabbed a bag out of the closet.

I had four hours until Mom expected to take me to my next appointment. But I wouldn't be here.

An extra change of clothing went into the bag. So did my toothbrush and a couple other small things. Flashlight, hiking med kit, matches, and pepper spray followed. Then my wallet. I picked it up and unzipped it. Thirty in cash and my credit cards … Not much, but it would have to work.

A door slammed somewhere in the distance. I heard the rumble of a car engine starting. A bird swooped across the window, followed by another, a swish of wings beating the air before they were gone. Silence fell.

I checked my phone. Three hours and forty-five minutes left. I surveyed the room. My eyes widened. *My sword and knives.* The police would have confiscated them. Disappointment threatened to knock me down. Was it wrong that I felt less whole now?

I threw on a long coat and left through the window, the same way I'd left when I'd visited Cam. Sure, Mom had her camera, but they would know I'd left anyway. Eventually.

My breathing was slow and deep as I paused a little way down the street and glanced back. They always say never to look back, but this had been a part of my life for so many years. I had grown up in that house, I had lost my brother while living in that house, and now I was leaving all of it behind. I had made so many mistakes, but I knew this wasn't one of them. *It's time to leave.* No longer did I belong in my world.

I brushed a loose tendril of hair behind one ear. Memories made me stronger, not weaker. My chin trembled. I spun on my heel and walked forward. I had pushed Adnan away before we even had time to really speak. He and Saya knew I had to learn from the past, not push it away. And yet that was what I'd kept doing and, if I stayed in my parents' house, in this world, what I would continue doing for the rest of my life. *The past shapes who I am, makes me who I am now.* It was time to face it.

No voice called me back. Not one inside nor out. I was free to leave.

Chapter Sixteen

As my house faded into the background, and I left the neighborhood for the busy street, I realized the portal was hours away ... by car. I had left the house without thinking it all through. *Think, Juliet.* I had been impetuous in the past, and now I was making the same mistake. A plan was needed.

I hiked the pack up a little farther on my back as the semblance of one began to form. It wasn't fully formed, but it was still a start. My steps quickened.

It was two miles to the bus stop, but the exercise was a balm to my head and body. Soft thuds from my boots on pavement accompanied me. There was hardly anyone about with the mist falling from the sky, and I was fine with that. Relaxing as the run was, I had every nerve on alert. My thoughts kept straying to home and whether Mom had found me missing yet or not. *How often does she check on me and I don't even realize it?* My teeth clenched.

Back in Ryujin, it had been so much quieter. As the drugs wore out of my system, it was becoming easier to remember, easier to see clearly what had happened there, but also here. *What a homecoming.*

I sighed and quickened my step. If I could just make it to the bus stop, I could catch the next bus to Tacoma and, from there, figure out the best way to get back to the Redwoods. To the portal. I saw the twisting roots in my mind—could feel the soft dirt floating about me as I fell—

It's part of a plan, at least. The knot in the pit of my stomach lessened as I focused on the next step. *What if my credit card doesn't work?* The pit grew. I pushed the doubt away. *Focus, Juliet.*

There, up ahead, the bus stop loomed into view. I checked the schedule on the wall. *No.* My jaw dropped. The next bus wasn't due to leave for forty minutes. *Shoot.* I had just missed the previous one. I chewed on my bottom lip. There wasn't anything to do but wait.

I leaned against the corner of the bus stop, watching as people came and went. Hands in my coat pockets, I kept an eye on the road, hoping I wouldn't see a familiar car drive down it.

Men and women continued to come and go, hardly giving me a second glance. Every now and then, I glanced at the desk assistant, who paid me no attention.

My stomach rumbled, but I ignored it. This wasn't the same world I had left. *Times have changed, somehow, since I left home.* My thoughts grew more hyperactive, and I struggled to slow them down, to be patient and wait. But my mind wouldn't stop. A groan escaped my lips. The more time that passed, the harder it became to remain calm, but I had to focus. Otherwise, I'd be lost to the chaos demanding to reign inside.

I checked the time on my phone. *The bus should be here any minute.* I rocked back and forth on my heels, loosening my stiffened muscles. Car lights loomed closer. *Wait.* I squinted as I leaned forward. It was the bus. My heartbeat slowed with relief as it pulled into its spot nearby. The doors opened with a squeaking hiss as a van pulled up to the curb. The passenger door opened. A short but broad man stepped out. *Detective Brockwell.* His eyes didn't leave mine as he approached.

"Juliet Barrows," he said, slowing. "You need to come with me."

I backed up a step. "Detective."

"Come with me, please. Your parents reported you missing, and—"

"Whoa," I retorted, backing up another step. "I'm an adult, not a minor."

"Yes, but—"

"And I've been gone just over an hour, so there was no need for them to have filed a missing persons report."

"Juliet Barrows," he bit out. "We know all the circumstances. No more. It's time for you to come with me."

The bus waited behind him. *It's so close.*

"Juliet?" He stepped back to his car and opened the back door. Even with the growing darkness, I could see the faint outline of another man on the passenger side.

I have no choice. I could feel each beat of my heart, and my head felt heavy. Each step felt like weights had been attached to my feet, holding me back. *I was so close.* I sat down in the car. The door slammed shut. Detective Anderson nodded to me from behind the wheel. *What now?* My thoughts raced, my body hot from the panic beginning to build from deep within. The air was stifling.

"It's too hot," I whispered, licking my dry lips. "How did you find me?"

"Huh?" Brockwell asked. "Oh." He turned a knob on the dash, and cool air began to blow through the vents. "We figured if you were trying to go anywhere, the bus stop would be a likely place to look for you."

The car pulled away from the bus stop, traveling back down the familiar street toward my neighborhood, my home ... my parents.

※※※※※ ※※※※※

A few minutes. That's all it took to enter my neighborhood. The two men hadn't spoken during that time, but nor had I. My body grew tenser as we neared my home. Something soft and white floated down past my window before another clung to it. My nose pressed against the cold glass of the window.

"Look at that," the driver said. "It's snowing."

I nodded even though I knew he couldn't see me. The flakes fell from the sky on the familiar streets of my neighborhood. And there was my parents' house, more charming against the backdrop of winter's touch.

With the car now at a standstill, the engine turning off with a soft purr, I slid open the door and stepped out. *I would rather face Creulon than this.* I froze. *No, Juliet. No, you wouldn't.* I took a step forward. *Or would I?* This world had changed. And now I knew that no one was good.

Another step.

I used to trust too easily ... and now, now I couldn't even trust my own loved ones. They had reported me missing less than an hour after I had left.

The door slammed open, spilling warm light out onto the front porch. Mom and Dad rushed toward me, their silhouettes dark against the bright backdrop. Mom grabbed me by the shoulders and almost shook me, Dad at her side.

"Where were you?" she cried out.

"We found her at the bus stop," Detective Anderson supplied as he stood nearby. He slid his hands into his jacket pockets. Brockwell remained in the car.

"What happened, Juliet?" Mom asked.

"Mel," Dad said, laying a large hand on her shoulder. "Let's just get her inside. It's cold, and we can talk just as well on the couch as we can out here." He began herding Mom to the door. "Come on, Juliet."

"I let the station know," Anderson called out, forcing Mom and Dad to stop. "We would like to question her ourselves."

I stood still, refusing to show the slightest hint of vulnerability.

Dad nodded once. "Very well." He continued walking, having to almost pull Mom up the steps into the house.

Anderson nodded and glanced once at me before beckoning to Brockwell. I watched as they approached, their dark clothing stark against the snowfall. The magical drift of snowflakes was numbed by what I knew I faced now. Gone was the freedom I had begun to feel in the past few hours, and gone was the security I felt at having a plan. Now I had no plan.

I took a deep breath and walked inside. My fingers slid over the worn wood as I closed the door after the detectives and spun in a slow circle to face the living room. Three men surveyed me. Mom had disappeared somewhere.

Dad shifted. "Your mom will join us soon."

"Why did you call the police?" I whispered.

Dad's face grayed. "Because you're not yourself, and it's not safe for you to be out on your own yet. Besides, we had a camera installed, and when Mom noticed you were missing, we saw you leave through the yard on the recording."

"I have some coffee ready," Mom said, her voice even. "Come into the kitchen."

That was quick.

I moved forward, following Dad. The detectives' footsteps were heavier and slower behind me.

Mom sat down and folded her arms. "Are you hungry?"

I shook my head. My stomach ached for food, but I had no appetite.

"All right, then." Mom gestured to the seat across the table from her. "Sit down."

Over my parents' heads, snow fell past the window, neither heavy nor light. *Snow. Maybe it was for the best.* The weather was cruel. A weariness settled over my shoulders. The detectives remained standing.

A flick of a match caught, and Mom lit a candle on the table. The soft, warm light shooed away the encroaching darkness, but it also brought flickering shadows. A lavender scent filled the air.

I glanced down at the mug of hot coffee in front of me. Steam rose in savage swirls. I took a sip and felt the heat travel down my esophagus and into the pit of my stomach like fire. The hot coffee fed my already taut nerves. My lips parted.

Mom's fingernails clicked against the table. Anderson's tall build was accentuated by the hefty figure of Brockwell as they regarded me. Something rasped. The chair slid back as Anderson pulled it out and sat down on the other side of the table from me.

"Juliet," Dad interrupted. He slid his glasses farther up his nose. "We're your parents. Please tell us what happened." His eyes blazed with impatience and a frightening fury. Anger built up within me in return. I bit my lip to keep it from spewing forth. *They don't understand. They never will.*

"Juliet," Mom began. "Tell us everything you remember." She didn't break her stare as she whispered aside to Dad, "Maybe the medicine is hampering things, Jeffery."

Anger flared brighter. My foot began to tap the floor. "I don't know." I couldn't think clearly enough; my brain had too much going on, too many thoughts oppressing my ability to discern what I should do. Evade. I had to evade them as long as I could.

Anderson spoke. "Juliet, we found you at the bus stop." He steepled his long fingers together in front of him and leaned his elbows on the table. "Why did you try to leave?"

"I just needed to get out for the day. There shouldn't be—"

"Why go out your window?" he pressed.

Surprise flickered over me.

"That makes you seem guilty, or like you had something to hide."

"No, I—"

"Did you give any thought to your parents?"

"Excuse me?" I managed. "No." I held up a hand. "Let me speak. I am an *adult*. Why do I feel like everyone keeps forgetting that? I have rights, *Detective* Anderson. Respectfully, I disagree with your line of questioning."

Anderson sat back and crossed his arms over his chest. "What will you do about it?"

"Excuse me?" *What is wrong with this man?*

"Juliet," Mom spoke. "These detectives are trying to help."

I stood up. "Trying to help how, exactly? I understand you two were the detectives on my case when I went missing?"

They both nodded.

"But I am no longer missing."

"No," Detective Anderson agreed, "but not only are we still hoping for some leads on your case, which is still open by the way, between the amnesia and the self-harm threats, plus"—he hesitated—"we *did* have to go looking for you today, considering you were missing."

"For an hour," I broke in.

"For an hour," he agreed. Regarding me with thoughtful eyes, he stood. "Very well. You and your parents talk, and we'll check in tomorrow."

My head tilted to the side. "No more questions?"

"Not for now. Mr. and Mrs. Barrows."

Chills ran over my body as I watched the two men file out of the kitchen. I hadn't missed the strange look that passed between them and my parents.

⚜

Back in my room, I lit a candle. The soft, warm glow beat back the darkness, causing the shadows to flicker. The candle was comforting. It helped estrange me a little from the world I was in. I looked at the window again. For days, I had tried to convince myself I belonged in the world I had come from, but I no longer believed that. My shoulders rose and fell. Gone was the war deep inside. I knew what I needed. And it wasn't here. For all of the dangers I had faced in Ryujin, I had found friendship, I had found loyalty, and I was my own person. I wanted to go back. Ryujin held so much of my life within its hands ... and pain—*so many have died*—but Adnan was there.

"I belong in Ryujin," I whispered.

"Why do you suppose you belong to a specific world?"

I whirled around, my pulse racing. "Natsumi!" I gaped at her. She stood before the window, which was now open. The rain fell louder now, but I hadn't noticed. The snow had gone. Too soon.

She took a step forward. "Hello, Juliet." Her simple dress fell to the floor in soft folds, an emerald sash gathered up below her bosom in a narrow strip. She perched herself on the edge of my armchair, her almond eyes darker in the glow from the candle.

I sank onto the edge of the bed. "When you were here last, you said no mortal on earth can know the future."

Natsumi nodded and folded her hands in her lap, her long fingers pale. Her melodic voice remained low and even, without a hint of emotion entering her tone. "Juliet, you left, or tried to, and now you are back." Her eyebrows rose a fraction.

"Is that a question?"

Natsumi shrugged. "It is merely a statement. Your mind and heart seem to be at war again."

"No, they aren't."

Natsumi raised her left brow in a gentle arch.

"I made the decision to go back. Adnan—" I hesitated.

"I know you want to be with him. You love him."

My hands clenched into fists. "I do," I murmured past the ache in my chest. "It's hard to leave here, my heart hurts, but I also know it's the right thing to do."

Natsumi sighed. "Oh, Juliet, if the years I've lived have taught me anything, it is that we can't always know what is right or wrong. Sometimes we make decisions for bad reasons, other times for good. I think it's more that we must try to use wisdom in all that we do, and whatever happens is how it was meant to be in the end."

I frowned. "Almost like fate."

"I suppose. I think there is something far more to it all, though," Natsumi said. "You are learning so much on this journey. You are learning life lessons that will be invaluable. You are learning *who* you are. Juliet Barrows, you are not the same girl who arrived in Umi no Machi that fateful fall day. You see that, don't you? When you look in the mirror?"

"And now I'm back home," I said.

"You have hope. You never lost it, even when you struggled to reach it, and when you needed help, it was there."

I sighed, not even trying to understand whether she was just trying to encourage me or if there was something else there. "Why are you here, Natsumi?"

"Do you want me to leave?"

I shrugged. "You're my tie to Umi no Machi. If anything, I think you always leave me with more questions than answers. But I do want to know why you've come to me twice."

"Do you think I come only to you?" Natsumi rose to stand before me. "I see others, too. There is more out there than you could possibly imagine, Juliet. The universe is larger than you grew up knowing. And now you know there is more than the earth you grew up on."

"Are there even more?" I asked. "More than just the other one and this one?"

Natsumi laughed, a clear, bell-like sound that spilled forth into the room, and I knew she wasn't going to answer the question.

"Can you take me back?" I asked.

Natsumi's face darkened. "No, I can't do that. Your future is in your own hands, relatively speaking. I try not to meddle as much as possible. It's too dangerous," she added under her breath.

I folded my arms. "Why is it dangerous?"

"Power is dangerous," Natsumi said. "No one has an easy path, Juliet. A piece of advice, though: Let the past in, but do not let it consume you. Don't hide behind a façade; otherwise, you will struggle all your life, and you will never begin to heal if you do not unlock the doors and let those you've lost in." She turned and strode toward the window. With a hand on the windowsill, she said, "We'll meet again. Just remember your time is not yet done; you have much to do still, I think. And Adnan has not given up on you."

What? But he left. My lips parted, but before I could speak, a soft bang echoed from somewhere else in the house. I glanced at my door before looking back at the window. Natsumi was gone. All that remained was the patter of rain and the slight wind that blew through the open window.

The open window.

I grabbed my coat and slid it on before the boots followed. My fingers shook as I rushed to tie the laces. I glanced in the mirror. Dark circles bagged my eyes. With a fingertip, I touched them, tracing the puffiness. I took a deep breath and glanced once more around my room. *How far will I make it?* But I shook away the doubt. *How long do I have?*

Folding my arms, I surveyed my window. It was possible to leave that way again. *A plan.* I strode over to my desk and opened the drawer. My wallet was gone. My heart fell. It shouldn't have come as a surprise. *Of course they would take that.* But it left me few options. No phone, no wallet—*I have to do this.*

I bit my lip and slid through the window. Within a few minutes, I found myself on the grass. The escape from my window to the covered porch roof to the ground was getting easier. My breathing was heavy as I strode down the sidewalk. My boots sent drops of water flying up from the cement with every quick step.

A silver van caught my eye, the glint of its headlights lying still, its windows tinted. *What if they're here to watch me?* I shook my head. *Don't be silly, Juliet.* I continued walking. As I turned the corner, leaving the van out of sight, the tension in my body began to ease.

I wasn't going to wait for the bus this time. I would hitchhike if I had to or walk. My breathing came quick and even as I kept up a fast pace. Something skittered out of my peripheral. I jumped. It was just a cat.

As minutes passed, I glanced behind me every now and then, but no one followed. One time I thought I saw the headlights of the van, but when I focused, there was nothing there. Adnan had taught me how to track, how to hunt—

My stomach rumbled. *Just get distance. Focus on not being seen.* Tracking and hunting weren't the only things Adnan had taught me. *Move quietly, but silently. Don't let anyone follow.*

The day was quiet, the roads silent. None of the cars that passed me slowed, but every now and then, I ducked into the shadows thrown by trees or into the awning of a store until a car passed. *Do what Adnan would do. Find the trail. Get across the bridge.*

It felt like forever before I reached the trail, but it only took four hours. I stood in the shadows thrown by a salon, watching the trailhead. There was no one in sight, just the sleepy neighborhood across the way, and on the other side of that, the busy I-5. I watched as the cars shot past, their lights on in the dreary gray afternoon. The constant thrum of car engines permeated the air.

I crossed the quiet street to the trailhead and peered down the path. It crossed over the water far below, in clear view of the cars passing to and from. I knew this stretch would be windy, confirmed by the warning signs nearby. Glancing up, I watched the dark gray cloud billow high above. *Will it rain again?*

I took a step, and then another. The metal railings were there to keep me from falling, yet I couldn't shake the pit deep in my stomach. I had fallen before. My wrist twinged. I hugged it closer to my body, forcing my legs to continue moving. Wind whistled by me. I tried not to think about losing my footing, of the long fall to the water—

Halfway there, I told myself. Lights from the houses and buildings built on the small hills to the right began to shine bright as the afternoon light dimmed. The wind was wilder here, more savage in its fury. It cut through my clothes, cold and damp, as it blew high above the water. My hair whipped against my face, stinging my skin. My journey had hardly begun, but the Redwoods were so far.

I've walked farther.

Deep breath in, out, in, out.

A van passed. It seemed to slow.

I froze mid-step.

When the vehicle left, I let out a breath I hadn't realized I'd been holding. It wasn't the same van. *There are plenty of vans.* It didn't have to be the same one.

I'd been hunted before, but this was different. I couldn't shake the fear beginning to grip me. They'd found me once, easily, and they could again. But I shoved my hands into my pockets to keep them warm, ignoring the way my wrist ached in the cold air. It was easier to find people here, but I could make it.

I glanced up. The other side of the Narrows was nearer now. The question slithered into my thoughts: *What if you can't cross it?* I shook my head. One step after the other, I continued forward. I never looked back. *Not this time.*

As I reached the end, my footsteps faltered. A figure stood off to the side, his back against the rail.

Keep going, Juliet.

I made to move past him. His head raised, and he put his phone back in the pocket of his coat. He straightened, taller than me, broad-shouldered, his hands at his sides. Then I was past. I don't think I breathed until I glanced back to see him still standing in the same spot. I breathed a sigh of relief. Before me began the long stretch of the outskirts of Tacoma.

Chapter Seventeen

A rock skidded across the concrete from where my foot had made contact. Somewhere nearby, a car's horn blared, angry and loud, before fading away. A trickle of sweat ran down my back as it began to rain. Soft and slow, the water ran down my cheeks and into my jacket. Pulling the hood up, I resisted the urge to look at the ground, and instead remained aware of my surroundings.

As I continued, my body weary, my pace slowed. The hours of walking, of trying to avoid main roads, of reminding myself to check for anyone following, took their toll. Energy sapped from my body, replenished by nothing, as I had nothing. No money, no food, no water, nothing but the clothes on my back. My stomach growled again, as it had so many times, too many to count.

Thoughts lay scattered through my mind, impaired by the drugs' dull slowing of them. But I knew this was different than when I'd been with Adnan and Saya. There, I hadn't been alone. They were my travel companions. There, I knew how to set traps, to catch food to eat … but here? I didn't know how to survive without money.

I looked around. There, forests stretched out before me with an abundance of wildlife. Here, Tacoma's city limits seemed to stretch on without end.

Light faded as the afternoon passed on by, and the earth continued its orbit around the sun. Still, I kept walking, heading south, heading for the Redwoods. My head spun from the lack of water.

A small gas station, nearly empty, stood just ahead. I watched a moment, waiting, but there was no sign of life other than a single car being filled with gas. *Water. Food.* Trying to look as if I belonged, I strode across the parking lot and entered the small building. The man behind the counter barely gave me a second look as he thumbed through a magazine.

In the back, I found a water dispenser next to the bathrooms. I gulped down the odd-tasting liquid as if it were fresh from glacial springs. After using the bathroom, I drank again until my thirst was quenched. My stomach growled at the sight of the racks of snacks. *No money.* I bit my lip. Glancing at the register, I watched the man continue to read.

A bag of jerky went into one pocket. Then a bag of trail mix. Next, a water bottle. With a deep breath, I walked past the register, assuming a posture of confidence. *Look like you belong.* Through the door, out into the fresh air, where I realized my neck was beginning to ache from being so tight. But it wasn't until I was across the street that I truly felt the tension ease away.

I stole. Shaking my head, I reminded myself it'd been necessary. Wishful thinking. The excuse did nothing to assuage the guilt.

I continued south.

So far, it was working. No one had come for me yet. And no matter how many times I glanced over my shoulder, there was never a sign of a silver van with tinted windows. With each mile that passed, the ember of hope within me burned brighter.

While the trees became a little more condensed in places, the people a little less, the roads a little quieter as night fell and I left the busyness of the city behind, I was never quite alone. Civilization wasn't gone, but I also stayed close to I-5. It was the easiest way to not get lost, to keep going in the right direction.

My legs ached. "Come on, Juliet," I whispered. "You can make it."

My water from the gas station was now gone, and my stomach had begun gurgling for want of food. Near an on-ramp, I found a copse of trees that hid me from prying eyes. I sat down, my back to a trunk, and watched the lights from cars stream past. My eyes drifted closed, heavy with weariness. It filled my limbs with a dull ache. There was nothing left in me to fight the exhaustion. I shivered from the cold. The night air rapidly cooled, and I had nothing to ward off the chill.

Breathing slowly, I observed the canopy above my head. A wind swept through the trees above my head. It had been a long few hours. And other than the sun having set, I had no way to keep track of time. It was a small comfort, for it reminded me of Ryujin. My eyes drifted closed.

This time, it will work.

I jerked awake, rubbing my eyes, and I peered around me. It was dark. Yet the lights from the freeway still flashed by, engines humming, and the faint thrum of nightlife provided a never-ending staccato effect on my ears. Emi and Kin had been with me in my sleep, walking in the familiar corridors of Creulon's fortress. But they were both dead, along with so many others. I wiped away a tear. *Tristan used everyone in his quest for power.* My breath caught. *But he lost; we won.*

"We won," I whispered, my voice hoarse. *Didn't we?* The question danced in my mind. With so many dead, so many lost, so much heartache and pain ... *had we truly won?*

A stick cracked nearby.

I stiffened, listening, watching, but saw nothing. Trees surrounded me, tall and dark. I shot to my feet, my head reeling as a wave of nausea swept over me. The air stifled me as it pressed in from all sides. There were too many places to hide, too many places eyes could be watching. My heart leapt into my throat. I swallowed, forcing myself to focus, to keep looking, to keep still. Too many ferns lay between the trees, breaking up the landscape, blurring it with the monotonous shades of green and dark brown.

Nothing moved. Not a flicker of movement, not a sound, nothing ...

I waited. And waited. Déjà vu cascaded over me.

This has happened before. I was the lookout while Adnan, Saya, and the townspeople from Umi no Machi rested. It had been a grueling night, but a daring rescue. The hooded stranger—Hirose—and Bagu had jumped me. *Kidnapped me.*

Running my fingers along my rib cage, I felt the imaginary stab of pain there again. Sweat pooled and ran in a single, thin rivulet down the side of my face. Salt coated my tongue as I licked my dry lips. Dark was the sky above, the stars masked behind clouds. There was no sign of someone nearby, yet I could've sworn I hadn't been alone.

Uneasiness stole over me, her fingers digging into every unsure part of my brain and locking in. Hands trembling, I glanced around again. Then a breeze blew through and, just as quickly as it had come, died. Goosebumps rolled over my skin. It started as a whisper, floating through the trees. *Run.* Over and over it came in the softest of voices, almost as though it wasn't there at all. A woman's voice, soft, ethereal.

It's not there, I screamed inside. *It's me! It's in my head. Get out! Get out!*

The voice didn't leave, urging me again: *Run!*

With a half sob, I ran. Leaves crunched under my boots as I left the small copse behind. A relentless pounding in my temples accompanied me. Sweat trickled down under my clothes. The cold air didn't feel so cold anymore.

My pace slowed. *No one was ever there.* Swallowing, I took a deep breath, my chest rising and falling in tandem. I glanced over my shoulder. *Am I going crazy?* My eyes blinked shut and opened.

Stone corridors surrounded me. I froze mid-step. The forest had disappeared. With trembling fingers, I reached out and touched the walls. The sides were smooth, ice-cold to the touch. I clutched my jacket tighter about me, shivering against the wind flowing through the narrow hallway. One step, and then another. My footsteps were a soft patter on the stones, the barest hint of an echo rebounding up and down.

A slow whirring filtered through from somewhere, and my head tilted to the side as I concentrated, listening. It was so familiar, yet hard to place.

There.

A woman's voice again—no, a girl's. High and soft.

Rounding a curve in the passageway, I froze. A girl knelt on the hard stones, facing a narrow window. The realization that it viewed brown, flat, barren lands hit me, yet I couldn't see out the window. *How do I know that?* My gaze lowered. The girl turned to face me.

I gasped.

Her eyes widened even as I remembered her face: *Emi.*

My lips opened and closed, my heart beating so fast it threatened to jump out of my chest.

"Juliet!" Emi pleaded, her cheeks wet with tears. "I need you! I'm scared. His voice is like honey, his face is alluring, but there is something terrible hidden inside. It's dark. It's so dark. You weren't here when I needed you. I can't get away!"

A sob threatened to spill out of me. My hands were wet. Another drop landed on them, warm and damp. Raising my hands, I touched my cheeks with cool fingertips. When had I begun crying? Emi didn't move. Her brown eyes were filled with grief, her dark hair hung over her shoulders ... My heart ached. It burned with a fire stoked by times past, a fire that now blew large enough to consume me from within.

"They're coming, Juliet," Emi whispered, hugging herself. "They're coming."

Boots ate up the ground, pounding as they came fast and close. "Who is it?" I whispered, my hair flying as my head swung back and forth.

"You still don't know."

What don't I know? The question hung in my mind.

"You still don't know," she repeated. "There's one more secret, Juliet."

Sounds ceased. It was just me and her. *One more secret.* He had one more secret to tell. *What is it? What don't I know?*

But Emi bowed her head.

And she was gone. The corridor had disappeared. Footsteps approached and stopped. I didn't turn around, still frozen, trying to make sense of what had happened, when a voice came from behind.

"Juliet."

Chapter Eighteen

A hand accompanied the voice, clamping down on my shoulder. The air was suffocating as I turned in a slow circle. It was dark, but I could see the tall silhouette of the man who stood before me.

"Juliet."

How could he be here? The air felt tight and heavy. "Adnan?" I whispered.

"Hi." A cloud exposed a sliver of moonlight, which lit up Adnan's face for the merest second. The light disappeared, leaving his face in shadow again. But it was him.

I reached up and touched his face with the palm of my hand. "Are you real?"

He chuckled and took my right hand in his left. "Yes. Come on." He tugged on my hand, urging me to fall into step next to him.

"Where are we going?"

He pointed just ahead of us, where trees bordered the road, stretching back in a blanket of darkness. "There. It'll keep us out of sight for now."

I shook my head as we entered the trees. My voice rose an octave. "How did you find me?"

"Natsumi."

"What?" I choked out.

Adnan's long strides forced me to quicken my pace. "We're almost there."

I reminded myself to be patient. He'd answer me later. "Is that—?" I hesitated. A light had appeared in the near distance, a faint glow that beckoned with a warmth I longed for. He led me into a small clearing, obscured from anyone on the road. It was surrounded by tall evergreens, and in the middle lay a small fire. I knelt before it, reaching out with cold hands, and sighed. The heat encompassed me with a soothing warmth. My body shuddered with delight. Something soft and warm draped over my shoulders.

I clutched it closer. "A blanket?" A grin split my lips wide open.

Adnan handed me a water bottle.

I laughed and opened it. The soothing liquid quenched my thirst. "Do you have food?" I asked, not wanting to get my hopes up. A growl emanated from my stomach.

Adnan handed me a couple bags of jerky.

I almost tore the first bag in my haste to shove some of the jerky it contained into my mouth. With a gleeful sigh, I forced myself to chew slower. "Where did you get all of this?"

He shrugged and sat next to me. "Let's just say I needed it more than they did."

"Of course." My shoulder grazed his own as I shifted into a more comfortable position. "I stole too," I admitted.

"Did you now?" His teasing tone was unmistakable.

"Oh, be quiet."

"What was that now?"

I butted him with my shoulder. Silence fell as we both stared into the fire. The food was simple, gas station steals, but it was filling. After a few more bites, I set it to the side and tilted my head to look at Adnan. His head swiveled, and I drank him in. His hair had grown even longer since the day I'd seen him at my parents', and his beard was a little fuller.

His eyebrow rose.

Running a hand through my hair, I searched for what to say. "I'm sorry I didn't come with you."

He shook his head and sighed. "You don't have to be sorry about that."

"Yes, I do. I didn't handle any of that particularly well. I didn't listen to you—or, at least, didn't want to." My tongue flicked over my chapped lips.

"I forgive you." His voice was halting, as though he were unused to saying that phrase. "And I'm sorry too."

"I forgive you." A heavy weight lifted off my chest. "You came back for me again," I whispered.

"Did you really think I'd leave?"

I shrugged. *Maybe? Yes ... ? I don't know.* My shoulders slumped. "Yes."

His jaw clenched.

Tears sprang to my eyes. *What if this is a dream? Like Emi ...*

His arm flexed where it lay across my shoulders. "Juliet, don't. I was wrong to try to strong-arm you. I was wrong to leave the way I did, though you didn't give me much of a choice." A hum of amusement escaped him, and he laid his free hand on my left leg. "You were being stubborn, closed-off, and irritating, but also loyal to your family—"

"Or at least the idea of what I thought it should be," I muttered. "No matter how hard I try, I can't make things happen just because I want them to."

Adnan's arm withdrew from around my shoulders as he leaned forward to add more wood. His silhouette was lean, his form strong. Peace filled me. His presence was familiar, comforting. He turned, catching me watching him. A warmth spread through my chest, weaving through my entire body until I felt I'd never be cold again. His lips parted. My body leaned forward. His lips pursed, and the moment passed. Emotion swirled across his face, in the slight cross of his brows as they drew downward, and in the way a muscle in his neck pulsed.

"You should get some sleep," he murmured.

My face creaked with a wide yawn. Sleep had never sounded so good.

He drew back. "We can talk more in the morning," he said, as though reading my mind. "Sleep."

⚥

Sunlight dappled the leaves above my head. The stillness of the foliage and the surreal peacefulness surrounded me. My mind woke slowly, quietly and relaxing, as the sleepy haze began to lift its fingers from me. The light was bright, piercing, and though I couldn't see the sun, I knew that it was well after dawn. *No nightmares.* For the first time in a long while, none had disturbed my sleep. *Why now?* The drugs were still there, but not dampening my system like they had before.

Warmth surrounded me. I didn't want to move, not ever. A drowsiness had claimed my body, not unwelcome in the least. A beat of a heart, steady, strong, relieving, somehow ...

With the slightest movement, I tilted my head. It lay over Adnan's heart, his arms wrapped around me. I stopped moving. The rise and fall of his chest was even. *And soothing.* Heat blossomed in my cheeks. Taking a deep breath, I enjoyed the scent of rain and earth. He smelled the same—the smell of the outdoors, clean and fresh, though a bit musty.

Don't wake up, I wished. My breathing slowed as I relaxed in his arms. He shifted below me, and his breathing changed. Tilting my head, I saw him looking down at me from under long, dark eyelashes.

"You were shivering," he explained.

I nodded, unsure of what else to say or do.

He moved, enough that I sat up and pretended to fix my messy hair. "I'll just stoke the fire," he muttered, eyeing me.

My head bobbed again, but I saw his eyes flick down to my cheeks. *Am I blushing?* I ran my fingers through my hair.

"It's cold this morning," I said in an over-bright tone.

He stirred the embers, slowly fanning them back into a small flame. "It is," he agreed. "There's some food left there if you're hungry."

I grabbed it but waited until he'd sat back before offering him some first. He chewed on a piece of jerky, watching the scant flames. His face, while content, was worn. Lines creased the corners of his eyes, as though he'd often worn frowns. His hair and beard were unkempt. He stiffened as he sensed my gaze on him, but I didn't look away when he faced me. His deep green eyes expressed the emotion trapped within. Grief and pain swirled within their depths, but also ... uncertainty?

His lips parted but then closed, as if he'd thought better about it. He took another piece of dried meat. "We'll stay and rest for a while, but then we'll need to come up with a plan and move on."

I nodded. "Last night, you said Natsumi told you where to find me?"

He pulled up one knee and laid his arm over it. "More or less. She visited me soon after I left, told me to wait here." He spread his arms out in a sweeping motion. "She said all would be answered in time, but that if I wanted to pursue ... my 'heart's desire,'" he said, "then I should wait here until the moon was but a sliver and night had fallen. So, I did. And last night, you came." He smiled, a genuine one that lit up his face like a sunbeam. "That woman is an enigma. She is the most infuriating woman I think I've ever met."

I chuckled. "And I'm not?"

Adnan ignored me. "She refused to answer my questions and then disappeared. It was as if she'd never been there."

I fingered the edge of my cloak. "She was like that back in Ryujin too. It was almost like she was noticed only when she wanted to be and otherwise forgotten. Even back in Umi no Machi, it had been like that. She would appear and disappear, yet she's always shown up when I've needed her, even when I didn't know I did." Taking a deep breath, I let a nervous laugh out. "I sound absurd, don't I?"

"No," he replied. "You don't." His attention wandered away from me, as though pulled elsewhere. But he shook himself and eyed me. "Will you leave with me this time?"

The fire crackled.

"Do you still want me to?" I asked, still as I waited for his answer.

"I stayed because of you, Juliet."

My breathing quickened.

"Now I'd like for you to follow me." His tone was serious, his voice clear. He scooted closer and took my hands in his large, calloused ones. They enveloped mine, a bit of bandage from my left wrist poking out under my sleeve. He had captivated me, and even with all his secrets, all the mystery, I knew I loved him. He had always come back, and I couldn't imagine my life without him in it. My lips parted. *Could I admit it now?* I wanted him to say them again first. *Is that wrong?*

Adnan pressed my hands. "Juliet?"

Say you love me. I licked my lips. "I'm coming with you. That's why I left." I hesitated again but forced myself to speak. "I want to be with you."

His faded white teeth flashed as he spoke. "Then come on. Let's get going."

"Go where?" I squeaked in surprise.

"Your portal. It's closer than where I came through."

I bit back the groan rising within me. *It's so far. We'll never make it.*

"Come on," Adnan reassured with a slight quirk in his lips. "One day at a time."

I gritted my teeth. "It's just—they found me so easily the first time."

He frowned and leaned back. "The first time?"

"Yes. This isn't my first time trying to escape since you left."

His eyes shone. "But now you have me."

I rolled my eyes. "Maybe you shouldn't be so cocky." Pulling my hands out of his, I fingered the hem of my shirt. "This is a different world from the other one."

"Yes," he replied, in as grave a tone as mine. "I know."

⁂

My heartbeat quickened, my eyes flicking here and there at every wavering shadow, at every rustle and crack echoing through the forest to our right. The chattering of birds in the distance was solitary and lonesome, as though calling out not to one another but to someone else. I moistened my lips with my tongue and slid my palms along my thighs.

My hands shook. I looked down as I flexed my wrist. It was healing nicely, the twinges barely noticeable now. Yet dirt coated the once-white bandage Mom had put on me.

Her face flickered into view in my mind. *"You're not well, Juliet. You need help—"* Her voice whispered through my thoughts, stealing through them with a brisk harshness. *"Don't go. If you do, you'll never come back. You'll never see us again."*

I imagined Dad laying a hand on her shoulder. *"Oh, let her go. Can't you see she doesn't care about anyone but herself? She never loved us ..."*

Loved us ... loved us ... loved us ... The lies blared inside my head, full of echoes.

"Juliet!"

At the brisk snap, air rushed into my lungs. I gasped and opened my eyes. Adnan stood in front of me, waiting. Tears slid down my cheeks.

"What's wrong?" he asked, his stance defensive as he peered around me.

"So much pain," I whispered, brushing away the tears. "I saw Mom and Dad in my mind."

His body relaxed. He held out his arms and I half-fell forward, melting into him. "That pain won't ever leave you, but you'll learn to live with it, and bear it with joy."

I sniffled and pulled away to look up at him. "Is that what you do?"

His eyes darkened. "It's what I've been told."

"Who told you?"

"Someone I knew a long time ago," he answered with a heavy sigh.

"Did it help?" I pressed, not wanting to move.

"I don't know." He pulled away and ran a hand through his shaggy hair. "Has something like that happened before? It's like you weren't here, Juliet."

Emi. The silence stretched out second by second. *The dreams, both awake and asleep.*

"What aren't you telling me?"

"It's happened before," I admitted, adjusting my stance. "I think it might be the drugs. Everything got worse then."

He handed me a bottle of water. "Need to flush them out. Drink."

I took it with raised brows. When I finished, I saw him watching me. "What is it?"

His lips pursed. "Nothing."

"No, what aren't you telling me?"

A harsh chuckle escaped his lips. "A lot."

My lips quirked. "Well, that's nothing new, but there is something."

Adnan raised his eyes to the cloudy sky above us and took a deep breath. "I didn't think I really had any reason to live, or that I would ever find—" He paused, and a dark look passed over his face as he battled something I couldn't see or understand.

My heart felt like it stopped a moment at the sight of the raw pain flaring there.

"That I would ever find joy," he continued, "or happiness. Until I met you. Even now, it doesn't seem feasible, or possible. I can hardly close my eyes at night for fear that when I wake up, it will have been my imagination and you but a figment that will fade away until I am left with but a memory." He closed his eyes.

I laid my right hand against his cheek, and he opened his eyes. "I'm real," I whispered. "Just as real as you. I can't say I won't ever leave, because I don't know the future. But Adnan, I know that I never *want* to leave." My vision blurred as I saw all the sorrow shining in his eyes that he'd been hiding from me. But even now, he could not be unguarded for long. His jaw clenched as he pulled himself together. "I love you too," I said, my soul eons lighter as soon as I replied. "I've loved you for so long, but I didn't realize it. I loved you when you came for me, but it was all so hard, and there was so much—too much for me to handle. My mind was foggy, and I felt torn between two worlds, between you and my family. I didn't turn you away because I didn't love you."

Adnan's hand slipped around my waist as he pulled me closer, forestalling any further words. "You don't know me still. You don't know what—"

"I love you," I said, shaking my head. "I know that more than I know anything else right now." My heart beat faster and slower as I watched his head lower. Time seemed to melt away as his lips met mine. Everything around me was forgotten in that moment.

He broke away, and I wasn't sure how long it had even lasted.

Not long enough. His lips were parted slightly, and his eyes shone. *More,* I wanted to ask.

His lips curved into a smile that reached his eyes. And my soul felt free. Sounds began to reverberate in my eardrums as I descended back into reality. *He kissed me.* I breathed in as he traced my cheek with an index finger.

"I'll always be there for you," he whispered, soft and low.

Chapter Nineteen

The birds sang, a brighter, sweeter note than the low croaking of frogs in the undergrowth, happy with the recent rain. A bunny bounded across the path before us, a path Adnan forged as he went. Above, the sun peeked through the gray expanse, pushing back the dreariness of the day. A spring still underlined my steps. I hadn't stopped thinking about that kiss. He had no idea how much that kiss meant to me. *How it felt.*

"It's been a long time," he said.

Quickening my stride to come closer, I wondered if the thoughts in my head had been spoken.

"You were humming," he explained, glancing at me over his shoulder.

My eyes widened. "I was?" *Humming?* A pinecone slid across the ground, dislodged from its place as Adnan passed.

"It's been a while since I heard you do that."

"Has it?"

He stopped and turned to face me. "It has." He handed me some water. "I like it when you hum. It eases some of what you carry away."

My throat tightened even as I drank. *But all those people and experiences remain, even if I don't want to remember them.* I handed the bottle back to him.

"What is it?" he asked, regarding me with a slight tilt to his head.

"Will I ever be able to face it all without feeling ... ?" I trailed off, unsure of how to explain what I meant.

His eyes darkened. "I can't answer that."

"Why?"

"Because there are things even I don't want to face from my own past." He made to turn around, but I reached out a hand to stop him.

"We'll find out together, then." I slid my hand into his, our fingers interlacing.

"I know you think you can face anything," Adnan said, his voice low. He rubbed small circles over the back of my hand with his thumb. "I just don't know if you can bear it. You already carry a burden; I don't want to add to it."

"But—"

He held up a finger. "I have so many sins in my past, Juliet."

My eyebrows rose and I made to pull my hand back, but he clutched it to him and didn't budge.

"But you need to remember that a lot of what happened to you was circumstantial and not of your own making." Emotion still rang in the huskiness of his voice. "Tristan—"

I flinched.

Adnan's face hardened. "Do you see him when you sleep?"

Trees surrounded us, the varying hues of brown blending in with one another as they stretched out around us. In the distance, the burr of car engines, but here, nothing.

"Juliet."

My shoulders rose and fell as I breathed in. "At times."

"Are they still as bad as they used to be?"

I shrugged. "Sometimes. I see all of their faces, not just his." My hand played with the hem of my shirt. "It's so vivid. And the guilt is eating me alive." My voice rose an octave. "I should never have been so blind! I was so *stupid*!" My lips trembled. "I let myself be manipulated by him. I *let* him. What was I thinking?" I tore my hand out of his grasp as I threw both up in the air. "What was I hoping for?"

Adnan shrugged and folded his arms across his chest. "We all make mistakes. We're all blind at times."

"I trusted blindly!" I retorted. "And I have to learn to live with the pain of trusting the wrong person."

Adnan shook his head. "Their deaths aren't your fault."

The seconds slid by as he waited for me to say something.

"I know," I whispered. "But part of me still feels responsible. The pain never goes away, and it's worse since—" I bit my lip before plunging on. "Since I stopped taking the drugs."

Adnan stepped closer. "Do you regret it?"

My lips downturned as I shook my head. "No. Nor do I regret leaving my family, and this world."

He stretched out his hand and I took it, enjoying the warm feel of his skin. "You're so much stronger and more resilient than you think you are, Juliet Barrows."

"Why, thank you."

He laughed. "I have to go relieve myself. I'll be back soon. Why don't you sit and rest for a bit?" He brushed my shoulder with his own before walking away. I sat down and watched the still, silent forest. A stick cracked, brush rustled, and a bunny popped into view. Its velvety black eyes peered at me. Its nose quivered, and it shuffled forward a couple of steps.

"Hi there," I muttered under my breath. "Did you come to keep me company?"

The bunny stood on its hind legs as a shadow fell over me from behind. I watched as its ears perked up and it bounded away into the underbrush.

"Adnan—" I began, glancing over my shoulder.

Natsumi inclined her head. "Hello again, Juliet."

I jumped to my feet and shivered. "You really need to stop creeping up on me." Taking a deep breath, I felt my racing heart slow.

"You don't have much time, Juliet."

I frowned. "Is that a threat?"

"No." Her eyes glinted. "It's a warning."

"Why don't I have much time? Time for what?"

"Time to get away. Time to leave this place behind, if that is what you want. Have you won the war you fight within your heart? Yes, but I still see turmoil inside you. So does Adnan. He worries for you, but you don't always see it."

"He hides many things from me."

Natsumi nodded. "From the world. It's his shield, and piece by piece, you are cracking what he has built around himself and maintained for years."

"Why would he worry so much for me?"

"Why wouldn't he? What do you think he is afraid of?"

I crossed my arms. "Is this why you came? To talk about Adnan?"

"Do you always have to question my motives?"

I glanced over my shoulder, but there was still no sign of Adnan.

"He'll be back soon," Natsumi murmured. "But there won't be much time for a decision. Do you hear that?"

"What decision?" I asked, but I heard nothing.

"You don't hear it, but they are coming."

"Who is coming?"

"You must face them." She ran a hand down her simple skirt. "You're strong and resilient, Juliet, far more than you realize."

Adnan spoke those words to me.

"Were you following us?"

Natsumi shook her head. "Believe, Juliet. Trust in what you know is right and true. But beware. They are coming." Something rustled in the forest, and she turned.

Flinging a hand out, I pleaded, "Wait, please, talk to Adnan."

"Why?"

I gritted my teeth. "Are you avoiding him?"

She snorted. "No. I have seen him twice before." She regarded me with her soulful brown eyes. "I know his life better than you do. I know his struggles, his desires, the war he wages with himself. He is strong too, but he needs you, Juliet. You need each other."

"What happened?" I asked, wondering where Adnan was. "How do you know all of that? Why will you not see him now?"

"You're always so full of questions." Her laugh tinkled like melodic bells, faint whispers upon the air—but I remembered as if it were yesterday, a dream which grew in clarity until it was as if I stood again on the path to Umi no Machi with Natsumi, the salt from the sea blowing in the wind, the fresh coolness surrounding us ...

"I want to understand," I said.

Natsumi lifted a hand and rested it against my cheek. Her skin was smooth and soft. "Be ready, Juliet. Be always on your guard."

Something rustled, drawing my attention. When I looked back, Natsumi had gone. I closed my eyes and took a deep breath, focusing on calming my pent-up nerves and suppressing the anticipation surging through my veins.

Minutes passed, and still my heart pounded, and my hands trembled at my sides. I stomped my foot and growled in frustration as I opened my eyes ... and stopped short. The bunny peered up at me and wrinkled its soft little nose.

"You're back again, are you?" I whispered. It rose on its hind legs as it watched me. For some reason, I hadn't realized until then how big it was.

A rock smashed into its skull, and I yelped as the bunny fell over, lifeless, not even twitching as it lay there, its eyes staring up into my own, so vulnerable, brown, so much like—

I stumbled back. Adnan strode up to the rabbit and picked it up.

"What did you do?" I demanded. "Why did you do that?"

He brushed it off and eyed me. "What's wrong?"

"What's wrong! What did that bunny do to you? Why did you have to kill it? It was just standing there, doing nothing!"

His hand fell by his side, his face troubled as he watched me.

"It was innocent! There was nothing done wrong, nothing it could do to defend, but you—it was over so fast, it happened too quickly, it—" My body shook as tears spilled forth and I sobbed, unable to say another word.

He dropped the rabbit and strode over to me. "Juliet," he almost yelled, taking hold of my shoulders. "Say what you're thinking."

"I can't!" I protested, unsure why I felt so angry inside.

"Yes, you can." His hands clasped my own and drew them away from where I clutched myself, rocking. "You have to say it."

I sank down, my heart feeling like it was being ripped into shreds. Adnan went down with me, his hands still gripping me. The torrent of anger that had taken over my heart and soul flared brighter.

"It's your fault!" I shouted. *It's not true. It's not him.* "No!" I yelled. *Stop, stop, those eyes ... it's all my fault.* "I can't!"

Adnan didn't say anything, but I could see his face redden through the sheen of tears blurring my vision.

Thoughts swirled around my mind in a whirlwind, snatching up snippets of memories and tossing them aside broken and dilapidated. *Emi. Those were her eyes.* The walls were breaking down, the barrier I'd erected began to crumble more now than ever. *She died, in front of me.*

"I can't do this!" I whispered, tasting the salt from my tears on my tongue. "I can't face this."

Adnan lifted a hand and brushed his thumb under my eye. "Yes, you can."

With a ragged breath, I opened my lips, terrified to speak, terrified to utter the thoughts raging through my mind. "It's not you, it's not the bunny, it's me!" I tried to explain between the half sobs. "Emi came into my mind. It was almost like I was watching her die all over again. I could see her eyes plain as day, see the pain flashing through them, the loss of hope dwindling when she knew I wasn't going to be able to save her, that no one was. Her eyes held my own even as the knife glinted in the sunlight, even as it slid from the left ear across her smooth throat, her face already pale, even paler as the life left her body. The light dimmed in her eyes—" Hesitating, I struggled to breathe, struggled to keep back the tears through the pain. I licked my lips and took a shaky breath. "I couldn't get to her. She died, and I did nothing. I couldn't do anything. She had tried to help me; she died for me! I can't live with that pain. It's too much. I see her, calling to me, running from me. Even in death, she is with me." I lifted my arm and wiped my wet cheeks. "She's dead."

Adnan watched me, his brow furrowed, his lips parted as though to speak, but he said nothing.

"I hide the pain away," I said into his shirt. "I try hiding the past so deep so that I don't have to feel, so that I don't have to acknowledge, but when I am least expecting it, when my guard is lowered, it all comes with all its pain and suffering." Before I knew it, I was standing. "I'm not crazy!" I said, flinging my hands in the air. "I'm weak! I'm weak because I don't want to feel the pain. I don't want to have to live with it, yet I keep living through it."

Adnan stood, but didn't approach me. "What do you feel?"

"I'm angry! I'm so angry!" I snapped, but no matter how much I tried, nothing more would come. Anything I could say was stuck inside me with his question rebounding over them.

"You're angry, yes, but you're also confused and scared."

"I'm not scared," I spluttered.

"You are. It hurts—*I know* how much it hurts—but you have to realize and try to understand the turmoil inside of you. You can't heal unless you do."

"And you do?" I regretted the question the instant it was out in the open air. Before my eyes, his shield built up and shattered all in one.

"Do I?" His voice was deathly quiet. He took a step back from me. "You need some time, and so do I."

"Maybe we do," I ground out, wincing at the hurt shining in his eyes.

He nodded toward the bunny. "If you don't want to eat it, fine—burn it, bury it, I don't care." He took a few strides, stopped, and glanced over his shoulder at me. "Emi doesn't deserve to be forgotten by you; nor does Mari, or any of the others."

"I'm not forgetting them. I'm burying the pain."

"And burying them along with it," Adnan bit out. "You're right. I don't talk much about my mistakes, some of which were made just within the past weeks. I haven't told you why I've shut myself away from the world, but know that if you go down the same path, it will change you, and you can pretend all you want that you are taking the right path, but it will be wrong. You can't bury the past, nor should you. Open yourself to it, and when you do, let me know how it feels." He turned as he finished. "Because since I met you, I've begun that path. It hurts, but it's needed." He turned on his heels and stalked off.

I stood there long after he'd gone and only the stillness surrounded me. Even the birds had stopped their chattering. A loneliness entered my soul, and my body ached with a dull thrum.

⁂

The light faded as the afternoon rolled by. My body hurt, my limbs stiff, from where I still sat on a cold fallen log. The rabbit still lay where Adnan had dropped it. Guilt filled me because of how I had acted. I wished Adnan would come back, but I also didn't want to be the one to find him. It would be easier if he initiated ... but I took a deep breath.

Footsteps shuffled behind me, heavy and slow, rustling leaves in their wake.

I sighed. "You were right," I said, without turning around, listening as they came closer. "I'm sorry for how I acted and for what I said."

"What is that supposed to mean?" a familiar, husky voice asked.

I jumped and whirled around.

Detective Brockwell laid a hand on the butt of a gun in a holster at his hip. "Well, Juliet Barrows, you were much harder to find this time." He grimaced. "You're definitely resilient, I'll give you that."

I took a step back. *Where is Anderson?*

"Now, will you come peaceably?"

I shook my head and backed up a step. "No."

"Fine." He cracked his neck. "We'll do it the hard way, then." He reached toward me, and I drew my hands behind my neck, angling my elbows toward him, and lunged, hitting him square in the chest. I brought my left hand down to rest on his shoulder as I pulled him toward me and kneed him hard in the groin. He grunted, his body going slack as I shifted to his left and wrapped my right leg around his right. With a quick twist of my body, I shoved, taking out his leg and driving him to the ground. He curled on his side, moaning.

"Get her, get her now!" he yelled.

I whirled around, my hair whipping through the air and stinging my cheek. A fist caught me, a glancing blow on my cheek, but I felt no pain. Anderson's arm wrapped around my shoulders and pulled me close to him, holding me in a vice. With a grunt, I brought my foot down hard on his and twisted, but he was quick and grabbed my arm, catching my sleeve as he yanked me back. This time, I felt pain burst across my jaw. Stars danced across my vision, and my hearing faded. Shaking my head, I tried to move my hand, but I couldn't. Something held my wrists together behind me.

Anderson shoved me onto the ground and panted. "Don't hurt her too bad, but do something to make sure she doesn't run again," he grunted to Brockwell, who was now standing.

"She's not going anywhere," Brockwell replied, tying my ankles together. "You good?"

"Fine," Anderson muttered with a groan.

"How did you find me?" I asked, my heart racing. *Stall them.* Where was Adnan?

"Oh, now you want to talk?" Anderson spat. He knelt in front of me. "Now, who did you think you were talking to when we arrived? Who was with you?"

I shook my head. "No one."

"Come on," he said. "It'll be easier to tell us. It'll save us all some time."

"Nah, I don't think I will, but thanks for asking."

He grabbed my shirt and pulled me up, his face inches away from my own. His breath blew against my skin as he hissed, "Don't try me. Did someone help you escape? Who was it?"

"No one. I was talking to myself."

He dropped me back onto the log. "She is crazy. It doesn't matter whether there was someone else or not. We're not getting paid to bring in anyone else."

"She did make it pretty far, for being so crazy," Brockwell pointed out. "And you said yourself she's a sprite. More like a little demoness, I'd say."

Anderson jabbed a finger at his partner. "Quiet. Go get the car, will you?"

"Let's just bring her along with us. It's not that far."

Where is Adnan? He thought I was angry before; I was angry now. My stomach turned as I was heaved upward. Pain throbbed in my jaw.

"Her skin looks a little reddish," Brockwell noted, peering at me from behind the flashlight. "You might have hit her too hard."

Anderson laughed. "We don't have to say it was us that did it. She could've done it to herself. She's crazy. They'll believe it." He shoved me, but as I fell, Brockwell swung me up and over his shoulder.

With every step, I expected Adnan to swoop in and rescue me, but he didn't appear. The seconds ticked by, turning into minutes, but still he didn't come. Something must have happened. He would've come if he could. He would've been here by now.

Silent tears dampened my cheeks. "I can't go back," I protested.

"What?" a voice asked over my head.

"I think she said she couldn't go back," Anderson answered.

"Too bad." Brockwell shifted me on his shoulder and continued walking. "Won't be long now before we can leave this godforsaken wilderness and head home."

I'm not going back. With a deep breath, I angled my head and bit the man hard on his fleshy back. A rancid smell of mildew filled my nostrils, and a sour old taste filled my mouth.

"Ow!" he yelled, dropping me off his shoulder. The air left my body when I hit the ground, and I lay there, looking up at the sky, unable to move or breathe. The earth reverberated, and a loud thud followed. With a quick intake, I gasped, my heart racing.

"What the—"

I turned my head, my jaw dropping as a black figure strode from the still form of one of the detectives to the other standing, fists raised. Within seconds, his body hit the ground, unmoving.

The figure turned to face me. "Miss me?" Adnan asked with a grin. He dropped down beside me and cut through the restraint binding my wrists. I sat up and flung my arms around him.

"Not so tight. You'll suffocate me," he said, but I could hear the teasing note in his tone. "You weren't afraid I wasn't going to be here, were you?"

"I wondered," I admitted, pulling back to look at him.

"I never really left." He ran a hand through his hair. "I heard you scream."

I pushed away from him and shoved my finger into his chest. "Then why didn't you do something sooner?"

He lifted his hand and pushed my finger away from him. "I was waiting for the right moment. When I arrived, they already had you bound."

I made to stand before realizing my ankles were still strung together, and so I settled for crossing my arms. "You let me be tied up and then slung across a back for several minutes?"

"You were already tied up when I arrived," he noted again.

"Argh! You're so infuriating."

His lips pursed, and he twirled the knife in his hands. "And they were right. You are a little demoness."

I glared at him.

He laughed, the chuckle starting deep within his belly.

"Thanks for rescuing me," I bit out.

"It's my pleasure, Miss Juliet Barrows. I couldn't let the damsel stay in distress."

I shoved at him but couldn't withhold a grin. "I'm so sorry for earlier, though. You were right. I was angry, and I never realized it. Emi and Mari should live on in my heart and in my thoughts. Even though I feel awful for what I said and how I acted toward you, I feel lighter somehow."

Adnan's hand found the side of my face, and he stroked my hair back. "We owe it to them. Don't ever forget what they meant to you and what they sacrificed. Healing takes time, but I'll be here with you."

Chapter Twenty

We huddled together for warmth, sitting under the branches of a tall evergreen. Raindrops pattered through the leaves in a soothing drum against the branches. Thousands upon thousands of tiny drops of water fell from the darkened sky, hitting the trees and ground. The birds were silent, all the little creatures hidden away in the downpour.

"They look like tears," I whispered. When silence met my words, I turned my head.

Adnan lifted his head from where it had leaned back against the trunk.

"Adnan?" I asked when he didn't respond.

His lips moved. "That isn't my only name."

The exhaustion tugging at me receded as I watched him.

"I didn't even mean to tell you that name. I had all but forgotten it. But that night, when you asked me what my name was, I remembered, and it slipped out. That was my birth name, given to me on your earth, this earth, but the couple who raised me in the other world—they named me Stian. They said I was a wanderer and that the name fit." He grimaced. "I've lived up to that name." Bitterness filled the air. His body tensed, and his eyes grew distant as he watched the rain. "I told the couple my birth name, but Adnan didn't fit in. I was different. I needed a name of their people."

"What country was that?" I whispered. "You said the northern raiders are from where you were raised, but ... ?" I trailed off, watching him intently.

"It's a group of smaller countries, in a way. Many tribes or small kingdoms, whatever you want to call it. We're at war with ourselves even though there aren't many differences." He took a deep breath and muttered, "Helps when you speak all of the languages."

I shook my head. "What do you mean?"

"Have you ever thought about how you understand everyone in Ryujin, and they you? Yet you're not from there?" His shoulder bumped against mine as he shifted his seat. "I can understand every language of every country I have been to in the other world. Best I can explain, it has something to do with how the portals work." He shrugged. "It's helped in my line of work," he added with a grunt. "It all sounds the same to me."

I frowned. "How does that make any sense?"

A chuckle burst forth from his lips. "How does any of it make sense?"

Shooting him a quick eye roll, I was about to speak when a drop of water landed on my nose. With a quick wrinkle, I continued, "So what happened next?"

"I was so young," Adnan explained. "There was nowhere else to go. I stayed with the couple who found me for a few years."

"Do you remember your real parents?" My voice sounded small amidst the patter of rain falling. Goosebumps spread over my skin. It was getting colder. "Do you miss them?" I added when he didn't answer.

He reached out a hand and laid it on my leg. "I think I miss the memory of them more than I miss *them*. I was raised in Helsingor, to the west of Illinach. It is a harsh, beautiful country." Light and dark intermingled in his face. "It's a hard country in a hard land. Life there is full of strife and difficulty, but it also has its moments of happiness. There are many who wish peace could be attained, and maybe one day it will." His fingers tapped my leg. "It's like I see my parents and my early childhood through another's eyes—someone else's life." His gaze wandered, and he nodded. "Looks like the rain is slowing."

He was right. It was more of a soft drizzle now.

"Do you want to go see your parents before—"

He shook his head. "No. It's been too long. Years have passed, Juliet. My heart isn't there. They wouldn't know me, nor I them." He grimaced. "All of that is in the past, and I want to leave it there."

"Are you sure?"

"Yes." His face hardened. "I'm sure." He pulled me a little closer as he spoke. "This world isn't my home anymore. I'm left with slivers of emotion, nothing more. You should remember the life before you came back. Leave the past couple of weeks behind when we go."

I flinched. "Maybe." The spatter of raindrops ceased. Taking a deep breath, I said, "Before we keep going, you should know that Natsumi visited me before you killed the rabbit."

"*What?*"

"I forgot to tell you," I admitted, glancing at him. "She said someone was coming, they were coming, and that time was running out. She said she could see the war I fight inside, and that I must face them—which I feel like had a lot behind it—and that the time was near, and I must believe and trust. It was cryptic, as always, but more so this time. I asked her to wait, to talk to you, and she said something about it not being your time."

Adnan stiffened, and I waited, holding back. "What were her exact words?"

"'It is not yet his time.'"

Adnan jerked, his face paling. "I've heard that before," he murmured, his voice faint. "A distant memory, one forgotten till now."

"She said she's seen you twice before, once a long time ago. That she told you it was not yet your time, and it still isn't. She wouldn't explain, and disappeared minutes before you came back. Do you know what she meant?"

Adnan froze. Turning, I saw Natsumi standing as though she had been there a while.

"Hello," she said, nodding to each of us. "I see I have perfect timing."

Adnan's arm fell away from me as he stood. My legs had stiffened, making it difficult for me to get up with any sort of grace.

She turned away. "Come with me."

"Where?" Adnan growled, edging slightly in front of me.

"Juliet needs to see something." Natsumi motioned to me to follow. "You may come as well, Adnan." She walked away without waiting for either of us to respond.

What must I see? I took a step forward, but Adnan's arm shot out, halting me.

The tendons in his arm flexed as his muscles grew rigid. "What are you doing?"

"Following her," I replied with a shrug.

"I see that," he gritted out. "But why?"

"Because while she is full of secrets and doesn't always make sense, she's also never given me a reason to mistrust her."

"And that has worked out so well for you in the past?"

My breath caught in my chest. *Tristan.* I ripped my arm out of his grip and followed Natsumi, ignoring the immediate apology shaping his expression after the accusation had left his lips.

"Juliet, wait!"

I listened as his heavier steps followed, but didn't look at him even as he kept pace at my side. Natsumi wove her way deeper into the forest and away from the main roads we had been shadowing.

"I'm sorry," he said under his breath.

I bit my lip. *I'm not ready to forgive you.* My chin trembled. *No, it's me I'm not willing to forgive.* I slipped my hand into his and squeezed. The words wouldn't come, but from the way he hovered next to me, keeping pace with my shorter legs, I knew he understood.

Natsumi stopped and stretched out her hands. "Each of you take a hand."

Dropping mine out of Adnan's, I didn't look at him as I took Natsumi's left hand in my right. Her skin was soft and smooth. A bird trilled nearby, reminding me of the day I had followed Natsumi to Umi no Machi. That day had been warm, sunny, the sky a brilliant blue, not like now. That time I felt I had no choice but to follow her. Now ... now I had a choice.

Adnan sighed, breaking me out of my thoughts. He took Natsumi's other hand. Together, we matched her as she took a step forward.

⁂

Sunlight streamed through a break in the clouds above. Natsumi let go of my hand and I started, feeling my eyebrows draw together in a frown. *Something is different.* The ground was dry. No rain had fallen.

"Where are we?" Adnan growled. "How did we get here?"

He's right. We were somewhere else. We were ... ? My jaw dropped. Across the street from the small park we stood in was one of the entrances to my neighborhood.

"Why are we back?" I pointed a finger at Natsumi as I faced her. My voice shook. "Why did you bring us here?"

Adnan stepped forward, a muscle pulsing in his jaw. "This is Juliet's home," he murmured.

"Yes," Natsumi said with a slow nod. "It is."

Flinging my hands into the air, I struggled to control the anger raging inside. Twice, I had tried to leave, and all she did was bring me back to the one place I didn't want to be. My cheeks burned. "Why. Are. We. Here. Natsumi."

"Because I think you should have some answers." She stepped onto the paved road. "Come."

I felt rooted to the ground.

"Juliet." Adnan took both of my hands in his. "We might as well see what she wants us to."

Shaking my head back and forth, I muttered, "No."

He traced my cheek with his finger before leaning down to kiss me on the forehead. "Natsumi said you'll have some answers, and while I still don't fully trust her, we *are* here, and if you do get answers, isn't it worth it?"

I shrugged and snorted. "Answers to what?"

Adnan dropped his hold on my hands and took a step back. "You won't know unless you come."

Infuriating man. He knew I struggled with curiosity, and here he was, playing me right into it.

I gritted my teeth. "Fine." I hurried to follow them, the knot in my stomach growing. With every step closer to my childhood home, nausea took over my body. My only comfort was knowing Adnan and Natsumi were with me. *Nothing can happen.* Music swelled over the air, classical, soft, and soon the low drone of happy voices.

A party. I stopped short, gasping. Cars lined the street, figures moved in the windows and out on my parents' lawn.

"Juliet," Adnan encouraged, his voice gentle. He took my hand, prompting me to keep going. As we approached, Natsumi leading the way, I watched as the lights strung through the yard and shining through the windows seemed to dance, tilting and swaying in time with my own messy thoughts.

Natsumi stopped. "Be careful," she warned. "Adnan, don't let them see Juliet."

Her warning didn't make sense in my mind.

"It's my birthday," I whispered, my body unresisting as Adnan led me closer. *February nineteenth.* I hadn't even realized. Around the side we went, to the gated part of the backyard. There, we stopped.

Adnan peered through the large knothole in the fence. "Is that—"

It took me a moment to register the way he'd been cut off. He looked at me, eyes wide. "Well, that's odd." He stepped aside, gesturing for me to see.

I stepped up and peeked through.

She stood there, a glass of wine in her hand, dressed in black jeans, a blue blouse—*my earrings.* She laughed, her blue eyes crinkling as she leaned down to whisper something to—I inhaled—Cam. And Cam, she grinned, her familiar face full of laughter and a secret joke lurking in her face. When was the last time I had seen her that happy?

The Redwoods, I answered.

But the other woman ... it was me.

"How is this possible?" I whispered.

"I don't know," Adnan said. Broken out of my reverie, I watched as he glanced back and forth between me and her. "She's—"

"More bubbly, more—"

"I was going to say she looks just like you," he replied, frowning.

"She is me." My hand waved through the air incredulously.

"You don't have an identical sister, right?"

"No, of course not! I would've told you." My fingers tapped against my thighs. "What should I do?"

Adnan crossed his arms over his chest and leaned against the fence. "Do you see your parents?"

I shook my head and peered up at the top of the fence. "Give me a boost."

"They'll see you."

"No, they won't. Please."

He clasped his hands together and waited as I laid my foot in his hands. With a quick jab upward, I looked over the top of the fence, just my eyes clearing it.

There.

They stood in the corner closest to me, engaged in conversation with Cam's parents. I almost stopped breathing. They were lovely.

"Let me down," I whispered, letting go of the fence. Adnan grabbed my waist and lowered me to the ground but kept his hands there as I clutched his arms. "It's them. But they seem different somehow."

Adnan cocked his head and brushed his hands over his pants. "How do you know?"

"I just do. I know."

"Then what about her? You have another woman who looks just like you, someone whom they are throwing a birthday party for."

"It doesn't matter. I don't have to talk to them. Why did Natsumi bring me here? To cause more confusion?" I chuckled, but it was dry and humorless.

Adnan sighed. "Remember, Natsumi said she brought you here to give you answers."

I peeped through the knothole again. *They're right there.* But as much as I wanted to understand, I knew I couldn't go through the gate.

Soft footsteps approached from behind.

"You see her." Natsumi's statement wasn't a question.

With my back against the wooden slats, I took several deep breaths of the fresh, evening air. "I'm not her anymore." I jabbed a finger over my shoulder. "She looks like how I used to. She *is* who I used to be." Shadows lengthened over the ground as the sun set. "Why bring me here?" I asked Natsumi.

"To give you answers."

"But you said you don't interfere!"

Adnan laid his hand on my shoulder.

Forcing myself to lower my voice, I continued, "You wouldn't help me leave before, so why bring us here now?"

"I had a vision." Natsumi shrugged her petite shoulders. "It was time."

My hand jabbed behind me toward the yard. "What is going on here?"

"This is your world," she replied, her voice soft and melodic.

"I know that," I huffed, crossing my arms.

"Your *real* world."

Feeling Adnan stiffen next to me, I didn't break away from Natsumi's stare. "What?"

She swept out a toned arm. "This is your world. I brought you both here so you could see and understand. The other world you've been in for the past two weeks—that is a mirror world to this one." She cocked her head as though listening to the voices filtering over the fence. "I haven't spent much time on that earth due to"—she hesitated—"its dark, oppressive nature." She glanced over my shoulder as laughter floated over the fence. "That girl is a mirror of yourself. She is from the other earth."

I shook my head, fighting against the waves of tension filling my shoulders.

"Essentially, you two swapped places."

"My parents, my real parents—they're still the same as I remember?" Without waiting for a response, I continued, "And you're saying that when Adnan and I went through the portal, we went to the mirror world? Why?"

"Now that, I don't know for certain," Natsumi said. "For some reason, you were both meant to be there, and maybe you will never know the true reason." Her shoulders rose in a slight shrug. "I have spent many, many years traveling and trying to understand how these worlds work, and while I know much more than I used to, I still don't fully understand them."

But those are my *parents.* My fingers clutched the hem of my shirt. *My real parents.*

"Then again," Natsumi continued, her nose wrinkling, "I do think there is someone who controls the portals—a higher power, you could say."

What? My arms folded across my chest, I leaned forward a little. Nausea crept in at the corners of my stomach.

"Juliet," Adnan said in a soothing voice. He slipped his arm around my shoulders.

"So when I went to Ryujin," I whispered, "she came here." After nothing but silence met me, I looked up at him. His eyebrows had drawn together, and a myriad of emotions crossed his face.

"Yes," Natsumi answered.

"And what happens if I stay?" I ignored the way Adnan stiffened against me, but he remained silent.

"Then she will go back to the mirror world."

That place. I leaned into Adnan. Closing my eyes against the thoughts warring internally, I took a deep breath. *They're happy.* My eyes opened. "They are a family," I whispered, pulling away from Adnan to go peek through the fence. That girl was me. *Is me.* My leaving would send her back to a world that was dark, a world that I couldn't wait to escape. *It would be like sending myself back there.*

I turned around to face Adnan and Natsumi. "I can't stay."

Adnan tilted his head as he examined my face. "Do you want to withhold the truth from them?"

Tears sprang to my eyes. "When does the truth hurt more than the lies? I don't think I can go back to the life I used to live." *And I don't think you would be happy,* I thought. *He would stay for me.* I took a deep breath, fighting against the whirling of turmoil threatening to uproot me from the ground. "I can't have both." Turning to Natsumi, I asked, "Is her personality like those on the other earth?"

Natsumi shook her head. "Yes and no. She is like you in every way, but she does have some personality differences."

"How does it affect my parents? My life? My friends?"

"I think that it is something that is changing even within her, being here, being surrounded by people who are lighter." Natsumi clasped her hands in front of her. "Just as you have changed by the people you have been with and the circumstances you have gone through."

Up above, the faint glittering of stars had begun to appear as the sky blackened. Hot, wet tears streamed down my cheeks, dripping off my chin without hindrance onto the ground. "I can't stay here," I repeated. "It would be like sending myself back to that world. I can't do that to her, to myself."

Adnan tugged on my hand, and I went into his arms, letting him hold me. Burying my face in his shirt, I let the tears fall. They were silent, a quiet grief filled with what had been and what could have been.

"My love just grew even more for you," he whispered into my hair.

His warmth pushed away the frosty grief pulling me apart. "We should go," I murmured.

"Go where?" he asked, still holding me, both of us ignoring Natsumi standing nearby.

"To Ryujin."

He pulled away so he could look at me. "Are you sure?"

"It hurts, and my heart aches, but deep down, I know that my life isn't here anymore. And now I have some peace. I know my parents love me, I know they're happy, and I know that to them, I'm not truly gone. They have her now, and she them." Smiling through the tears, I watched as his face softened, his eyes crinkling at the corners. He leaned down and brushed a lingering kiss across my lips.

He nodded to me and angled his body to face Natsumi. "You appeared to me when I was a child, in Helsingor."

Natsumi inclined her head.

"I didn't realize it until just now. I thought you were a figment of my imagination then."

Her tinkling, bell-like laugh filled the clearing. "You are not the first to have thought that, but I am no figment. I am as real as either of you."

My face scrunched. "How old are you?"

"Old," she replied with a laugh. "I have been blessed, or cursed, depending on how you look at it, with a very long life. I am aging, very slowly. Yet as far as I know, none have seen the length of life I have." Natsumi beckoned, her hair slipping down over one shoulder. "I see so much, but it's because of the power I could have that I try not to involve myself unless I see the need."

Adnan frowned. "How do you determine that?"

She laughed. "I'm not going to answer that. This is about Juliet, and you, and these worlds you all have been part of, brief as some have been." She glanced back and forth between us. "Juliet, you have some answers now, and some peace."

My head bobbed in agreement. *In less than an hour, I went from the home I thought was mine to the home that was mine.* I focused on the rich blue of Natsumi's dress. *And now I need to find my new home.*

"You know what to do, don't you?" she asked, drawing my attention back to her.

"I do."

"What?" Adnan stepped forward so he could better look at the two of us.

"Stian," Natsumi uttered, and Adnan froze. "I once told you your time had not yet come."

She told me that about him as well, I remembered.

Adnan's hands clenched at his sides. "I was searching for a way back home. I now think you meant that my time in Helsingor, on that earth, was not yet done. You knew then that I wasn't from that world." He ran a hand through his hair. "My time wasn't yet done."

Natsumi's face brightened. "Yes, but time is an interesting concept." She sighed. "It is—complicated."

"I was gone for roughly the same amount of time in Ryujin as I was missing in the mirror world."

"Yes," she agreed, her full lips pursing. "As I said, it *can* be complicated."

"Who are you?" Adnan interrupted, growing taller as his back and shoulders straightened.

"You are not the first to ask that of me. Juliet did not receive the answer she wished."

Here we go again.

Resisting a pent-up sigh, I listened.

"Do you know the future?" Adnan pressed, so focused on her that I wondered if he even remembered I stood next to him.

"Perhaps not in detail, but I know many things that will happen, some that could happen but do not, and others that are mere possibilities swaying back and forth."

Adnan took a step closer to her. "Are you a god?"

She laughed again. "Are there gods? Is there one? Are there many?"

I gritted my teeth just as Adnan's features darkened. "I don't know."

"Juliet?" she prompted.

I shrugged. "I don't know either."

"Well, then I won't give you the answer."

"Why not?"

"Because it is so easy to be given an answer without searching your heart and mind on your own first, and it is even easier to cast aside an answer when you have not given it much thought. Yes, Juliet, I know you have wondered, but you need to find out and understand what is true. It is not for me to say. Adnan, the same goes for you."

Putting my hands on my hips, I leaned forward. "I'm even more confused now."

"Then perhaps I am leaving you with more questions than answers."

"Which is what you want," I retorted.

She nodded. "To think, you must have questions. To contemplate, you must have things to think through. Now, do you want to know the truth of this world?"

Adnan and I exchanged glances, and we both inclined our heads.

"The girl from the mirror earth is living here now, in your place, taking your name and your life," she begins.

I swallowed and wished for water. My body stiffened as I imagined her living my life.

"But she does not know that she now lives in a different world," Natsumi continued. Her eyes narrowed as she swept them up and down my body. "Now, Juliet Barrows, you chose to leave, but are you content with that decision?"

I clutched Adnan's forearm with my hand. "They don't need me."

"But Juliet," Natsumi whispered, raising a delicate hand. "Do you need them?"

Do I? The past five months since I had gone through the portal into another world flashed before my eyes. I took a deep breath. "No, but it won't stop me from missing them."

"And mourning them," Natsumi said. "You will mourn them as though they have died, even though they have not. I see that you are decided. And though you still feel torn, deep down you know this is the right decision. Just remember that there are times you will ache and hurt so much that you will second-guess yourself."

"I do now," I muttered.

Natsumi leaned forward and tucked her index finger under my chin. "But you have the strength within you. And you will not be on your own. You have never been on your own." She turned to Adnan. "And you?"

The silence stretched out before Adnan shifted. "I knew long ago that my life was not in my old world, and it has not been for many long years. I'm at peace with that."

"Yes, but you fight a different war within you," Natsumi said. "One that you have not won, and one that you will never win. But you must keep on fighting. You have changed; your heart is lighter, and your burden will become easier with time. You are leaving behind one battle for another, as you have oft done in the past."

My eyes flickered between Adnan and Natsumi.

He squeezed my hand but did not lower his eyes from Natsumi's. "I am not deserving."

"Cryptic," Natsumi noted. "'Deserving' is a concept many use lightly, others too heavily. Many deserve more than they receive, and others less than they receive, whilst many more align their hearts and deeds with what they should get out of life, yet life does not work that way. You do not do a good deed so that you may reap the reward; you do it anyway. You do not expect the reward, for then you may be disappointed. If every person were to examine their lives and hearts in comparison to what they deserve, then no one would receive anything joyous or anything they wished, for every person shares a common ground." She inhaled. "So do not push away what you think you do not deserve. Never stop striving to be the person you wish to be, and never give up. The desires of your heart may lead you down a dark path, but follow the ones that will lead you out of the dark and into the light."

Adnan nodded, but still did not look my way. Natsumi's encouragements repeated themselves in my mind, and my soul felt heavier with the weight of what she'd said.

"Now," Natsumi said, taking a step back. "We have talked about much, and the hour grows late. Are you ready?"

"What?"

"Are you ready?" she repeated.

Adnan glanced at me and took my hand, turning me to face him. As I turned, I saw Natsumi walk away to the edge of the trees.

"Juliet ..." He hesitated. "I—you—" He let go of my hands and raked through his hair. "You're not wanting to leave solely because of me?"

I nodded. "I'm leaving because I want to."

His eyebrows formed a *V* shape as they came together.

I took his hand. "But I also would not be able to stay without you. Natsumi is right. My heart already begins to break inside me. The wall I erected around it is crumbling faster than I can stop it, and the pieces pierce my soul. The grief of saying goodbye to them is shattering me. They are adding to what I already feel, but I still know it is right. I do." At the look in his eyes, I pressed on. "I'm not just telling myself that. I know it, and I think you do too."

He nodded and, with a gentle motion, stroked my cheek with his thumb. "I love you, Juliet Barrows, and would not leave without you, or have you taken from me. Marry me?"

My jaw dropped, and my mind and body froze.

He stepped back and raked his hand through his hair. "Did I do it wrong, then?"

My lips moved without a sound. "No," I managed as I found my voice again.

His jaw tightened. "No, you won't marry me?"

"No, you did it fine."

His shoulders relaxed.

"I'll marry you," I said, feeling my face flush with excitement.

He took a step forward and I met him halfway, burying my face in the crook between his neck and shoulder. Joy blossomed in me until it threatened to spill forth at the seams. Then, at the same time, we both loosened our grip, and he stepped back, holding my hands between us.

"That wasn't quite planned ..."

"It didn't need to be," I replied. He let go of my hands and cupped my face with his warm hands as he dried my tears. My eyes closed. The knots within me had begun to loosen, and a tiny flame of hope and peace grew deep within, pushing back the overwhelming darkness. He kissed me, a quick burst across my lips, before he pulled back.

I opened my eyes. "This is not a conventional proposal."

A sheepish expression crossed his face. "I don't have experience or knowledge in conventional. I want this, and I won't have you slip away from me."

"Not so suave, but sweet."

His teeth glinted through a saucy smile.

"Though you'll have plenty of time to learn the finer nuances," I murmured with a wink.

A glint entered his eyes. "But you agreed to marry me even with my rough ways, and I think you found me suave even then."

Warmth filled my cheeks as I tried to keep the laughter locked down. Natsumi's soft voice humming reminded me that we weren't alone as she returned from the tree line.

"Are you two now ready?" she asked, her chocolate eyes filled with mirth.

"Yes," Adnan confirmed, smiling down at me. "We are."

She beckoned. "Come, then."

"What's going on?" I asked. "What do you mean?"

"It's time for you both to leave."

My lips parted.

"You will both arrive safe and sound. Come with me."

Chapter Twenty-One

Snowcapped mountains lay in a haphazard range in the backdrop of a sea-blue sky. Before them, and looming in front of us, towered a city. Sharp-angled roofs etched in red, gray walls, varying heights, all crowded together around a huge building.

"The palace," Adnan explained in an undertone.

I gaped, my eyes wide as I took it all in. *Cities like this exist?* It was so much bigger than I'd ever imagined.

"Why did she bring us here?" I asked.

Adnan shrugged. "My guess is that's where Hirose is now. It makes sense. He needs to get the country under control as fast as possible before chaos ensues. The best place to do that is in the capital, where he can not only control everything from, but where he'd also be in the center of attention."

"So that's where we're going," I assumed.

"Yes." Adnan clasped my hand in his. "That's where we're going. This is where Natsumi brought us, and I can't think of a reason other than it being for us to find Hirose." He walked forward, forcing me to follow.

And Saya.

Hope flared within me.

"The palace is the southernmost city in Ryujin." Adnan pointed at the mountains I'd noticed earlier. "Those won't be capped with snow for long. Legends have talked of them spouting fire and ash many, many years ago. Now, not even a bit of smoke rises."

The palace. My feet had a little spring in their step. A few weeks ago, I wouldn't have thought of seeing the palace, not while it was still connected to Creulon, but things had changed. Creulon was gone, and so was Tristan.

We hadn't far to go. I hadn't noticed before now the people streaming in and out of the double gates leading through the outer wall. They regarded me strangely, and I realized it was because I wore clothes from the mirror earth. Again, I didn't look like I belonged. *Just like in Umi no Machi.* The same looks, the same curiosity, the same inclinations of heads. *I really am back.* When I had first arrived in Ryujin, the attention had bothered me. It had been unnerving, but now I could brush it off. *Do they even know who I am? Or does the Otherworlder die with Tristan's downfall?* This time, Adnan walked close beside me. *I'm not alone.*

I let Adnan take the lead a little as we neared the gates. He didn't let me go, nor did he look back at me. The guards at the doors barely gave us a second glance. We were through. Noise blared from every direction. Stalls full of food, clothes, and other wares dotted the street to the right. I caught a glimpse of what looked like a large, square courtyard at the end of it. Flashes of color danced together as people wove their way around one another.

My heart beat faster with the thrill. Here, there were so many people. Some full of laughter, enjoying the sunny day and the busyness, and others frowning in concentration as they went about their business.

"Market day," Adnan explained, calling over his shoulder. He tugged on my hand, leading me up a street that was broad and wound straight through to what I assumed was the heart of the city. A man brushed past me in the crowd, his eyes dark with irritation as he spoke to someone else. I glanced back over my shoulder. It was English, and yet there was a heavy sort of accent behind the words. Adnan's comment about understanding languages flitted into my thoughts. He could understand everyone, and be understood, without trying. So could I. It was something about the portals. I frowned, concentrating. Pressure on my hand pulled me back to the present. Adnan's eyebrows rose.

"I'm okay," I called over the noise of the crowd. He nodded and continued forward, somehow seeming familiar with the path we trod. "Have you been here before?" I asked, having to raise my voice to be heard over the din.

"Yes."

There was nothing more in the way of explanation. *When had he been here? And why?* The questions swirled through my mind. His grip tightened. *I'm going to marry him.* It hit me for the first time since he'd proposed. So much had happened, I still hadn't had the chance to really let it sink in. Something had happened here. Adnan had history here. I filed his reaction away to question later.

Someone bumped into me, hard, and I bit back a yelp.

"Sorry." A grunt followed, the person already lost in the crowd.

It's all right, I thought back. Taking a few quick, mincing steps, I shadowed Adnan as close as I could. His strong, trim build wove its way through the crowded street with ease. It was like people saw him coming and moved away from him. I would too. He was different now, at least to me, but I still remembered the way I first saw him in Umi no Machi. Tall, dark, quiet—the Unknown.

My future husband.

I wasn't sure whether to smile or just melt into a puddle of confusion. *Juliet—wait.* The realization that I didn't even know his last name hit me. *What would I be called?* I shook my head, trying to focus on the present, to push it all to the side. *Focus, Juliet.*

"We're almost there," Adnan yelled over his shoulder. "Over here." He led me through a side street, which then opened into what was more of an alley, through a curtained door into a small square, and then out onto another broad street. This one was quieter, with fewer people. The surrounding houses and buildings seemed to dampen the sounds coming from the rest of the city.

"Just a bit farther," he said. "There."

Before us lay another double gate. Guards flanked it, this time a set of four, with more manning the towers to either side.

Adnan pointed. "The palace." He let go of my hand as we approached. I followed suit as he bowed.

"We'd like to speak with Hirose."

All four guards eyed us. Black-clad, they reminded me of the old king's private guard.

"*Emperor* Hirose, you mean," one said, stepping forward. His hand clutched at a sword hilt. "What do you want?"

"I'm the one known as Benkei, and this is the Otherworlder."

The man's eyes widened as he listened to Adnan speak. "*Benkei*?" he repeated with a note of panic. He snapped something under his breath to one of the other men, who slipped through the gates.

Names have power.

I peered around Adnan, watching as the man practically ran up a path and into the palace. Then came a waiting game. While still winter, the sun was warm, and it beat down on us without remorse. My mouth tightened with thirst. Each alley we passed reeked of human body odor and waste. My nose wrinkled. The warm sun made it worse.

To my relief, the man came scurrying back. He whispered in the ear of the guard nearby, who nodded and turned to us. "Please, I will escort you in. Emperor Hirose will see you." He inclined his head and gestured for us to follow him.

Here we go. A spring entered my step as I fell in next to Adnan. *The palace!* I could have squealed. Creulon's medieval fortress had been impressive, but it was nothing like this. I ached to wade through the market we'd left behind, to mingle with the people there and get a taste of what life was like here in the capital city.

"Come on," Adnan urged, waiting a couple of yards in front of me.

I hurried my step to catch back up again.

He grinned down at me. "We'll get a chance to go explore. Don't worry."

"Is it that obvious?" I whispered, my mind already being drawn back to the succulent smells from the market carts.

"Yes." He laid his arm over my shoulders.

"Have you explored there?" I chewed on my lower lip. The question was out.

Adnan's gaze grew a bit distant, and he removed his arm. I found myself missing the weight of it.

"Yes." His reply was short and clipped, a not-so-subtle hint that he wasn't ready to say anything more about it.

"In here," the guard said, ushering us through a side door into the palace. His step was quick, and I barely noticed the path we took, other than it felt like a maze. "Through there." He pointed at the doorway we stood in front of. "I must get back to my post."

We watched him go.

"Ready?" Adnan asked with an eyebrow raised. The snappish attitude he'd had a few minutes earlier seemed to have dissipated.

Had he already forgotten? *Because I haven't.* What had happened here, to him, would have to wait.

Seeing me nod, he opened the door and led the way through. Beyond lay a large, square room, full of wood paneling—

My eyes widened.

"Saya?" I exclaimed, freezing in shock.

"Juliet," she greeted, hurrying forward. It was her. Petite, curvy, and with long hair, black as midnight. We met in the middle of the room, both of us laughing as we hugged. "Juliet! I can't believe it's you!"

"Nor I you!" I squealed back. We stepped back and regarded one another. A light tread approached, and the slight rustle of leather.

Hirose inclined his head, first to me, and then to Adnan. A shiver ran over my skin. Memories collided: him, hooded and cloaked, my captor; then later, in the palace as head of Creulon's Black Guard. He stopped next to Adnan, and I was reminded yet again of how similar their heights and builds were. *No wonder he reminded me of Adnan.* He had played the part well. Swallowing, I watched him as he watched me. *He has his own aura of mystery.*

"Juliet Barrows," he said in his quiet, suave way. "And Benkei. What a surprise. It seems we have much to talk about."

"Yes," Saya added. "Hirose said that you had left this world. What happened?"

I swallowed and my lips parted, but Adnan spoke first.

"We'll answer your questions, but first, do you think we could eat?" He gave a sheepish grin. "We haven't eaten much the past couple of days."

"Of course!" Hirose beckoned to us to follow. "Come, sit. I'll send for some food. Unless ..." He glanced between the two of us. "Do you want to eat, bathe, and rest before we talk?"

A bath. I almost shivered at the thought. *Please say yes.*

Adnan peeked at me before turning back to Hirose. "Yes, and thank you."

Hirose nodded. "Good, because unless there is something pressing, there will be plenty of time for us to speak later." Though his tone was calm, I could see the curiosity radiating from his raised shoulders and tense form.

Saya turned to me and pressed her hands over my upper arms in a quick squeeze. "I can't wait to talk," she whispered. "But get some rest. You look like you need it."

You have no idea. My stomach gurgled. "Will do," I replied with a chuckle as I placed one hand over the offending anatomy.

Hirose waved, and an attendant appeared, as though out of thin air.

Where did he come from?

"He'll take you. When you're ready to speak with me, just let someone know."

"Emperor, huh?" Adnan said, one eyebrow raised.

Hirose's nose wrinkled. "Yes."

Adnan inclined his head. "Sounds like we have a fair bit of catching up to do."

⌇⌇⌇⌇ ⌇⌇⌇⌇

Steam rose up in thin curlicues from the surface. The last maid left after having poured the hot water into the basin built into the floor. Hearing the door slide shut behind her, I slipped out of my clothes, leaving them in a pile on the floor, and slid in. I shuddered, feeling the heat against my skin. It was almost too hot, but it felt wonderful. I sighed and lowered myself farther into the water. Leaning back, I let the back of my head rest against a rolled-up soft towel that had been placed along the rim. My eyes drifted shut. I inhaled and let the scent of roses waft over me. Rose ... and something else. I couldn't quite place the other scent, but it was heavenly.

The minutes ticked by, but there was no rush. The water was warm, the air smelled of flowers, and the room was peaceful. Silence reigned. I felt more at home than I had in a long time. *Not like on the mirror earth.* Keeping my eyes closed, I frowned. Were showers a thing of the past? With slow movements, I rolled my neck in circles. *I'm here. I'm back.* My muscles ached from tension, but that all began to fade away as I relaxed. Yet it took time. My mind and body wanted to hold it all in.

Let it out.

With another deep breath, I relaxed a little farther into the water, letting my head slip off the towel and into the water. My long hair swirled through the water as it dampened.

I'm back. In two weeks, I had traveled three times. First to the mirror world, then to my real world, and now to Ryujin. *Three times and three different worlds.* I shook my head. I never imagined I would ever visit another planet, much less versions of my own world. So much change for me.

My mind drifted to Adnan. *Where will we live?* We hadn't talked about what we'd do after we were married. We hadn't even talked about what we'd do leading up to being married. *When? How? Where?* The questions built up, and I could feel the tension beginning to rise.

So much had happened. In one morning, I had been on three different worlds. And now I was back in Ryujin. My pulse raced. Taking another series of deep, calming breaths, I focused on what was at hand. The hot water, the scent of rose, the bed awaiting me in the other room. *And food.* The maids had promised there would be food waiting when I was done.

My stomach growled, low and deep.

After washing, I took the robe that had been left for me and slid the door open into the other room. Savory scents assailed my nostrils. I almost melted. The food waited on a low table, a plump cushion next to it. Sinking down onto the pillow, I took in the generous helping of food before me. Fire crackled in the grate nearby, warming the small room. It was simple, but cozy. A teapot sat on the table as well, with two cups. With a shrug, I reached for the chopsticks. A knock rang on the wooden door from outside.

"Come in?" I called, wondering who it was.

The door slid open with a rasp. Adnan stepped through, wearing a new set of dark clothing.

I pulled my robe tighter around myself. "Adnan, what—"

"May I join you?"

The two teacups. Swallowing, I nodded and watched as he closed the door and sat down across from me.

"Your clothes fit well," I remarked, wincing at the professional tone.

He grinned.

And his beard ... it's trimmed short. My face burned. His hair had been cut back to just above his shoulders and was tied back in a half-do. I swallowed again. The room felt hot.

He gestured to my robe. "Did they not bring you clothes?"

"Um, not yet." I watched as he poured the tea into the small cups. Steam rose from the surfaces. "How did ... ?" Trailing off, I realized I was unsure of how to ask him about his clothes. The black material encased his muscular arms and chest in a perfect way.

"Hirose," Adnan explained, breaking through my thoughts.

I nodded and took an absent sip of tea. The tea burned my tongue, only slightly, but still enough to almost splutter.

"What's wrong?" Adnan peered at me over his bowl of rice. "You're acting a little strange."

I shook my head. *Nothing. Nothing at all. Oh, but you are so—* I blinked. *So distracting.* Taking a bite of meat, I chewed and swallowed.

Adnan set his bowl down and regarded me with his head cocked to the side. His jawline showed off even more now that his hair and beard were trimmed, and his eyes—they sparkled as he watched me.

"I've seen that look before." His lips curved into a smirk.

"What look?" I swallowed the bite of rice I'd been chewing.

He motioned to my face. "That look. I've seen it on plenty—" He hesitated. "On some faces before ..."

"Women?" I supplied, keeping my tone neutral.

Some sort of affirmation came from his throat.

"*Plenty* of women?" I questioned, not letting him back out.

He shook his head and muttered, "It doesn't matter. Have you tried these vegetables? The sauce is delicious."

Eyebrows raised, I grinned at him and reached for the dish.

"We are engaged."

At his words, I froze. He had laid down his bowl and chopsticks and watched me with a careful, but intense gaze.

"I know," I whispered when I realized he'd been waiting for an answer.

"You don't have to hide your attraction." His voice was slow and measured.

Air whooshed through my lips as I sucked in a breath. *Oh, you don't know how much I am.*

"I like seeing it," he added under his breath.

How do I answer? My mind raced. "I know." My voice grew stronger as I spoke, but I wondered if my face was as red as I imagined it to be. "You're just *really* handsome," I squeaked, unsure of where I should look.

"You're blushing." Adnan picked up his teacup, his eyes twinkling. He took a drink, set it back down, and reached a hand across the table. Laying my hand in his, I watched as his long fingers intertwined with mine. My heart skipped a beat.

"Do you realize how captivating you are?" he asked.

I inhaled, wondering if he could see into my soul.

"I'm sorry I teased you." His thumb rubbed slow circles over my skin.

I let out the breath I'd been holding. "You're fine. You should be able to tease me." Shooting a quick glare at him, I added, "Within reason."

He raised his glass in a sort of salute before focusing on the food in front of him.

My lips pursed as I lifted the teacup to them. *But he has so many secrets still.* Taking a sip of the green tea, I set it back down on the table. *What was his life like before he met me?* Other women ... I knew without a doubt there were some in his past. A part of me wanted to ask him about it, to know the extent of his past life. *He'll tell me with time.* His thumb continued to brush across my skin. *Or will he?* Tension built behind my ears and in my shoulders. Did I need to know before we married? Or was the past always supposed to stay in the past?

"Juliet?"

I looked up.

Adnan regarded me with thoughtful eyes. "What's on your mind?"

Shaking my head, I murmured, "Nothing." *A lie.* I winced. "No. It's not nothing."

He let go of my hand and slid around the table to sit next to me. "We're going to be married. I know I have struggled with opening up to you." He hesitated, each word conveying so much weight, and yet I could sense the internal struggle inside of him. "You deserve to know. You have the *right* to know, to ask me questions."

My tongue flicked out to moisten my lips. *Do I?* Part of me believed he was right, and the other part was afraid. *What if he thinks because I want to know, that I'm judging him? That I'll end our engagement?*

"What do you want to ask?" His question hung in the air, backed by his serious expression—the slight cross of his eyebrows, the set of his jaw, and the darkened, yet gentle, depths of his green eyes.

"Relationships." My answer hung in the air between us before I plunged on. "What relationships lie in your past?"

His Adam's apple bobbed as he swallowed. "Ah." He raked a hand through his hair—a habit I'd noticed whenever he was uncomfortable, or nervous. He didn't meet my eyes. "How much do you want to know?"

When I didn't answer, he sighed.

"I was thirteen when I left Helsingor, or at least, when I left my parents." His shoulders stiffened as he continued. "I was drafted. I saw much, much more than I should have seen. I focused more on training, on becoming the best out of those I was with. It was a couple years before I first had a relationship with a woman. One older than I." His head jerked as he watched me, as though wanting to catch my reactions. "There were more after her. I never married, never carried on a lasting relationship. They were flings."

When the silence fell, I searched for what to say. "How long ... ?" I trailed off with a shrug.

"About two years." He exhaled and laid an arm across his drawn-up knee. "That was about when I began to long for more. I was dissatisfied with my life, and that dissatisfaction grew. It was then that I began spending more time in Umi no Machi, being more selective with the jobs I took, and—" He paused and leaned forward. "Then I met you."

Goosebumps ran over my skin at the way he said those words.

"I was drawn to you, Juliet Barrows. You were like a fly buzzing around—annoying, but also—" He grinned, one of his rare smiles that lit up his face. "You became so much more to me. I've never felt about anyone the way I feel about you. I can't imagine my life without you in it."

My cheeks burned. Happiness took wing within me, and I felt as if I could soar.

"I love you. I'm sorry for my past, I'm sorry that though I didn't know you then, things I did hurt you now."

"I know," I breathed. "And I know there is awkwardness between us." My arms came up as I rested my elbows on the table. "It just—" I hesitated. "What now? It's just been one thing after another since we first met in Umi no Machi. Will it ever stop?" My voice cracked, and I realized that my eyes were welling with tears.

"I don't know." His reply was quiet, but there was a deep ache hidden under his words. "I wish I could give you answers. Time is what we need and have never been given. And you—I need *you*, Juliet. But there is much to process, for both of us."

My lips opened and closed. *So many questions.*

"Ask."

Ask. One simple request. "What if something else just comes along? What if we don't get the time we need?"

Adnan sighed. "Then it does, and we'll take it day by day, as we have done the past few months. But it's different now."

Where is this going? My heart thumped.

"We have each other in a way we didn't before. I've asked you to be my wife." He reached forward and traced my cheek. "I know that was sudden, and there is still much about me you do not know. Do I need to prove myself to you? We can wait longer—"

No! I shook my head. "You already have! Adnan, I *want* to marry you." Leaning my head into his hand, I continued, "I can't imagine my life without you in it either." If there was anything that I felt confident in, it was that.

Adnan leaned forward, his breath hot on my face. His lips met mine, full of promise and longing.

Chapter Twenty-Two

Ornate hangings covered the walls, decorated with strong brushstrokes filled with color. The dark wood panels on the walls starkly contrasted the bright décor, the hand-printed vases on shiny stands, and the lighter bamboo flooring. Wide-eyed, I took it all in as we passed, following the guard who had arrived to bring us to Hirose. *Emperor* Hirose.

"Beautiful, isn't it?" Adnan whispered, glancing down at me.

I nodded. There were no words for the old feelings surrounding me.

"Not as beautiful as you are, though."

My face warmed as I took in the way Adnan watched me with those green eyes, almost emerald now as they shone. "You've said that before." *Please don't let that be the only reason you want to marry me.* The thought burrowed its way deeper into my mind before I could halt it.

He frowned. "It is a compliment. And you are more attractive to me because of *who* you are, and how much I love you and grow to love you more and more."

A door opened with a hiss, and the guard gestured for us to go through. Again, our conversation would be cut off. *When will we be able to talk again?*

The guard closed it behind us.

Ahead, I saw Hirose sitting at the end of a long, rectangular room. *We're here.* Our shoes tapped against the floor as we walked forward, keeping pace with one another. Saya sat on a cushion nearby, her face bright with excitement. My eyebrows drew together. *And relief?*

"Good morning," Hirose greeted, inclining his head. Silence fell as we bowed in response. He gestured to a couple other cushions before the low table Saya sat at, before getting up himself and sitting with us. On the table's surface was tea and biscuits.

Saya poured each of us a steaming cup. "How do you feel?"

I took the cup she offered. "Much better."

"Good." Hirose's typical black clothing with light leather armor rustled as he shifted. "It is good to see you both, though my mind has been busy wondering why exactly you have returned. We have much to discuss this morning. Why don't we begin with you two?"

Looking to Adnan, I wondered who should start. He gestured for me to begin. Taking a deep breath, I filled them in on the events of the past couple of weeks. When I finished, I swallowed down the rest of my tea, now cold.

Hirose studied the table, his expression unreadable, but his fingers tapped the table's surface. "So there *are* mirror worlds."

I glanced at Adnan, who leaned forward. "What?"

"Mirror worlds," Hirose repeated. "Surely you have heard the legends. Well, not you, Juliet, but you, Benkei?"

Adnan shook his head.

"I have." Saya's voice was quiet. "Though I didn't think of it until just now."

"What legends?" I asked.

"Old, old myths, stories," Hirose explained, rubbing his jaw as he thought. "That mirror worlds do exist, copies of this one. But they can be dark, oppressive—"

"Like the mirror world I went to," I muttered. *A mirror earth. Like my real world, but not.* "There are really legends around that?"

"Yes," Hirose confirmed. "And now I believe that they stem from those who have visited those other worlds, and somehow stories became myths and legends, as they often do. I never believed it to be true, but it just goes to show how there can be truth in what we think of as tales." He stopped stroking his jaw, a light dawning in his eyes. "That world you went to, Juliet, is a mirror of your real world, but it is a dark version. You wanted to go home. You thought you returned to your roots, but it was false."

"And then Natsumi brought me—us—to my real world," I finished for him.

Saya clapped her hands together. "Now I wonder if there is a mirror world to this one."

Hirose shrugged. "Perhaps there is. Maybe we will never know."

"Even on my earth, we have legends of other worlds," I began, "built into the myths of various cultures. Now I wonder how much of those stem from reality as well."

"Fascinating," Saya breathed. "This is a lot to take in." She glanced between Adnan and me, her eyes wide.

My shoulders fell as I hunched over. "Yes."

"A lot," she repeated, and gave herself a small shake. "But what now?"

Hirose looked up then. "That's what I would like to know as well. If you both want to stay in Ryujin, you are more than welcome. You'll always have a place here—" He held up a finger as Adnan made to speak. "Or if you would rather live elsewhere in the kingdom, just say where, and I will provide you with a house and all you require."

My heart warmed within my chest.

Adnan bowed his head. "That is generous."

Hirose's lips quirked. "It is little thanks for what you both have done for Ryujin."

A door opened, and footsteps approached. The conversation stilled as we all watched a maid replace the pot with fresh, hot tea. I licked my lips in anticipation as Saya poured more into my cup. The steaming liquid was comforting and helped ward off the cold chill pervading the room.

"What say you both?" Hirose asked, laying a hand on the table.

"I—" Adnan glanced at me.

They don't know about us.

Leaning forward, I listened for what he would say.

"May we give you our answers later?"

"Of course. I suppose there wasn't much time for either of you to consider the future, was there?" Though Hirose phrased it like a question, neither of us answered.

I sat back a little, distracted, as I wondered why Adnan hadn't wanted to tell them of our engagement. Ignoring the frown Saya sent my way, I faced Hirose. "What has happened here?"

Hirose sighed. "That will be a shorter story than yours. We left the fortress the day after you and Adnan left us. As you can imagine, there has been much unrest. Rumors spread fast, and there is much confusion on the part of the people. And many don't know what to think about my taking the throne. Haniel—"

I perked up. *Haniel?* Was he here?

"—while in custody, has backed my rule. He holds some sway with those familiar with the rebellion. He has also signed a statement that we sent out all over the kingdom last week with the truth behind Tristan." Hirose inhaled and gathered his thoughts. "As you can see, we did away with the more Western idea of kingship and went back to our old tradition of having an emperor rule." He glanced at Saya, who nodded. "Saya has been invaluable. She agreed to be one of my advisors."

I grinned. *Of course she did.* "Wait," I interrupted as Hirose began to speak. "What is the difference between an emperor and a king?"

"Good question." Hirose's eyes gleamed. "As of now, not much. It is more historic for us, and a way for us to go back to our ways and cast off the rulers we have been under for so long."

Nodding, I sipped at my tea, cooler now.

Hirose picked up his own cup. "We have not yet had to deal much with other kingdoms, but I know that will come at any point."

"What has your focus been?" Adnan asked, so still he seemed like a statue as he listened to the emperor.

"To reinforce our borders, pacify the people, and be ready for what may come," Hirose answered in a grim tone.

I set my cup down, my head cocked to the side. "What do you mean?"

"It's not just the northern slavers," Hirose explained. "If any of the other countries that have an interest in us see weakness, then we are prone to an attack. We must be ready in case of an invasion." His fingers flexed. "I am afraid one will come."

What does he mean?

Before I could ask, he continued, "Every day brings hope, though. Day by day, we are growing stronger. Even here, things have begun to return to normal." He swept out a hand. "More than normal. I have not seen the people this happy and carefree in a long time. Rumors have spread already, both from my men and Tristan's, of the day he fell. While some are not helpful, most have been sowing good seeds."

"When we passed through yesterday," Adnan said, "I had not seen the market that loud and boisterous in a very long time. It is as though a cloud has lifted."

Hirose nodded. "I forgot you have been here before." His hands twitched as he faced me. "Juliet, I would like for you to see it while you are here."

"I'd like that," I replied. The echo of voices and laughter flitted through my mind as I remembered our brief walk through the city. Biting back a sigh, I returned my attention to the present.

"Adnan," Hirose said, a frown marring his face. "Would you be willing to advise me if needed while you remain here?"

Silence fell. If a pin dropped, it would have sounded loud in the tense quiet reigning through the room. *It's happening.* I wanted to protest, but couldn't seem to say anything.

"Yes."

It was a one-word reply, but I saw Hirose's shoulders relax even as tension radiated through mine.

"Good. There is much yet to be done."

It was then that I noticed the lines around his eyes. And not just him, but Saya too. She had a pale, drawn face, as though sleep was difficult. *Maybe it is more than just the busyness of running a new empire. Maybe their sleep is plagued just like mine.*

The room grew darker as though a cloud had passed beneath the sun. Just as fast, it grew brighter again, and light once more streamed through the windows.

Hirose rose, and we all followed suit. "I appreciate that. Now I must go and attend to a few things, but will you both join us for a meal later?"

Still wondering at the tense silence of a couple minutes before, I nodded, only half paying attention.

"Take the rest of the morning and afternoon to rest, explore, whatever you would like to do. I will send someone to you when it is time for dinner. I have also ordered more clothes for the both of you." He smirked. "Adnan, as good as my clothes look on you, I would like you to refrain from sharing my wardrobe."

Adnan smirked. "Why? Because they suit me better than you?"

Hirose rolled his eyes and drew himself up. "Because I am emperor and you are not." With that lighthearted jab, he rotated on his heels and left the room.

"I must go too," Saya said, placing her hand on my arm. "But I'll come find you as soon as I can." She gave me a quick hug and followed Hirose.

I turned to Adnan. "What was that about?"

He raised an eyebrow. "What do you mean?"

"That moment between you and Hirose, when he asked if you'd be willing to advise."

Adnan sighed. "Oh, that. I believe he was afraid I would say no, given our past."

My lips pursed as I frowned. "Your past?" I echoed. *As in him pretending to be you, or … ?*

"It's complicated," Adnan replied.

"So uncomplicate it," I suggested, crossing my arms.

He chuckled. "Part of it is how he pretended to be me, part of it is what he did to you, part of it is his past service to Creulon …" He hesitated. "As I said, it's complicated. While I suggested he sit on the throne, he didn't know—until now—whether I had his back, so to speak."

"Okay." Shaking my head, I threw my hands up in the air. "Maybe I just won't understand court politics."

Adnan stepped closer, surveying my face. "Is there anything else?"

Just say it.

"Yes, why did you say yes? Isn't this just one more thing now? Are we now being drawn into things without knowing if we want to be part of them?" The questions rushed out of me like a dam broken. *We chose to come back.*

His pallor deepened. "I'm sorry. I should have spoken to you first—"

"How could you?" I asked. "It's not like you told them we are engaged."

Adnan's arms crossed. "Is that what this is really about?"

I threw my hands up in the air. "I don't know."

"You really don't?"

I recoiled as though stung. "In the space of one day, we've traveled between three different worlds, we've become engaged, I've given up my parents for my mirror-self, and now we're here, and yet we haven't really talked about any of it." My foot tapped the ground. "You didn't tell Hirose and Saya about our engagement, which I don't understand why not, and now you've agreed to become Hirose's advisor without us even speaking about it?"

Adnan regarded me for several long moments. "It has been a lot," he admitted. "For you more so than for me, and for that I am sorry. I should've been more thoughtful, more caring about how you feel about all of this." He reached out and waited until I slipped my hand into his. "I didn't tell them because I realized I hadn't asked you if you wanted to let them know yet."

Oh. I could have smacked myself. *He was trying to be thoughtful.*

"And I am sorry that I agreed before talking to you. This is new for me, and I know—" He hesitated. "I know it is a weakness of mine. I am used to doing things my own way without caring about what others might think or have to say about it."

Realizing he was waiting for me to say something, I muttered, "I forgive you."

"I can tell Hirose—"

"No." I shook my head. "No, just leave it for now. I need to trust you too. We're a bit of a mess, aren't we?"

His eyes twinkled and his face brightened. "No more than many others." He led me toward the door. "How do *you* feel about Hirose?"

Peering up at him, I wondered what he meant by that. "As in when he and Bagu kidnapped me?"

Adnan grunted in affirmation.

"I try not to think about it," I confessed. "It's easier that way."

His grip on my hand tightened. "That's still not answering my question."

"Fine!" I stared at the floor as we continued walking. "All right, I suppose it's still hard when I look at him and remember, but otherwise, I'm fine, really. I think he's changed since then. He's a good man to sit on the throne ... I know he cares about the country and the people within. Perhaps more, now that he can do something about it." Taking a deep breath, I leaned into Adnan as we strode along. "Deep down, I wish he would have said something about taking me, though, even acknowledged it." I shook my head. "It's probably silly."

"I don't think so," Adnan murmured. "But let's not speak of it anymore unless you want to. Look." He led the way out of the palace into a large, terraced garden surrounded by stone walls. The sun beat down with a gentle warmth, and birds sang from their treetop perches.

Letting go of his hand, I spun in a circle and laughed. With my head tilted back, I took in the sky. It was a clear blue. When I looked back down, Adnan stood, silent and still, regarding me with an intensity. Raising my eyebrows, I tilted my head to the side.

"What?"

He grinned and shook his head. "Nothing."

I jabbed a finger at him as I stalked closer. "No, it's not nothing."

A quick laugh escaped his lips. "You're just rather enthralling."

"Oh."

"And you're so unaware of how much you are," he teased as I stopped in front of him.

"Maybe because it's just you," I retorted.

His expression grew more serious. "Want to go on a walk with me?"

"Is that a date?"

"A date?" he echoed. He slid his hands over his shirt, as though straightening some imaginary wrinkles. "What is that?"

"It doesn't matter," I replied, slipping my hand into his. Tilting my head back, I grinned up at him, freezing as I took in the intensity filling his eyes. He captivated me as he leaned forward and brushed his lips across my own. As he pulled back, I sucked in a breath, feeling lightheaded. *I could get used to that.* Though I tried not to, I couldn't hide the bright airiness filling me. I didn't have to, but I leaned into him as we walked silently along, enjoying the feel of his strong figure there beside me.

❧ ❧

More than an hour had passed while we meandered around the gardens. It wasn't just the walled terrace we'd walked out onto. A gate had opened into another, which had opened into another. Beyond the tall walls, I could hear the faint sounds from the city. It was peaceful. It was the first time Adnan and I had walked without trying to get somewhere or fearing who could be following. The courtyards were full of plants, trees, stones, and some were raised, giving a view of the mountains lying in the distance behind the palace. It was also the first time our conversation held nothing of the darker nature of our pasts.

When I saw a servant approach, head bowed, my heart sank.

"Lady Juliet," he greeted. "Lady Saya wishes to know if you would join her for a light repast."

"Go ahead," Adnan said, letting go of my hand. "Besides, it looks like you're not the only one."

Seeing a man approach, I felt a knot of tension form.

"Benkei." The servant refused to meet Adnan's eyes. "Emperor Hirose requires your presence, if you would be so kind."

"See?" Adnan gave my hand one last squeeze before letting go.

"Why does it feel like we're already being sucked back into everything?" I whispered, wrestling with the weight of everything. "It's happening so quickly."

"What?" he whispered. "Did you just want it to be the two of us for eternity?"

I bumped him with my shoulder, my cheeks warming.

"So, you did," he teased, giving me a quick kiss. "Enjoy your time with Saya. Don't worry about me. I'll come find you when I'm done."

I nodded, turning to follow the servant who waited. Behind us, I could hear the faint patter of boots on stone as Adnan went the other way. *Don't think that way.* Taking one last breath of fresh air, I followed the servant through a side entrance back into the vast, maze-like palace. *It's just tea with Saya. Nothing is going to happen.*

⁕⁕⁕

"Juliet!" Saya cried, her face beaming as she ran forward to embrace me. "I'm so happy you're here!" She turned to murmur thanks to the servant, who bowed and left us alone. "Come, sit! I wasn't sure if you would be hungry, but I had some food brought. I didn't eat lunch."

"Nor did I," I replied, grinning as I watched her bouncy enthusiasm.

She clapped her hands together. "Good!"

Following her lead, I sat down at a low table, sinking into the cushion on the floor. It was a typical fare for this country: meat, rice, and a bowl full of some steaming liquid … I leaned over and smelled. My stomach growled as the savory aroma wafted into my nostrils.

"It's one of my favorite soups," Saya explained, picking up her own bowl. "You should drink it while it's hot."

Neither of us spoke until our bowls were drained. I set mine down and wiped my lips with a napkin. "That. Was. Delicious."

Saya nodded with a grin.

"I want more."

She laughed. "Sorry, maybe there will be some at dinner." Chewing a bite of rice, she swallowed before speaking. "How is it being back?"

How is it? Had I really given it that much thought? It had only been a day since Natsumi had brought us through the portal. Three worlds in two weeks. I sighed. "It's good, but different and kind of weird all at the same time. I feel like I just haven't been given time to really let anything sink in."

Saya set down the glass she'd drunk from. She swept her long black hair over her shoulder. "I know what you mean. Just two weeks ago, you and I made our escape from Tristan, unaware of what was going on with each other. I headed one way, and you another—" She held up a hand as I made to speak. "You don't have to tell me what happened, unless you want to," she added. "Hirose filled me in."

The hairs on the back of my neck prickled.

"It might help, though." She took a sip of tea. "I could use someone to talk to, and I think, maybe you even more so?" When I didn't say anything, she continued, "You've been through a lot."

Has it only been two weeks? My throat tightened. "What about you?"

Saya eyed the small cup in front of her. "For me, while it's been busy and I've helped Hirose with a lot, I've also had time to just begin to ... to *process* everything that has happened." She tapped a finger against the table. "You haven't had that. If anything, there is just more and more that keeps happening to you and around you." She leaned across the table as she spoke. "I'm so sorry, Juliet."

My head bobbed, but I couldn't say anything.

"I'm here when you want to talk about anything. I hope you're able to get some rest while you're here. I'd like you to stay." Her brown eyes were large in her face. "But I know you might not stay, and I don't blame you."

I knew she waited for a response, but what to say? *We haven't yet decided. We haven't even talked about it.* I took a drink of water. "I'd like to stay for a little while, at least," I said. *Do I? Didn't I just tell Adnan I wanted to be alone with him for eternity?* My nose wrinkled.

"What?" Saya asked.

"Nothing." *She's right.* We hadn't had time to speak before I left, to reconnect, and yet our paths had become intertwined in Umi no Machi. "I will talk, soon, but not now."

"Good." Saya took another bite of food. Her face paled a couple of shades. "There is something I think you ought to know."

The way she spoke made my pulse quicken. *What is it?* I screamed inside. *Something is wrong.* Each second that passed felt like an eternity.

"Tristan is still alive."

Saya's concerned face blurred before my eyes. My leg tried to nervously bounce even as I sat on the floor. I set my bowl down and focused back in on Saya.

"He's here," she offered. "He's to be executed."

Still, I couldn't speak as my mind tried to wrap its way around what I was hearing. *He's somewhere within these walls.*

"I'm sorry. I thought you should know." Saya's voice filtered through my dazed mind again. "Juliet?"

"He's here," I whispered. My right hand gripped the edge of the table, and my knuckles whitened.

She nodded. "You don't have to see him, not at all. I—I just thought you should know, especially with his execution in a few days."

My head bobbed in the affirmative. I stood up, my legs aching from how tight my muscles had become. "I'm sorry."

Saya stood as well, her complexion grayer than usual. "Are you all right?" She reached out an arm.

I stepped back, away from her. "I'm fine. I just need to be alone."

She didn't say anything as I turned and fled.

I wandered through the palace in a haphazard way, meandering from one room to the next, from one hallway to the next. *Lost, lost, lost.* I had no idea which way my room lay. *Adnan!* I screamed his name internally, wishing he were here with me. *Juliet, calm down.*

Taking a deep breath, I stood with my back against a wall and focused on taking deep breaths. No matter how much I tried to persuade myself I was fine, the other part of me disagreed with a vengeance.

"Juliet."

With a half-sob, I turned toward Adnan's voice and saw him standing at the entrance to the room I stood in. The moment he opened his arms, I knew he had found out the same thing.

Tristan was here. And so was his secret.

Chapter Twenty-Three

After my rant about Tristan, Adnan set me back a little, his hands still on my shoulders, so he could look me in the face. Footsteps approached and receded as someone passed the room we stood in. His lips pressed together, and his brow furrowed in thought.

"Juliet," he began, his voice low. "Saya told you?"

I nodded, not trusting myself to speak.

"He's to be executed."

I drew back a little. *Is that supposed to be reassuring?* "I know." The man with blond hair and blue eyes would be dead in a few days. How did I feel?

"You don't need to see him or watch the execution."

"How long?"

"Four days," Adnan murmured. "But Juliet—"

I shifted out of his grip and stalked to the window, looking out on the palace gardens. It was another beautiful day, with pale white clouds floating across the blue sky.

"Juliet?" he asked, his soft tread following me.

My hands shook as I tried to take in deep breaths, to control the panic threatening to overtake me. "I didn't expect this, is all," I muttered, feeling him step up even closer behind me. "To know he's here, somewhere—" Laying a hand on the wall, I took a deep breath as a wave of dizziness overtook me. "I wish ..." *What? What do I wish?*

"That he was already dead?"

Hearing Adnan's question, I couldn't help but wonder. *Do I? Is that what I'd hoped?* The pit in my stomach grew deeper. "No, it's more than that." Rotating on my heels, I looked up at him. "He knows something."

Adnan frowned. "What—" His eyes cleared. "The final secret he whispered to you that night."

My head bobbed. "He didn't tell me what it was."

"Because that night he was baiting you. He'd been captured, and he saw no way out."

"Yes," I murmured. "But now ..."

"You want to know what it is." His body tensed, and he threw his shoulders back. "Why?" he growled.

I took a step back.

"Why do you care so much? Why can't we just leave it all in the past? Haven't there been enough secrets?"

Anger rose within me. "You're one to talk," I bit out. "You're *full* of secrets."

Adnan's chest rose and fell as he inhaled. "But *him*?"

I could see how much this was bothering him. He didn't want me to have anything more to do with Tristan. Could I blame him? Besides, I had known all along that Tristan could have been messing with me. He might not have any secrets to share. If I could have left it alone then, I could now. But I chewed on my lower lip. My heart raced in my chest.

"Never mind," I said, unsure how convincing I was. "You're right. It should be left alone."

Adnan's eyebrow arched.

Again, footsteps sounded in the hallway outside the door. A servant revealed himself for a moment as he passed by and continued, his head not turning to acknowledge us. I waited until I knew he was out of earshot.

"How did it go with Hirose?"

"You're trying to change the subject," Adnan noted. He sighed and folded his arms across his chest. "I know it's bothering you."

Shaking my head, I widened my eyes, trying to show it wasn't. *Because it isn't.* I pushed away Tristan's beckon, the curiosity inside me that hadn't been quenched. But my curiosity had been the cause of many issues before this. I didn't need to know everything. Natsumi's reminder floated through my mind. I couldn't know everything. Even she, with her long life, didn't know everything. *Because we're not meant to.*

I focused back in on Adnan, who scrutinized me. "Hirose?" I prompted him.

Adnan shot me a look that told me he wasn't convinced. "We spoke of current matters. He's doing a good job bringing stability to the country." He shrugged. "While he didn't plan on becoming emperor, he's a man of action, so he's not wasting time letting the country fall to ruin while he figures it out. There is still much to do."

"And it probably won't ever stop," I murmured. "I can't imagine he'll ever have downtime trying to run a country, especially one that has been under opposition for over a century."

"No, it won't," he agreed, letting his arms fall to his sides. "I'll help as able while we are here." He paused and eyed me, the green of his eyes sparkling. "We still need to talk about *our* plans."

Our plans. Thoughts of Tristan faded to the outskirts of my mind.

"I don't think we should stay here," Adnan admitted when I didn't respond. "We need time. Time away from government, from this place, time to process and to get to know one another."

There was a more serious underlay now.

Tristan.

Will I ever be free of him? My heart plummeted in my chest. *Yes, in four days' time.* The hem of my shirt wrinkled as I played with it between my fingers. Tristan had no hold over me. *But his secret.* I shook my head.

"Juliet?"

My body jerked. "Hmm?"

"I asked you about our getting married."

"What?" Tristan was pushed down in the recesses of my mind as I focused on Adnan, who stood before me.

"We should get married before we leave."

Leave as a married couple. I knew what he didn't say. Hirose could perform the ceremony. We wanted to get married, so why not do it now? *But where would we go?* Part of me didn't want to leave Saya. She was the one friend I had here. Things had already changed since I had told Adnan I wanted an eternity with him, alone. Saya and I had just reconnected, and it meant more to me than I realized it would.

"I'm not saying we can't ever return."

He knows. Something of my inner turmoil must have shown on my face.

He reached up to cup my face with his hands. "I love you, Juliet Barrows. Will you come away from here with me, at least until we both feel we are ready to return?"

"Yes," I whispered, savoring the thought of being with him—always. "Yes," I repeated, stronger now. "I'm not sure how Saya will take it though." A hint of remorse made its way into my tone.

"It's not just her," Adnan noted. "It will take some time anyway. We have to speak with Hirose, and there are arrangements to be made. Besides, Tristan's execution is in four days—"

I stiffened.

"—And I don't want that to be a shadow over our wedding."

"It won't." *But his secret? No.*

He leaned down and brushed a soft kiss across my lips. "Good."

Waves crashed against the shoreline, pushing up across the sand with a spray of white foam before receding back into the depths of the ocean. Birds wheeled, landing on the damp ground to peck at what the water washed up. With each wave that came, they flew up into the air, waiting for the ocean to pull back.

My toes curled beneath me, feeling the warm, dry sand. Air blew through my lips as I exhaled. Out in the water, something bobbed. I squinted, raising a hand to block the sun's rays. The black object disappeared. Another wave rolled, and it reappeared. Something flashed up over the top. My eyes widened. An arm. A hand.

Recollections flashed through my mind: a girl and a boy playing in the water, the depth increasing, the force growing, the boy being pulled out.

Eddie.

My scream ripped through the air.

My feet plunged across the sand, throwing dust clouds up with every pounding step. My heart raced, threatening to explode out of my chest, and my breaths came in gasps.

Eddie.

I reached the water's edge. The water lapped my toes as I continued forward, every part of me locked on the boy bobbing in the waves, being pulled farther out with every second that passed. It was cold, so cold. And strong. I continued on. I could see his face now, his eyes wide with terror, spluttering as water went into his lungs.

Somehow, I couldn't shout for him. My voice was frozen.

He went under—and back up, his thrashing slower now.

Another wave.

He disappeared.

No! *I shouted in my mind.* No!

When he resurfaced, I caught him by the arm. He was a deadweight. I felt myself being dragged under the water. I couldn't hold him.

I can. Please. Please. I can hold him. He'll be all right.

His head—I couldn't get his head up. I went under and bobbed back up, my movements panicked. Instinct kicked in. I let go of him. When I came back up, I couldn't see him anywhere.

He was gone.

Kicking, my arms pumping, I made it back to where I could stand. Tears streamed down my cheeks. The ocean stretched out before me, vast, empty—

The room was black. Jerking up out of bed, I slipped out of my covers and felt the cool air from the open window meet my skin. My breathing came in rapid gasping breaths. A dream, I realized. My body shook. It was nothing more—but it was everything. I'd let go of my brother. Sobs wracked my body. I'd never been able to see him in the mirror world, where he'd been alive. My sobs morphed into soft crying. *Why? Why have those nightmares returned now?*

I raised my head from where I'd held it in my hands. Wiping my face on my sleeve, I rose from the bed. *But what if things have changed? What if my decision has changed everything?*

Grabbing a robe where it hung over the edge of the bed, I threw it on and sniffled as I ran out of my room.

It didn't take me long to find a guard.

"Where is Saya?" I blurted out as I approached him.

He eyed me up and down. "I would assume in her rooms."

"Show me."

"But—" He stopped and regarded me. "This way."

I paid no attention to the path he led me down. All I knew was to follow the guard through the maze of darkened hallways and rooms, lit here and there by torches in the brackets on the walls. Always corridors. I shivered. The underground tunnels in Tristan's first hideout, where he had forced us into helping him, the mountain with its dark, dank maze cut deep within the rock, and then Creulon's fortress with its maze of rooms. There, I had also been escorted by a guard dressed in black. *That was a different time,* I told myself. *I'm free here.*

"There." He motioned to a set of doors just ahead. A guard stood outside them. "She needs to see Lady Saya," he said.

The other guard frowned. "At this time of night?"

"Yes," I replied, moving past him to knock on the door. When nothing came, I rapped my knuckles against the wood again.

This time, soft footsteps approached, and the door creaked as it opened.

"Juliet?" Saya murmured through a yawn.

"I need to talk to you."

Her eyes widened, and she held the door open without a word. After I entered, she closed it and led me to a small sitting area. "What happened?"

"I had another nightmare." Air hissed through my lips as I inhaled, forcing myself to calm down. "About Eddie."

Saya dropped onto her cushion. "All right."

"Why now?" I whispered, sitting as well. "He was alive in the other world. I should be happy that he is, even if he's not my Eddie."

Saya frowned and shook her head. "I'm not following."

Taking a deep breath, I forced myself to speak slower. "Why would they come back? If anything, shouldn't I have even more closure over his death? I got to speak with my brother! Eleven years after he died."

Saya nodded, but I could tell she wasn't understanding. "But he's not the *same* Eddie."

My hands flew up in the air. "I know! I know. But what if something has happened? What if my leaving my real world and my mirror-self there instead of sending her back to her world has changed things somehow?"

"Oh," Saya breathed, sitting back a little. "But I don't see how ..."

"Eddie was there, I had him, but I had to let go. He disappeared," I explained, still feeling the terror I'd felt when I'd woken up.

"He drowned, Juliet," Saya replied, her eyes soft and sad. "And I don't understand why you think something has happened just because of what you saw?"

"No!" I shook my head. "No," I repeated. "I mean, yes."

Saya drew her knees up and rested her chin on them.

"I'm sorry," I admitted. "I'm not making much sense, am I?"

Saya shook her head. "Here, why don't you drink some water. It might help."

I took the proffered glass. "I don't believe it was a premonition of what's to come, and I really do feel like I moved on from Eddie's death. I learned to not blame myself for his death. Yes, a lot of that came rushing back in after I found out my brother was alive, even though at the time I didn't know it was a mirror Earth."

Saya nodded again, her brows drawn together as she concentrated.

"But what if I made a decision to leave my mirror-self in a happier place, a better world, but didn't consider the consequences of what that would do to the mirror Earth?"

Saya sat back and groaned. "Oh, Juliet. It's late, I'm tired, and you're making my head hurt."

"I've been guilty of making hasty decisions," I continued, calmer now. "And I don't want to keep making the same mistakes."

Saya's lips pursed. "What are you doing right now?"

"What?"

"From what you've told me," she said, "my *understanding* is that you sacrificed so much in leaving your mirror-self. You could have stayed with your family, your *real* family, and sent her back to the mirror Earth, but you didn't, because you felt like you couldn't do that to her, to *yourself*." Saya cocked her head to the side as she regarded me. "Is that true?"

"I suppose, but—"

"So yes, you don't know what's happening on the mirror Earth. Why do you need to know?"

The truth that I had suppressed began to fight back. My hands shook.

"Why do you want to know about mirror world Eddie?" Saya asked.

"So that I might have some peace about it." *But that's not the whole truth. You already have it.* I repeated it inside my head. "I know that Eddie is not my

Eddie," I said. "But I still want to know." *Do you?* The question rang inside my head.

Saya swept her long, dark hair over her shoulder. "I suppose I could try, but—"

My face brightened. "When?"

"It will take some time ... I don't know."

"That's fine. I don't expect anything more."

"I can't make any promises, though." She reached forward and gave my hand a quick squeeze. "If I find something out, I'll tell you. But I don't know how long that will take, if ever. I'm just trying to be realistic."

"That's all I ask."

Saya wrapped her arms around herself and shivered. "Now, I really do want to go back to sleep, but I think we should talk more tomorrow. Your apparent struggle with sleep for one, and two—" She hesitated. "Two, I think you should talk to Benkei about all of this."

"I will, but why?"

"Because I think you're fixating on Eddie rather than letting him go."

I recoiled as though gun-shot.

"It's true," she whispered. "And it's not healthy." She stood up, and I rose as well. "I love you." Her arms went about me in a hug, but I felt frozen. She drew back. "Try to get some sleep."

Eddie. Tristan. Eddie. Tristan. The two men circled through my thoughts. "I might go talk to Benkei first. I don't know if I can sleep right now. There's too much going through my head, especially with ..." *Not now. Don't think of Tristan now.* But he was there, he was always there.

Saya's jaw locked as she gritted her teeth.

I stepped back, toward the door. "I should go." But I knew it was too late. Saya knew what was on my mind. She knew Tristan haunted me. *Will I ever be free of him?*

"You're letting him," she whispered, her brown eyes holding my own blue ones.

I froze.

"You're letting him get to you. Don't give him the satisfaction."

I am. He always has, hasn't he?

"Think of me, the country, yourself. Think of Shizukana." As she spoke his name, I watched as her eyes widened, and her jaw dropped. She peered at me. "Are you and he—" She shook her head. "Never mind. We'll talk more tomorrow."

I let out the breath I'd been holding, listening as she followed me to the door.

"Try to get some sleep, Juliet. Tomorrow is another day."

The guard nodded to me as I stepped out of the room. The door clicked shut behind me. *Another day.* I could wait to talk to Adnan. *Eddie … Tristan … Eddie.* I took a deep breath and wrapped my robe closer around me. *It will never end.* There was always something. Natsumi knew that. *She tried to tell me or warn me.* Was Saya right? No more could I convince myself that I had let Eddie go. The past weeks had been dredged back up, weeks and experiences that I hadn't even begun to process. Was it all because of Tristan?

CHAPTER TWENTY-FOUR

No sleep came to me. I had paced my room, waiting for the first rays of dawn to spread over the horizon. When they arrived, I'd dressed and left to find Adnan. But my search was fruitless. He wasn't in his chambers. The guards and servants I asked hadn't seen him. I managed to find Saya's room again, thanks to a servant, but she had also gone.

So breakfast was a lonely affair. I ate by myself in my room, the food a little tasteless. All I was left with were my thoughts, and two men—Eddie and Tristan—vying for prominence in my mind. One who should have been dead, and the other who would die soon.

When I finished, I watched as a maid removed my plate and straightened my bed before leaving. Unable to remain, I roamed the fortress. I was just nearing the main doors into the palace when one was opened by the guards outside. Adnan's familiar tall figure entered. He straightened when he saw me.

"There you are!" I exclaimed. "Where—?" My question died as I saw him hold out a bouquet of flowers.

"I had some business to take care of." He held out the colorful wildflowers with a sheepish look. "Then I thought you might like some flowers."

Taking them, I inhaled, smelling the fresh, sweet blooms. "They're pretty." My face warmed with delight. Stepping up on my tiptoes, I kissed him. "Thank you."

His joviality faded as he regarded me. "Something happened."

"How do you know that?"

He shrugged. "You're happy, but you have the same look you always get when something is plaguing your mind. Your eyes have a layer of sadness to them, and they're dark, as if you haven't slept. You haven't, have you?"

I shook my head. "Not really."

He tucked my arm into the crook of his. "Come on. Let's go talk." Rather than leading me inside, he led me back outside into the dreary, cloud-filled day. I shivered as a gust of wind blew across us. It had been winter when we'd left Ryujin, then continued in the mirror world, and now we experienced Ryujin as spring approached. A pulsing grew in my temples as I wrestled through the cloud of thoughts.

Adnan led me through a small wrought-iron gate into an intimate courtyard. A brazier burned bright at the center, and a stone bench lay nearby. He sat, drawing me beside him, and angled his body to face me. In here, the wind was almost nonexistent, cut off from the high surrounding walls.

It should have been breathtaking, with the high stone walls, the trees, the lush plants, and the warmth from the fire. I remembered the cherry blossom trees that had begun to bud back in Creulon's mountain fortress. It was so early. *How?* I shivered, already feeling colder from the stone bench we sat on. *This would've been Tristan's if he'd won.*

Adnan shifted, scrutinizing me. "All right, tell me what happened."

I shook the thought away. *It's Eddie, but what about him?* Welcoming the heat from the brazier, I listened to the faint whistle of the wind high above. Saya's sentence still blazed at the forefront of my mind: *"Because I think you're fixating on Eddie rather than letting him go."* I tucked my hair behind my ears. Wood glowed below the flames. Its searing heat warmed my body, pushing back the chill.

"Is it Tristan?"

"No." *Yes. No.* Shaking my head, I licked my lips. *But he's part of it.* "I had a nightmare about Eddie last night."

Adnan frowned. "The Eddie from the mirror world."

"No. I mean the Eddie from my world." I took a deep breath and plunged on. "It made me realize I didn't really think about the repercussions of leaving, of letting my mirror-self stay in the real world instead of returning to her world. What if that's changed things?" The more I spoke, the harder it became to remain incredulous at Saya. "My Eddie is dead, but what if something happens to him on the mirror Earth because of the decisions I made?" I stopped. *Oh. She's right.* Saya was right. I shook my head.

Adnan stroked his jaw. "I suppose that's possible, but—"

"Saya was right."

Adnan frowned. "What?"

"I went to her last night, after I woke up. I asked her to look for Eddie, to make sure—" I bit my lip. "To make sure he's all right," I finished. "I'm not letting him go, am I?"

"Hold on," Adnan said. "You're being too hard on yourself either way. You have had *no* time to process what happened on the mirror Earth. That Eddie isn't your brother, though, Juliet. Not the one that you remember, not the one who died eleven years ago."

Every word he spoke drove into my heart like a spike, but I knew he was right.

"You do have to let him go, just like you had to let your brother go."

I sighed and leaned forward. "I could be wondering and asking Saya for updates on him the rest of my life, couldn't I?"

He nodded. "Yes. Is that what you want?"

No. It began as a small trickle of a thought. One word. *No.* It came stronger now, flaring bright, dominant. I shook my head.

"What now?" Adnan asked, his scrutiny so deep I wondered if he was trying to see into my soul.

"I'll talk to Saya, tell her that I shouldn't have asked, that I don't want to know. My brother is dead. He died eleven years ago. Nothing will change that. I don't know the mirror. Eddie."

Adnan stretched his legs out. "And your decision to come here?"

I knew what he was asking. My desire to know about Eddie, seeing him, had caused me to question everything. But I also knew the answer.

"Juliet?"

"Sorry." I sucked in a breath. "It was the right decision. The other Juliet will be better off in my world, and my parents have their daughter." A bug crawled up over the bench. "And now I've gone and created more drama where none needed to be had."

Adnan raised a hand but lowered it just as fast. "You're not sleeping well. It's been"—he paused—"five months of harrowing adventures for you. You're not sleeping well, and then you saw your brother's death. I wouldn't be too harsh on yourself."

I sighed. "You're right."

He nodded. "I know I am." The statement was softened by a twinkle in his eyes. "All right. Now, about—" He was forestalled as the gate behind us opened, and Hirose and Saya stepped through.

Now what? Forcing myself to relax, I inclined my head to Hirose.

"Do you mind if we join you?" he asked.

Adnan gestured in response.

"We want to ask you something." Saya's lips twitched. "You are together now, aren't you?"

My lips parted in surprise.

"Yes." Adnan shifted closer to me.

"Very well." Hirose's eyes twinkled. "It's about time."

Still, I couldn't speak.

"You wish to be married?" Saya asked, her head bobbing.

Warmth flooded my cheeks. "Saya!"

"What?" Her teeth flashed as she grinned.

"We'd like to be," Adnan replied, trying to hide his own smirk.

Hirose waved a hand. "Would you do me the honor of letting me perform the ceremony?"

"Whoa, whoa," I sputtered. "Wait. This is all moving so fast."

All three looked at me, Adnan with a slight frown.

"I'm not trying to rush you," Hirose explained. "I know you had not planned on staying here, and I wanted to offer. Please don't feel obligated to accept my offer."

"It's not that." *Then what is it?* It was a struggle to find words for what I warred with. *We just got engaged, and so much has happened, and will happen.*

Saya's face paled. "Is it Tristan?"

Only the fire crackling filled the air, and my silence was response enough.

"Ah." Hirose glanced at Adnan. "Tristan is to be executed in three days."

Adnan switched from looking at me to Hirose. "May we speak of this after the execution, then? We don't need his death to cloud talk of our wedding."

Hirose nodded. "I should have considered that," he said by way of apology. He bowed. "That was my mistake."

Remorse clouded my heart as I saw how my behavior affected what should have been a happy, joyful conversation. "I'm sorry. Hirose, I think we'd both be honored if you performed the ceremony," I said. *But that's not all,* I thought. "Yes, let's talk about it after the execution. I know I shouldn't let him—" I stumbled over my words. "I—"

"No need to explain," Hirose interrupted. "Do you want to see Tristan?"

My eyes shot to him. *See him? Speak with him?*

Adnan stiffened next to me. "She doesn't need to see him," he growled.

Isn't that my choice? My skin grew hot.

Hirose's leather armor creaked as he moved. "Juliet?"

Tristan's secret. "I don't need to," I whispered. *Do I mean that?* "But does he know I'm here?"

Hirose shrugged. "I gave the guards strict orders not to let him know you or Benkei have returned."

Adnan's tone was brisk. "Let's leave it at that."

I don't need to know his secret. I don't need to see him. In three days, he would be executed. He had no need to know I was there. So many had died because of him, and now death would be his punishment. A just ending. He wouldn't get out of this, not this time.

"Why don't you two take the rest of the day and just try to distance yourselves from what is going on here?" Hirose suggested.

I had a vague awareness of Adnan responding, but I was concentrating on Hirose as I studied him. His long black hair was pulled back into a bun at the nape of his neck. Not a hair was out of place. His thin brows rose as he shot a wordless question at me.

They were *all* watching me.

"What?" I asked. *Did I miss something?*

Adnan's full lips thinned, but he said nothing.

Is he angry at me? Even Saya wouldn't look at me. "What's wrong?"

"We all know," she began, frowning, "that you carry a lot of weight when it comes to Tristan. This is not going to be easy for you."

"He'll be dead in three days, and I'll be happy about it." My tongue felt thick.

A sharp hiss rent the air as Saya inhaled. The three of them continued watching me, Adnan with resignation, but Hirose with widened eyes and a sort of curiosity about him.

"You're not the same girl who arrived here five months ago," Saya murmured. Were those tears?

"No, I'm not. And he's to blame for that."

The gate behind us creaked as it opened.

I froze at the sight of the woman hesitating on the threshold. *Miya.*

"Come in, my lady," Hirose said in a somewhat suave manner.

"Am I intruding? I didn't realize anyone was in here." Miya stepped forward, her dainty slippers barely showing under her thick cloak.

"No," Hirose assured her in a soft voice. "Please join us, Lady Miya."

"Miya?" I spluttered as she approached.

She inclined her head. "Hello, Juliet."

"What? How? What are you doing here?"

"I'm here by Emperor Hirose's invitation. I stay here." She shrugged her petite shoulders and stepped up to the brazier between Hirose and me. "It's not like I have anywhere else to go," she murmured under her breath.

"No, that's not what I meant." I shook my head. "You're *here*."

She laughed, a bubbly sound that I wasn't sure I had heard issue from her lips before. Tendrils of dark hair flew as she shook her head. "I know. And so are you."

I turned to Hirose. "Who else is here?"

"Many of the harem lodge here. I offered to let them stay if they had nowhere they wanted to go."

Many of them. *Amarante.* The woman with the fire in her eyes and the color of red crept into my mind. "Is Amarante here?"

"Yes."

I sucked in a breath. It seemed everyone was here ... except Creulon and Master Hitto. *At least they aren't alive.* I winced at the delight I'd felt with that thought. Creulon had died before me, killed by Tristan in a rescue attempt. But it hadn't just been a rescue attempt. Tristan had used me to take over the fortress, to bring down Creulon, and take the throne. So much was being dug back up. An emptiness warred with hurt and pain inside of me.

"I'd like to see Amarante," I announced. Miya didn't look surprised—something that I filed away to ask her about later. Ignoring the way Adnan brushed against my shoulder, I fixed my focus on Hirose.

He inclined his head. "Very well, I will send for her. When and where?"

"Inside." The air was cold, and I wasn't sure how much longer I could stand being outside. "Wherever would be best, but I'd like to see her now."

Miya's gentle face paled a shade.

What am I doing? Miya's expression said it all.

"I'm sorry," I added to Hirose, softer now. "I shouldn't have spoken to you like that."

He waved a hand in dismissal. "When we get to the palace, I'll have a servant lead you and will send another to fetch Amarante."

The realization that he used 'Lady' before Miya's name but not Amarante's hit me. *Why?*

Hirose turned to leave, Miya's arm tucked inside his own.

Ah, now I know. The flicker of joy I felt at seeing Miya and Hirose together pushed away the oppressive darkness I fought against. Adnan took my arm as well and extended his other to Saya, who took it. His warmth and care drew me back into the present. These were the people who cared, whom *I* cared for. They were the ones who mattered.

Hirose glanced over his shoulder at the rest of us. "Benkei, Saya, would you two join me while Juliet speaks with Amarante? I received a letter by courier this morning from one of the northern countries. The northern raiders are gauging our strength and my new rule. They must be dealt with before unrest grows."

"I'll come," Adnan said, sparing a quick glance toward me.

His home country. His people. I leaned into him, listening to the sound of silence filling the air as we walked. *Would he ever want to show me the northern country? Would I want to see it?* Images of the night of the raid in Umi no Machi flashed into my mind. The accents, the rough speech, the large, burly men—fear settled in the pit of my stomach. *Should I ask him? No.* There wasn't anything to say. Not now. I had questions, but they would slowly be answered. First, Amarante. She was yet another piece that had been left by the wayside. She was another tool used by Creulon. She was another fallout from Tristan's actions.

An enigma. And I wanted to know if Amarante still hated me, or if we could come to some sort of reconciliation.

⸙

The soft footsteps halted behind me, accompanied by gentle breathing. My shoulders rose as I inhaled and straightened my back. My slippers slid as I turned. Amarante stood before me, as resplendent as ever, in a gown of deep red, with a sash of an even darker red below her bosom. Her eyes were different than what I remembered. Her eyes. They were ringed purple, and her pallor had grayed. The jubilant life her face had always seemed to contain had faded.

"Amarante," I greeted, gesturing to where a servant had brought some tea and snacks. Without waiting for her, I sat on the cushion and poured us both some tea.

"Juliet Barrows," Amarante greeted as she sat down.

Her voice doesn't hold the same enigmatic power.

I handed her a cup full of steaming liquid.

She took it. "You're back. I wondered who had called for me when Hir—*Emperor* Hirose had summoned me. I wouldn't have expected it to be you." She smirked. "My understanding, if the rumors were to be believed, is that you and *Benkei* left this world for your own."

While her words had been spiteful, the tone hadn't been. *What is she about?* My guard was up—had been before she had even walked into the room.

"So." Amarante set her cup down on the table and regarded me with her large brown eyes. "Why did you want to see me? And *why* did you return?"

Setting down my own tea, I rested my hands in my lap. "How do you know for sure I left?"

"I don't." She shrugged. "But considering you both have been nonexistent in one of the most important and influential times in the past few centuries ..." She left the rest of the sentence dangling as she watched me.

"We're back now," I replied, ignoring her prompting. "And I wanted to see you because of how things were left."

"You mean when you found me down in the dungeon, where Tristan had placed me and everyone else. Yes, I survived." She waved a hand down her body. "I can't say I wasn't surprised."

"You look well."

She guffawed. "Do I?" Her eyes glinted as she leaned forward.

I took a sip of tea, letting her wait while I thought. "Well," I replied, my voice quiet, "you have dark circles under your eyes that were never there before. Nor do you hold the power you did when you were head of the harem, and it shows in your bearing and your voice."

Amarante blinked. She sat back and drew herself up. "I have a question for you. If you are here, does that mean *Adnan* is as well?"

I focused on her emphasis. *Adnan.* My eyes widened. "How do you know that name?"

A sly smirk slid across her face.

"Amarante, how do you know?" I demanded, clutching the edge of the table. *Names have meaning. He doesn't want anyone to know his name.*

"You told me." Her eyes drifted down to my bandaged left wrist. A question flitted across her face, but she said nothing. But she didn't have to.

"No, I didn't," I protested, but even as I spoke, my mind raced, searching the conversations I'd had with her in Creulon's mountain fortress.

"Remember that night you visited me when I was in the cell? We spoke of Benkei then, of how he had been here several times before the time he rescued you. Before you left, you called him Adnan."

My lips parted. "Why didn't you say anything then?"

"I filed it away. There was no need then. You would have denied it."

Stupid, stupid, stupid.

Amarante sipped innocently at her tea.

I took a deep breath. "What are you going to do?"

"Do?" she echoed, tilting her head. "I'm not going to do anything. His secret is safe with me."

A knot formed in my stomach. *Is it, though?* She hadn't proven trustworthy in Creulon's court, so why would she now? The room wasn't small by any means, but it felt small now. The other furniture served only to make it feel crowded.

"It really is safe with me, Juliet." Amarante's shoulders lowered. "There is nothing in it for me."

"And if there were?" I shot back at her. No matter what she said, I couldn't forget her vindictive nature or her hunger for power.

"All I can keep telling you is that you have nothing to worry about. It's up to you if you believe me or not." She rose and clasped her hands together. "Now, is there anything else you wished to speak to me about?"

"Are you happy?" The question flew out before I could stop it.

Amarante's cheeks reddened, bringing a little color into her face. "I am content. Emperor Hirose is providing for everything I need. But that isn't the real reason you're here. Why do you care about my happiness?"

"We were at odds while I was in Creulon's court."

Amarante snorted.

"For many reasons, though now you know I had no plans of actually trying to take your place," I finished. "But it is through my actions, along with others', that your life is completely different."

"You want to see if I am angry with you? If I resent you?" Amarante took a step back. "No, I am not angry with you. At first, yes, but I harbor no ill will against you. Now, is that everything?"

I nodded and stood up.

"If you wish to speak to me again, I am at your service." Amarante bowed. "Until next time."

I watched as she left the room. Now I had to figure out what to tell Adnan. And not just him, but the others. She knew Adnan's name. Her life had changed, and while she said one thing, I still wasn't sure she could be trusted. Perhaps she had changed. *Maybe Creulon's death and Tristan's actions really did break her.*

A sigh escaped my lips as I left the room.

Chapter Twenty-Five

Adnan stood in front of the crackling fire. The flickering flames thrust dancing shadows upon the floor and the walls. He said nothing, and I didn't blame him. There was something hypnotic about watching the fire in the hearth. Its warmth filled the room.

It had only been a couple of weeks that I had spent between the two other worlds, and here but a few days. It wasn't until I overheard a maid speaking of spring approaching that it fully sank in how it was still February, which made me realize once again how quickly everything was happening. The mountain fortress, the mirror world, my real world, and now the palace in Ryujin. My head ached.

Adnan stirred, drawing my attention back to him. "I think Hirose has ironed out what he'll do to address the northern raiders."

"Have there been more raids?"

He looked at me. "Yes."

"Will all the people they've taken as slaves be returned?"

Adnan sighed and stroked his chin. "No."

What? My heart thumped, and my lips parted to speak.

"There's no way of getting them all back. The raids have been going on for years. And Hirose, as much as he wishes, does not have the resources to get them all back. What he *has* done is declare that all raids are to stop."

I licked my lips. "Will they listen?"

He shrugged. "I don't know. Time will tell."

"And if they don't?"

"If they don't, Hirose will be forced into declaring war. He must solidify his rule, and he *cannot* make empty threats. It would be detrimental to Ryujin's future."

"Did you have advice for him?"

"Some, but I mostly just reminded him of what he already knew."

The nagging question of whether Adnan was being sucked back into everything plagued me. *Don't ask.* Was I afraid of the answer?

"Juliet." Adnan took my hands, urging me to look up into his face. "I'm only giving advice, nothing more."

A half-chuckle escaped my lips. "How did you know what I was thinking?"

"Because I'd probably be fearing the same thing in your shoes. I'm *done*. I'm giving advice, but nothing more. Soon, we'll leave."

"You can't promise that," I said, my voice soft, watching as his green eyes darkened.

"I—"

"No." I shook my head. "You can't promise that. Sometimes you fight. While I was drawn into the uprising, and then after, against Tristan, I *had* to fight. What we do is sometimes done for the right reasons or because we have no choice at all."

He traced a finger along my cheek. "I don't want to hurt you."

I frowned, my arms crossing. "I knew when I agreed to marry you that your past might follow us—"

"It shouldn't. It won't follow us."

I exhaled. "You don't know that for sure." My thoughts shot to Amarante. She was another loose end. Two people were alive who knew Adnan's name. And even more knew his past occupation and how dangerous he was.

"I'll do everything I can to keep you safe," Adnan promised. He straightened his shirt and sat down on the floor, his back to the wall near the hearth. "I don't plan on doing what I used to, but you're right, if the time came ..." He inhaled. "We'll talk."

"And we'll keep talking." A grin flashed across my face. "We'll communicate. I don't want to keep any secrets from you." *Amarante.* My cheerfulness faded.

"Nor I you."

A secret.

Taking a deep breath, I said, "There is something, though."

❧ ❧

After Adnan left, I dressed for dinner. It didn't take me long. No servant had yet come to lead the way, so I paced the floor, alone with my thoughts. Adnan had taken it well. He thought that, in the end, it might not matter so much since he was leaving that life behind him. But he also didn't trust Amarante, just as I hadn't. Now he needed to decide whether to tell Hirose and Saya about my conversation with Amarante.

I was beginning to feel restless. There was too much downtime. But it was more than that.

Tristan.

My wrist twanged. He still haunted me. I gritted my teeth.

A knock rang through the air. *The servant.* Going to the door, I slid it open. My jaw dropped. "Hiro— Emperor Hirose."

He nodded to me. "When it's our inner circle, Hirose is fine, Juliet. May I come in?"

I peered around him. He was alone. Nodding, I stepped aside and let him walk in before closing the door.

Hirose turned to face me. "I know Benkei has told you about my role in your kidnapping."

Whatever I had expected, this wasn't it. The room felt hot, and my skin flushed.

"Creulon idolized Benkei—*Oniwaka*—and wanted me to become him. There is so much behind that name. The legends behind it, the rumors ..." Hirose sighed. "And he had heard you might be traveling with him. That was part of the reason I was to emulate him. We wanted to sow a seed of doubt in you about who Benkei was and what he was doing with you." Hirose's gaze never left my own. "I was cruel, unnecessarily so."

The memories of Bagu's knife slicing into my ribs, of the beating, the drugs, the lack of food and water—all of it washed over me. I shivered, feeling the scar over my rib cage tingle.

He laid a hand over his heart and lowered his head. "I began to resent what I had done. But then when you did come to Creulon and I carried out his orders"—he paused—"I know I can use that as an excuse, but it doesn't change the fact that it was wrong." He bowed. Deeper than he needed to, deeper than was required of an emperor to someone like me. "Will you forgive me?"

Listening to him, I hated the way he brought everything back. But, sucking in a breath, I regarded him. Did he expect me to say yes? A sense of peace descended over me. I had forgiven him, but his asking was like the last piece of the puzzle that I didn't realize how much I wanted.

Without moving, I answered. "Yes, I do."

I stood in front of the closed doors to the dining room. My hand rose, but I didn't slide back the doors. The guards waited on either side, silent. *Another time, another place.* Fighting to even my breathing, I slid my fingers through my hair, slipping loose tendrils back into place. The air felt stifling. *This isn't the same. It was different then.*

"Juliet!"

I jumped, my heart racing.

Adnan stepped up beside me, his brow wrinkled. "What's wrong?"

My eyes flicked between him and the doors. *Not the same.* "Nothing."

He tilted his head to the side, his lips pursing.

"Just something I remembered," I explained.

"Are you ready?"

Behind those words, I knew he meant more. *Am I ready to face others? Am I ready for what's to come—Tristan's execution, Adnan being an advisor—*

I sucked in a breath and nodded.

Adnan slid the doors open and warm candlelight spilled out, illuminating Adnan's dark hair and sending more dancing shadows upon the floor as we took a step forward, and then another. This wasn't the same as those nights I had joined Creulon for dinner. Then, I had been a prisoner, and now, I was free.

Hirose waved us forward from where he sat before a low table with Saya and Miya. "I thought we could have a cozy meal together, just the five of us."

The sight of Creulon sitting there, with Amarante, Hirose, and the other advisors and ladies flashed through my mind. I flinched.

"Juliet?" Saya asked, standing. "Are you all right?"

I smoothed down my skirt. "Yes."

She frowned, but sat down as Adnan led me to the table. After we sat, Hirose cleared his throat.

"I did not believe we would all be here now, like this. More than that, that we would all be more than just acquaintances, much less enemies. There is a friendship blossoming here."

Miya grinned, the years of hardship shedding as her face took on a youthful glint.

"What?" Hirose asked.

She shrugged and took her glass in one small hand. "I didn't know you to be so eloquent."

Hearing the chuckle escape Saya, I couldn't help my own mood lightening as the merriment drove away the past. Adnan took my hand under the table and pressed it.

"On a more serious note, though." Hirose's voice changed to a deeper tenor. "You and Amarante spoke. May I know how that went?"

My lips parted, but I hesitated as the door opened and servants brought the food. Steaming plates were set down, piled high with seafood, meat, and vegetables. Before each of us was placed a bowl of rice. My stomach rumbled.

The servants went back the way they'd come, and we were left with hot food and savory aromas wafting through the air.

"My apologies, Juliet," Hirose began, not touching his food. "That was an indelicate question. The last thing I want is to cast a shadow over our meal."

Did he just apologize? Another apology. From him? I stared at him, wondering if the shock I felt showed. "It's fine, Hirose." *It's the norm now. When do dinner conversations ever not involve difficulty?* "She told me she's changed," I began.

"Do you believe her?"

Leaning forward, I craned my body slightly. "Why? Has something happened?"

He shook his head. "No, nothing. Yet I don't see any reason to believe she would just give up everything she fought for. Her position has been lost. She holds nothing now."

"And she's always been a viper," muttered Miya. "Her claims mean nothing."

The clink of a dish turned my attention to my other side, where Saya ate. She looked up, and her shoulders rose. "What? I'm hungry."

"Do you have concerns about Amarante?" I asked Hirose, ignoring Saya. "There might be war. Is it wise to have her around?"

Hirose sighed. "And that is the crux of the matter. I've offered asylum to any of the old harem who have no place to go. Could I just kick Amarante out?"

"Yes." Adnan's answer was given almost before Hirose had finished speaking.

Shaking my head, I said, "I'm not so sure. What would that do? What if she is telling the truth? That might just destroy any loyalty she does have. It could *make* her into an enemy."

"Or it could save this country."

The others faded as I focused on Adnan. "How?"

"She could do something similar to what you did in Creulon's court. You were instrumental in the end, even if Tristan was using you for reasons other than what we knew. Amarante could feed information, could help sneak someone in—"

I snorted. "*If.*"

"I don't plan on removing her from the palace," Hirose interrupted. "These are all possibilities, but we have no way of knowing, and I won't punish her for something she hasn't done—or has *yet* to do," he added as Adnan made to speak. "Maybe that is wrong, but it *is* my decision."

"Why don't we change the conversation?" Miya asked. "Otherwise Saya will have eaten all the food before we even begin."

I nodded and picked up my bowl of rice, avoiding Adnan. He was watching. I could feel it. Miya and Hirose took the lead in providing conversation, but I didn't listen. Eating gave me something to do, and a way to focus my annoyance. *He's wrong. But you don't trust her yourself, so why take her side?*

The question ate at me.

CHAPTER TWENTY-SIX

The window was a door into another life. It was only when the breeze swept toward me that I could hear the faint sounds of voices. The city beyond the palace walls was filled with people, living, laughing, talking, breathing. Theirs was a life different from mine, removed from the palace, from the concerns Hirose, their emperor, carried.

In two days, Tristan was to be executed. So many had already died. But out there, through that window, there was life. It wasn't market day, but still the city was busy.

Adnan and I hadn't spoken since dinner the night before. Our argument was unresolved. *Maybe it'll stay that way. We won't always agree on everything.* I crossed my arms over my chest, trying to ward off the unsettling air descending on me.

Footsteps approached, quiet, almost imperceptible. *Adnan.*

"Hi," I said without turning around.

He brushed my shoulder. "Are you still upset?"

"No," I murmured, leaning into him. "I can't say I understand you, though. I don't trust Amarante either, but she also hasn't done anything—"

Adnan snorted.

"Fine. I agree that she could, but I just don't see how sending her away solves it all."

"It doesn't," he said, patiently standing his ground. "I've always had to think about the worst possible outcome. Hirose says Amarante has not had communication from anyone outside this palace, as far as he knows. Given the possibility, though, he is keeping a closer eye on her now."

"Do you really think she could do something like that?" I asked.

"I don't know." Adnan laid his arm over my shoulders. "What would be her incentive? A position again? Power? But is that a strong enough reason?"

"So far, she has kept your name a secret."

He nodded, his hair bouncing a little with the movement. "Yes, but it's not enough to convince me."

I tilted my head to rest against his shoulder. "What now?"

"About Amarante?"

"About everything. You, me, what our plans are ..."

Adnan stepped away so he could face me, his green eyes striking against his dark features. "I haven't given it much thought," he admitted. "I plan on marrying you, as soon as ..." He hesitated. "As soon as we can plan a wedding after Tristan's execution." He took my hands and rubbed his thumbs in slow circles over my skin. "Let's talk after that."

My brow wrinkled. "Why not now?"

"Because I have some other things to go over with Hirose today, and they're on my mind."

"What things?"

His thumbs stilled.

"Adnan?"

"Nothing for you to worry about." He leaned down as though to kiss me.

I pulled away. "Why can't you tell me?"

His hands rose, palm up. "It's just nothing for you to worry about."

"Is that all? Did Hirose tell you not to tell me?"

Adnan's face darkened. "No—"

"Then why can't you tell me?"

"You just don't need to worry about it. That. Is. All."

Anger seethed inside of me, and my hands trembled. "So let me get this right. The only reason you're not telling me is because you don't want me to worry about it?"

Adnan's face tightened. "I don't understand why you're so upset."

"Because you're keeping secrets from me. Again."

He flinched. "I'm not keeping secrets from you."

Oh, really? I gritted my teeth.

"Calm down."

I held up a finger. "One, do not tell me to calm down; if anything, that makes me angrier." *Stop this.* The thought was unspoken but sounded loud to my own ears. *Be honest with him.* "No, you're right. I'm sorry. But Adnan, if you want to be in a relationship with me, then you need to be more open. Don't keep things from me."

A range of emotions flew across Adnan's face as it darkened, paled, and then flushed.

My heart beat like war drums inside my chest.

"You're right," he said in a quiet tone. "I'm sorry." His eyes shone with suppressed emotion. "I have a history of keeping things from you. It is something I am fighting against. I should have told you if you wanted to know."

I bounced a little on the balls of my feet. "I forgive you."

Adnan's lips parted. "What you wanted to know—Hirose is concentrating a lot of his efforts right now on the military and shoring up defenses. There are two possibilities of attack, one by Nordik and the other by Helsingor. Ryujin has not had the strongest military presence since Nordik defeated them a few centuries ago." He took a deep breath. "So, Hirose's job right now is to shore up defenses as much as possible."

"And where do you come in?"

"I know the country. I know people. I've been giving Hirose my advice as to numbers, strategies, and areas that are more vulnerable to attack. He has a lot of work cut out for him, but he's already made immense progress."

"He's working hard," I murmured, remembering how tired Hirose appeared.

"They all are," Adnan replied. "Saya too. And the other advisors—they have good heads on their shoulders. Hirose chose well."

"Do you think Ryujin will be attacked?"

Adnan motioned to the city below. "I don't know. It's very possible. Nordik won't let Ryujin go easily, but it's also possible they have not heard yet."

I knew Nordik lay somewhere to the west, but not how far. "How long would it take?"

Adnan shrugged. "Depends. Something of this nature? It would travel along the gossip chain. There is no way Creulon would have been able to alert them, so my guess? In the next two weeks, they'll know."

"About a month total," I muttered, thinking.

"Yes."

"And Helsingor?"

"Helsingor is more complicated," Adnan replied. "I think they will abide by the attacks, but it may take a harsh measure to make them aware first."

"Why?"

"Because they will want to test Ryujin first, test her strength, see how serious Hirose is." Adnan turned from the window. "Because of that, Hirose has sent extra patrols to the northern border."

My thoughts turned to those who had already been taken. All those attacks, all those people—and there was nothing to be done.

"There isn't anything we can do for them," Adnan reminded me. "All Hirose can do is protect those who are still here. He doesn't have the power or men to demand the slaves be returned, and Helsingor knows it. Besides, many of those taken aren't even in Helsingor anymore."

"I know," I whispered, but I also knew one slip-up that night, and I would have been amongst those taken.

"Juliet." Adnan reached forward and took my hand, interlacing my fingers with his. "I hate to see you hurting like this." He hesitated, and a note of longing filled his voice. "I wish I could take you away from here, from all of this. I believe a life exists where we can be together, without always looking over our shoulders."

"But that may not exist for us," I whispered.

"It may not," he admitted. Reaching forward, he cupped my face with both hands. "But we will have each other, no matter what happens."

A movement over his shoulder drew my eye. A flash of red against the dark wood walls. A flurry of movement as whoever it was hurried around the corner.

Amarante.

I pulled away from Adnan and rushed down the corridor.

"Juliet!" I heard Adnan hiss after me, his footsteps following.

Rounding the corner, I halted. It was her. "Amarante," I called.

She stopped. Standing a few yards farther down the hallway, she turned, her hands upturned in an innocent gesture. "Juliet, what a surprise."

Adnan stiffened from where he stood beside me, his arm brushing mine.

"You were listening." There was no question behind my words.

Amarante laid a hand over her heart. "Me? I saw you both, but I continued on my way."

My head shook once. "What did you overhear? How long were you standing there?"

Amarante smirked. "Nothing. And even if I had, haven't I shown you I can keep a secret?"

I glanced up at Adnan, who walked forward, and I followed.

"Benkei," Amarante greeted him with a silky greeting. "It's been a while."

"Juliet asked you a question."

Amarante's mirth disappeared.

"How long were you standing there?"

"Just a moment, no longer." She smoothed down the skirt of her dark red tunic. "It is interesting," she began, her voice slow. "The two of you, together at last. What a turn of events. Makes one wonder what happened in your world, Juliet, for you both to be back here. And on the brink of war, no less."

"What do you know?" Adnan asked. The air grew stifling. I watched the two of them eye one another, Adnan with a masked insistence, and Amarante with her usual devil-may-care ignorance.

"Me? Whatever do you mean?"

"Amarante." His voice was as sharp as steel. "You walk a fine line. You're a smart woman, you know this. Yet you continue to play games. Your power disappeared with Creulon's death. Why continue?"

Her face reddened, paled, and reddened again as Adnan spoke.

"Emperor Hirose has given you asylum here, cared for all your needs. So why?"

Her tongue flicked out over her lips, and she grew taller as her posture straightened. "Why do you care?"

For the first time, I saw her eyes darken. Was that pain?

"Either of you? You both got what you wanted. What am I left with?"

"Your life," Adnan replied.

Chapter Twenty-Seven

Soft footfalls and the rustle of clothing came from behind us. I turned to see Hirose approach, a katana hanging at his side. His hand dropped to its hilt as his gaze traveled past Adnan and me to Amarante. Behind him were two men dressed in black—his guards. They both wore swords.

Mine was missing. It had been left back in the mirror world along with my two knives. I found myself missing the weight, the comfort they had brought me. I shook my head. *They're gone.*

"What is this?" Hirose asked, bringing me back to the present. His tone was different from what I was used to—confident, regal, a demand for an answer.

"Emperor," Amarante greeted, bowing. "We were just speaking of some trivial things."

Trivial? My lips parted to blurt out what we had *really* been speaking of.

"You're dismissed."

Turning from Hirose, I saw Amarante's face whiten once again. She bowed and retreated down the hallway. One of Hirose's men followed and stood vigilant where the corridor ended.

"Now," Hirose said. "What was all that about?" His shoulders relaxed a little, matching the less serious tone of his voice.

"We caught her eavesdropping on us," Adnan replied.

"Ah." Hirose's brow furrowed. "What did she overhear?"

"We're not sure," I put in.

"I shared what I have been helping you with," Adnan interrupted. "So if she heard anything, then she knows what you're working on and what we fear Nordik and Helsingor might do."

Hirose tapped a finger on his sword's hilt. "I'll have someone keep an eye on her since I take it she wasn't honest with you?"

Adnan shook his head. "No, she played her games, or tried to."

Hirose sighed. "Very well. Well, I must go train. Have you gone into the city yet?"

"Not yet," Adnan admitted.

I butted him with my shoulder. "Hopefully soon."

"Market day is coming up. Even if you go before then, make sure you see the city then. It comes alive in ways you can't imagine." Hirose's eyes glistened. "I'll see you both later."

We watched him go, his lithe form quiet and cat-like as he strode out of sight.

"Why do we always seem to get interrupted?" Adnan asked me with a mournful tilt of his head.

"Whatever do you mean?" I teased, trying to look confused in the way my eyes widened. "With Amarante? Or when Hirose came up?"

He snorted. "You know what I mean." He stepped forward, closing the distance between us. My breathing quickened as I laid a hand on his chest. His hair fell forward as he leaned down. I rose on my tiptoes to meet him, warmth surging through my veins as his lips met mine.

⊱ ⊰

The sun continued trekking across the sky, the afternoon passing by. But I didn't feel it. While I knew time continued her slow tick, it didn't feel like it was. Adnan had gone to train, and while I considered joining him, my wrist still ached from when it had broken trying to escape Tristan. Exhaustion crept into my limbs. Back home, I would have drunk a cup of coffee, looking for that extra surge of energy, but here, I resorted to a cup of tea.

It was fragrant. Rice. Nutty. Savory. Sweet. The tastes hit my palate with each sip. I relaxed in front of the window. There were so many times over the past couple of months when windows had been my gateway. This was different. I was free to go outside if I wished. This time, my room was no prison.

A knock sounded on my door. It opened. A maid entered, her dark hair pulled back into a high bun.

She bowed. "I've come to inquire if you would like to join Lady Saya in the baths."

The baths? Oh. The last time I had joined someone in a customary bathing chamber, it had been while in Tristan's mountain fortress.

"The chamber is within the palace," the maid prompted. "I could escort you there?"

I nodded and set my tea down. "Let me grab something to change into after."

"No need," the maid replied. "We have finished sewing some clothes for you. An outfit for tonight will be brought, and the rest will be placed here." She stood to the side of the door.

As I passed her, I murmured my thanks. She bowed again and stepped out of the room. I waited while she closed the door and led me down the corridor.

The way was meandering, though the maid seemed sure of her path. The farther we went, the deeper into the palace we headed. I was blown away a little by how big the palace felt. After we descended two levels, she led me to yet another stairwell headed down.

"I thought we were on the main floor," I said, trying to think if I had miscounted how many stairwells we had gone down.

"We were."

The air grew colder, danker, and the hallway stretching out from the bottom of the stairs was dim. Torches hung in brackets every three yards or so, each burning with a bright flame. The walls were no longer wood. I glanced over my shoulder. It was a corridor cut into the earth. *Tristan's underground hideout.* It smelled similar, musty, earthy, and still. *So quiet.* With the next step, we neared and crossed into a pool of light, before exiting and continuing down towards the next torch. *Where are we going?* A seed of suspicion was sown. The maid almost marched, her posture maintaining the rigidness she'd had since she showed up at my door.

The corridor split into two branches, one veering to the right and the other to the left. We went left.

"Here we are." The maid opened a door set into the wall.

Dank.

The air was even wetter now. I stepped inside, past the maid, and saw Saya sitting in a pool of water, with steam curling up in gentle tendrils. The breath

I'd been holding whooshed past my lips in relief. I heard the soft click of the door closing behind me.

"Juliet!" Saya greeted, lifting her arm to wave. "What do you think?"

At least it wasn't a trap. I glanced about the room. It was a cavern, large, oval, with a man-made ceiling above—at least, I thought it was man-made, but the torchlight failed to reach that far. I strode toward Saya. She sat in a large pool of water, with another nearby, lower, so that the water from the first cascaded into the second.

"It's a lot bigger than the one in the mountain."

Saya nodded. "There is a place there for you to wash up." She studied the water while I undressed, washed at the flowing basin set into the wall, and walked over to the pool.

My fingers touched warm rock as I slid over the rim. "Ahh," I said as the water swirled about my legs. I sat down near Saya and felt tension slide from my body.

"I know," Saya said. Her long, dark hair flowed in the water about her shoulders. "It's a perk of living in the palace."

"So anyone can use this?"

"All right. It's a perk of being an *advisor* in the palace. Only the emperor, his family, and his closest advisors and their families have access."

"Guess I shouldn't be here." My hand slid over the surface of the warm, clear water.

Saya laughed. As the sound died away, her face hardened. "Your side seems to be healing nicely, but what happened to your wrist?"

I glanced down. The weightlessness of the water and the calming heat soothed the pain. "I broke it."

"How?"

My thoughts flashed back to when Adnan had asked the same question, and I had told him. Then to when my parents asked, and I told them I didn't remember. *And Cam.* She had also asked, and I'd told her the truth. A truth that had made my life more difficult.

I focused on Saya. "I jumped from the castle wall."

"*What?*" She leaned forward. "You did *what?*"

I smirked, pride and daring replacing the fear that surrounded that night. "Tristan chased me to the top of the wall, and I jumped."

"Why aren't you dead?"

"There was a rope," I admitted.

Saya shook her head. "Start from the beginning."

So I did. I told her about what happened after she and I had parted ways that night when we'd sought to escape Tristan. How Hirose and his men were blocked in the courtyard, and the moment Tristan saw me, I became his target. There was no way out. It had only been a few weeks since that night, though it felt like a lifetime ago. As I finished, I gestured, and my wrist twanged with pain. It had all happened. It hadn't been that long ago.

I took a deep breath as Saya's face flickered with pain, with amazement, and followed by pity as she processed what I had told her.

"You jumped from the castle wall."

I nodded.

"How did you know to put a rope up there?"

I shrugged. "When I was planning our escape, I thought it would be best to have a backup plan. So I placed a rope up there, just in case. It sounds daring in hindsight, but it was terrifying."

Saya studied the water. "It wasn't like that with me. I got away easily," she said. "It wasn't difficult. I was one of the first to leave. Had I only known—"

"No." I shook my head. "I have had to learn that hard lesson. You can't do that. There was no way for you to know, and there was nothing you could have done."

"You hold no guilt?"

My heart skipped a beat. *Emi.* She had haunted me in the mirror world. I had seen her face in reflections. I had felt her looking over my shoulder. She crept into my nightmares, joining Mari and so many others.

"You still do," Saya whispered. "Emi."

I recoiled as though gut-punched. It was the first time Emi's name had been spoken in a long time. Hearing her name lingering in the air doubled the pain I felt.

"Hirose told me," Saya continued, her tone soft in the cavernous room. "Her death isn't on you. Tristan killed her. There was nothing you could have done."

"I know." Scooting over, I leaned against the rock wall, feeling the sharp edges jab against my back. "I do know that. But it doesn't erase the pain."

"War is never without death, Juliet."

"It's one thing to know that and another to live it," I replied.

Saya grimaced and tucked her long hair back behind her ears. "Yes, but what Hirose is doing, what we all are doing, is building a better life. One where hopefully there won't be any more pain of lives lost."

I thought of the city, of the people of Ryujin, of Saya and Hirose. "And if there is to be war?"

"Then at least this time it will be in true defense of the country, of Ryujin, and of the rightful ruler, an emperor who has a heart for his people. Hirose will sacrifice everything for them." She inhaled, her hands clenched into fists. "Ryujin is ours again."

My head bobbed as I thought. "You believe in him."

"Hirose? Yes, I do. These past few weeks have shown me where his heart is. He has made mistakes, but who hasn't? His goal is the peace and stability of the country—of *his* country and *his* people. I trust him."

"You respect him."

Saya tilted her head back. "I suppose I do. Yes. And I think you will, too, once you get to know him better. I know what he did—"

I flinched.

"And I can't imagine how hard it is to see him and have the past dredged up. I don't believe he is the same person he was then." Saya came closer. "He has good men around him too."

"Ones without any ties to Creulon?" I joked. *Or am I serious?*

"Of course," she said. "None of the advisors served under Creulon. I know it will take time, but he is still working on weeding out anyone who could have any loyalty other than to him. But you can rest assured, these men are honorable."

I stretched my legs out and relaxed. "And you? How are you?"

Saya shrugged. "Better than some, and worse than others, I suppose."

"That's not an answer."

She threw her hands up in the air. "No, you're right. Sometimes I wonder if I'll ever stop thinking of Drielle's death and Tristan's betrayal. They creep in when I'm relaxed, when I least expect them to. It's best to keep busy."

"Do you have trouble sleeping too?"

Saya reached up to touch the dark circles around her eyes. "Don't we all?"

Chapter Twenty-Eight

My boots thumped against the floor, my stride quick and sure. By now, I was fairly confident of the path to the gardens, and I needed fresh air. My conversation with Saya still dwelt in the back of my mind as though it were echoes rebounding in the far recesses. It had helped. Saya had begun to open up. We had shared in tragedy together. Yet there was still the mirror world and my real world, and those mixed with the past five months jumbled together inside my brain.

I turned a corner and almost ran into a short man. His long robe brushed the floor as he bowed, presenting me with a clear sight of his sleek black hair bound into a tight bun on the top of his head.

"My apologies," he muttered, rising back up, his eyes downcast.

"It's all right. I took the corner too fast."

"No, no, my lady. It was my fault." He moved aside and I stepped forward, his steps like echoes to my own. His voice was so deep, strange coming from such a small man. I glanced over my shoulder, watching as the slight figure continued moving away from me. A silver streak went from the left side of his hair up into the bun he wore.

With a shrug, I continued down the hallway.

Ahead, a guard stood next to the small door, a side entrance into the palace gardens. He opened the door as I approached, and I stepped out into the brisk afternoon. The sun lay hidden behind clouds, cooling the air. I clutched my cloak tighter around me, glad for its warmth.

My feet wandered, as did my mind. It felt safe. The stone walls surrounded the garden, keeping people out, but they didn't keep me in. *I could leave.* That assurance meant so much after being kept close by Tristan, by Creulon, and by my parents.

My footsteps slowed. Before me lay the deep green of a large bush along the path. Bright yellow buds adorned its leaves. Leaning down, I inhaled. *Jasmine.* The flowers weren't white, but that heady scent was undeniable. *Mom.* She wore jasmine. Tears glistened in my eyes. Lifting a hand, I touched the smooth firmness of the buds. It was like she was with me. There was some sadness, but intermixed was a shroud of peace. It fell over me like a comforting blanket. My shoulders dropped as my body relaxed.

"Juliet!"

I turned around.

Adnan strode along the path, his long legs eating up the ground. His face darkened. "Are you all right?"

I reached up and dried my eyes on my sleeve. "Jasmine," I explained, gesturing behind me. "Mom wears that scent."

"I'm sorry."

I shook my head. "Don't. It's all right. It's like she's here with me."

He fingered the plant. "Primrose Jasmine. It blooms earlier than other varieties."

"Primrose," I murmured, also turning around. "How soon do you think the buds will open?"

He shrugged. "Give it a couple of days."

"Really?"

"No." A gleam entered his eyes. "I'm no gardener. I have no idea."

I butted him with my shoulder. "You're ridiculous."

"We could find a gardener," he offered.

"No." I slid my hand into his. "I'll just come out here every day to check. It's like a piece of her is out here. Nothing can take those away."

He pulled on me as he stepped away, his pace slow and relaxed. "How was your time with Saya? I heard you were with her."

"Good. It helped."

"I hoped it would. You two have shared much, and she's"—he hesitated—"a woman."

My eyebrows rose. "What? I mean, yes, she is, but what do you mean?"

"You were right. We must be able to talk with one another and be open, but I think having a friend would be good for you also. She needs you as much as you need her."

We passed another Primrose Jasmine bush. It filled the air around it with its perfuming scent.

"Oh," Adnan began. "I'm to tell you that Hirose wants us to join him for dinner tonight. But it won't be just Saya and Miya there."

"His advisors?"

"Yes, as is another." His face, already tan, shifted into a darker hue as he stopped walking. "Afkar Nilsson."

"Afkar Nilsson." I rolled the name around my mouth. "But that sounds like—"

"Yes, he's from Nordik."

Nordik. Tristan's country. "Why is he here?"

"He was sent as an envoy."

"But they haven't even heard yet—"

"No," Adnan said. "No, they haven't. Afkar Nilsson arrived without knowing the events of the past three weeks."

My lips parted.

"*But* he is still due the courtesy of an envoy. Hirose's men will keep a close eye on him, but it does make things more complicated, not only with him being here, but the fact that he brought his own personal guards and staff."

So many eyes.

Adnan studied the ground a moment. "Nilsson has extensive political and military expertise, so he could be valuable to keep around. He's also very knowledgeable of Ryujin, as he has been here before."

"Why did he come?"

Adnan shrugged. "He has not said. Perhaps Nordik knew of the civil unrest and thought it was time to send an emissary."

"The timing though." I chewed on my inner cheek.

"Yes, but it could be circumstantial. He does hold lands here. When Nordik invaded Ryujin and won, Nilsson's family was gifted lands—lands that had been taken by one of the daimyos."

"And those are still his lands?" I questioned as a bird swooped low over our heads to land in the blossoming branches of a cherry tree. It cocked its head as though listening to our every word.

"For now, though, I doubt it will remain that way. This country is Nordik's no longer, and so the lands do not belong to them. He no longer has a claim. They will be returned to the family who owned them before, or gifted to someone if there are no living descendants."

The bird spread its wings and dove off the tree before flying back up to disappear over the high stone wall. A gust of air blew through the garden and I shivered, burying my hands under my cloak.

"Tonight should be interesting." It was all I managed to say. *What else can I say?*

"Yes. Hirose has a bigger part to play now."

"And he's only been emperor a few weeks."

Adnan peered up at the sky. "I don't envy him." He looked back down. "It might rain. Ready to go back in?"

I nodded and walked alongside him, my arm brushing his every now and then. "How did you know where to find me?"

"When you weren't in your room, I figured this might be a good place to look. The fresh air helps you think, doesn't it? Same for me." Adnan slowed and touched my left arm. "Juliet?"

I stopped, and time seemed to still. The air around us grew heavy with anticipation. "Yes?" I breathed when nothing was said.

"You're more resilient than you realize."

I fought to hold back the mirth bubbling up inside. *Resilient?* Somehow, I had expected something serious, heavy, and wasn't prepared for what he did say.

"I mean it." He pulled me closer. "I've never met a woman quite like you."

I flipped my hair over my shoulder. "I'll take that as a compliment."

Adnan let out an exasperated sigh. "I mean it. You are a strong, brave, loyal, *wonderful* woman, Juliet Barrows."

As he spoke, the glee I felt faded and was replaced by yearning. "I think I love you even more now," I murmured.

He leaned closer. "Do you?"

"Aw, there you both are!"

Adnan broke away from me with a muffled oath. "Always interrupted," he muttered.

Saya waved as she walked toward us.

"Guess we should leave," I teased.

"Glad I found you!" Saya called as she approached.

Adnan murmured something under his breath that I couldn't catch.

"You could've sent a maid," I said.

"I wanted the fresh air," she retorted. "Though it looks like it's going to rain soon."

"That's what I said." Adnan threaded his fingers through mine. "We were heading back when you found us."

"Hmm, yes, it looked like it."

My face warmed.

"What is it?" Adnan asked, changing the subject.

Saya tensed. "Word came from Mongul." She glanced at me. "It's a nation that borders Nordik. They've asked for confirmation as to who now rules Ryujin if the rumors are true."

Adnan muttered another oath. "Which means Nordik will have found out by now."

"Yes." Saya glanced between the two of us. "But it's not enough time for a rescue attempt. Tristan will be executed soon."

"Why not give him back to them?" I asked, and saw Saya and Adnan almost glaring at me. "What?"

Adnan crossed his arms. "So he can just come back and try to take over again?"

"We *cannot* do that," Saya said. "He knows too much. No, whatever happens with Nordik, Tristan dies in two days' time."

I stiffened as I stood there. "Does the envoy know that?"

"He hasn't been told," Adnan answered, his voice low. "But it's not impossible."

"That's not all."

Not all. I waited for Saya to speak. *What's next?*

"I had a vision this morning." Saya hesitated, as though unsure of her next words.

There was something in her tone. Something that was heavy, deep, as though an inner turmoil. *She's holding something back.*

"About Amarante."

Time seemed to slip by faster as I unfroze. Thoughts flickered faster through my mind, and my body felt looser. Yet I didn't think that was what had been holding Saya back. There was something else.

"I don't know what it means," Saya admitted. "She was—" She hesitated again. "It seemed like she was in a compromising position. I couldn't see the man's face, but she wanted something—information, it seemed. Afterward, she was satisfied with herself, like she had gotten what she wanted."

One of Adnan's thick eyebrows rose, and he stroked his jaw.

I threw up my hands. "And?"

"Who and why?" Adnan asked.

"I don't know," Saya confessed. "I know it's not much, but—"

"It's enough to bring more suspicion on her," Adnan finished.

"Yes."

My head shook from side to side. "What are you talking about? I'm lost here."

"Amarante wanted information—*needed* it," Saya explained. "She got what she wanted from the man she was with. She was up to something in my vision."

Ah. I chewed on my inner cheek as I thought. *For someone else or for her own gain?* History had shown her to do things only for herself. *Why change now?* But visions were hard to decipher sometimes. We had already seen that in the past few months. One thing looked like another, and so on.

"Hirose is considering taking your advice," Saya said to Adnan. "She's dangerous, and now, with that vision, we don't know what to expect."

"Does she know?" I asked, crossing my arms over my chest. Adnan grinned, and I realized I was mirroring his stance. Rolling my eyes, I returned my attention to Saya.

"Yes. Hirose has already spoken to her. He didn't give her any details about the vision, just that I had a vision about her. She denied doing or planning anything that would jeopardize this country or Hirose's rule."

"And now she knows she's under suspicion." Adnan sighed, and his shoulders relaxed. "We'll see what happens now."

Chapter Twenty-Nine

My image reflected in the clear glass. Behind me, the maid who had come to help me dress fluttered about the room, tidying up, paying no heed to me. Squaring my shoulders, I drew my head up and took a deep breath. A knock sounded on the door.

It was time.

I nodded to the maid, who slid the door open. Adnan stood there, dressed in dark green, almost black in hue. His hair was sleek and shiny and was half-tied up in his normal hairdo. I walked forward to join him, enjoying the way his eyes traveled over me before lighting on my face.

"You look lovely." He bowed and offered me his arm.

My insides warmed, and I could feel my face reflecting that. "Thank you."

He tucked me in closer to his side. "Hirose has good taste or knows someone who does. Blue is my favorite color on you."

Not green? I wanted to ask, but felt frozen even though we still walked. *Green was Tristan's favorite.* I licked my lips. "Why blue?"

"Because blue brings out the blue in your eyes." He reached over and tapped the intricate bun holding my hair. "And it brings out the lightness of the blonde." His hand lowered. "And did I mention your eyes are actually more green than blue, so when you wear blue, they appear darker?"

I chuckled.

He smirked and stopped. "Now, my lady, are you ready for dinner?"

I started in surprise. A double set of doors stood before us. I hadn't even noticed until now the guards standing on either side. *Hirose's private guard.* As one, the two men each slid a door open. The room was rectangular, formal, dark, and yet inviting. Hangings adorned the walls, depicting flowering plants, birds, and other things from nature. They lay in shadow, barely reached by the light flickering from the candles arranged on and near the table.

We stepped into the room. There were two empty seats at the almost-full table. Several dark-haired faces turned to us, and amongst them, I thought I recognized Hirose's advisors. A couple of women sat in their mix. Wives, maybe?

Hirose gestured, welcoming us, and Saya and Miya sent us welcoming looks. These were our friends. Except one.

Afkar Nilsson.

He watched us with a wan wariness, his face long and weathered.

My step faltered. Brown where Tristan was blond, but sharing the same build. The light from the candles flickered in those blue-gray depths. He didn't look away as we neared, and it didn't break, even as I sat across from him, on Hirose's right. I felt Adnan brush against my side as he sat next to me. The man across the table reminded me of a hawk: strong, swift, sure. *A man used to being listened to.*

He blinked, long and slow, and turned his head to Hirose, who began speaking.

"Benkei, Juliet, this is Afkar Nilsson, an envoy from Nordik."

The man in question must have sensed someone watching, as he swiveled his head like a bird to look back at me. I couldn't look away, Hirose's voice filling the room as a sharp background noise. Nilsson's eyes were blue—a startling blue. *Like Tristan's. Like mine. We're all from the west.* The innkeeper's probing came back to haunt my thoughts. He'd been the first to wonder if I was from the west. It had taken me some time before I realized he meant Nordik.

"Nilsson is here as a guest and is under my protection while he remains here." Hirose's voice was steely. "Please treat him with the courtesy an envoy of another nation deserves."

Nilsson arched one thin brow.

I'm the one who isn't looking away. A shiver passed over my body. *Why? He's just a man—a man who reminds me of Tristan.* My hands trembled.

"Benkei, Juliet."

It was the first time he'd spoken, and his voice was deep and low, burly for one so tall and slender. It was the strong, piercing sound of a great bird calling its challenge across the skies.

"I am glad to finally meet you." His voice was slow and meticulous.

"Afkar Nilsson."

I shook myself as Adnan's voice rent the air. He bowed, a sign of respect. A finger jabbed me in the thigh. I bit back a muffled protest and inclined my head also. The back of my neck prickled. Someone was watching me.

Afkar Nilsson.

"Juliet Barrows, the *Otherworlder*," he said.

My body froze. That name had been spoken once, by the guards at the palace entrance, but this was different. The emphasis brought back all the ways Creulon and Tristan had both used it—me—for their own gain.

A hand brushed my leg. A question stirred in the depths of Adnan's green eyes, and a muscle pulsed in his neck. I licked my lips and turned back to Afkar Nilsson.

"Yes, Juliet is the *Otherworlder*," Hirose began. "But that is a title we need not use."

My heart thumped. *How does he know?* Those words, spoken by Hirose, closed the rift between us even more. I nodded to him, hoping he could tell how grateful I was. For all he had done to me, he was setting aside what had been and was protecting me.

"Of course," Nilsson said, inclining his head to me. "I meant no disrespect. It is a title I had heard overseas, and rumors circulate still, even here. It is a title of mystery, and I confess I do not fully know why you have that title, or what you did during the Uprising, or in the events since." He turned to Hirose. "But I know that is a weighty topic, and one that we do not need to dwell on while we eat."

No. This man could know the truth, what had happened, how I was instrumental in bringing down Creulon, and then Tristan, but not from me, and not here. My hands clenched into fists in my lap, hidden under the table. Creulon was dead, but Tristan was now in the dungeons awaiting his death. And above him, an ally dined with the emperor. I swallowed, the room appearing darker in hue to match my dampening mood.

Hirose shook his head. "No, not now. Let us speak of other things."

I breathed out a sigh of relief. Pressure on my leg reminded me of Adnan's hand still there. The others began speaking in loud voices and drank their wine.

Adnan leaned over and whispered in my ear, "Are you all right?"

"Yes," I murmured.

"You seem tense."

I forced my shoulders to relax and took my glass. "To whatever comes next."

The suspicion radiating from Adnan's posture didn't dissipate, but he did raise his own glass. "Together."

We drank. The rice wine trickled down my throat, cool and sharp. Over its rim, I regarded Afkar Nilsson. He was a man who had been expected to come to a country under the rule of another. Now he had to embrace change. I knew how that felt, and on a far larger scale than he. *He doesn't know what it means to survive.* He hadn't had to endure what I did, what we all did. *I* had changed. Almost every one of us sitting at this table had—Hirose, Miya, Saya, Adnan, and I. There was no going back. There was only forward.

This world.

Ryujin.

My roots were no longer in one world, but two.

⚜

Food helped. So did conversation. Nothing more had been spoken of Creulon, or of Tristan, or of me being the Otherworlder. I listened to talk about the country, of good times past, of hopes for the future. As we ate and drank, my fears faded.

Nilsson spoke little. A smooth and confident talker, he helped spur the conversation forward and would listen attentively while others spoke.

I could almost forget where he's from, who he is. I took another sip of wine, also listening. The wine had softened my tension, each sip erasing a little more, until all that was left was me wishing I had a chair to lean back in.

Not like at home. No. I winced as I realized I had been shaking my head with the thought. Setting the glass down, I eyed it. *No more. You've had enough, Juliet.* I moved to set my elbows on the table so I could rest my chin on them, but resisted. *Not polite. You're not home.* My place, in my world, was one without emperors. *A place with chairs. Chairs with backs.* I nodded and fought a yawn. *I said goodbye to that life.* The conversation around me was but a blur.

The only way forward.

Another girl stood in my place, in my home, in my world. *She's me, and yet not me.* Peace filled my heart. *My parents have her.* I had run from reality. Now I embraced my memories. They were all I had from home.

"Juliet?"

I jumped. Adnan stood above me, his hand stretched down. Everyone else had also risen and was heading for the door.

"Are you coming?" he asked.

I took his hand. It was strong. Firm. My thoughts all drifted away with the wind as his grip grounded me. He pulled me up, and I swayed a moment before finding my balance.

"Too much to drink?"

"Shh," I blurted out, glancing over my shoulder. No one paid us any attention.

Adnan snorted but threaded my arm through his and led us out of the room. "Do you drink much?" His face was void of expression. "Trying to figure out if this is a side of you that I haven't seen before, and is normal, or if this is—"

"No, no." I shook my head and felt a pin loosen. My hand rose in a dramatic wave. "This is *not* normal for me." My lips curved up. The smile on my face froze. *Though it happened at Creulon's court.*

Adnan frowned. "I—" He was interrupted as Saya almost jumped in front of us.

"Juliet, could I speak to you?" She shot an apologetic glance at Adnan. "Sorry if I'm stealing her away from you."

"Of course not," he replied.

I nodded to Saya, my curiosity piqued. Adnan moved away from me, and with him went the warmth I'd felt having him at my side.

"What is it?" I asked, following her down the hallway. "Is everything all right?"

She rolled her eyes.

Like Cam. The thought tore through my mind before I could stop it.

"Yes," Saya replied. "Nothing's wrong. I just—" She paused as we strode through a doorway into a small, empty room. "I just wanted to tell you, to ask you ..."

"What?" I asked again when nothing was said.

"Will you stay longer? Please? I need you," she whispered. "I'm not asking you to stay years, or even months. Just please stay at least another week or two. You're my only friend." Wetness shone in her eyes. "I've *never* had a friend, Juliet. Not a real one. Not like what we have."

"Saya—"

"I know I can't make you stay, even if I wish I could." She chuckled. "And the day after tomorrow—" Tears ran down her cheeks as she continued. "I know you'll be leaving soon. And you should, you and Adnan both, but please consider staying longer."

My eyes mirrored hers as tears threatened to fall. Throwing my arms around her, I drew her into a hug. "Saya, I love you. I wish I could stay," I whispered over her shoulder. "But it's best for us if we leave. Maybe not forever, but for a while at least."

Saya pulled away. "I know." A shaky laugh escaped her lips as she brushed away her tears.

An idea dawned. *The innkeeper. Umi no Machi.* "Why don't you take time and go away too?"

She shook her head, tendrils of hair escaping from her bun. "No, no."

"Why not?" I pressed. "Go back to Umi no Machi, see the innkeeper—"

"Juliet!" Saya replied. "I can't leave right now. Hirose needs me. And I need to be here." She tucked the loose hair behind her ears. "I think I will go crazy if I go back to Umi no Machi," she admitted. "I'm not ready to face the questions, the nosiness. Here, I'm accepted for who I am. I'm one of Hirose's advisors. He values what I think, and I'm *helping*." Her shoulders and face softened. "Here, I'm needed. I think you know how much that can mean."

I bit my lip and nodded.

"The innkeeper knows I'm all right," Saya said. "I invited him here, but he's too afraid to visit. Says the city is too big, and the palace is not for him."

"It is big, at least in comparison to Umi no Machi," I agreed.

Saya laughed and dried the last of her tears from her face. "You'll write, won't you?"

I fought to keep my voice from breaking. "Yes."

"Good."

"And you?" I questioned, reaching up to brush the tears from my cheeks with my thumbs. "Mongul, Nordik, Helsingor ..." The names felt foreign on my tongue. "You'll be all right?"

"Ryujin has endured much. We can endure more."

I nodded but couldn't erase the doubt stretching its fingers into my soul. *Ryujin needs Hirose and Saya. But what about us?* How could we leave while danger lurked on the doorstep of those we love?

"I should go," Saya admitted. "We have an early council in the morning, and I am *exhausted*." She motioned to the open doorway. "You coming?"

"In a moment. You go. Hope you sleep well."

Saya's eyes blackened. We both knew how nights were. We both knew how much lingered in the shadows, in the quiet silence that darkness brought.

"You too," she said and turned. Her footsteps faded on the wood floor as she walked out of sight.

I threw my head back and drew in a deep breath. She was right. Our days here were ending. And with that, my wedding was approaching. I thought of my fiancé. *My fiancé.* My left hand rose. There was no engagement ring there. Nothing to show that I was to be married. *Not like home,* I reminded myself. The blue of my tightly fit sleeve caught my eye. *His favorite color.* A gentle heat blossomed in my heart and soul. Soon he would be mine, and I would be his.

I spun in a slow circle.

His wife. Forever.

My slipper-like shoes caught against one another, almost pitching me forward. Catching my balance, arms stretched out, I straightened. It was time for bed.

A yawn threatened to split my jaw.

I headed for the door and rounded the corner. Thump. Something firm and unyielding stood in my way. With a yelp, I backed away a step. Not something. *Who.* I swallowed.

Afkar Nilsson.

"Sorry," I murmured. "I should have been paying attention." *Why is he here?* My neck popped as I craned my neck to look around him. *Why is he alone?*

He didn't move a muscle. "Nothing to worry about. It was a simple mistake. No harm done."

I nodded and made to move past him, but he didn't budge. "Is there something you wanted?"

"No." He gave himself a slight shake and moved to the side. "If anything, only to say that you are as breathtaking as the rumors have said. An exotic creature."

A shiver ran over my skin.

He inclined his head. "Have a good night, Otherworlder."

Chapter Thirty

"There is something about Afkar Nilsson," I murmured, folding my arms across my chest. "I can't place my finger on it. Something just seems off."

"That's not surprising," Adnan said. "The man is an enemy."

"I know, but there's something."

"What?"

I grunted. "That's just it. I don't know."

"His loyalty is to Nordik, but he also has lands here. He might be convinced to play both sides." Adnan laid his hands on my arms. "I know it's all more complicated now, but this isn't on you. Avoid him if you can, and let Hirose handle it."

"I know, I know." Shifting my weight, I shrugged. "You're right. It's just, something about him." *He reminds me of Tristan.*

"Is there something else?" Adnan asked, examining me.

I winced.

"Juliet?"

Shaking Tristan out of my head, I replied, "Nothing."

Adnan watched me with a grim twist to his lips. "Hirose has assured me that he's keeping an eye on Nilsson. Try not to dwell on it."

My skin tingled where his hands touched me.

Rap, rap, rap.

Adnan's hands dropped away. The knock came again.

It's not the maid. She would just come in.

Adnan glanced at me before walking to the door. He spoke to someone in a low voice. I stepped forward, craning to see who it was, but the door slid closed.

"I have to go. Hirose needs me," Adnan said, turning around to face me. My heart sank. *It won't be long. Just find something to do.*

"Wait!" I ran my fingers through my hair and twisted it back into a low bun. "Let me come too."

Adnan hesitated.

"Please."

He nodded. "Come on, then."

There was a spring in my step as I ran forward to join him.

"This way I can keep an eye on you."

My neck craned as I looked up at him. "What is that supposed to mean?"

"You *do* have a propensity for getting into trouble." The smirk he sent my way softened any sting. His words were an echo of what he had said weeks before to me. A different time. A different life.

It's better now. I slid my arm through his as we walked the palace hallways. *We have each other.* A happy fog hung over me, distracting me from the path we took. When Adnan stopped, I realized we stood before a door.

"Where are we?" We stood in a small anteroom, with a square opening behind us and a dark paneled wood wall beyond that. The room was bare, as though not in use. It was yet another corner tucked away in the palace.

"Hirose's council chamber. The less formal one. Ready?" Without waiting for an answer, he opened the door, and we entered. Five heads swiveled: Saya, Hirose, and three other men—Hirose's advisors. All three had been at dinner the night before.

"Benkei," Hirose greeted before nodding to me. "And Juliet. You are welcome here."

One of the advisors shifted his weight. "But she is not—"

Hirose held up a hand, forestalling the man. "She is always welcome within these chambers."

The advisor's face reddened, but he said nothing more.

"I can leave," I murmured, hesitating, trying to remember the names of the advisors.

"No, come." Hirose beckoned to me. "I'm glad you both are here. Two days ago, we received word from Mongul, requesting confirmation on the change of"—Hirose paused, considering—"leadership. We have yet to send word, though it is prepared and ready."

"Why wait?" I asked. *Juliet!* It was too late to take back the question.

The advisor, who had spoken before, snorted.

"No, it's a good question," Hirose said. "While it is very likely that Nordik has already heard the rumors as well, we want to give as long as we possibly can to confirm said rumors. Once Mongul receives our reply, there will be no doubt that Nordik will know shortly after." Hirose swept a hand over the table's surface. A map sat on its surface, larger than any I had seen, and covered with fine lettering and intricate drawings. "The northern borders are shored up. That was one of the first moves we made after I was crowned emperor."

"My lord—"

Shuji. The name snapped into my thoughts.

"We already know this," the advisor, Shuji, said.

"Juliet does not, and I would like for her to be acquainted with the details before we begin what we are here to discuss."

Shuji inclined his head without looking at me.

I shouldn't have come. Now it was two advisors who had reason to dislike my interference.

Adnan's shoulder brushed against my own.

"But the reality is that it was by ship that Nordik took Ryujin centuries ago," Hirose continued. "The south is still our weakest point. They may know this, and if they attack, may come the same way."

I lurched a little. *But…*

"Juliet?" Hirose asked, motioning for me to speak.

"Wouldn't they think you *would* think that and so attack elsewhere?"

"Possibly," he agreed. "But we must consider it, nonetheless. Now." He pointed down at the map, drawing our attention. "Helsingor is still in negotiations with us, so while the north is protected the best it can be with the resources we have, we don't need to overtly worry about an attack. They may try a small raid, but it would be to test us, and we are ready for something of that scale." Hirose moved his finger to the west. "Here is Mongul, about a two-week journey." He again moved his hand and tapped on a large country just northwest of Mongul. "Nordik."

I leaned over, peering at the country. It was larger than Ryujin. *Tristan's country. Has he ever even been there?*

"Now we come to why we're meeting here." Hirose swept the six of us with his dark scrutiny. "Our army is almost nonexistent. Whilst under the rule of Nordik, we have had very small reserves, and the training has been deficient. Those men are currently holding the northern borders under the command of a few of my men."

The Black Guard. The elite. The men Hirose had commanded, and who now were his personal guard.

"We need an army, and quickly. I can spare more from my guard to train them."

Shuji tapped his chin with a thin finger. "It is time to recruit once again. It is something we have not done in many years."

"Where do we begin?" It was the advisor who had questioned Hirose. He crossed his arms over his chest, his face reflecting the flickering light from the torches ringing the square room.

Shuji laid his hands on the table. "What about Tristan's men?"

Hirose shook his head. "I thought about that, but no. They have disbanded back to their homes, or wherever they came from. Their loyalty was to Tristan."

"Isn't it to their country?" I asked.

Saya cocked her head to the side as she considered my question.

"Go on," Hirose encouraged.

"They fought for Tristan because they wanted a better life. They wanted freedom. Isn't that the same as why you want an army? Ryujin is threatened. If you have the resources to offer payment, then wouldn't they come?"

"Does anyone disagree with Juliet?" Hirose asked, gazing around the table.

Shuji steepled his fingers. "In essence, it makes sense, and yet why would they trust us?"

"You hold a lot of sway in your lands," Adnan said. "If the daimyos could be convinced, if they have backed the new emperor's rule, then they could encourage the able men in their lands to join."

"But that would take time," Shuji replied. "Time we don't have."

"Is it the only option though?" I pressed back.

"Unless—" Adnan began, but hesitated. "Unless you have the money to hire an army."

"Mercenaries?" someone spat. It was the other advisor, one who hadn't spoken until now. His eyes were stormy with spite. "Benkei, we know your past, but—"

"Enough." Hirose raised his hands in the air. "I, also, have considered mercenaries. But that is a short-term solution only. Even if we do so, we need to put into effect a long-term solution. And Juliet is right." He gestured to me. "We need an army. A functioning force for defense."

The advisor who had lashed out spoke. "We have the resources, the funds, to build an army. It will take time, but we could put all of this into motion today."

"It's a good plan," Shuji said. "Rather than targeting Tristan's followers directly, we could use the daimyos to let the people know."

I watched as Hirose nodded, his lips thin as he concentrated. *He wants this,* I realized. He had his own plan, but he wanted the advisors to be involved, and he was pleased that they were going exactly in the direction he wanted. *Smart play.*

"Training grounds," Shuji added. "And we also need ..."

His voice faded as I turned my attention to Adnan. Serious, bold, and dignified. He belonged here, amongst the advisors, planning the future of the nation. No, he belonged at my side. Pride filled my heart. His silhouette was different than the others. The light from the torches lit his face, accentuating the green of his eyes and the brown, almost black, close-cropped beard covering his cheeks and jaw. *Tall, dark, and handsome.*

Sensing me watching, he glanced down at me.

What? he mouthed.

I shook my head and returned my attention to the table. *Nothing. Nothing at all. Because I'm at your side.*

Chapter Thirty-One

I pulled my cloak on, a well-made, thick piece of material. The dark gray-blue matched that of the skies outside as the sun rose, casting its pale light through the dreary clouds billowing across the sky.

Miya had invited Saya and me to go riding. I hadn't ridden since being in Creulon's court, but I found myself looking forward to it. New experiences needed to be forged. Horseback could be something pleasurable, not shaded in darkness and need. Always, riding a horse had been fraught with trepidation, danger, or a sense of urgency.

Not now.

Flicking my loose hair over my shoulders, I tied it back in a half-updo, keeping most of my blonde locks out of my face. With a quick glance in the mirror, I nodded, satisfied that I was ready. As I turned to go, I froze. A piece of white paper lay on the floor, partially under the doorframe.

Tristan.

He had left me notes like this. Today was his execution. Air hissed through my clenched teeth as I inhaled. It couldn't be his note. The air felt heavy, as though threatening to suffocate me. *Stop, Juliet. It's just a piece of paper.*

Breathing once more, I forced myself to pick up the paper. My hands trembled as I opened it.

You might want to know that Tristan is planning an escape.

~ A

A? Tristan. Crumpling it in my fist, I bolted out of the room. I ignored the looks of surprise on the faces I passed as I flew down the hallway, through a split into another one, and came to a stop before Adnan's door.

Thump, thump, thump. The sound was muffled as it carried into the bedroom beyond. It repeated. This time, I heard faint footsteps approach on the other side.

The door opened, and I pushed my way past Adnan, half-hidden behind the door. I turned around and froze. He stood there, shirtless. My eyes wouldn't leave his shirtless torso. He was lean, but his muscles rippled. My heartbeat quickened.

His eyes traveled down and back up. "Ah. I'll fetch a shirt." He slid the door closed. Feeling my cheeks burn, I waited, my foot tapping on the ground.

His eyes narrowed as he returned. "What's wrong?"

I handed him the piece of paper.

He scanned it and turned, calling over his shoulder, "We need to speak to Hirose."

"Do you think it's real?"

Adnan grabbed a shirt and pulled it over his head. "Better safe than sorry."

❦

Hirose's hand drummed on the table next to the note. "Adnan, please alert the guard. Juliet, do you know who gave this to you?"

Adnan walked away as I shook my head, feeling my hair swirl through the air with the motion. *Wait.* Frozen, I stared again at the *A*. There was only one who could've written that, whose name began with an *a. How did I miss it?*

"Amarante."

Hirose's eyes widened. "Give me a moment." He shoved the paper into his pocket. "We'll address that later." He donned black leather over his tunic and strapped on his katana. "Come."

I followed him to the doorway, where Adnan waited.

"One of your men went to gather others and will meet us there."

"Where are we going?" I asked.

"The dungeon." Adnan laid his hands on my upper arms. "Why don't you stay here?"

I shook my head. "No, I'm coming with you."

"Juliet, please—"

Hirose shook his head. "We don't have time for this."

"I know I don't need your permission to go," I hissed at Adnan. "But I'd like you to be okay with it."

Adnan sighed. "All right, but stay close to me."

Both men were silent as we followed Hirose's remaining guard deeper into the palace. Our step was quick, and as I watched Hirose's hand firm on his sword's hilt, I wished for my own weapons back. They had rarely crossed my mind since I'd left the mirror world, and them behind, but now? Now I realized that I would never really leave them behind.

We descended two levels, down to the main floor. At the end of a corridor, I saw half a dozen black-clad men clustered around a doorway. They stood to the side, quiet and ready, as we approached.

"Emperor," one greeted with a bow, stepping forward. "The men are ready—"

Hirose's eyes narrowed. "Where are the guards?"

"They weren't here." His words, while quiet, seemed to ring through the narrow corridor. Behind him lay the open entryway into the dungeons.

Hirose's face darkened. "Let's go."

Two men grabbed torches out of their brackets on the wall and led the way.

"Stay close," Adnan whispered.

"Juliet!"

My name rang out from behind us. Craning my head, I saw Saya approaching at a run. Seeing Adnan hesitate, Hirose and the guards disappearing down to the dungeons, I motioned. "Go. I'll wait here."

He nodded and ran after the emperor and the Black Guard. His footsteps mingled with those of Saya as she ran up, her breathing heavy.

"I saw you come this way, but you didn't hear me call out. What's going on?" Her eyes roved between me and the empty doorway behind me. "I was looking for you. You didn't meet Miya and me in the stables."

The horseback ride. I'd forgotten. "A note was left under my door this morning. A warning of Tristan attempting to escape."

Saya paled, her ivory complexion in stark contrast to her dark hair framing her face. For once, she wore it down in a relaxed fashion, matching that of the simple cloak and tunic beneath.

"That's where they've gone." I gestured over my shoulder.

"You think he has escaped?" Saya trilled, her tone higher than usual.

"We'll soon find out." *Please, please, no.* My lips parted, but I froze as Saya's eyes widened. She was focused on something behind me.

"Well."

"Juliet!" Saya shrieked almost at the same time as the voice uttered that one word.

Chills ran over my body as I spun around. *Tristan.* Two guards stood next to him, their weapons raised. Light glinted off the blades. Muffled footsteps pounded, but they sounded distant to my ears as I backed up a step, fighting the terror as I locked on the man who had betrayed me. All else faded away, but I could hear my heartbeat thrumming inside my chest. Figures filled the doorway and Tristan lunged. A hand caught his shoulder. The guard at his side spun.

So did I.

The hand, small but strong, pulled me away, and I lost my footing. Walls. Ceiling. My head cracked against stone. Saya crouched over me, her hair falling to cover her face.

Someone yelled. Or maybe multiple people. Black surged in at the edges of my vision.

No.

Chapter Thirty-Two

There were sounds first. Distant, as though I heard voices at the end of a long tunnel. My eyes drifted open. Blurry. I blinked and things began to come into focus. Propped up a little, I saw the wall beyond first. A slight breeze blew through the room from the open window.

My bedroom.

"Juliet." A strong hand grasped mine, where it lay on the quilt. "I'm here."

Adnan.

My eyes fluttered shut and opened again, focusing in on Adnan, who sat next to my bed.

He reached up with his free hand to smooth my hair back from my face. "How are you feeling?"

The dungeons. Tristan.

I lunged upright and my head began to throb.

"Whoa, careful now." Adnan eased me back down. "Just take it easy."

"What happened? Is Tristan—"

"Back in the dungeon," he supplied. "Saya pulled you back from him, but you cracked your head in the process. It was enough to make you pass out. Hirose had his doctor look you over." Adnan rubbed slow circles on the back of my hand with his thumb. "And here I thought you'd be safer waiting with Saya."

I rolled my eyes. "See? Better if we're together."

"Always."

"What did the doctor say?"

Adnan cocked his head to the side. "Said you'll be fine."

The bedroom door slid open and Saya peeked her head in. Seeing I was awake, she rushed in and fell to her knees beside my mat.

"Juliet! You're awake. I'm so sorry!"

"It's all right!" I protested, pulling my left hand out of her grasp. "How long was I out?"

"Just a few minutes," Adnan replied. "We didn't know if you were badly injured, though, so we brought you here. The doctor left just a couple of minutes before you woke up, but he'll be back to check on you later."

Saya and Adnan exchanged glances.

"What?" I asked, peering between the two of them. "What's going on?"

Saya shook her head. "Nothing."

"Tell me, please," I added.

Adnan sighed. "There is still the issue of the letter to be resolved."

"Amarante."

Adnan and Saya gaped at me.

"It was signed with an A. Who else could it have been?"

A light dawned in Saya's eyes. "Of course. The vision I had, we thought that meant she was up to no good, but what if what I saw was her trying to get the information?"

I nodded. "And by you and Hirose confronting her, she knew even more that she was on a fine line and that she needed to prove herself."

"We'll need to question her," Adnan broke in. "How did she suspect there was going to be an escape attempt? Is there something else she hasn't been telling us?"

"There is one thing more." Saya's face seemed paler. "Hirose has delayed Tristan's execution."

My heart skipped a beat. "When?"

"Two days, but I think it's tentative. He wants answers first."

"It's a delay tactic," I murmured under my breath.

Saya leaned closer. "What?"

"A delay tactic," Adnan repeated for me. "Could be. Though I very much believe his escape attempt was in earnest. But either way, yes, his execution does need to wait until after he's questioned."

So much to do. Fear pulsed in every part of my body. I pushed back the covers, along with the numbing feeling fear spread over me. "Let's go, then."

Adnan let go of my hand. "What are you doing?"

"We need to speak with Amarante."

Adnan regarded me.

I felt he could see into my soul, see the fear lying there.

"Hirose will take care of that."

"He's right," Saya agreed. "And if Hirose requires us, he'll send for us. As for you, I've sent for breakfast for the three of us. It should be here shortly."

"But—"

Saya chuckled. "The *emperor* will take care of things. Don't worry. All you need to do is rest, recover from that headache I'm sure you have based off that pinched expression on your face, and eat. I'll stay with you, and I'm sure Benkei will too."

My head turned so I could look at Adnan. He nodded.

"I'm not leaving."

⚹⚹⚹⚹

The food had been cleared away and was gone. I cupped the porcelain mug in my hands, enjoying the warmth seeping through onto my skin. The tea was comforting and relaxing. Adnan and Saya nursed cups of their own. We were all silent, enjoying the feeling of full stomachs and hot tea on a crisp morning. Adnan's shoulder brushed my own from where he sat on my mattress, our backs to the wall.

A knock preceded the door opening. Hirose stepped through, and as one, we all straightened.

He held up a hand. "No need to rise." He sat down on a floor mat near Saya, facing Adnan and me. "Tristan is refusing to talk, which is no surprise. The guards are also proving resilient and stubborn. My men are working on them."

A shiver ran down my spine at the ominous way he'd spoken.

"As for Amarante, she refuses to talk without you there, Juliet."

"What? Me?"

Hirose nodded. "Yes. If you are feeling up to it, I would like you to come with me." Seeing me nod, he continued. "Benkei, Saya, you may come as well, but I would like for you to remain in the outer room." He rose and waited as we all followed.

Why me?

⁕⁂⁕

"Juliet Barrows." Amarante knelt on a floor mat. She barely spared a glance at Hirose once she had bowed. Now we sat before her, Hirose and I, with the door behind us closed. There were no guards. Just the three of us.

"Amarante."

"You have many questions, I know. How did I find out? Why the note? Why leave it under *your* door?"

I nodded. She was asking all the questions I wanted answers to. Silent, I waited as Amarante folded her hands in her lap.

"First, how. That one is simple." Amarante's lashes brushed her cheeks in a demure manner, but she didn't redden in the slightest as she proceeded. "After being told that Lady Saya had a vision, I realized I was walking a fine line here, and I did not want to be sent away. So, I sought after something that could prove myself—"

Hirose motioned for her to continue.

"Or begin to," Amarante said. "I had heard the rumors, same as everyone else, about Tristan's execution. There had to be something planned. Would he—or anyone, really—not try an escape? So, I began to work on the guards and soon set on one whom I found to be a little shiftier and more close-lipped than the rest." Amarante shrugged. "I found out the information I needed."

"How?"

Amarante cast Hirose a sly look. "Do you really want to know? Fine. I worked my womanly charm upon him. It's worked before, so why not now?"

I squirmed a little even as I came to the realization. She had lived out Saya's vision. She'd seduced the guard to get information—information she could give us about Tristan. What Saya had seen had happened, but we had been the instigators.

"Now, the note. It seemed simple enough, and best for getting the information to you in a timely manner. Juliet had to have been in her rooms at the hour, and I needed her to be the one to receive it."

"Why?" Hirose asked. "Why her and not me? Or even one of my guards?"

"Because I knew *she* would take it seriously."

She's right. Whether Amarante had signed her note or not, I wouldn't have just dismissed the warning. Not when it came to Tristan.

"I think it is a little dramatic," Hirose noted. "Tristan almost did make his escape. What if Juliet hadn't been leaving when she did? What if Juliet hesitated? Or Benkei, when Juliet told him?" His voice grew. "What if *I* had hesitated when they came to me?"

"Then Tristan would be gone," Amarante supplied in a smooth voice. "But it didn't happen that way."

"No, it didn't, but your antics could have been detrimental." Hirose rose. "I'll think further on this."

Amarante's face paled a shade. "You do believe me, don't you?"

Yes. It fit her. The drama, the drive, the determination.

"We'll see." Hirose turned away.

He doesn't believe her.

Rising, I followed him, unable to escape seeing Amarante raise her hand as though about to call us back. But she didn't speak. Her hand fell to her side.

It was then that I believed her more than ever before. She'd meant no harm. *But her theatrics almost got the best of her.* Hirose's back was rigid as we exited the room. *And they might still.* The door slid closed behind us with a soft rasp. Hirose's guards stood on either side, silent and brooding.

"Well?" Adnan asked from where he leaned one shoulder against the wall of the narrow anteroom.

"She's telling the truth," Hirose said.

My jaw dropped. *He believes she is.* "You're not sending her away?"

Hirose clasped his hands behind his back, his legs in a wide stance. "No, much as I am tempted to," he added under his breath. "But I don't mind letting her stew for a little while. Perhaps it will help her realize the dangers of her antics." He looked at Saya. "You should know that the vision you had played out. What you saw was her getting the information about Tristan's escape."

Saya's lips opened in an *O*.

"Turns out that our warning to her served as a push for her to provide valuable information. If she hadn't taken the steps she did, who knows if Tristan's escape attempt would have been thwarted."

I glanced at the closed door over Hirose's shoulder. We had Amarante to thank. Never did I think I would thank her for anything, but now she had not only kept Adnan's name a secret thus far, but she also had revealed Tristan's plans.

"Do you think there are others?" Adnan asked. "Besides the two guards who were caught with Tristan?"

Hirose grew rigid. "I don't know. Saya, perhaps you could try to have a vision about this?"

Saya inclined her head, her face pale, but said nothing. I squinted at her. Her arms were crossed over her chest, but she was still, her shoulders raised as though tense and holding her breath.

She's hiding something.

"For now," Hirose said, nodding to the two guards behind him, "we'll leave Amarante here for a little longer. Benkei, would you accompany me?"

To the dungeons. I knew what he didn't say. *Saya and I are being left out of this.* A sense of relief washed over me.

"Yes." Adnan watched as Hirose strode toward the door, Saya trailing behind him.

"Juliet," Adnan whispered. He drew me into a quick hug and pulled away. "This time, stay. I'll find you as soon as we're done, but you aren't going to want to be there."

"I wasn't planning on going."

Adnan arched an eyebrow.

"I wasn't!" I protested, before tilting my head from side to side. "Well, not this time, for once."

He snorted. "Just watch yourself. We don't know who else may have been in on Tristan's plan."

"I will," I whispered. His jaw clenched, but his soft green gaze shone with love and care. I watched as he left. It was just me and the two guards behind now.

Saya.

I needed to find her. Something was going on. Something was wrong.

CHAPTER THIRTY-THREE

There she was. I caught a glimpse of her petite figure, a stark contrast in bright blue robes to the dark wood paneling on the walls. Her steps were quiet and slow as she walked up the hallway.

"Saya!"

She turned, her face paler than usual. "Juliet." She glanced back up the way she'd been heading.

For a moment, I wondered if she would continue walking without waiting. My step quickened. But Saya didn't move. She nodded to me as I stopped near her.

"Want to tell me what's going on?" I asked in a quiet tone.

She chewed on her lower lip. "I suppose it's time to tell someone," she replied with a sigh.

My heart fell at the troubled look crossing her face.

"Since Drielle died and everything happened with Tristan ..." She hesitated, her eyes swirling with painful emotion. "I've had a hard time seeing anything." She watched me, as though waiting for my reaction.

Seeing anything? Oh. "You mean visions."

She nodded.

"But you had a vision." I shifted my weight to my right side. "You saw Amarante—"

"I've been able to see occasionally. It's just, it's not the same. It's harder. I don't know what's going on, what's wrong with me." Her chest heaved as she inhaled. "Hirose doesn't know."

"Saya, have you ever thought about how this could just be some sort of reaction to trauma? You've been through a lot in the past few months. Maybe you just need to give it some time."

"I've thought about that," she admitted. "It's the best scenario. But what if ..." She trailed off as she tilted her head to look up at the ceiling. "What if I'm not needed?"

"Hey." I reached out and touched her shoulder. "Don't do that. Give it time."

She nodded again.

"And maybe you should consider telling Hirose," I added. "He should know."

"You're right. Let's go." She walked forward without a second look.

"Wait, what?" Running a couple steps to catch up, I fell in beside her, matching her quick stride.

"I'll tell him now."

"With me?"

"Why not?" She didn't try to hide the snideness sneaking into her voice. "It was your idea after all."

Biting back a groan of frustration, I said, "Fine. I'll be there for support. I don't see what there is to be afraid of though."

"He *is* the emperor."

True. There wasn't anything I could say to that. "Isn't he with Tristan? Benkei left a little while ago to join him."

Saya stopped. "Right. Let's wait in the hallway, then." She started walking again. And again, I had to run a couple steps to catch up.

"I'd rather not, you know."

"Why?"

"The last time I was there, Tristan escaped, and I passed out."

"Good point. Let's wait in Hirose's council chamber. I'll send a maid to let him know I'd like to speak with him."

"Much better," I agreed.

We had been waiting in the darkened council chamber for what had seemed like forever, though it had been no more than an hour. I paced the floor, fighting against my mind dwelling in the dungeons far below us.

The door behind me rasped as it slid open. Saya jumped to her feet, and I heard the footsteps as I turned. Hirose nodded to the both of us, Adnan following close behind.

"Ladies," Hirose greeted, his eyes slightly dark with what seemed like exhaustion.

Or anger?

Adnan came up to me and slid an arm around my shoulders.

"You wanted to speak to me, Saya?" Hirose prompted, sitting down in his chair. "Considering I see Juliet here, I figure you are all right with Benkei being here as well?"

Saya nodded. "Yes. I wanted to—need to—tell you that ever since Drielle's death, and what happened at the fortress with Tristan, I've been struggling to see." She spoke faster. "I'm not sure why, but having visions is difficult right now, as though I've gone backward in my abilities. I should have told you sooner. I'm sorry. But I'm hoping that it's just a phase."

Hirose held up a hand. "I'm not angry," he said. "I wish you had felt like you could tell me sooner, but I also know I am still working on building that bridge of trust between us. Saya, you have no need to be afraid." His fingers drummed on his thigh. "I'm assuming this is trauma-related?"

"That's what Juliet thinks, and I'm inclined to think that as well."

Adnan's arm tightened around me. *She's not the only one. We all struggle with it.*

I focused as Hirose began speaking.

"Well, there isn't much we can do other than give it time. Just keep me informed from now on."

Saya bowed.

"There is something else we need to speak of." Hirose beckoned to us and waited as we all sat down on floor cushions. "I will loop the advisors in later, but for now, this needs to stay between the four of us."

The hairs on my arms tingled.

"We believe there is an informant or traitor of some kind." He paused.

Saya and I had similar reactions, but Adnan didn't move a muscle. *He already knows.* I swallowed.

"I don't believe Tristan was able to do this on his own. I think he had help. Besides, one of the guards reacted a little when we pressed in on the idea, though we haven't yet broken them."

A shiver ran over my body.

"For now, we are creating a list of possibilities. It could be someone whom we do not suspect at all, but we have to start somewhere." Hirose gestured to Adnan. "Benkei?"

"Lord Gorm, who has been living in the northwest. Hirose had already sent men to remove him and allow him to sail back home, but his time allotted to get his affairs in order doesn't end for another two days. Because of that, he is still here and could be helping Tristan. Then there is Nani, Tristan's nanny, who loves him and is loyal. The advisor, Shuji—"

The one who doesn't like me.

"Why him?" I interrupted.

"He has second-guessed me quite often," Hirose said. "Good question though."

"But isn't that a good quality?" I ignored the way Adnan's eyebrow rose. "I don't like him, but at least he's not afraid to question as an advisor."

"True," Hirose replied. "In essence, I agree, but I have been wondering if it is that he just isn't afraid, or if there is a lack of respect for me and the position I hold. That in itself could give him opportunity for playing both sides."

"The last person on our list is Afkar Nilsson," Adnan finished. "The newest arrival to this court, and one who has direct ties to Nordik."

The room went silent. *Four people.* The list of names played in my mind as I ran through them.

"Well," Saya said, breaking the silence. "At least it is only four, but they all have reason to help Tristan."

"Yes," Hirose agreed.

"And what if it's none of them?" Saya asked, her hands dropping to rest on her legs.

"Then none of them are. But we have to consider them, and perhaps as interviews go on, we will add more to the list. I have already given orders for my taisho to interview the servants who have any interaction with the prisoners and guards, as well as to quietly begin to investigate the three men and Nani."

"What are we to do?" I asked.

"Do?" Hirose echoed. "Nothing, for now. Benkei has been very helpful in dealing with today's events, but I have tasked him with your safety, Juliet Barrows."

I froze. *What?*

"Given there is most likely someone on the outside, and you have been a target of Tristan's before, we must make sure you are not a target again. Benkei's only job is to protect you."

"Isn't it more important for him to—"

"No," Hirose broke in, his voice gentle. "I have the rest handled. My men are trustworthy, and they have already proven themselves before, that night you rescued us. We will get to the bottom of this."

"What about me?" Saya asked, almost seeming to shrink in on herself.

"I want you to rest and keep trying. If you see *anything* that could be related to Tristan and the escape attempt, let me know immediately." He rose. "Now, I have someone waiting for me, and that is not an appointment I want to miss." His eyes sparkled.

Miya. I struggled to hold back my mirth. Rising to my feet, I slid my hand into Adnan's as we followed Hirose and Saya to the door.

Saya turned to face us. "I'm going to my rooms."

We nodded and watched her go.

"Are you all right?" Adnan asked me.

"Do you really think I'm in any danger?"

He shrugged. "I don't know, but I agree with Hirose—it's best to be safe."

Than sorry. It was left hanging between us, unsaid.

"So what now?"

"Now, I think we plan on a city outing."

"The city? Now?"

He chuckled. "Yes, are you not up for going?"

I stepped forward with a little spring in my step. "Oh, I'm ready."

He let go of my arm and faced me as he walked backward. "Grab your cloak and meet me at the entrance we used to get in. Do you remember?"

"I think so," I called over my shoulder, already heading for my room. *The city.* A small squeal escaped my lips. *And with Adnan.*

There he stood, waiting, tall and with a dark gray cloak slung over his shoulders. His posture relaxed the slightest as he saw me coming. "Ready?"

"Yes," I replied with a nod.

"I hope you're not disappointed," he said with a chuckle as we exited through the door. The guards closed it behind us with a small clang.

Rock crunched under our shoes as we meandered down the path. "I doubt it," I replied. "You know, back in my world, I never left the United States, but I always wanted to. Here in Ryujin, I've seen the darker sides, but now I want to see the people, see the life!"

"The heart of the country," Adnan said. "It's here. Here, there are people from every corner of the country. Remember, it will take time for the people and country to heal from the oppression they've lived under for the past few centuries." He paused as we neared the small side entrance. Nodding to the guards, we waited as they pulled the heavy gates open. Through the ever-widening crack, I saw the city outside. My heartbeat quickened.

"Benkei, my lady!"

My heart sank as we turned as one to face the servant hurrying up. "Lady Saya sent me to find you. She has news."

I glanced at Adnan. *We just saw her.*

"Can it wait?" Adnan asked the small man.

He shook his head. "No, my lord. Please, if you will follow me."

I cast one lingering look over my shoulder as we followed the man. The gates closed and the narrow view of the city beyond was cut off.

"I'm sorry," Adnan whispered.

"It's all right," I said, but I didn't voice the deep disappointment I felt settling over me. *You're just being selfish,* I told myself. What did Saya want? It had been no more than an hour since we had parted ways. The servant's wringing hands and hurried step suggested it was something urgent. Had something gone wrong? *Tristan.* I tried not to think of all the possibilities that could have happened.

Just inside, the servant stopped. "Please, follow me." He rushed off without another word, his robe-like tunic rustling with the quick movement.

Isn't that what we are doing? While I felt a little like he was wasting our time, Adnan didn't seem the least bit perturbed.

"I believe we're going to the gardens," Adnan noted. "We haven't headed deeper into the palace."

The servant's head bobbed. "Lady Saya is waiting!" he reminded.

"Her waiting in the gardens doesn't seem that urgent," I muttered to Adnan. He shrugged as the servant led us through the entrance into the gardens. The air smelled fresh and clean, wafting with the scent of jasmine as the buds bloomed.

"Through there," the servant said, gesturing to an wrought iron gate set in the side of a wall. He turned and left.

Adnan swept out an arm. "After you."

I entered a square courtyard, even smaller than the one Adnan and I had spoken with Hirose and Saya in a few days before. A single stone bench sat in the middle, surrounded by trailing plants and shrubs. A small fountain bubbled with water. It was an oasis. Saya sat there, her eyes closed and her dark hair loose about her shoulders.

As Adnan stepped in behind me, her eyes opened, and she nodded to us.

"I'm glad you're here. I sent a note to Hirose already, but I wanted you both to know."

I tapped my foot, impatient at the slow way she spoke. "What's wrong? What happened?"

"What do you mean?"

"The servant made it seem this is of a very pressing nature," Adnan replied. "He caught us just as we were leaving to go into the city."

Saya's cheeks reddened. "Oh. It isn't really ... it could have waited. That is my fault. I was excited, and so impressed that on him without realizing." She pulled her hair over one shoulder. "But since you *are* here now, I'll tell you. I *did* have a vision."

I exhaled. "That was fast."

"It was," Saya agreed, eyes shining. "There wasn't much, but I did see a retinue arriving, shadowed figures in dark corridors, a hand reaching through a cell door, slightly ajar, and then an item." She paused and took a deep breath. "The ax, it is of Nordik make. And there is one here, even now."

"Afkar Nilsson," I murmured under my breath.

She nodded.

"How do you know it's his axe?" Adnan asked.

"Because it was taken to the treasury when the retinue arrived, along with any other weapons they found. The ax has a distinctive symbol on its hilt. I've already been to the treasury … it's the same one." She shook her head. "My vision points at him."

"Your visions have been wrong before," I noted. "And besides, what if the vision is about something else entirely?"

Saya shrugged. "Yes, which is why we can't do anything definitive yet. It could mean something else, but I do think it points to him. I was *trying* to see anything having to do with him."

"But how?" I asked, raising my hands. "He didn't arrive until a short time ago."

"And he is closely watched by the Black Guard," Adnan put in. "And why Tristan? Even if it is Nilsson behind this, why Tristan? Yes, Tristan is from Nordik and has claim to the throne, but Nordik could just put someone else on the throne. Nilsson has power—he could try for it himself. It doesn't make sense."

"I don't know," Saya admitted. "We don't have any evidence, but my vision has given us one person to focus on. Hirose has already had the watch around him doubled, and we are leaving the other three names alone for now."

"The escape attempt didn't work," I murmured, thinking. "Tristan's execution is in two days, so if he is going to try something, it would have to be soon."

"And it will be harder now," Adnan said. "If it is him, which is likely, he'll know our guard is up as well. It wasn't easy the first attempt, and it will be less so the next."

Saya glanced between the two of us, her dark eyes wide. "I *am* sorry I kept you from going into the city. Why don't you go now?"

Adnan looked up. "It might be just as well you stopped us."

Above us, the clouds had darkened and begun to billow across the expanse that we could see. The tall stone walls kept us from seeing what lay in every direction but directly above. I breathed in deep. The sweet scent of an incoming storm infused the air.

"Yes," Saya said, drawing my attention back to her. "The thunderstorms here are just as strong and wild as the ones in the mountains."

I remembered them all too well. Those nights had helped me. The rain had beaten against the stone walls, silenced when broken by the strike of lightning followed by the crack of thunder. It had been hard to sleep anyway. *And those storms held so much power.*

"Shall we head in?" Adnan asked, offering us each an arm.

A drop of rain landed on my nose.

"Yes," I agreed, taking his arm and grinning. "The city can wait another day."

"Hirose will not want to raise suspicion," Adnan said. "I believe we will be having an interesting dinner tonight."

I groaned. "With *him*?" I had already felt repulsed by him, but now with him the likely culprit of Tristan's attempted escape, I didn't want to be near the man. "Why can't we just question him?"

"Because he is an emissary, thus we must tread carefully."

"But how is that wrong or out of line?" I asked.

Adnan sighed. "There are nuances, nuances that Hirose will consider. It's his call." He shrugged. "Do you want to sit out tonight?"

"You've held it together in worse times," Saya noted with an eyebrow raised. She peered around Adnan at me. Another raindrop landed, this time on my hand.

"True," I murmured. *But I don't want to have to do so anymore.*

CHAPTER THIRTY-FOUR

My body jerked as I woke up. Sweat dampened my skin and clothing. Swiping the bedding away, I sat up. The room had darkened, the fire now a bed of glowing red coals. Hours had passed since I'd gone to bed after dinner the night before.

A dinner in which nothing had happened. Afkar Nilsson had given no sign of even *knowing* of Tristan's escape attempt or impending execution. If anything, the evening had been almost fun, with lively conversation and stories of lives past.

Tilting my head back, I took a deep breath before exhaling, trying to calm my racing heartbeat. The cool air bit at my skin. Tendrils of hair clung to my neck, wet with sweat. I drew it up into a messy bun before securing it.

Another night of tossing and turning.

Tomorrow was Tristan's execution. And I knew then, if I didn't speak to him before he died, I would always wonder. *I need closure.* Standing up, I dressed with shaking fingers before leaving the room. Tristan had seen me, and I him. Things had changed now. There was still one more secret. *And who helped him?*

The hallways were dark, but I knew the way. It wasn't far. Questions accompanied me, but the answers remained in the shadows.

Once there, I rapped my knuckles on the wood and waited. It didn't take long. The door slid open with a soft rasp.

Adnan stood there, bleary-eyed. "Juliet?"

Again? I really needed to stop doing this, but my eyes wouldn't leave his shirtless torso. He was lean, but his muscles rippled. My heartbeat quickened.

"You're making a habit of this," he muttered, sliding the door closed behind us. "Not that I'm complaining." His arms flexed as he crossed them over his bare chest. "You're up early," he noted.

My foot tapped against the floor with nervous energy. Clutching at the cloak I wore, I wrapped it closer about me. "I need to speak to Tristan."

Adnan sighed and ran his hands through his hair. "How did I know this was going to happen? Are you sure about this?"

I nodded.

"Very well." He strapped on a dagger before taking his cloak. "Let's go."

We walked in silence, me trusting he knew where he was going. In the distance, I heard faint sounds of the castle stirring with servants beginning their day.

"Here," Adnan said, leading me through a door into a narrow corridor. At the end was a door flanked by two guards. "We'd like to see Tristan," he explained to them.

The men glanced at one another, their stances unmoving.

"No offense, Benkei, but we're under orders from the emperor not to let anyone down there without his permission."

"Then please go get his permission." Adnan's expression was neutral, yet his tone was unrelenting.

One guard nodded to the other, who left without a word. *At least we know these men are loyal,* I thought. While we waited, I ignored the way Adnan watched me and brushed aside the concern weighing in the tilt of his head. My trepidation grew the longer we waited. *I need to do this. It's the only way to move on.* Yet I knew what Saya and Adnan would say.

As the minutes ticked by, I found myself shifting from foot to foot, not a little admiring of how Adnan and the guard never once moved. Nervous energy zapped through my limbs.

Then the door at the end of the hallway opened to reveal the returning guard. He gestured as he reached for his belt. "The emperor has granted you permission to go in. Follow me."

His keys jangled as he opened the door to the dungeons. Taking a deep breath, I lingered close to Adnan's shadow as we stepped through. No light illuminated the halls other than from the torch the guard had brought with us. At the end of the hallway was another door. He took a torch from beside it, lit it, and handed it to Adnan. Using another key, he unlocked the door and led us through it into another hallway filled with doors.

When he stopped before one of them, my breath caught.

"Are you sure?" Adnan whispered in my ear, his breath warm.

I nodded, unable to speak.

"Do you want me to stay with you, or wait just out of sight?"

As much as I wanted him to stay with me, I knew Tristan would be more likely to speak if Adnan wasn't there. "Out of sight," I whispered, wishing my voice carried more confidence.

"He's chained up," the guard muttered. "I'll wait just outside the door with Benkei, but leave it cracked open just in case."

Adnan's hands clenched into fists. "Are you ready?"

My jaw locked as I gritted my teeth. *Find out his secret. Play to his ego.* As air blew through my lips, my shoulders dropped, and I straightened them. I bobbed my head once. The guard handed me his torch and opened the door. A creak shrieked through the air. The entrance was black. Lifting the torch, I entered, stopping just inside the small room. The bare stone walls encompassed me, but I could feel the draft from the hallway on my back. I shivered and took a deep breath, squaring my shoulders. A dark form sat against the far wall.

Tristan.

Forcing my breathing to remain even, I waited. His head rose, his shaggy blond hair dirty and hanging about his face.

A moment of silence passed.

"Juliet."

Our history resurfaced with the sound of my name on his lips. I shivered again, but this time, it wasn't from the cold. All the manipulation, the cunning, the romance—it tasted sour in my mouth.

"I assumed you would be long gone."

My tongue flicked out to moisten my lips. "I'm here."

"I see that." Tristan drew up a leg and rested his hand across it. "Why?"

Why? As much as I wanted to have this conversation, it was still a struggle. *Pull yourself together.* He would do everything possible to gain the upper hand in this conversation, and I couldn't let him. I cleared my throat. "Why do you think I'm here?"

He chuckled, a raspy sound. "You missed my company." He leaned forward a little, his voice even smoother as he continued. "Do you think of me often? You must have, if you are here now. When? During the day?" He paused and let a silkiness creep into his voice. "At night?"

I forced myself to stand still, to keep my disdain hidden. The awareness of Adnan behind me, just out of sight, strengthened me.

"Aw, Juliet." My name was a caress on his lips. "You aren't broken; you never were."

Against my will, I stiffened, my lips pursing as I frowned. *Broken.* Wasn't that the question that had been raging inside me? *Don't play into his hand.*

"You see"—Tristan grimaced, his teeth, once white, now yellowed, glinting in the torchlight—"you could have it all. No matter how much you try to run, you can't. You know how much you've tried to push me away, yet I'm still there with you." He pointed a thin finger at my chest. "You can't be rid of me," he whispered. "Think of everything we could do together."

I took a deep breath. "No, Tristan. You think you understand me, but you don't, and you never will."

Tristan relaxed back against the wall and raised an eyebrow.

"I'm only here for one reason." I watched as his eyes narrowed. He gave me a searching look. Recognition flashed across his face.

Drawing his head back up from where it had lain against the wall, he grimaced. "You want to know my last secret." He shrugged. "What if I don't have one?"

"You do."

"How do you know?" he almost snapped. "How well do you think *you* know me?"

"Enough, Tristan. You're a manipulator, but when it comes to lies, you tend to twist the truth to fit what you want. And with me, you've always edged closer to those truths, especially when you think it could get what you want from me." I adjusted my grip on the torch, my palm sweating. "So what is your secret?"

Tristan laughed. "Are you sure you want to know?"

I waited. *Give him time.* My time with Tristan had given me one advantage over him. He couldn't stand to let someone else be in the spotlight. If his telling a secret would put someone in awe, whether for good or bad, he would spill the secret. *He won't be able to resist.* Gritting my teeth, I waited, fighting against the urge to tap my foot against the ground, to plead with him, anything to get him to stop looking at me the way he was. His eyes were hungry, penetrating, but his posture still held some of the same proudness he had always possessed. *It's as if he wants to eat me.* Nausea settled in the pit of my stomach.

Tristan waved a hand, his manacles clashing in a sharp ring with the movement. "Very well. You really want to know? Here it is. I'm not Tristan Gorvenal." His voice echoed in the small room.

My lips parted in surprise.

Tristan's blue eyes glittered in the torchlight.

Pulling myself together, I snapped, "What do you mean?"

"Have you ever wondered why I believed you had come from another world so easily? Or why I wanted to know everything I could?"

My brain threatened to implode as the pieces began to fall into place.

"I'm not from this world either, Juliet Barrows. You and I, we are more similar than you thought." He held his head high. "We've *always* shared a connection."

It was a struggle to comprehend as he spoke. "Where are you from?"

"You're not the only *Otherworlder*," he explained with a wink. "When I got to Ryujin, I ended up becoming friends with the real Tristan Gorvenal. He had everything—or would soon. I had nothing—no friends, no family, no one." His voice took on a bitter tone. "He would inherit the land, the family, the throne. So one night, after careful planning, I had the whole family slaughtered."

Twisting the truth like always. The first time I had met him, he told us of how his family was killed by Creulon—his cousin—and then later, that it had really been him. And that had been the truth all along, but not for the same reasons.

Tristan continued, "I was young. I played my shot too soon because Creulon survived. He was older, wiser; he would've known I wasn't the real Tristan. So I hid away, biding my time, waiting until I grew older and could build an army to take back what was mine."

I shook my head. "It was never yours. You're not Tristan."

"Oh, but I am." Tristan tilted his head to the side with a smirk. "I *became* him."

"What's your real name?"

"Tristan Gorvenal."

"No, it isn't," I growled, my voice reverberating off the walls. "Your *true* name."

"Tristan Gorvenal." The man I had known as Tristan for months now laughed, but it quickly faded into a hoarse croak, which he bit off. "I am he. He is me. We are one. The other Tristan is no more; he was merely a placeholder."

You're sick. Trembling, I gripped the torch even tighter. Its flames sent shadows across Tristan's grubby face.

"What name did you have here? Who were you before you had Tristan and his family killed?" The man before me used to be a boy. He had been so young. *How could you? How did you?*

"It does not matter." He shook his head. "For all anyone needs to know, *I* am Tristan Gorvenal."

"And the nanny?"

Tristan smirked. "She was Tristan's nanny too. She mothered both of us, took me under her wing with even more love and care than she had for Tristan. I was without anyone, you see, and he had everything."

"You were a boy."

"So? I had a brain. It is amazing the things you can do when you have one." He studied his dirty fingernails.

"How did you do it?"

He frowned as he focused back on me. "What do you mean?"

"You said you were from another world, you came to Ryujin, a mere boy; how did you manage to kill an entire royal family?"

"Well," he said, "I *did* miss one." Seeing my confusion, he added, "Creulon?"

"But how?"

"I found some willing to help, obviously. *I* did not kill them. You think *I* would be capable?" His voice was saturated with a silky innocence.

"No, I know you didn't do it with your own hands. But you had it done, so you were responsible for all of their deaths."

Tristan shrugged.

There is something more here. I watched as Tristan avoided me like I wasn't there. There was something he didn't want me to see. *How did he do it?* A light began to dawn. "Tristan," I said. "You don't just have one secret, do you?"

He laughed so loud it filled the small cell. "Oh, Juliet. I have far more than one. But it was the one *you* really wanted to know. It is the one that is important. It is the one that you and I share."

"But there is one other," I whispered. *Come on, Tristan.*

He leaned forward, and it took everything I had not to step back. His eyes smoldered with a sort of fire. "My escape attempt."

Yes and no.

"Imagine my surprise when I saw you here. You wanted to return home, to your world, so why did you stay?" He cocked his head to the side. "Or did you go? But why come back? It has barely been, what? Three weeks? Four?"

I ignored his questions. "When you were a boy, you needed help, Tristan. You couldn't kill the king's family on your own. Yesterday, you needed help to escape, much like you've needed it before."

Tristan drew himself up a little, back against the wall. His chains clanked. "I do not need anyone's help. I am behind it all. I *use* others."

"So who was it, then? Who was it who helped you?" *Could it be the same person?* Silently, I urged him to answer, to give up his secrets, to make sense of everything.

Tristan didn't say a word.

"Afkar Nilsson."

Tristan blinked, and I knew. He had heard that name before. *He knows that name.*

My heart thudded, my pulse rapid. "Truth bent obscures the lies ..." I whispered under my breath.

Tristan leaned forward, his broad shoulders straining against the chains holding him against the wall. "What?"

"It's why you were able to get so many to believe you. You always relied on the truth." My left hand flexed, a slight twinge of pain reminding me of the night I'd escaped him. "But I don't understand how you could do any of it."

This time, his face remained serious. "Because I want power. I want everything I lost."

He was a child. A sick feeling stole over me, and my stomach churned. "And now you really have lost everything."

Tristan's face reddened, a burning accentuated by the flames held high above my hand. He lunged forward, a feral growl emanating from his throat, and his chains rattled. Heart racing, I backed up but hit something solid.

Adnan stepped around me and stopped next to me, angling his body just in front of mine.

Tristan's lips curved up. "Never without him, are you, Juliet?" he spat. He leaned his head back, drawing my attention to his blond hair, now a dirty gray sort of color.

"You already know you die tomorrow." Adnan's hand didn't leave the dagger he held at his side. "Juliet is right. You have lost everything, and soon you'll lose your life as recompense for all you have done."

Tristan's grin was wild. "No, no. My country will come for me."

They have come for him, and he knows it.

"Your country isn't even yours," Adnan said. "You said it yourself. This world is not yours."

"They don't know that," Tristan hissed. "They won't let you execute me or lose this country. It has resources."

"People?" Adnan asked. "First Creulon and then you. All of you have used this country only to further your own power."

Tristan sat back with another rattle of chains. "So? Sheep must be herded."

Adnan took my arm with his free hand. "Your life is forfeit, Tristan." He stepped back, and I went with him. "You became friends with the real Tristan Gorvenal, won the affections of his nanny, and even the king. You could have had everything. A father, mother, brother—but you gave it all up."

I froze. *No, he didn't.* It all clicked. He had to have help. He had to have a way to worm his way into the king's family. The how had been driving me to distraction.

"Juliet?" Adnan whispered, brushing my arm as he came to my side.

"Yes, Juliet?" Tristan echoed, my name a caress on his lips.

Adnan tensed at my side.

"You weren't giving up any of that." I watched as Tristan's brow wrinkled. *Adnan wasn't the only one taken in.* "You had a family. You came here, and you found one. Someone close to the king, someone who probably shared your same thirst for power."

Tristan's face grew stormy.

"Or maybe they were the ones who really shaped you, turned you into the man you've become."

"No!" Tristan almost yelled. "I am the one who pulls the strings."

I shook my head. "Are you sure about that? They were the ones who orchestrated the death of the king's family, they were the ones who paid for the assassins, and they were the ones who tried to rescue you today." I paused, my breath held. They were guesses, but guesses that had a ring of truth to them. *Afkar Nilsson.* He arrived before we knew to expect anyone from Nordik. *What if he had been sent for?*

Tristan laughed again. "I used *him.* He was just a means to an end."

"And now he wants the throne," Adnan said, stepping in front of me. "This man you've relied on, he didn't really want you to escape, did he?"

Tristan's face darkened, and his shoulders rose.

"You are to be executed tomorrow," Adnan pressed. "Are you just going to let him take it? Let him take the power?"

Tristan's eyes roved from side to side. "He's here."

I had to strain to hear his voice.

"It's because of me we came so close. It's because of me our power has grown. I am the heir he didn't have." Tristan lunged forward again, and I shrank back, glad for Adnan who didn't budge an inch. "Leave."

"Is it Afkar Nilsson?" I asked again.

Tristan leered at me before he settled on my face with a cold gleam. "Go."

Adnan nodded and, taking my arm, backed up. I went with him. There was nothing more to be said. I knew his secrets now. But I shivered as I heard Tristan's laugh ring through the dungeon.

"You think you are so smart?" he challenged.

Without another word, we stepped out of the cell, and the guard closed the heavy metal door. I gave him the torch, my hands shaking. Adrenaline coursed through my body. All the pent-up nerves began to release. Sweat coated my skin, and I almost stumbled as my legs threatened to give out.

"Whoa," Adnan murmured as he steadied me. "Let's go."

"Afkar Nilsson," I breathed.

"Yes," Adnan agreed. "But we still don't have confirmation." He grimaced. "There still isn't enough to do anything against him."

"But it has to be him! Tristan said the man was here."

"Or it's someone we haven't even considered yet." Adnan stepped up the corridor, past the guard standing there. "We need to speak to Hirose."

But what went wrong? What happened that night Tristan attempted to take the throne?

Chapter Thirty-Five

A dusky orange shot in rays across the sky, a bright herald of morning. Dawn had arrived, bringing a close to the night. After Adnan had escorted me back to my room, I hadn't slept. I knew it wouldn't come, so I remained alone with my thoughts the last couple hours, until day began to draw near.

A soft knock preceded the door opening. I turned to see Adnan poke his head through. Seeing I was awake, he stepped in and joined me at the window. When he didn't say anything, I stiffened. "What is it?"

"I spoke with Hirose. He's moved up Tristan's execution. It will happen in a few minutes."

"*What?*"

"He doesn't want to risk what Tristan said about his country as being possibly true. Tristan is still not speaking anymore. This way, there won't be any extra time to warn anyone of the timeline changing. And it doesn't change Tristan's fate."

"It's just a few hours."

"Dawn instead of sunset," Adnan agreed.

My jaw hardened, and my fingers drummed on the windowsill. My eyes closed. *This is it.*

"Do you want to go—"

I shook my head. "No."

Adnan nodded and leaned his shoulder against the wall. We stood in silence as the sun continued its trek up and over the horizon. "It's done," he murmured, still not moving.

My breath left my body. *It's done.* "The final chapter," I whispered.

"For him, not for us." Adnan smiled, but it was filled with a weary sort of sadness. "At least not yet."

We had just finished eating breakfast when a guard popped through the door and surveyed the room. His eyebrows relaxed as recognition crossed his face. The man wound his way through the room towards us.

"Adnan," I whispered, motioning with my head. Adnan set his tea on the table as we watched the man approach.

"Benkei, Miss Barrows," the guard greeted with a bow. "Emperor Hirose requests your presence."

Even as I stood and followed in Adnan and the guard's wake, I screamed inside. Something had happened, and we were being drawn into it. *What if Tristan hadn't died? What if something had happened?*

Out of the dining hall, through a small side door into a windowless inner corridor, up a flight of stairs, through two more corridors, and then we arrived at the throne room. It was a blur as I followed the guard, happy for Adnan's strong presence beside me. A flash of dark hair, hair high, the figure slight, caught my eye. I hesitated.

"What is it?" Adnan asked.

"That man," I said, pointing. "I ran into him a few days ago." *In the hallway.* There was something about him then—his voice. He had his hands hidden within his robes and was fidgeting as he peered down the opposite corridor from where we stood.

His head swung around, and his dark eyes met my own. He ran.

Adnan snapped, "Fetch him."

The guard ran down the corridor, one hand on his sword to keep it from swinging. We waited, silent, watching. A flurry of motion appeared as the guard dragged the slight man back around the corner toward us. He protested, his voice higher than it had been last time as he strove to loosen the guard's hold on his robes. As the guard approached us, he shoved the man toward us, his grip remaining like steel as he propelled the man in front of him.

"What are you doing?" Adnan asked.

"My lord, nothing, nothing at all. I was waiting, waiting for someone."

Adnan frowned. "Why here, outside the emperor's council chamber?"

The man's eyes flicked between Adnan and the door nearby.

"I ran into you the other day," I said.

"No, no, not me."

Adnan sighed. "Bring him inside." He stepped forward and threw open the doors to the council chamber.

Inside the throne room, Hirose and Saya waited, but also the other advisors with them.

"What is this?" Hirose asked, straightening.

"Found him lurking in the hallway," Adnan replied.

Hirose's jaw hardened. He stepped around the table and walked up to the smaller man, quiet and somehow deadly in his movements. "Why?" That one word, spoken softly, was of steel.

"My lord—"

The guard shook him. "*Emperor.*"

"Emperor, I—" he stuttered and went silent.

"Were you spying?" Hirose asked, his voice barely above a whisper.

My heartbeat felt loud in my chest as I strained forward to listen.

The man's eyes widened, but he said nothing.

"Your silence says all," Hirose said. "There is one link we have been missing. Tristan needed help from the outside, someone with power and money. Afkar Nilsson. But there had to be someone else, someone from Ryujin, someone people would overlook. A go-between."

The man paled as Hirose spoke.

"You."

He spluttered, looking like a fish.

"Take him away." Hirose returned to the table as the man was dragged back out of the room by the guard.

It was so quiet. I exhaled as Adnan joined me, brushing against my shoulder with his arm.

What will happen to him? My lips began to part to ask the question, but closed. *No, I don't want to know.*

"That part is done," Hirose began. "I'm sorry you are here for all of this."

As if we had a choice. I kept quiet. *We don't have a choice.*

"This morning, as you both know, Tristan was executed."

I let out the breath I was holding. *He is gone. Is it wrong to be relieved?* Before I could examine that new feeling stealing over my heart, Hirose continued, drawing my attention.

"Soon after, a courier arrived from Nordik."

I glanced at Adnan. *So soon. What if we had waited? No … Tristan is dead.*

Hirose glanced down at the table, where a long piece of paper lay. "They have asked for Tristan to be released."

"Under what terms?" Adnan asked, his voice terse.

"War."

"Wait, what?" I felt my cheeks warm as all eyes turned to me. "How do they know Tristan is still alive? Or what happened to Creulon? Was it Nilsson?"

"We don't know," Hirose replied, nodding. "He was never alone, but there are ways to bribe servants, pass a note." He shrugged. "As for their request, obviously this is no longer possible. I believe war would have been inevitable, no matter if we'd handed Tristan over to them or not. They will not let go of Ryujin so easily."

I watched as Adnan glanced between Saya, the other advisors, and Hirose. When no one spoke, I asked, "What now?"

Hirose sighed. "I have stalled the messengers for now, asked them to give me a day to send a response back with them. That gives me even one day more to prepare for the war that will come."

War. A sick feeling ate at me. It felt like déjà vu. They wanted Adnan. They needed him. *We'll be sucked right back into it all.* There was no getting away now. My skin began to feel feverish as I fought to keep the panic from overtaking me. *But shouldn't we help them?* A wave of nausea swept over me. *Another war.*

"Benkei," Hirose said. "No disrespect, but I do not wish for you to be one of my advisors—"

What? My eyes widened. I inhaled, unable to speak.

"—in any official capacity," Hirose finished. "I would appreciate your help as you have done so since returning here."

Adnan frowned. "I—"

Hirose regarded me. "Only until you both leave, if you are willing."

With those words, I felt some of my tension ease.

"I know neither of you wants part in this war." Hirose's shoulders bowed a little as he spoke. "I don't blame either of you. I think it important that we stand on our own two feet anyway. You have been used by both sides before this. But if you are still determined to leave"—he paused—"I suggest you do it soon."

Clothing rustled as Saya shifted her weight.

What does she want? My brows furrowed as I studied her.

"Let me speak with Juliet a moment," Adnan said, and pulled me to the side, away from the others. "I'd like for us to be married before we leave," he murmured, his green eyes capturing my own. "But if you want to wait longer, we will."

This is happening so fast. I shook my head. "No."

His eyebrow rose. "No, what?"

"I want to marry you." Even with all the confusion inside, that was something I knew for certain.

"You're sure it's the right time?"

I flicked my hair over my shoulder as I shook my head. "Is it ever?"

His lips quirked upward in a teasing way. "Very well." He took my hand and led me back to the group. Addressing Hirose, Adnan clutched my hand. "We'd like to be married by you first."

Hirose's face lightened. "Good."

"Two days."

I stiffened. Those were the first words Saya had spoken.

"It is time enough for a proper ceremony and celebration."

Hirose nodded. "Two days then, if that is agreeable to you both?"

Joy bubbled up within me. *In two days, I'll be married.* I barely heard Adnan's agreement.

Hirose's face darkened. "I wish I didn't have to follow up this joyous news with something darker, but we must speak of it. This morning, we took Afkar Nilsson into custody, along with his men."

Adnan stiffened. *He hadn't heard either,* I thought. *Why now? What evidence surfaced?*

"Just before his execution, Tristan declared Afkar Nilsson to be his adoptive father."

I knew it. Even though it was what I had suspected, the news still hit me like a thunderclap. *I was right.*

Adnan crossed his arms. "Why now?"

"I think it is because he wasn't going to let Nilsson have the power when he couldn't." Hirose took a deep breath. "They used each other. Nilsson was obviously not going to save Tristan; he was prepared to let him die when the escape attempt didn't work. Tristan saw that, and so responded in kind."

Adnan shifted and crossed his arms over his chest. "Have you spoken with him?"

Hirose shook his head. "Not yet. I will later today."

"What will happen to him?" I asked. *Death?* The question whispered in my mind.

"We'll send him back to Nordik. He has not been found guilty of any crimes other than an attempted escape, so we will let him go. Perhaps sending him back will be a soothing gesture to Nordik."

"And if it is seen as weakness?" Adnan asked.

Hirose stiffened. "It is a possibility I have already considered, but I have made my decision."

"And if he returns?" Adnan asked.

"Then we will be ready."

A shiver ran over my skin at Hirose's words. *And we won't be here. He doesn't expect us to be here.* Hirose's confidence was catching. I studied him closely. There was no guile hidden there. *He doesn't believe he needs our help.* Hirose turned to Saya, who spoke under her breath. He nodded and turned to speak to an advisor. Adnan stepped forward to join them.

Feeling a flutter of movement near me, I saw that Saya had drawn near. She tucked a stray tendril of hair behind one ear. "Can we talk?"

"What about them?" I whispered.

Her hair swung over her shoulder as she gave a quick shake. "I told Hirose I would be back soon."

"All right," I replied, letting her lead the way out of the room. Adnan and Hirose were the only two who noted our disappearance, their eyes watchful.

"Where are we going?" I asked once we'd left the throne room.

"Outside, if you're willing."

Already I could feel the cold air I knew would be out there, but I nodded anyway. I had no cloak, but neither did she—and I followed in silence as she led the way through the palace until we reached a side gate into the gardens. Even then, it was the crunch of her slippers on gravel and the trill of birds in the air that filled the silence.

She took a deep breath. "You were right, you know. I do have things I have to work through, but I didn't want to admit it. You do as well. You should leave, you and Adnan." Her steps quickened. "But come back. I don't want you to go, but I understand why you are." Her gait slowed. "I'll miss you."

"I'll miss you too." Emotion clouded my tone. *I'll miss you more than you could know.* War threatened Ryujin, threatened Saya yet again, and I was leaving. My eyes closed a moment before reopening. *Will it ever get easier?*

"Where will you go?" she asked, hugging herself to ward off the chill.

"I don't know," I admitted. "We haven't really had time to talk about it." *Not while we keep getting drawn into everything.* Looking up from the narrow path, I almost missed a step. Cherry trees filled the grounds, their buds dark pink as they began to fill the branches. *Just like back at the mountain fortress.* But this time, they were blooming with life. There were so many of them.

"Gorgeous, aren't they?" Saya asked, spreading her arms out wide. "This is one of my favorite places to go."

"Isn't it early?" Aspects of the conversation I had with her pierced my mind in a numbing way. She'd warned me about my parents. She'd seen me looking on as though I no longer belonged. She saw the cherry trees before in a vision, and that had been true. She had seen me leave my family behind, and that had been true as well. Tears stung my eyes.

Saya laid a hand on my arm. "What is it?"

"I just realized ..." Taking a deep breath, I continued, "You saw my parents, you saw me leave them, knowing I no longer belonged, and you were right."

Saya's eyes fell, and her chin trembled. "I didn't know you would leave. I didn't understand exactly what I saw until you told me your story."

"It all worked out in the end, though not the way I expected," I said, watching the branches wave in the breeze. "Now I'm getting married."

"Yes, you are." Saya clapped her hands together. "A wedding! I just wish we had more time ... but no matter. I'm going to order a dress made for you."

"That's not necessary."

"Yes, it is." She frowned at me. "Just because you're getting married in two days doesn't mean you can't have a wonderful ceremony. We will give you a celebration worthy of our culture and customs. You'll see."

I chewed on my lower lip.

"What is it?" she asked.

"I just—what *are* the weddings here like?"

Saya's shoulders fell. "I'm sorry. I should've thought, realized, that you might want something different." She clasped her hands together in front of her. "There are a few things we should go over, then. Your dress, we can figure out when the maids come to get your measurements, but the wedding will take place in the gardens, if that is all right with you."

I nodded.

"And there will be music. I think the part you might want to change, depending on what you think, is the ceremony itself." She eyed me. "I know Adnan is also not of my country, so he will probably be happy with whatever you want."

Again, my head bobbed.

"So the ceremony." Her hands flung out as she explained. "A typical ceremony is dedicated more to the gods than to the two being married. The vows are spoken to the gods, and rice wine is drunk from cups symbolizing three different things." Her lips parted, closed, and parted again. "No, I won't explain that yet."

My mind sorted through what she had said and the possibilities of doing something different. But not too different.

"What do you think so far?" Saya asked.

"I'm fine with drinking the rice wine, but more as a symbol of our impending union versus anything spiritual or religious. I just don't believe in the same gods you do. And I'd like for us to say our vows to each other, not to the gods."

Saya exhaled. "I'm not surprised. I figured you might want to do those differently, which is fine!" she added as I made to speak. "I'll talk to Hirose, tweak the ceremony a little. Is there anything else?"

"Yes. I haven't talked to Adnan about it, but back home, a couple exchanges rings as a symbol of their union, their promise to one another, and I'd like to do the same. But I don't have a ring, and my guess is he doesn't either—"

Saya's teeth flashed as she grinned. "Don't worry about that. Is there anything else?"

"No."

Saya clasped her hands together in front of her and glanced over her shoulder. "I should get back." She beckoned for me to follow. "Already our time together shortens."

I fell in beside her, listening to the wind blowing through the shrubbery.

She laid a hand on my arm and applied pressure for a moment. "I'm going to try to keep tabs on you, you know. And I promise I'll write faithfully." Her dark eyes welled with emotion. "I'll miss you."

Again, the tears threatened to come. "I'll miss you too."

"We'll keep in touch," she affirmed again, though I wasn't sure if she was trying to convince herself or me more.

We neared the door back into the palace.

"Saya, wait, there's one thing more. I should've told you, but I didn't."

She stopped, listening, her stance relaxed.

"I think Natsumi is a seer."

Saya laughed. "I'm not sure what I expected, but it wasn't that. Yes, I've suspected that as well."

"For how long?"

She shrugged and hugged herself as a cold breeze blew over us. "I don't remember. For a little while. It just started to make sense the more I learned about her. And then I began wondering if she could be ..." Saya's voice grew in excitement. "Well, there are legends about the first seer, what she can do, how powerful she is, and I can't help but wonder ..."

"If she's the first seer?" I finished for her. My eyes widened.

Saya raised her hands in the air. "No need to be so incredulous. Think about it. What if?"

My mind raced. It made sense in a weird sort of way, and I didn't even know the legends like Saya did. "You might find out eventually. I don't think that's the last we'll see of her. She always seems to come around when you least expect it, but when you need her the most."

"Why so often here, though?" Saya turned to continue walking. "What is it about Ryujin?"

"I don't know, but somehow she's strongly connected to this world. Maybe she was born here." I glanced back over my shoulder at the cherry trees we were leaving behind. *Just like the trees. Their roots have grown and spread beneath the ground.* Natsumi would be back. Maybe after we had left, but she *would* be back.

Chapter Thirty-Six

The sun had risen over a cloudless sky. It appeared warm out, inviting, and I itched to get outside. Saya had ordered a dress, as promised. Two women, one older and one younger, had come in and fitted me, promising to have it done by nightfall. I sat in front of the fire, wishing for a book to read or something to do. Briefly I had considered going to look for Adnan, but I wasn't sure if he was busy with Hirose, being an advisor, or what I would say.

Hey, we're getting married tomorrow. What do you think of that? How do you feel? I groaned. We were getting married, and yet it still felt strange sometimes to be honest about what I thought and felt. *Not good.* My lips downturned. Stretching out my legs, I flexed my toes toward the fire. If there was anything I had seen in the strong marriages around me growing up, it was communication. *Like we're so good at that.* I sighed. But we were getting better. *What will it be like to spend time together without war looming over us?*

A soft knock echoed from the door. Head tilted, I turned. "Come in!"

The door opened, and Adnan stepped in. Grinning, I sat back on my hands and watched as he approached. He leaned down for a quick kiss before offering me a hand. "I want to show you something."

"What?" I teased as I stood.

"Come with me."

Grabbing my dark gray cloak from the wardrobe, I put it on and laced up my boots.

He took my hand and led me out of my room. I recognized the way he led me: We were heading toward the main palace entrance. Excitement grew within me, even though I tried to suppress it. *Are we going to the market?* I knew he was aware each time I'd glance at him because his lips would twitch, but he said nothing. I tried to dampen my hopes, knowing they might well be dashed if it was something else he had in mind.

When we walked outside, I almost jumped with glee. The sun was almost as warm as it had looked when I'd seen it earlier through the window. I breathed in deep. Spring was coming. With it, hope also flourished, even on the eve of war. It was that deep-seated something that linked to the sun shining, the birds twittering, and the plants beginning to bloom. It drove away the depression of winter, the dark and the dreary grayness. Our lives were changing. Tomorrow we would begin a new journey together. A new future was being laid before us.

Adnan pressed my hand, his calloused palm rough but strong. The moment we passed through the gates onto the street in the city, I knew it. I leaned into him, brushing against him with my shoulder and arm.

The noise grew as we walked. Sounds filled the air, a babble of voices here and there, the laughter of children, the shouts of those trying to get attention, the clatter of households we passed ... it all added to the symphony of life in the city. People went about their day, trusting others to watch over them. The thought of war assailed me without provocation. All this joy was fleeting. My heart twinged. They didn't know what was coming.

"Juliet," Adnan whispered, leaning down to look at me, his gait slowing. "Don't. Just enjoy the day and leave the rest to Hirose."

I nodded and forced myself to let it go. He was right. We were to be married tomorrow, and nothing would be gained by my fretting over something that had not yet happened.

"That's better." He pulled me closer as we continued. "Now, let's explore the city." His eyes twinkled. "Emperor Hirose was quite generous with some money for us to enjoy the day."

I laughed. "Was he now? What's first?"

He pulled at my hand, his stride lengthening. I had to half-run to keep up with him, my cloak fluttering about me.

The street was a blur as we rushed down it, ignoring the way people rolled their eyes in polite indifference, before Adnan stopped in front of a dark building. I was a bit breathless, and the day was warmer than I had expected. After sliding my cloak off my shoulders, I laid it over my arm.

With eyebrows raised, I gestured toward the dingy building with my thumb. "Here?"

"Why not?"

"It's—" I hesitated. "It's not that inviting. Is it safe?"

Adnan let go of my hand. Throwing his head back, he laughed. "Why? Do we tend to haunt better places?" His scrubby cheeks reddened. "Sorry, I shouldn't have said that."

"Wait, why?"

"Because—" He ran a hand through his hair. "I forgot for a moment that you don't, you wouldn't—" He laughed. "The people of Ryujin have a lot of superstitions, and one of those is not to joke about spirits or haunting. It's unnecessary."

I shrugged and switched the heavy cloak to my other arm. "It doesn't bother me."

"Should we go in, then?"

When I nodded, he led the way into the dilapidated building. Beyond candelabras gleaming with soft candlelight, a large fire roared in the stone hearth, and soft chatter filled the room. It was warm, inviting, the opposite of what I had expected. Tea and light finger foods lay on the tables. *It's some sort of teahouse.* I glanced at Adnan, whose eyes twinkled. He had already removed his boots while I had stared at the room.

Reaching down, I quickly unlaced my boots and slid on the slippers. A small man whose dark hair was gathered into a high bun came forward with a bow. Without a word, he led us to an empty table in the corner, where we had some privacy and yet were still part of everything going on. He bowed again and left us to be seated.

"Not like that tavern we visited after we left Umi no Machi, huh?"

I shot a glare at Adnan. "No, not like it at all."

The man came back bearing a tray with tea and food. As he laid the things on the table, my stomach growled. I hadn't realized how hungry I was until I saw and smelled the food.

"Hungry?" Adnan teased, pouring a cup of tea.

"Very." I grinned and took the cup from him. Setting it down, I took a slice of raw fish. It was smooth, soft, and melted in my mouth. My eyes rolled back in my head a little as I let out a sigh of pleasure.

As Adnan continued eating, I set down my wooden utensils. His eyes narrowed. "What is it?"

"What's your favorite food to eat?"

An eyebrow rose. "Meat," he answered.

"Which doesn't seem to be as common in Ryujin," I noted, picking up a bite of fish. "They eat a lot of seafood."

He nodded. "Yes. In Helsingor, we ate a lot of meat: deer, beef, pig, and occasionally sheep as well. I miss the heartiness of it."

I swallowed the fish. "Favorite drink."

Adnan leaned back on his cushion. "Ale, though I have to admit I tried something in your world called coffee." He stared ruefully at his cup. "It's better than tea."

A giggle escaped my lips. "And your—"

He held up a hand. "Your turn to answer both questions."

"Mexican food," I answered, not having to think about it. "And it used to be coffee, but I've come to really enjoy the tea here."

"Mexican food?" he echoed.

"It's a lot of rice, beans, corn, meat, spices," I explained. "Comfort food. Though I also love seafood." I took a bite of rice, chewed, and swallowed. "And your favorite thing to do?"

Adnan stared at me.

"What?" I asked, glancing from side to side. No one was watching. "What's wrong?"

"I'm not sure," he admitted. "Your question. My life has been war, spying, and other things ..." He trailed off. We both knew what had gone unspoken. "The time I have in between jobs, I hunt." His green eyes lightened. "So hunting. I enjoy that. And ..." He hesitated. "I enjoy the time I have with you."

With a soft sigh, I felt myself relax. This was what I wanted. This was what I wanted with him. A life without the threat of war looming over us. I sat back a little on my cushion. "Adnan?"

"Hmm?" he grunted around a bite of salted fish.

"It's easy to forget all the dark things here." At first, I spoke haltingly, as though finding it difficult to say what was on my mind. *Do I even know?* Taking a deep breath, I forced myself to keep speaking, to try to explain. "I want more days like this."

Adnan swallowed and rolled up his sleeves a little. "So do I," he admitted, laying his muscled arm across the table in a relaxed stance. "It won't ever quite be perfect for us, though."

"I know." With that admission, I realized what I was afraid of. What I had always been afraid of. *I can't control what happens. I can't see the hardships that will come.* "Why is it so easy to be afraid? I feel like I shouldn't be scared. Look at everything that's happened to me the past few months, everything I've done, everything I've experienced, and yet I'm still afraid of what I don't know. I'm even more afraid now, I think, because I *do* know the darkness more."

"But you've fought against it," Adnan reminded. "And you'll keep doing so."

It was my turn to sit back on my cushion, shifting so that I sat cross-legged. It was not the custom, but I could only sit on my heels for so long.

"I don't want to live life with anyone else," Adnan said. "I want to face whatever comes our way with you by my side."

"So do I," I whispered. "Are you okay with leaving?"

Adnan's head cocked to the side with one eyebrow raised. "Leaving here? Yes. Hirose and his advisors have things handled. This country is not ours to save. And I believe he'll call for us if he truly needs to." He stood and reached down a hand. "Come on. There's more I want to show you."

⚘

The sun was setting when we finally headed back to the palace. Energy still coursed through my veins. The colorful market had been filled with the music of voices, laughter, haggling, and arguments. It was a place where you could just stand and drink it all in. My cheeks hurt from how much I had laughed.

Adnan glanced down at me, his own body more relaxed somehow. It was something in the set of his posture, his facial muscles, and the way his eyes didn't constantly dart here and there as though searching for an unknown enemy.

As we passed through the gates, pebbles crunching beneath our feet from the path we followed, I glanced to the left and stopped short.

"What is it?" Adnan asked.

"Is that Miya?"

"With Hirose," Adnan replied with a slight chuckle.

Miya's head tilted as though she felt someone watching. Seeing us, she murmured to Hirose and beckoned. Hirose motioned to Adnan as he took a different path, which, if Adnan continued, would intersect with our own.

"Go ahead," Adnan murmured. "Seems Lady Miya would like to speak to you."

I watched as Hirose waited, his stance expectant in the way he held his arms at his sides. "And Hirose with you," I replied. "See you later."

Turning, I slid my cloak over my shoulders as I walked. Now that the sun was setting and shadows lengthened over the ground, the air was rapidly cooling. Miya watched while she waited, her rich green dress accentuating the browns of her hair and eyes.

Though it suited her, I wasn't sure I could ever wear green again after Tristan. It was his favorite color on me. He had manipulated me through that color. But blue was different. Mari had worn that color and had died. Wearing it would be like an ode to her. *Never forget.* Clutching my dark gray cloak tighter around me, I stopped in front of Miya.

"Juliet," she greeted with a slight inclination of her head.

I returned the gesture. "You and Hirose … ?" I prompted with a twitch of my lips.

She laughed. "Yes. He is pursuing me."

Taking in the happiness radiating in her expression, I felt my shoulders relax. "I'm happy for you both."

"So am I." Miya's ivory skin reddened as she blushed. "I don't feel I deserve him."

"Is it about deserving?" I whispered, glancing down at my hands. If Saya did as I'd asked, soon there would be a ring on that finger. A piece of my own life, a custom we could make anew here. "Do we ever deserve anything?"

Miya's head tilted to the side. "I suppose I don't know. The gods give us what they will when they will, and I must be content with that. If they are giving me Hirose, it is not my place to question, I suppose." There must have been something in my expression, because she rolled her eyes and took a step closer. "You still don't believe in the gods, do you?"

Taking a moment to choose my words, I replied, "No, I don't. I'm not trying to offend or disappoint you, it's just"—I took a deep breath—"I don't feel like it makes sense to *me*. Ryujin has its gods, Helsingor with their Nordic gods, and back in my world, there are many different religions and beliefs too." I shrugged and felt my hair loosen a little from its binding. Ignoring the tendrils that had begun to fall, I continued, "I'm not sure what I believe. With the portals, the other worlds, there must be some higher power, a god, but I just don't think that it's all these different gods who watch over various peoples."

Miya listened to me, her face open.

"I don't know if that makes sense," I added.

She gestured with her hands through the air. "It doesn't have to. You must come to your own understanding in your time. Just because I believe what I do doesn't mean I can make you believe it as well." She clasped her small hands in her lap. "But I do hope you figure out what you believe in, Juliet."

"Me too," I murmured. With that, my hair fell out of its binding. I reached down to pick up the supple leather that had fallen to the ground and tied it loosely about my wrist.

"Tomorrow you are to be married," Miya said, changing the subject. "We will give you a wedding according to our customs, if that is all right with you." Seeing my nod of agreement, she continued, "Also, Hirose has spoken to me of Amarante."

My breath caught in my throat. "About what?"

"Benkei spoke with him. Don't worry. You both are our friends, and your secrets are safe with us. We will keep a close eye on Amarante."

I stared at her. Adnan had shared his name with them, and he hadn't told me. He trusted them with that information. Not only that, but Hirose trusted Miya enough to share with her even when they were not official yet. *Not that I can blame him.* Miya had always had a sort of trustworthy aura about her, even when I had known her in the mountain fortress. How close I had come to sharing with her why I had been there. Bright shades of fine dresses, glittering jewelry, and the tension of always being afraid for my life washed over me in a drowning wave. I inhaled, fighting for air past the memories assailing me.

"Juliet?" Miya laid her hand on my arm. "Are you all right?"

I gulped and forced myself to speak. "Do you ever struggle with the past?"

"Yes." Her hand dropped away, small and pale at her side. "I think of my time in Creulon's court more often than you could know. Sometimes I wonder if I'll ever be able to leave it all behind me, but then I remember that it's been mere weeks. It's also a part of me. I can't ever *really* leave my past behind me." She gave me a weak smile. "We all carry burdens, Juliet. We all carry mistakes, things we wish hadn't happened to us, or things we've done. I wish I'd never been part of Creulon's harem, but then again, if I hadn't, I wouldn't have met you or Saya or—" She hesitated. "Or Hirose. And that makes me bear it all a little easier." She linked her arm with mine and drew me along with her as she walked down the path. "I'm here for you. I know you and Benkei must leave soon, but know that I'll always be your friend. My prayers are for your happiness, your safety, and your peace in the days, months, and years to come." She applied pressure on my arm as she glanced up at me. "If you ever need anything, all you need to do is ask. *Anything*, Juliet."

Even as I left behind my world, with my parents, Cam, and my other friends, I had gained new people. I wasn't alone. I withdrew my arm from Miya's grip and hugged her. "Thank you."

⁙ ⁙

Soft, warm light glowed from the dozens of candles on the table in the small, intimate room. The rich, dark hues of the wooden table shone against the ivory plates filled to the brim with meats, vegetables, seafood, and rice. Rice wine filled glasses, and dishes gently clinked as we ate.

It was a small party. Hirose sat at the head of the table with Miya at his right, me at his left, and followed by Adnan and Saya. There was no talk of war, of what had been or what would follow. Instead, lighthearted conversation filled the space, permeated here and there by teasing barbs at Adnan and me about our impending nuptials. Sometimes my face reddened, and I hid myself behind my glass. Other times I laughed and joined in on whatever had been said.

It was the type of evening to let the sorrows of the past melt away, to encourage joy and hope of the present and the future. We could almost forget the danger lurking on our doorstep.

Finishing my food, I sat, twirling my glass, watching the others. Adnan and Hirose still ate, but Miya and Saya had also pushed their bowls of rice away and talked of the way the palace was currently decorated.

Décor, furniture, hangings ... how long it had been since conversation between us had been that light. *Had it ever? Until now? It really is over, for us.* The voices, filled with lighthearted but passionate opinions, continued. Hirose shook his head and took another bite of food before turning to Adnan with some whispered comment about women and households.

I rolled my eyes. *At least we care.* A slight chuckle escaped me.

Adnan and Hirose both turned to me, each with one right eyebrow raised.

Freezing, eyes wide, I shrugged. *They do have similarities. It goes beyond their height and build.*

"Why the laugh?" Adnan asked, pushing his plate away from him a little as he leaned his elbows on the table.

"No reason."

"Oh, there is a reason," Hirose exclaimed, draining his glass. "Adnan, you are about to leave me with these ladies, all by myself."

Adnan glanced at him. "No, I'm not."

"No?" Hirose echoed.

"No, you have your advisors and your guards. You have plenty of masculine company."

Hirose's face darkened. "But they aren't the same as having friends about whom I can trust."

The table went silent with his words. It was the first time I felt a heaviness descend in the room. *Especially with a war coming.* A pang of guilt tore through me.

Hirose's face reflected an inner war as he tried to lighten the mood. "But never mind me."

Adnan's hand gripped my leg under the table. "You'll find plenty of good people."

Miya laid a small, gentle hand on Hirose's shoulder.

He shook himself and laughed. "You're right. But the hour is growing late. We should all retire. You two have a long day ahead of you tomorrow." He winked, and I felt my face warm. Standing, he held out an arm to help Miya up. Clasping her hand, which rested on his arm, he inclined his head to us. "I hope you both get some rest tonight. Good night."

Curling my toes, I rose and watched as Saya followed. After giving me a quick hug, she left Adnan and me. We walked along the corridor with a slow, meandering tread. Neither of us spoke, enjoying the peace and quiet of the palace halls. When we reached my door, Adnan leaned against the frame, his long legs slightly crossed. "Good night." His green eyes appeared even darker in the dim light.

"Night," I murmured.

He reached forward, cupped the back of my head, and kissed me. "See you in the morning."

I watched as he walked back down the hallway, his footsteps soft. *This is my last day as a single woman.*

Chapter Thirty-Seven

My reflection stared back at me. Blonde hair pulled back with soft curls framing my face, my blue eyes ringed with charcoal to darken my lashes and brows, and my dress ... I swayed, turning a little as I took in the rich blue—almost as dark as the ocean roiling before a storm—and the sash, almost black it was so dark, tied at the start of my torso. It was a dress to be envious of. Rather than opting for the many layers that went into a traditional dress, I had chosen something light, form-fitting, with a sweetheart neckline. That neckline had turned out perfectly, even though it had been difficult to explain to the seamstresses.

Reaching up, I traced a finger along the light blue gemstones sparkling on pins in my hair. Another change. I didn't want to wear a hat, so Saya had come up with these jeweled pins that, when placed, gave the illusion of a tiara on the top of my head.

"All the blue brings out the blue of your eyes," Saya whispered, coming up to stand next to me. "I'm surprised. I thought it would be green."

"I used to wear green a lot more," I whispered.

Saya's shoulders tensed. "Tristan," she breathed. "Green was his favorite on you." She touched me lightly on the arm. "The pins are a gift. Don't give them back."

"What? No—"

"Yes, by Hirose's orders."

I touched them again.

Saya leaned a little closer. "How do you like how you look?"

My lips pursed as I grimaced. "Is it prideful of me that I think I look nice?"

Saya laughed. "No, of course not. You should look beautiful on your wedding day, but more importantly, you should *feel* beautiful. It means we've done our jobs well." She glanced over her shoulder at the three maids who had helped me get ready. I murmured a word of thanks to them. Saya waved her hand at them and watched as they bowed and left the room, leaving us alone. She straightened one small strand of my hair that had come undone and laid a hand on my shoulder, still looking at me through the mirror. "All right, you ready?"

Inhaling, I drew myself up and nodded. "As ready as I'll ever be."

"Nervous?"

My head tilted to the side. Shaking my head, I replied, "No, I'm not. I'm excited."

"Good." Saya grinned and ran her hands down her own dress, smoothing invisible wrinkles. "Just follow Adnan and Hirose's lead. I know you haven't witnessed a wedding in Ryujin before, but it is simple. No need to worry about anything."

I nodded, letting go of the sudden trepidation I'd felt when I heard her speak Adnan's name. I still wasn't used to her, Hirose, and Miya calling him by his given name, even though it was only done in private. And even this had all been done in one day. There weren't five weeks of preparation like I had made up to convince Creulon to give me more time before he'd force me to join his harem. My nose crinkled as I remembered what had gone into those first few weeks, how my doubts had increased the closer I got to the end.

"Hello?" Saya said, waving a hand in front of my face. "Whatever you're thinking of, let it go. Today is all you need to think of." She stepped back. "It's time. Let's go." She watched as I turned to face her. "You're a perfect bride, Juliet. May the gods watch over you both as you begin this new chapter in your lives."

She knew I didn't believe in her gods, but she meant well by her wishes.

⚜ ⚜

I stood outside the side doors leading outside, alone but for the two guards who flanked the closed doors. My foot tapped the ground as I stood, my hands clasped in front of me, waiting for Saya to come and say it was time. Out there,

I knew it would be a small company, just those I loved and trusted—those *we* loved and trusted. In a few minutes, the ceremony would begin, and I would be married. I glanced at the guards, but neither gave me any attention, their gazes fixated on a point on the wall somewhere behind me.

A rasp hissed as one of the two doors opened. Saya peeked her head through. "We're ready."

My heart raced as I watched the two black-clad men open the doors and fall into place ahead of me and Saya. Her eyes shone as she surveyed me. Pebbles shook as we meandered down the path, following the guards. This was a part of the garden I hadn't yet seen, and it must've rained during the night, because everything was misted with a dewy glow in the morning light. The luscious plants were vibrant in their green hues.

Saya brushed against me a moment before drawing away a few inches to the side. "You look very nice."

"Thanks," I murmured.

"You look so different than the brides I am used to seeing, but it's a good look."

I rolled my eyes.

"You're the Otherworlder," Saya said, her voice more serious now. "You are a cross between that world and this one, between traditions and cultures. And you wear it well." She jabbed a hand in the air. "Seems we're here." Her voice held a hint of laughter.

Following her gesture, I saw the guards had stepped to either side, revealing a red-and-gray archway at the end of the path, the stone wall behind it covered in vines and budding flowers. Before it stood Hirose—and *Adnan*. They hadn't noticed Saya and me yet. The two men spoke in hushed tones, but there was a lightness about their stances and in the way Hirose smirked at something Adnan said. I breathed in deep.

There was an emptiness at my side. My father wasn't here to walk me down the aisle. I fought back the tears, turning my attention instead to Adnan, and took a step forward. My dress rustled about my ankles as I walked. The two men quieted and faced me. Adnan watched me approach, his beard trimmed short again and shaped in a way that just served to accentuate his jawline. My breath caught. His lean figure stood tall in dark gray, almost black clothing. But the undershirt was the same shade of blue as my dress.

All else faded away as I walked toward him. Hirose, Saya, Miya, the guards … they were a passing shadow. It was just Adnan and me. As I neared, the green of his eyes sparkled, and his face softened.

My attention strayed from him as I realized music had been playing. The sound of flutes cascaded from somewhere over the side of the wall, where unseen musicians gave this ceremony an even more intimate feel. The music was soft yet shrill, gentle yet aching. It drove into my soul to the point where I thought I might fly.

Adnan held out a hand once I approached, then turned so that we faced Hirose. I glanced to the side to see Miya and Saya standing nearby, watching us with joy shining on their faces.

I returned my attention to Adnan as Hirose began to speak. In a distant sort of way, I heard his words, but my focus was on Adnan. A hazy joy settled in the air. It was a short speech, but one that spoke of times to come, of love, of finding joy and happiness in one another, and of living our lives with one another.

Then came the rice wine. When Hirose handed the small cup to me, I drank, letting the strong but sweet wine swirl around my mouth. I swallowed. My nose crinkled as I fought not to cough. Adnan smirked before Hirose took the cup from my hands.

"It's time for the vows," he said, looking between us. We faced one another, and I waited for Adnan to speak. We'd agreed beforehand to keep it simple.

"Juliet Barrows, I vow to love you in sickness and in health as long as we both shall live. I vow to love you in all that life brings us, to watch out for you more than I would myself, and to serve you. I vow to love you first and foremost, and to be faithful and loyal to you as long as I live." Adnan's hand trembled a little as he finished.

Inhaling, I licked my lips and spoke. "Adnan, I vow to love you in sickness and in health for as long as we both shall live. I vow to love you as we live life together, to serve you, and to cherish you always. I vow to remain faithful and loyal to you until death do us part." Every word was true and came from my heart.

"Very well." Hirose threw a questioning glance. "The rings?"

Saya stepped forward and handed a ring to me. I glanced down at the small weight in the palm of my hand. It was gold, smooth and glossy. Feeling Adnan take my hand, I watched as he set something smooth and cool over my ring finger.

"Juliet, I love you and give you this as a symbol of my love." He set a delicate gold ring, with little diamonds and emeralds sparkling over the surface, on my finger. It was elegant and beautiful. Steadying my hand, I placed the ring I held on his finger.

"Adnan, I give this ring to you as a symbol of my love."

Hirose clasped his hands together. "Very well. Before the gods—" He cleared his throat. "Before these witnesses, I give you Adnan and Juliet Taira."

Taira? My nose crinkled.

"Juliet," Hirose began, raising his hands, "by marriage, is now part of my family. Let this be known."

My lips parted. *What?* I glanced at Adnan, but he shot me a look that seemed to say he'd explain later. The music began again, the flutes accompanying us as we walked back down the pebble path to the palace.

"We're married," Adnan whispered to me.

"I know," I replied, grinning. "What now?"

"Now, we celebrate."

"No," Hirose interrupted from behind. "First, you two shall have a few minutes to yourselves. *Then* we will celebrate."

I lifted the hem of my dress a little as we walked into the palace. It was warmer in here, out of the cold, dank air.

Hirose pointed to a small side room. "There is something hot to drink and a fire in there. A guard will fetch you in a few minutes."

Miya and Saya gave a small wave as we entered the room. The door closed behind us.

Adnan exhaled and turned to face me. "Kiss me?" he asked with a laugh.

I fell into his arms, letting him hold me as we shared our first kiss as a married couple. Pulling back, I touched a finger to his chest. "Now what was that about? Hirose's family?"

"Ah." Adnan loosened his grip a little to see me better. "Hirose has adopted me into his family. It's an honorary thing. His last name is Taira." He must have seen the confusion shining on my face because he let go of me and turned. "See?" He jabbed a finger at the crest on his robe. "It's traditional to place your family crest here. I have no family, not here at least, so earlier this morning, Hirose asked me if I'd do him the honor of joining his family."

My jaw dropped. "Just like that?"

"Well, there was a small ceremony involved. And then when you married me, you became part of the family as well."

"And you didn't ask me first?"

His face darkened and his voice deepened. "Do you not want to be part of his family? Is this about the kidnapping?" He drew back from me. "By the gods, I didn't think. Juliet, I would never have said yes if I knew it would hurt you."

"Adnan, that's not it."

He frowned. "It isn't?"

"No. I just wish you had talked with me first. That's a big request—of-fer—from Hirose." I stumbled over my words, trying to make sense of how I felt and say it. "Why didn't you speak to me first?"

His eyebrows drew together. "It's up to me to make the decisions, and I didn't see how you—" He paused and grunted. "Now that I say it, it sounds foolish."

"The marriages I'm used to seeing," I said softly, "are a union. One. Yes, you are responsible for the final decision and the consequences, as the man of the house, but we make them together. I want to make them *with* you."

"It's not done that way here," Adnan said. He held up a hand. "Wait. I'm not saying that means it's right. I want you by my side, Juliet Ba— Taira. I'm sorry I didn't speak with you first."

"I forgive you." I leaned my face up, waiting for a kiss, which he bestowed with a grin. "So I'm royal now? If so, I think I could get used to it."

Adnan's eyes twinkled as he leaned down again. "It's honorary, but yes, I suppose we are. I hadn't thought about it like that."

Someone knocked on the door.

He quirked one eyebrow. "You ready?"

I leaned up on tiptoes and gave him a quick kiss. "Now I am."

"All right." Adnan held out his arm to me. "Wedding celebrations can last all day, so be prepared."

I couldn't help the grimace that crossed my features as the door opened. "All day?"

"All day," Adnan reiterated with a wink.

⚬⚬⚬

I didn't need to be nervous. It was just the five of us and some servants who came in and out bearing food and drink. It was a cozy room we had been brought to, full of windows, large floor cushions, plants, and wall hangings depicting wildlife and outdoor scenery. A large fire burned, warming the room and chasing away the drafts from the windows.

I sat back, a glass of wine in my hand, my shoulder brushing Adnan's, as I watched Miya and Saya giggle over something Hirose had said. Last night had been the first time I had begun to see this side of him. Seeing how he looked at Miya gave me flutters in my stomach. It was the same way Adnan looked at me. And I could tell by the way she drank in what he said that she loved him.

Love. My eyes sought Adnan. His dark hair hung gleaming, just to his jawline. *I have a husband. A husband my parents won't ever meet.* My fingers clenched around the glass. Why did that thought have to come now? I stared at the floor, tracing the grains in the wood with my eyes. *They won't ever meet him. But that's okay. I have a new family now.* But still, the pain persisted. I knew they weren't going to be here, that my dad wouldn't walk me down the aisle as I always thought he would. But they would be there for when my mirror-self got married, and she would have them. A better life ... a better world. My *old* world.

A hand slid over mine. "Juliet?" Adnan whispered. His brows furrowed as he watched me. He knew something was on my mind. Forcing myself to be more cheerful, I shrugged at him.

"Do you need some more wine?" Hirose asked, drawing my attention. He held up the porcelain jug.

I nodded and let him refill my glass, trying to ignore the feeling of Adnan's eyes on me.

"Juliet?" Adnan whispered again when Hirose turned back to his conversation with Miya and Saya.

"It's nothing," I murmured, sliding my hand down my skirt.

"Are you sure?"

"It's just—" I gulped and reached for some water. "I realized my parents won't ever meet you."

Adnan's face darkened. He laid his hand on my leg. "I'm sorry," he said under his breath. "I truly am. I wish it would've turned out differently for you."

"But I'm still happy," I protested, glancing over to make sure the others were still caught in conversation. "I love you, and I can't imagine my life without you in it. It's just hard ..."

"I know." He clinked his glass softly against mine. "This won't be the last time you feel this way."

I nodded and picked up a glass of water near my wine. I drained it. The soothing liquid refreshed me and helped me feel a little resolve about keeping what might have been from dampening the day.

❧ ❧

Hours of conversation intermixed with food and drink. It was relaxing, but also tiring. I couldn't keep back a yawn as I tried to stretch my legs out. They were beginning to cramp from sitting, even though I had stood several times to walk around a little.

Hirose set his glass to the side and stood. "Normally the celebration would have lasted all day, but given we are a small company, I think you two are ready to retire."

I tried to hide my surprise. *Wasn't this all day?* Glancing at the windows, I realized the sun had not yet set, but it was close. We had to have been here for at least five hours. Adnan stood up and reached down with a quick flash of teeth. *Is he laughing at me?* My eyebrows furrowed as I glared at him.

"Need some help?"

I rolled my eyes but took his hands. Letting him pull me up, I smoothed down my skirt and watched as Miya took Hirose's arm. *What now?* I was ready to be alone with Adnan. It had been fun but long, and I was so tired. Adnan's arm flexed beneath my fingers.

Miya ducked her head. "We don't want to press in on your day, but we do want to share something." She chewed on her lower lip.

"Miya has agreed to be my wife," Hirose murmured, his dark eyes shining.

I clapped my hands together. "What?" Taking a couple steps forward, I enveloped Miya in a hug. "Congrats! I'm so happy for you both."

Adnan stepped forward and inclined his head to Hirose, then to Miya. "May your life together be filled with happiness."

Realizing that Saya hadn't said anything, I peered at her. She raised both shoulders. "I already knew. Hirose asked her last night."

Shaking my head, I pressed in closer to Adnan, wishing he could hear my thoughts. *Now can we go?* I was happy for them, but it had been a long day, and I was ready for it to just be the two of us.

Even if he hadn't, Hirose certainly did. He smirked and gestured toward the door. "We have placed you in a suite. We'll show you."

My face reddened. This had already felt awkward, and now waves of it washed over me. In the movies, I could laugh, but this was my wedding night, my life. Biting my lips, I forced myself to move as Adnan fell into step behind them. I glanced up. He didn't seem perturbed in the least.

With each step, I knew we drew closer to where Hirose, Miya, and Saya led us. With each step, I felt both excited and embarrassed. *Get ahold of yourself, Juliet. You're married. That's it. Don't overthink it.* I inhaled. Saya glanced over her shoulder at me with a quick grin. *Did she hear that?* I frowned and chewed on my lower lip.

Turning a corner into an area of the palace I hadn't been to before, they all paused before a door.

"This is in a quieter part of the palace." Hirose patted Miya's hand on his arm. "It's in the family wing, so you won't be disturbed. It looks out over the gardens. Everything you need should be there, but if it isn't, then alert the guard." He jabbed a finger over his shoulder. "There is one down the hallway, and you saw the other one we passed when we entered this wing."

Miya stepped forward and opened the door, moving to the side to give us clear entry.

My hands trembled. At this point, I was glad for Adnan taking the lead and beyond relieved that he could just lead the way into the room, past the expectation and the faces watching. Inside, he let my arm go and turned back to the door. Glancing over my shoulder, I caught a glimpse of Saya and Miya giggling before the door slid closed and we were alone.

The awareness that we were alone, and married, seeped through me until every nerve danced in eager anticipation. A warm glow from candles provided some light in the dim room, and a fire burned bright in the hearth. Adnan's face lay in shadow, his eyes on me. His arms were relaxed at his sides, but I saw his fingers twitch.

I'm married ... to that man. Happiness and love almost bowled me over in their intensity. *So begins a new chapter.*

Chapter Thirty-Eight

Silence met my ears as I woke up. I yawned and rolled over, beginning to drift off again. Exhaustion tugged at my mind and body. Sleep pulled at me. *Wait.* The thought drifted through like a slow eddy. *I'm married.* My eyes snapped open. I rolled over again and took in the other side of the bed.

Empty. Adnan was gone.

Sitting up, I peered around the cozy room, taking in what I hadn't noticed before. While it was full of furniture, another smaller door, and plush rugs, there was no sign of Adnan. But the fire had been stoked, and the room was warm. Frowning, I sat up and pulled my legs to my chest, resting my head on my knees. My hair fell in waves about my shoulders. Stifling another yawn, I pulled my robe close around me and stood up. The floor was cold on my bare feet.

I padded to a wardrobe against the wall and opened it to find my clothes hanging inside, along with some new outfits. Running my hand over the fabric, I chose a long gray tunic with some sort of blue shimmer and a pair of dark gray pants.

At the bottom of the wardrobe, I found a couple different belts. Buckling one on, I smoothed down the tunic. It felt good to be out of a dress and in something that was both comfortable and functional, as much as I liked dressing up. The wardrobe doors closed with a click. Hands on my hips, I waited, trying to make a decision. I hadn't quite planned on venturing out, especially not first thing in the morning. *But where is he?*

A knock came.

"Come in," I called.

The door opened, and a maid stuck her head through. "Good morning, my lady," she greeted, coming in with a full tray. She set it down on a table and bowed. Her head swiveled, and her lips pursed as she saw the bed and empty room, but she said nothing. With a bow, she turned and left.

Still unsure of whether to leave or not, I noticed the door hadn't been closed. With a frown, I stepped forward but froze as Adnan walked through and closed it behind him. He ran a hand through his hair, which was loose about his face, and grimaced.

"I hoped to get back before you were awake." He held out a bouquet of flowers I hadn't noticed he'd been holding. "I picked these for you."

Approaching him, I took them and sniffed. "Where did you find flowers?"

His face blanched a little. "I had to go to a flower vendor I know. It's just—" He stumbled over his words. "I'm not used to ... I needed a walk."

My face fell. "Is something wrong?"

"No!" His eyes widened. "No," he repeated in a gentler tone. "I woke early—I usually do—and thought some fresh air before anyone else was up and about might help me clear my head."

I set the flowers on a nearby table and perched myself on the edge of our mattress.

Adnan groaned. "I'm not explaining myself very well, am I?"

Shaking my head, I clutched at the bedding under my hands.

He strode over and kneeled in front of me. "Juliet, I love you, and I love that we're beginning our lives together. But I'm used to being alone, to living where and how I want, and to getting up at the crack of dawn. After watching you sleep for a while, I felt restless and wished I could give you something. I hadn't planned on being gone when you woke up, and for that I'm sorry."

"I just want to make sure you aren't regretting—"

"No!" he replied vehemently. "No, I don't regret it at all. Please don't think that." He took me in his arms. "Juliet, I could never regret marrying you."

I felt my features soften. "Thank you for the flowers. It was sweet."

He leaned down and kissed me. "Juliet Taira. You're my wife. Don't think I'll ever forget that. Now"—he raised an eyebrow—"how about some breakfast? I'm famished."

"I'm also hungry." I laughed, feeling my stomach gurgle in response. "Are all our meals to be delivered?"

"Yes." Adnan walked over to where the maid had set our breakfast. "Sit by the fire. I'll bring this over there." He slung his cloak on the bed before picking up the tray. "We aren't expected to leave our rooms."

My stomach fluttered. That was okay with me. "What's in there, then?" I pointed at the smaller door.

"A bathing room."

"Well, that's good." My face warmed. *We're married.* There was no need to be embarrassed about sharing a bathroom.

"And through that is another door to a balcony."

Fresh air ... also good. I watched as Adnan sat down. The way his hair framed his face, his beard, still shining with some sort of oil ... I inhaled. Would he ever stop having this hold over me?

⁘ ⁘

Rap, rap, rap. The sound flitted through my mind. I shook my head. *Rap, rap, rap.* Bedsheets rustled, and the mattress moved. Opening my eyes, I watched through bleary vision as Adnan pulled a robe about him to ward off the chill. He strode to the door, slid it open, and whispered to someone on the other side. I propped myself up on one elbow.

"What is it?" I asked as he came back.

He got back in bed and leaned against the wall. "A response to Hirose's letter has come from Nordik. It is to be war."

I sat up, sleep forgotten. "War? What happens next, then?" Hugging myself, I felt the cold shiver travel the length of my body.

Adnan shrugged. "Preparations must be made in an even greater hurry now. And it's time for us to leave."

"Is that right?" I whispered, wishing I could take it back, but also knowing it needed to be said. We *needed* to be on the same page about this. *I want to leave, but does he?*

Adnan crossed an arm behind his neck. "Yes, it is. We're not being asked to stay, nor are we responsible for what happens next. We've already given so much to this country."

"So have they," I murmured. *Why am I fighting this?*

"Do you want to stay?"

My body jerked. "No." The thought of staying filled me with such dread that I wasn't even sure I could put it into words. Nightmares still haunted me. I didn't want any part of the oncoming war.

"Then why do you argue?" Adnan reached forward and traced the side of my face with a finger. "Why do you think we should stay?"

I let my frustration ring through my voice. "Because we're part of Hirose's family now, aren't we? And he, Saya, and Miya are our friends, the closest we have—the *only* ones we have. Is it right to leave them when their lives could be in danger?"

Adnan sighed and let his hand drop. "We don't owe them anything. They don't believe we do. You and I need to leave because I think we both know that is what we need, both for our marriage but also in our own lives as we begin to heal from the past." He scooted closer and enfolded me in his arms. "Would it make you feel better if we speak to them of this?"

I bit back a muffled sob. "I don't know."

"You shouldn't feel guilt over this. Have they once made you feel like we should stay? Like we are abandoning them?"

"No," I muttered into his shirt. *Not once.* Even Saya, though wanting me to stay, had urged me to go. *Heal.*

I could feel him smiling even though I couldn't see him. His lips ruffled the hair on my head as he spoke. "Get some more sleep if you can. We have a long day awaiting us."

I shook my head against his broad chest. "I don't think I can."

"Then I'll just hold you."

⚜ ⚜

A much more somber party met this time. Dark purple edged Hirose's eyes. The table before him was strewn with papers, but taking up the center of the table was a map. I'd seen maps before, but not like this. This showed the world in which I had chosen to stay, a world which looked eerily like my own but with some notable differences.

Ryujin was not an island, not like Japan. The northern countries above were all small and clustered close together. To the east, an ocean, to the west, more countries—and Nordik, Tristan's homeland, or at least the homeland he claimed after he'd murdered the real Tristan.

A movement arrested my attention. Miya rubbed her small hand along Hirose's arm. He jerked a little before forcing a slight smile to his face.

I glanced at Adnan, who also studied the map, his hand stroking his jaw as he thought. Continuing around the table, I took in Saya, who had her eyes closed, her fingers pressed to her temples as though fighting a headache.

Two days ago, we had been celebrating my wedding. Now, war was coming.

I still don't know what we're doing here. It was easy to keep my expression neutral, waiting for someone to speak. We'd only been here for a few minutes, yet it felt like far longer. Adnan and I hadn't had long to wait after the servant had come. We all were running on little sleep.

Hirose laid his hands on the table and leaned forward to look at Adnan. "What do you think?"

Adnan's hand dropped from his face. "I think that you're doing the right thing in shoring up the border between yourself and the northern countries, especially considering the threat of raids from there. But I think you need to figure out a way to guard the whole coastline without spreading yourself out too thin. You know they'll come by sea, but not how or where." Adnan pointed at the map. "Before, Ryujin had ships to help fight them, and now we have nothing. They long ago took or destroyed the armada."

Hirose sighed. "I know we are very vulnerable along the coastline."

"But if they come by sea, at least you know it will be a while yet before they arrive."

"A small relief," Hirose murmured with a groan of frustration. "I knew this would come, but it doesn't make it any easier." As Miya pressed his arm, he oriented himself. "As for the two of you, I suggest you leave tomorrow."

"Tomorrow?" I echoed.

"Yes. It's best you get out before they arrive, and—" He hesitated. "The longer you stay, the harder it will become for you to leave."

He's right. I knew he was right, but still my lips parted. *And Adnan knows it too.*

"You two *don't* want to leave?" It was the first time Saya had spoken.

"We do want to leave," Adnan replied. "But it's not so simple."

"And why not?" Hirose asked, folding his arms. "Do you feel we can't handle things by ourselves?"

"No, it's not that."

"Or that we must have the *Otherworlder* and *Benkei* to win our battles for us?"

Adnan ran his hand through his hair and glanced at me. But I had no words. That wasn't the reason, but how to explain what it was when I struggled to put it into words with my husband?

"Neither of you wants to betray your friendship with us." Saya's eyes narrowed. "And you're torn now that you are part of Hirose's family. But you also want to have the chance to heal, to get to know one another, and to have some time together that isn't impacted by war or strife."

My jaw dropped. She had driven the point home with ease.

Hirose's furrowed brows relaxed, and his hands unclenched. "See, was that so hard? Neither of you could have said it?"

Adnan and I glanced at one another in confusion.

"I wanted you to say it," he explained. "I was trying to pull it out of you both." He pointed at each of us in turn. "But you aren't required to serve this country, you aren't required to defend this country, and you certainly aren't being made to do so. Not by me." His voice rose an octave. "If you *wanted* to stay, I wouldn't stop you. However, I don't think that is the best decision. What Saya said is right. You both need to get away from here, for a while at least. Maybe one day you'll return. The gods know I would like to see you again." He swallowed like he was suppressing the emotion surging through him. "You are not only friends, but you are family now. We want you both to take time to yourselves."

Adnan's hand slipped into my own. "I plan on taking us to Helsingor."

My eyebrows rose, and my hand clenched around his. *The country he grew up in. Why there?*

"I want to show her where I grew up, and I think it's time I see if the couple who raised me are alive and well. They haven't heard from me since the day I left over a decade ago." His hair fell forward as he tilted his head to look down at me. "Is that all right with you?"

A new longing grew within me. The same love of adventure, of wanting to see more, do more—the way I'd felt leading up to when I came to Umi no Machi through the portal—began to blossom in me once again.

"I'd love to," I whispered. *As long as you are with me.*

Adnan looked to Hirose and the two women. "There you are, then. That's where we'll go. Once we're there, we'll send word."

Hirose placed an arm around Miya and drew her close. "If it makes you feel more at ease, then know that if we *truly* need you, we will know where to look."

My heart rose and sank all at the same time. Knowing that if the war took a turn for the worse, that we would know, that we could possibly help ... *then it's what's needed.* All my strife faded away. I placed my free hand on Adnan's upper arm as I leaned into him.

"I'll make preparations for you both, with Miya's help."

"What about your wedding?" I asked, remembering their engagement. "When will that happen?"

"It will happen." Hirose pressed a gentle kiss to Miya's forehead. "For the sake of the people, we will hold an official ceremony, something they will be invited to. It will be as soon as we can plan."

"As soon as *I* can plan it, you mean," Miya put in. "It won't be while you are here," she added, regarding me with her large brown eyes. "I'm sorry."

"So am I. I wish we could celebrate with you both."

"Write to us when you arrive," Hirose reminded. "Now take the rest of the day to yourselves if you can. We'll handle all the preparations for your leaving."

CHAPTER THIRTY-NINE

Adnan and I drank in the fresh air as we leaned on the balcony rail. It was quiet. The gardens lay below, far larger than I'd realized. Warm afternoon sunlight lay over everything.

"It'll probably rain tomorrow."

Eyebrows raised, I looked at Adnan. "Why? It's gorgeous out, no sign of any clouds."

"Exactly." He leaned his elbows on the edge of the balustrade. "So it'll probably rain tomorrow. Given that we're leaving. Seems to happen that way." He turned to me, and that's when I realized he'd been grinning.

I shoved him with my shoulder. "Doubt it."

He shrugged and encircled my waist in his arms. "Well, *wife*, should we go inside?"

My ears perked. "What's that?"

Adnan groaned and let me go. "The door." He proceeded the way back into our room and opened the door. Rotating on his heel, he said, "We've been summoned."

"Again?" I mouthed.

He nodded and waited for me to join him. The servant bowed his head to me. This time, the polite gesture felt more like spite, even though the servant had done nothing but bear the summons.

"Do you know what it's about?" I whispered as we followed the man down the brightly lit hallway. Adnan's silence was answer enough. Dinner was still a couple of hours away, so it wasn't that.

I chewed on my lower lip as we walked, not paying attention to our surroundings. *What could it be?* An arm was thrown out. I grunted as I came to an abrupt stop.

"Sorry," Adnan murmured with a crooked grin. "You were about to walk straight into him." He motioned with his head to the servant, who turned to face us. I hadn't realized he had stopped. The man bowed again and opened the door. *Oh. Hirose's office.* We had been to the small room a couple of times now. As we entered, my eyes had to adjust to the dim interior. I stopped still, feeling the draft at my back disappear as the door closed behind us.

Natsumi.

I knew it even before she turned.

"Hello, Juliet, Adnan." She inclined her head to each of us. Her almond eyes held Adnan's. "I understand that you have grown more confident with your name."

"Yes, I have." Adnan stepped forward to join Saya and Hirose, and I stopped at his side.

Hirose's hand clenched into a fist. "I'm beginning to think there is even more going on than I wish to know. Well, Natsumi, you are full of secrets, and I think it's high time you begin to tell us what those are."

"My lord." She bowed. "I cannot tell you all, but I will share what I can. I understand there is not much time, given that Adnan and Juliet are to leave and you have war looming on your doorstep once again."

"How did you know?" Saya asked. "We are sending out word later today—"

Natsumi turned to Saya. "I am a seer like you."

Saya's eyes shone, a look I had seen before. *She already knew this though.* But that look was so similar to the one she had given Drielle. *This is different,* I told myself. *Natsumi is not Drielle, and Tristan is no longer here to control anyone.*

Inhaling, I forced myself to pay attention to the conversation. It was not a surprise to me, seeing Hirose's blatant suspicion radiating from his tense shoulders and piercing gaze.

"I will stay here awhile," Natsumi proclaimed, her announcement having a different reaction on everyone in the room.

Stay? The word repeated in my mind. *Stay and do what?*

"Saya, I will help train you. I know you had some help from Drielle before she was killed, but I have much I can teach you."

"Wait." Hirose's command cut through the air. "Why?"

"Because Saya shows talent, and I have seen enough to believe that she means the best for Ryujin and its people. I also think she shows enough humility and carefulness to not let herself be consumed."

"Consumed by what?" Saya's small voice asked, the previous excitement having gone.

"Consumed by greed, power, whatever you'd like to call it." Natsumi shrugged and inspected the folds of her sleeves as they billowed down over her arms. "Seers have either been killed or driven out of this country, yet most did no wrong. But every gift can be abused, and perceiving the future is no different. I will teach you, Saya."

My eyes flickered between the two of them. This was a conversation the rest of us could only listen to.

"Natsumi." Saya inclined her head in a gesture of respect. "Are you the first seer?"

Natsumi threw her head back and laughed. By the look on the men's faces, I could tell not only that had they never heard her truly laugh before, but that the bell-like sound had some sort of effect on them. Their faces took on a slightly dreamy look, and they leaned closer, as though wishing to hear more. I frowned, disgruntled, and stepped up closer to Adnan.

"I am."

I almost missed Natsumi's answer, as preoccupied as I was with wondering why her laugh had more of an effect on the men.

"How?" Saya asked.

"Now that is not something I will share. I have told Juliet that I have been blessed with a long life. But yes, as far as I know, I am the first seer to have existed."

"You're hundreds of years old."

Hundreds? My eyebrows rose. My jaw dropped.

Natsumi waved a dismissive hand through the air.

Saya tucked a loose strand of hair that had fallen behind her ear. "Why don't you help more than you do? Why didn't you help during Creulon's tyranny, or even with Tristan? You must've known, must've seen more."

"Ah." Natsumi sighed and let her eyes travel over all of us. "This is a question you have all been asking?" Seeing the affirmative, she steepled her fingers together as she thought. "I do not want power to consume me. My goal is truth. I will keep searching for it as long as it takes. For a long time, I have made every attempt possible not to meddle in affairs unless it is necessary."

Hirose crossed his arms over his chest, his head tilted to the side. "Who are you to determine that?"

"Good question." Her almond-shaped eyes widened in appreciation. "I have to make choices, but every choice I make is to guard myself."

"Why?" It was my turn to ask.

"Because if I didn't, I could become the most powerful person in Ryujin, if not the world. My abilities are more than you could imagine." She nodded to Saya. "They are more than yours will ever be. Never have I met another seer like me. I do not want the temptation to take anything and everything I could possibly want." With a sigh, she continued, "That is all. None of you may understand that, but it is something I must live by; otherwise, I will not live at all."

Hirose took a half step forward. "Then why help now?"

"Because training another seer is not wrong, and she needs it. But it's also more than that. I helped where I could with Creulon and Tristan, even if none of you see it, and there are ways I may be able to help again. I love Ryujin. It is my home, my country, and no matter how long I live, it will always be in my heart."

Hirose retreated a little ways and sat on a cushion. He leaned his back against the wall and stretched out his legs, the most informal pose I had seen him take other than the celebration after our wedding. He gestured for us to join him. When we had all been seated, he rubbed at his eyes before asking, "So, Natsumi, may we know in what *ways* you were helpful?"

While I knew his question could be taken as a personal attack, he'd asked it with a sort of resignation, as though he knew Natsumi would give him the answer, no matter that he couldn't see her efforts now.

My knee brushed Adnan's as I leaned forward, waiting for her to speak.

"I suppose it first begins with Juliet."

My jaw dropped. *With me?*

"I saw that she would be instrumental in what was to come. I brought her to Umi no Machi to let the events begin to play out."

"You brought me to this world?" I gaped at her, not caring that a note of bitterness underlined my words.

She shook her head. "No, I didn't, but I saw what would happen after the portal brought you through. I was there to meet you. Creulon was used to my coming and going. It was no difficulty to leave for a few days."

"What else?" Hirose ground out. "You had a vision, you knew Juliet would be helpful in some way, but what else?"

"I helped her along the way, when I could—"

"You were confusing," I muttered under my breath.

"I told Creulon to seek out Juliet."

"What?" Adnan burst out, almost rising. Hirose raised a hand to still him.

"She needed to be at his court. I set that in motion. It was through Tristan's spy in Creulon's court that he, too, learned of Juliet's existence in this world. He didn't know why Creulon sought her so strongly, but he figured if she would be useful to Creulon, then she must be to him as well." Natsumi's full lips thinned as she grimaced. "That wasn't according to my plan necessarily, but it worked out in the end. As for Creulon, I was the distraction you needed to do what you had to."

My eyes widened as I realized she spoke to me now.

"He was determined to have me as his queen. But you—you had much to do, and it wouldn't have been possible if you were his sole focus, so I gave him reason to be distracted."

My head shook from side to side. "This is crazy."

Natsumi's bell-like laugh rang through the air again. "As crazy as it must sound, it's all true."

"Wasn't there an easier way?" I pressed, shifting.

"Perhaps." She shrugged. "But this was the way I saw forward, with the least amount of interference possible."

The silence that followed her words was deafening. My ears buzzed as my head tried to wrap around it all. *It's because of her... Or is it?* Natsumi had helped set everything in motion, but she wasn't the one responsible.

"I can't say I begin to understand you," Hirose muttered, his voice rising as he continued speaking. "But I do respect what you are saying. We would be glad of your assistance in whatever way you see fit to provide, and I believe Saya welcomes your offer to train her. As you already know, Adnan and Juliet are to leave in the morning."

Natsumi raised one shoulder. "That is good."

I leaned forward. "Have you seen something?"

She laughed. "No, but you both have been through much. You need time."

So much was behind that word. Time to get to know one another better, time to live in peace, time to learn more ... *Maybe it's just because I'm not meant to know the future.* I felt the tension seeping from my body. *I don't want to know the future.*

"Adnan, Juliet, this time I truly do not know if I will see either of you again. Neither of you has shown in my visions of the future." She shifted on her heels, her posture ever perfect with a straight back and thrown-back shoulders. "Maybe our paths will cross again, and maybe they will not."

I swallowed, examining the strange feeling in my stomach. "This is goodbye, then."

"Yes, for now."

A dull pulsing began behind my temples. I stood and bowed low. "Natsumi. Thank you for everything you have done."

Natsumi inclined her own head and watched as Adnan rose. "Take care of her. You have quite a special gift in your care."

He nodded to her. "One that I cherish with all I am and have."

She smirked. "Safe travels."

I bowed to Hirose, turned, and walked toward the door. The buzzing in my head had worsened. I needed fresh air and water, and there was no need to stay. Adnan's quiet footsteps followed behind me. Hirose, Saya, and Natsumi had much to talk about, and for once, I didn't need to or want to be part of it. My curiosity was satiated, and while I could wonder at what they would speak of, I didn't feel the need to listen in and find out.

Adnan placed his hand on the small of my back.

We're done.

Chapter Forty

Tears rolled down Saya's cheeks. She sniffed and swiped at her nose, which was already a little red. My own eyes glistened in response. It wasn't like back on my earth. There were no phones, no video calls, no getting in a car, or even an airplane to visit someone. Here, we didn't know when we would see each other again.

"I'll write to you," I reminded her. "As soon as I can."

Miya stepped up next to Saya and put an arm around her shoulders. "Don't worry. I'll watch out for Saya. We'll take care of each other."

Saya's shoulders hunched a little further, and she let out a half-sob, half-chuckle. "I didn't think I would act like this." She hiccupped. "This is ridiculous."

"No." I shook my head at her. "No, this is you showing how much you care."

Miya let go as I drew Saya into a tight hug. My voice was muffled against her hair.

"I'll miss you—both of you," I added, looking up to include Miya. She opened up her arms and wrapped them around Saya and me.

I knew I'd miss them. After a few drawn-out seconds, I drew away and stepped back.

Leaving Hirose's side, Adnan approached. "Ready?"

I nodded, taking the reins of a long-legged, dapple-gray mare.

"These mounts will get you through the mountain passes," Hirose explained, watching us. "They're some of the best in the stables, and are sure-footed." He held out a hand for Miya to join him.

Her face shone. "We have some gifts for you."

My eyebrows rose.

"Haven't you already done enough?" Adnan asked, looping his horse's reins back over the neck. "We don't need anything."

Hirose laughed. "In your saddlebags, there is not only food, but also money for whatever expenses you both have."

Adnan's lips pressed together before he let out the breath he'd been holding. "But—"

Hirose held up a hand. "No. I hope the money makes things easier for you both. Adnan, I'm not asking what you have put away and where. It's not whether I think you have money or not; it's that I want to make sure you do not have to worry about where money will come from for your needs. And Miya, while not yet queen, has gifts for you as befits her upcoming station."

Miya turned to me. "Juliet, not only are the emerald hair clips from your ceremony in your bag, but also some other jewelry I thought you might like." She grinned as she saw me open my lips. "You will accept these, just as Adnan will accept the money from Hirose. You are family, and these are gifts we give freely."

I glanced at the saddlebags. "I don't know what to say."

"You don't need to say anything," Miya exclaimed with a giddy delight.

A snort almost escaped me, but I managed to turn it into a resigned laugh. "Thank you."

"Yes, thank you." Adnan bowed low. "We'll send word when we arrive in Helsingor."

"Wait." Hirose held up a hand, glancing to the guards who stood just out of earshot. "There is one more thing."

We all watched as the guards approached, each bearing some sort of object below a cloth.

Hirose revealed what the first man held. "Adnan, you still have some of your weapons, but these replace the ones you have lost over the past weeks. I know you like to carry seven, as the legend goes, so I hope you will accept these."

My breath caught as I saw the weapons Hirose held out to Adnan. A fine dagger inlaid with silver, a new bow with a quiver of arrows, and a couple of throwing stars.

Adnan didn't take them, but his fingers twitched.

"I could be wrong," Hirose noted, "but I believe these are the ones that you have mislaid."

Adnan shook his head, but his eyes shone a dark green. "These are finer than the ones I no longer have."

Hirose grinned and shrugged. "They'll serve you well, better even, as they do look prettier."

Adnan shot a glare over the weapons at Hirose. With a grin, the emperor turned to the second guard. His wrist flicked, and another cloth fell away.

"Juliet," he said, "I know you had some training with a katana, as well as daggers. This katana is the lightest and most durable in the armory." He held out a sword in an elegant sheath.

I took it and turned it over in my hands, admiring the silver etching on the hilt. Hirose's family crest was inlaid right above the blade, a small thing that would be almost invisible if you weren't looking for it. My head shot up.

"Yes," Hirose replied with a soft inclination of his head. "You are part of my family. That blade belongs to the royal family, and now to you. Bear it well, though I hope you never have to use it." He turned back to the silent guard. "And these are yours as well."

Buckling on the sword, I felt a sense of satisfaction at feeling the weight at my side and against my leg. Taking the two daggers Hirose handed me, I clutched them to my chest. "Thank you," I murmured. "I'm sure Adnan will keep training me."

Hirose laughed. "I'm sure he will, as he should. There are many dangers in this world, as you both know all too well." His voice grew more somber. "Now it is time for you to leave. Gifts have been given, prayers have been offered, and wishes for a safe journey have been made." He bowed to each of us.

I hugged Saya and then Miya again. "Goodbye," I whispered. Feeling Adnan's hand on my arm, I let him draw me back to the mare. As I vaulted into the saddle, I sat back, reins loose in my hand. I flexed my other wrist, which was still bandaged. It twinged, but the pain was faint now. The smooth leather was held loose in my fingers. *How far I've come since the first time I sat on a horse.* Still, I winced internally at the thought of how sore I'd be at the end of the day.

Adnan settled on top of his sturdy black mount, his saddle creaking. He wheeled his horse around in a slow circle to face the gate we'd ride out of. Chains rattled and creaked, followed by a hiss as the door opened.

Raising a hand in farewell, I fought to keep the tears at bay. "Goodbye," I called, taking in one last look of the three friends we were leaving behind. "Stay safe," I whispered, my heart aching in my chest. My throat hurt worse as I realized Miya was now crying as well. My chin quivered, and I turned away to follow Adnan down the path and through the gate. Tears now slid down my cheeks freely.

Adnan glanced over his shoulder at me and shot me a sympathetic look.

I took in a deep breath and straightened. The ground moved past at a slow rate beneath me. *Thud.* The gate closed. Ahead lay the city, but behind us was the palace. It was the second step in our final farewell. While the tears still welled silently in my eyes, I felt the yearning sadness deep within my soul. Soon we'd leave even the city behind. *And then it will really be goodbye.*

But think of what lies ahead. We were setting off on an adventure. Time would continue to slide by. We were free now. Free from Tristan, free from Creulon, free from anyone telling us what we had to do.

I watched as Adnan's strong form rode easily atop the horse, as though he'd been born to the saddle.

And I'm not alone.

ACKNOWLEDGEMENTS

This debut trilogy has finally come to a close. So many people have helped me get here, and I am sure I will miss some. But there are several to whom I wish to give special mention.

My parents, for encouraging me to keep writing ever since I began at the age of ten.

My friends, Hannah, Emily, Sydney, and Caylee, for wanting to read my books, and for letting me talk your ears off about my ideas. Thank you for all your suggestions and questions that have helped me shape this story.

Inkblots, thank you for being the first and only writing critique group I've had the honor of being part of. Thank you for encouraging me to keep going and to hone my craft and for being the early beta readers for parts of *A World Within Roots*.

My sister, Chloe, for always being one of the first to buy the books as they came out, even though the genre isn't up your alley.

My sister-in-law, Em, thank you for being so interested in *The Roots Trilogy*, for reading the earliest drafts, and for being such a stalwart supporter.

My children, for being so patient with your mommy as I wrote and tried to figure out how to turn my hobby into a business. Thank you for still being patient with me as I continue to figure it out!

My editors, Bri, Cheyenne, Deborah, and Caitlin, thank you for all your hard work and for helping this trilogy become better than if ever could have in my hands.

My husband, Andrew, thank you most of all for encouraging me to do one of the things I love, to write and craft these stories, to pursue publishing, and for being the best person to bounce ideas off of. I wouldn't be doing this without you, or at least would have probably waited a lot longer before pursuing my dreams. I love you.

ABOUT THE AUTHOR

Anne Elizabeth lives in the beautiful PNW with her husband and two children. Inspired by the grandeur of the world around her and the works of authors such as Tolkien and Lewis, Anne joyfully gifts her imagination and storytelling as she establishes her niche in familiar genres. Along with her literary pursuits, she enjoys adventures outside, a variety of arts and crafts, and is an avid board gamer.

Instagram: @anneelizabethwrites
Facebook: @AnneElizabethAuthor
Tiktok: anneelizabethauthor
&
anneelizabethbooks